COLLATERAL FRANKLINS

Trenchcoat Investigation – Two

Chuck Emerson

One Drum – Houston

Copyright © 2014
by Charles Stephen Emerson, Jr.

All rights reserved. No part of this publication may be produced or transmitted in any form or by any means, electronic or mechanical, without written permission.

ISBN-13: 978-1500442705
ISBN-10: 1500442704

+

Special Thanks to these kind and patient Beta Testers who made it all the way through an earlier version of this novel and gave their considered and insightful feedback (in reverse surname order):

Elizabeth Zajic, Andrea Tantillo,
Marina Olson, Amy Lightfoot-Moniz,
Margarita Kanavy, Pam Howell,
Ashley Helms, Randy Edwards,
Terri Divine, & Guy Avellon

+

Please visit my web presences
www.ChuckEmersonTX.com
www.Facebook.com/ChuckFiction

Much of this novel takes place near a body of water called Clear Lake bordering the Texas counties of Harris and Galveston. However, this is a work of fiction. Names, characters, places, and incidents are products of the author's imagination or used fictitiously. Any resemblance to actual events, locales, or persons, living or dead, is entirely coincidental.

DEDICATION

Andrea Johnson Tantillo

Thanks for finding the screwups in my throughput.

COLLATERAL FRANKLINS

Trenchcoat Investigation – Two

*Name is Trench. Nate Trench.
Trenchcoat Investigations. My world.
Twenty years.*

*8:30 – 12:00, 1:00 – 5:00
Monday through Friday*

Chapter 1
– April, 2013

I arrived at my office half an hour early, behind on reports. Seriously behind. It was the last Monday in April, my sixth year in business.

At 8:12 I heard a light yet lively knock on my office door.

Lynnette's knock.

She knew better.

Trenchcoat Investigations opened at 8:30. And she was to call first before sending anyone down the hall.

The United States Secret Service had visited the Thursday before – without an appointment. No call; no text; no email. Just turned the knob and walked in.

Lynnette had witnessed that invasion. They'd walked right past her.

And Lynnette was good help. Very good

help.

I wondered: had she stopped by early that morning to sit and visit, figuring we wouldn't be busy? She'd tried to visit the week before. Frustrating: just moments after she settled her warm smile into one of my chrome-framed office chairs (Sam's Club), the hotel call bell on her desk summoned her with its demanding tone.

I waited to see if she knocked again.
Nothing in thirty seconds.
Nothing in forty-five seconds.
Nothing in a minute.
I resumed adding keystrokes to the report.
A minute or two after that, I heard a commotion echo down the hall, maybe from Lynnette's desk in the waiting area.
A moment later, a thud-thud-thud.
Then, a female screamed; expletives, maybe.
Not Lynnette, I thought.
I pushed the keyboard tray back, looked toward my door. Should I lock it?
Waited.
No knock.
Waited some more.
My Blackberry Z10 chimed.
Executive Suites main number calling.
"Hi, Lynnette."
"Nate, I am so sorry." She sounded really nervous, really hassled. Usually quite calm. "I know you don't open for another ten-fifteen-twenty minutes."
"What's up?"
"There's this lady out here. Knows you're here. Knows the Forester. Told her you weren't

open yet. Won't take no for an answer."

"Does this 'lady' have a name?"

"Doesn't care to identify. I've not seen her before."

"Describe."

"Seriously?" she said in a whisper.

"Seriously."

"Okay, a little tallish, five-six easy. Sculpted. Tanned.... high maintenance."

I got a strong hunch.

"Early middle age?"

"Yes. Sure."

"Well kept?"

"Absolutely."

"Okay," I said. "I'll open a few minutes early, walk on down and get her."

I tapped the Blackberry Z10 off. Pulled the keyboard tray out. Returned to the report.

More thuds.

Another minute, two more thuds.

Enough.

I pushed the tray back under again; powered down my monitors; stepped to my door.

Screaming.

I eased the door open, stuck my head out. Looked down the hall toward Lynnette's area.

No one.

I stepped out in the hall, called out as loud as I could without shouting, "Do you have a warrant?"

Shriek. Another.

Not what a woman wanted to hear.

Another thud.

"I'm coming," I said, still loud. "Be right there."

Collateral Franklins

I heard scuffling, then a loud rapid-fire female discussion – that's two women shouting at the same time.

It had to be her. Had to be.

I slowed my pace, rounded the corner and laid eyes on Candice Faith Pence Franklin.

My client.

Chapter 2
– Monday morning

"It's about time!" said Candice Franklin, punctuating her shout with a heel stomp.

"Good morning," I said, cheery as I knew how. "Would you like some coffee?"

"I want your ass in your office. Now."

How rude.

"Lynnette, this is Candice Franklin. She's a very important client. Would you be able to bring us two cups of coffee? I think Ms. Franklin takes cream."

"S-s-sure," said Lynnette, looking like she'd agree to anything just to have Candice leave her space.

"Good. Thanks. Now, Candice, let's go on back."

My client charged right past me without so much as a nod.

I mouthed "thank you" inside a smile to Lynnette, then took my time walking back down the hall.

~ + ~

Candice had arrived looking for a fight. No doubt about that.

If I hurried after her, she'd assume she had me under a thumb. Not good.

If I took my time, her anger would rise

toward rage. Not good either. Yet on that count, there was an outside chance that when I entered the room she'd be nothing more than an expensive gray business suit folded over a lovely lavender blouse – horizontal on the floor.

Sudden heart attack.

Still not good, but my favorite at that moment.

~ + ~

Candice had left Trenchcoat's door wide open.

She stood, arms crossed, at the far right edge of the wide picture window that was the charm of my office.

I shut the door behind me.

Her glare tracked me as I walked to the left and my desk.

I maintained eye contact and sat down.

I waited.

Daggers soon erupted from her eyes. Honest. Silver ones.

I put up my invisible shields. Didn't flinch.

A good old-fashioned stare down.

I waited a bit, maybe two minutes, said, "Candice, you go on ahead and say what you came here to say. I'll –"

"You didn't call me all weekend."

"Ma'am, I sent you two emails on Sat –"

"Yes! And one yesterday. What have you been doing?"

I waited a few beats before saying, "That's what reports are for."

"I've been most busy. Tell me what's in the emails."

I wondered what her real beef was.

"The reports."

"Yes..." she said, the "s" tailing off like a deflating tire.

"Well, over the weekend, first I put in quite a bit of time working on those reports attached to those emails I sent you – in good faith. You, howev –"

"We're talking about your failure to –"

"Candice, you did not pay –"

"And I'm not going to pay –"

"Then we're done."

My stomach flopped.

Candice's mouth fell open and stayed there.

My stomach couldn't believe my mouth had said "done." Must have been my brainstem's autopilot trying to keep me alive.

Over the prior two weeks, Candice Franklin had paid me ten grand plus another four to reimburse my expenses – all in cash, in hundred-dollar bills: Ben Franklins. I'd gone full in on her case, worked more hours than I could count, and had borne my client's severely erratic and highly dramatic behavior with a smile.

Talk about "high maintenance"!

She owed me another five G's retainer for that week which had begun the prior Friday, plus last week's expenses.

Trenchcoat Investigations was not going under if she didn't live up to our agreement. I had retired U. S. Navy Senior Chief Petty Officer after twenty years, and had been doing just fine working a second career for more than five years without her kind of work.

Candice's eyes had gone from mean and

penetrating to those lifeless black dots found on the creatures gracing the covers of vampire novels – and somehow she had bent forward at the waist a little and gone white and rigid as a Marble Statue.

She understood. She'd played a lot of contract bridge.

Maybe five minutes later, Statue's feet inched the white marble statue step by short step over to my desk where a newly-awakened hand retrieved Prada purse from chair. Feet then inched statue half way around, made one step toward door, and stopped.

If she walks, she walks, I remember telling myself over and over.

~ + ~

Candice Faith Pence Franklin was, well, complicated. She had entered my life three Fridays back, late in the afternoon. It was just minutes before The Great Wall of Texas was due to rise up in Harris and Galveston counties and block out the dull work week crap so we could all head out and have some fun.

She'd hired me to track the activities of her husband, Benjamin Ivan Franklin, to follow him around, watch him. She suspected he'd been skimming money from their chain of eight restaurants. A week later she wanted me to catch him in the arms of another woman.

Seventeen days after Candice Franklin had hired me, I arrived at my office that Monday bent on clearing my desk and developing a game plan to get stuff done for Candice – and, yes, figuring to still get paid. The Feds had told me to.

Except... the Feds had made doing straightforward surveillance of Ben Franklin a major no-no when they paid me a courtesy call four days back, gave me strict orders not to follow Ben Franklin any more.

Agent Torville of the Secret Service had sat in front of my desk and made things clear: Ben Franklin was their baby. National security and all that. Torville wouldn't tell me why or how a mid-ticket restaurant owner-manager and caterer could affect national security. Mr. Secret Service Man *did* tell me he could make my life miserable if I didn't comply.

What did he care? I'd be just another piece of collateral damage. The Feds were notorious for referring to innocent bystanders, the accidentally or casually involved in their operations as "collateral damage." The Patriot Act gave them even more leeway – not quite a license to kill. More like lock you away and lose the key.

Even worse: Torville told me I couldn't tell my client, Candice Franklin, that he and I had met; that her husband was associating with the Secret Service; and that I had been told not to monitor Ben Franklin. I could tell her everything else my investigation had churned up – which was nothing, except Ben Franklin wasn't screwing around – but certainly not that the house I had tried to electronically monitor was the local Patriot Act's safe house. It was not the rendezvous point for Ben and his lovers like she thought it was.

If I left Ben alone, followed Torville's explicit orders, I'd be lying to Candice, my client, my boss day in and day out. The lady with The

Franklins.

If I told her, I'd be locked behind bars or lost in some clandestine vanish house as soon as she confronted Ben.

I had never had such a bizarre set of circumstances cross my life. I was used to dealing the cards face up. I wanted to do right by Candice Franklin and I wanted to do right by the good old U. S. of A. Uncle Sam was paying me, too, being retired U.S. Navy.

~ + ~

Candice the Marble Statue cleared her throat, waking me out of my nightmare.

She didn't speak right away.

I waited.

She cleared her throat a second time, said, still standing that one step forward facing my door, "I'm not giving you any more money until I see some dividends."

I let the air dry that one out a little bit, then stood.

"Well, like I said, we're done. I'll fax you a final billing by end of the workday tomorrow."

"I never!"

Feet took statue to door where Prada hand turned knob. Feet resumed walk, shuffled out the door and down the hall. Yes, statue left door open.

Was Candice Faith Pence Franklin a mostly unhappy female wherever she went? Was I her most recent whistle stop?

I flopped back into my executive chair, mumbled, "I said 'We're done' again. Damn."

Chapter 3
– Monday

Trenchcoat Investigations was quiet most mornings back then. Folks started dropping by after 9:30 looking for help locating someone – usually a person who'd made them angry, lied to them, or disappeared owing them money, usually child support.

I was good at finding folks for folks. Had cutting edge cyber assets, native and cloud. I had retired a communications technician, a geek, from the U.S. Navy six years before. The Internet, HTML, and special gateways were old friends.

The Houston area had four million folks back then. My far southeast corner, the Clear Lake City development and surrounding areas, had a quarter million. Local folks hated to drive inside the I-610 loop. They happily brought their worry and anger to little ole Trenchcoat Investigations, even though I looked like a middle-aged Dick Butkus, buzz-cut and bulky, only shorter – not Tom Selleck, not Mark Harmon.

I was a Licensed Private Investigator, yes, but mostly I was a Geek.

I had little experience as a true gumshoe, out on the streets talking to people looking for clues; not used to drama, and no experience dealing with the Feds.

Things could worry me, like:

How could I possibly comply with Agent Torville's orders?

How could I not?

How could I perform an investigation for Candice Franklin in an ethical fashion, earn my fee?

Comply with Feds invoking the power of the Patriot Act – a piece of cake. Not.

I found myself in the midst of real life espionage – where bad people go underground and clueless bystanders like me lose their lives, becoming "collateral damage."

I needed to talk to somebody who walked in my shoes. Somebody who'd worn some shoe leather out on the streets. A true gumshoe.

~ + ~

Candice Franklin was not my first true gumshoe case. She was the first who paid enough to make working out of the office worthwhile.

During my first five years as a Licensed Texas Investigator, I didn't resole a single pair of shoes. Almost never needed to leave my desk. Rarely worked nights and weekends. I used a few pricey data access subscription services plus the Internet's vast resources to do my job, to investigate. Nobody else did the work. No rich, eccentric, and/or bored old drinking buddy. No college roommate. No best friend from the marines. No retired cop. No Dr. Watson wanting a thrill.

I did have one other resource: fellow investigators who lived outside of Texas, members of a professional association, Golden

Gumshoes – no, they didn't look like James Bond nor were they silver hairs on Medicare. Just veteran investigators who'd seen much of the seedier side of life and liked to solve puzzles.

The Gumshoe I had found most cordial, <u>islandgenius,</u> might not want to talk to me that Monday. He'd chewed my ass raw the week before, trashed what he called my "confused professional conduct" in the Franklin case. I had wondered whether he intended his tongue lashing to be understood as "Never cast a shadow on my LCD screen again" or "Maybe you should consider another line of work – have you ever sold used cars?"

As I sat there in my office that Monday morning, the aftermath of "We're Done" short-circuiting the ether, I got to where I figured I might as well chat him up. What the hell could he do, hang up? Not answer my emails? Block me in Chat? At least it wouldn't take much to bring him up to speed on the Franklin case.

Then, again, <u>islandgenius</u> had threatened to have me delisted from the Golden Gumshoes....

He lived in Hawaii, their clock some five hours behind Houston so I had four hours to toughen my hide. I'd call just after lunch. If Golden Gumshoes denied my login, I'd know.

~ + ~

My hide didn't get real thick so after lunch I shucked the telephone and direct email for the Golden Gumshoe's chat room.

On the third try I typed my password correctly and got in.

<u>lakesleuth </u>> heya Genius

I waited.

One minute.
Two minutes.
Then,
islandgenius > oh, it's you
lakesleuth > seemed you wanted me to report back

Okay, I lied. Good one, no?

islandgenius > i must have been delirious
lakesleuth > is now a bad time?
islandgenius > well, it was a good chat room until you showed up
lakesleuth > nice
islandgenius > not the best time. hold on if you want. may take a bit.

I got busy and culled through my snail mail. There was one piece of valid correspondence: my insurance rate was going up.

He was back in seven minutes according to the logged time stamp.

islandgenius > sorry about that. was in three chats at same time. what's up?

No slams? No threats? I froze. Will he zing me later?

lakesleuth > ummm, feds paid me a visit.
islandgenius > oh, now this is fun. go on go on
lakesleuth > last thursday
islandgenius > you been holdin' out on me

I was trying to settle my fingers on the home keys when he continued,

islandgenius > what's up?
lakesleuth > secret service agent says I can't follow client's husband around, can't do my job for her. national security.
islandgenius > what, he protecting patent

rights of fettuccini alfredo
    lakesleuth > agent won't say
    islandgenius > you did ask more than once
    lakesleuth > yes. three, maybe four times.
    islandgenius > national insecurity as patriotically frickin' usual. feds. what else he say?
    lakesleuth > not much. one thing -- said I had to continue to work for wife
    islandgenius > okay, so you're supposed to do the impossible; typical fed. not so unusual. heard of worse.
    lakesleuth > it was way he said it
    islandgenius > sure. start over. How did it go down?
    lakesleuth > secret service sent a convoy after me

I typed, with few islandgenius interruptions, for what seemed a half hour, giving him chapter and verse.

    islandgenius > man, you have worked yourself in a corner. how do you plan to get out of it?
    lakesleuth > don't have a corner.
    islandgenius > wth
    lakesleuth > she refused to pay me. no retainer. no past expenses
    islandgenius > you said?
    lakesleuth > told her we were done.
    islandgenius > you sure you're lakesleuth
    lakesleuth > hey, this is a secure site.
    islandgenius > I can break in.
    lakesleuth > okay okay. you're the genius
    islandgenius > jk you have a right to be paid
    lakesleuth > u think Secret Service will agree

Collateral Franklins

<u>islandgenius</u> > do your regular stuff. if they don't like it, the Explorers will be back. gotta go

Bastard had baited me, then cut the line.

Chapter 4
– Monday afternoon

Lynnette's call refocused my mind on my electronically-accessed information and research service. I powered down my monitors in time to answer her knock.

As I opened the door, she gave me a wink, momentarily rebooting my focus. Where had that wink come from? Who else was waiting in the reception area?

"Mr. Worthington, come on in," I said as I swung the door wide.

A slender man of gaunt features, perhaps in his late seventies, padded toward my desk. He wore a plaid short-sleeve shirt of pale green and light yellow stripes, jeans old and baggy. His shirt sagged under the weight of a clear pocket protector containing seven writing instruments.

A retired NASA engineer.

He stopped in front of my desk. Seemed hesitant to sit.

"Have a seat," I said. "Either one."

I landed in the high back.

He took the Sam's chair nearer the door.

"Did Lynnette offer you coffee?"

"Can't drink it. No more. Too much acid."

His voice was scratchy like mine would likely be at his age. I should have stopped smoking sooner.

"Water perhaps, sir?"

Collateral Franklins

"Already had some. Nice young lass."

Most walk-ins would begin talking about what they want help with one foot in the door. Not Mr. Worthington. I was going to have to take the crowbar out of my desk drawer.

"Sir, how can I help you?"

His jaw slid left and right like a camel chews. I guessed he was thinking.

"Saw your name on that list near the elevator."

My office was on the first floor and I'd heard that same response from Candice Franklin the first time she was in my office. I wondered – naw, this guy was too genuine to lie.

"Go on, please, sir."

"I'd like you to find somebody."

"My specialty."

"Good."

I powered up the desk monitor he could see and handed him a four-by-six card with my general fee schedule, then said, "Let me open a new case and I'll input your narrative and data as we chat – okay with you?"

"Used a spiral notebook for notes. Had one at my desk always. Phone rang, I picked up the pen. Forty-one years. New one every October first."

I thought I might have guessed his age too low. Sounded more like eighty.

"Good plan, sir. Who would you like me to find?"

"A friend."

He was too old to be looking for a runaway lover. I'd helped folks look for lost relatives but never in five years a simple friend.

"Okay, great. Name?"

"Marie Worthington."

"Your sister?"

"No, she's never been my sister."

His choice of words gave me pause.

I let a moment pass then said, "What has she been, to you, Mr. Worthington?"

He sat back in the Sam's straight back chrome office chair, and smiled. "Wife."

"Right. Sure. How about her full name, including maiden?"

"I suppose you've got to have that. Her full name before I married her was Marie Anne Baumgartner, so you can add Worthington on the end."

"Where was she when you last knew of her whereabouts?"

"Brenham."

A city northwest of Houston, about an hour and a half's drive on US290.

I entered that and then mined Mr. Worthington for the technical data computers found so critical to a valid search outcome. He had an address in Brenham, a phone number, her date of birth of course, even her social security and Texas driver's license numbers. Maybe five minutes of data gathering — I typed and moused fast.

"Okay, sir, now when did you last see Marie?"

"Not so long ago."

He sounded forlorn. She was his best friend and his wife.

"Mr. Worthington, could you be a bit more specific. Would help us find her more quickly."

"Not very long."

Things just didn't feel right. Most older folks I had dealt with would lay down the law, be very specific as to what they wanted and how much they were willing to pay for it, so Worthington was clearly a different animal.

"Okay, sir, let's assume I locate her. How would you want me to proceed at that point."

Mr. Worthington shook his head, looked left and right a couple times, then twisted around in the small chair and looked behind him, before turning back around, a look of panic on his face.

"Mr. Worthington, are you alright?"

"Worthing-ton?"

"Yes, sir."

"That's my name," he said, sounding a bit unsure of things.

"It's the one you gave Lynnette when you arrived."

"Lynnette."

"The receptionist."

"Oh, right." He looked left and right again. "I've got to go."

He rose from the chair more quickly than you'd figure he could, headed for the door."

"Mr. Worthington?" I said, standing up.

"Don't know him."

"Sir? Mr. Worthington, are you alright?"

"Name's Baumgartner."

And he was down the hall.

I chased after him, thumbing thru the Z10 for the name of the assistant director of the social service agency that officed on the third floor.

Lynnette helped me get the older gentleman

to agree to sit on the sofa in the reception area with me until a counselor came down and took him upstairs in the elevator.

Chapter 5
– Monday afternoon

Two everyday-type clients came by right after that so I didn't have time to dwell on what exactly was up with Mr. Worthington-Baumgartner. It was maybe three when Lynnette called, right after the second client had left.

"You have a delivery," she said, a tease in her tone.

"I haven't ordered anything."

"From where I'm sitting I'd say that's true."

I didn't need any more code that afternoon.

"What is it?"

"Come up here when you're caught up."

"Just have the deliveryman bring it on down the hall."

"Already gone."

I got up out of my chair and started walking, Z10 to my ear.

"Lynnette. How'd you let that happen? You been real busy?"

"Something like that. Gotta go."

In another twenty seconds I was round the corner and at her desk.

I didn't see a brown box or carton or anything like a delivery anywhere on or near Lynnette's desk or the reception coffee table or floor.

I stationed myself directly in front of her desk, said, "You messin' with me?"

"Who's your new girlfriend?"

Girlfriend? I didn't date much. Had been single for over fifteen years; not seen anyone regular since the year I opened Trenchcoat. Once a quarter or so I got to go play with a banker friend who liked to wear those gray suits and chase money all day but was one hundred percent female hormone unit in the evening and on weekends.

"Lynnette, it's been a rough day. You know this. Yours, too. Can we cut to the chase?"

Her phone rang and she held up a finger.

I looked around the other side of her desk and then over behind the couch. Nothing.

Could it be a big item? I headed toward the lobby.

"Nate, stop. Over here," said Lynnette.

I looked back. She had her hand over the phone and was pointing to a small flower arrangement on her desk.

"Aren't those yours?" I said. She liked flowers. Had said so many times.

She hung up the phone, said, "Delivery man verified name on card. Nate Trench."

"You messing with me?"

"No, but maybe this somebody is," she said, again pointing to the flowers.

I reached her desk.

She pointed at a small envelope pinned to a ribbon tied around the slender glass vase.

I looked. My name. No question.

"You can have them," I said.

"You sure?"

"Why not?"

"Read the card."

"What card?"

"In the envelope."

"Right." I couldn't remember the last time I had received flowers – or even given them.

I struggled to get the card out, my good-sized hands not liking little card inside little envelope.

Lynnette slapped my hand, removed the pin from the envelope, separating it from the ribbon.

"Here."

I tore open the back of the envelope and slid out the little card.

Printed with a kind of a purple gel ink on both sides: "Dear Mr. Trench, Perhaps I was a bit hasty this morning. I have not been myself. The weekend was not pleasant. Can we meet at Valdo's for dinner? On me, of course. Say six-thirty?"

It had been signed in a messy cursive I made out to be "Candice." Not Candice Franklin, but Candice. Just Candice.

"So, you going to take her back?" said Lynnette.

She had such a mischievous grin on her face.

"You read this already, didn't you."

Lynnette shook her head, one eyebrow raised.

I said, "You did. I know it."

"Mr. Trench, I am a trained business professional and would never violate the privacy of one of my tenants."

She laughed. I fought a laugh but gave in as Lynnette continued to jiggle her chair with laughter.

As I walked down the hall back to my office,

Chuck Emerson

I wondered why I laughed. There really was nothing funny about Candice Faith Pence Franklin.

Chapter 6
– Monday afternoon

Candice had sent three yellow roses, accented by a few tiny branches with fragile little flowers that had something to do with a baby breathing – go figure. Two ribbons around the vase.

Lynnette explained yellow roses stood for friendship. She probably meant that information to be comforting but Lynnette wasn't around when Candice and I had met at Marble Slab a couple of weeks before. My client had stormed off. Seemed I didn't "get" what she was expecting. Later it seemed to me that Candice had intended that meeting to be more like a "date" in an ice cream shop, like in high school or maybe the old black-and-white movies.

So, were the flowers and offer to buy dinner her idea of a date yet again? A make-nice? Or a sincere apology? My guess: Candice was not the type to give out anything even remotely resembling an apology. I *would* be expected to "get" the magnificence of her offer, though.

Drama.

Well-to-do female drama.

I did not need drama. Had not seen much in the Navy. Fights, hell yes. Ongoing drama, no.

Guys are lazy. Fights are short. Blowing off steam. Drama is like – forever.

And I never did a good Don Juan. My

database lacked a folder for pickup lines. And I wasn't in the wind tunnel of social life anywhere I was stationed: mostly overseas, on shore. Some places you could try to date the local women. Others, like on the Atlantic coast of southwestern Spain, local girls were locked away. You never saw them without their entire family.

Candice Franklin, though, had slam-dunked me into the whirlwind that was a family and Secret Service drama. I was billing five G's a week retainer, doing the Tango with the Patriot Act.

I thought about ignoring the flowers.

I could have been out of the office the rest of the day, right?

In fact, I was supposed to be out of the office, shadowing Benjamin Ivan Franklin, Candice's husband and co-owner with her of Shrimp-Steak, Inc.

Secret Service Agent Torville had banned surveillance of any kind by anyone so I didn't want to get anyone else arrested.

And I was supposed to have another five G's in the bank already and at least two G's for the expenses I fronted. Since I didn't, I needed not worry about working, right? – or showing up for dinner. No pay, no play – errr, work.

Candice Franklin had a different view, of course.

Should I draw the line and hold to my mind's utterance, "We're done"?

My mission statement never anticipated a Candice Franklin. Had to be a reason she wasn't in there. Oh, yeah, I wanted to enjoy my work.

Did Candice own a gun?

I had put a daily reminder in my Z10's contact manager software, scheduled it to pop up every morning at 8:15: "Think hard, think hard three times, Dude, before you take on another female cash client."

~ + ~

I fiddled around until four, then received a call from a law firm and accepted a short gig.

Seemed a partner in a Clear Lake area engineering firm had not returned from his Cozumel weekend. And seemed the firm was a NASA contractor with high level security clearances. And seemed he was contractually required to get approval to leave the country. Of course, he hadn't or they wouldn't be calling me.

The walls came tumbling down evidently when said partner didn't make his appointment with NASA senior staff three hours earlier.

His wife met his plane. He had not.

So, where was he? Playing in the sun, lime wedge in his Corona? Nursing a hangover in Mexico? Getting a quickie divorce in Jamaica? Answering questions in Venezuela? Handing over documents in Cuba?

The State Department had begun reaching out through diplomatic channels, the CIA through its not-so-diplomatic channels.

I was to search cyberspace for said business partner activity, accessing my investigator links and such, kinda double-checking NSA efforts through their secret portals to the world and links no doubt piggybacking apps in said partner's cell phone. I guessed the NSA was checking two years back. The law firms told me to go three months back.

An electronic task involving the government and such would usually go to the Big Firm inside The Loop (Interstate 610 loop around central Houston). Why me? Sure, the Johnson Space Center was close, a mile away. In cyberworld there is no long distance, though. I asked my usual contact at the law firm what I had done to deserve such an honor.

Seemed the law firm's usual Inside the Loop contractor for that kind of search had disconnected its Internet portal temporarily. It was investigating how its encrypted and vaulted data had been accessed by an outsider many many times over the past two years. Just discovered Friday. Yes, the chickens were nervous.

I asked if they had a suspect – I needed to be watchful as well.

Was told I didn't want to know.

I set about putting all my resources in motion so I could play with all my decks – and bill for it. Heaven for a geek to use his toys for fun and profit!

Unlike Candice Franklin, the government-contracted attorneys cleared invoices in four to six weeks, except for December and May, when they deferred to the following month. Those firms didn't seem to work around holidays. It really wasn't fair since they wanted work completed on their timeline or they'd go elsewhere. I did bill them at a higher rate and they didn't care. The government rate was so much higher back east, even rates in Houston's economy were a bargain.

~ + ~

What about making dinner at my favorite restaurant with my least favorite client?

I decided to let my Subaru Forester decide. If it drove me home and asked to be parked in the garage, well that would settle it. And Zip would confirm. If he was happy to see me when I got home, then I'd stay there. Dogs are wonderful psyche stabilizers.

Chapter 7
– Monday evening

Dog Zip and I went for a boat ride – actually, I paddled us around the neighborhood boat channels in the skiff. I'd only had him nine days yet he'd already come to love the tiny boat and checking up on the neighbors. Great dog. Lucky Nate.

We reached the outer limits of my neighborhood's residential canals at six – a half hour before Candice wanted dinner. By the time I paddled me and Zip back to our bulkhead, then drove down to Valdo's, I'd be late. Candice, *she* could be late. I could not.

Had my subconscious, the part of me that said, "We're done," gone and set things in motion for me to waste time until it was too late?

I could just call and say I couldn't make it.

Except there was no way in Timbuktu I wanted to talk to her. That was it, plain and simple. I didn't want the meeting, in person or on the phone. Not before I had figured out a way to deal with the situation the Feds had put me in four days before. I had been on a guilt trip to the max with her.

I didn't want to lie to anyone.

I didn't want the Feds to lock me up.

I really didn't want Candice mad at me.

I really did want to do my best work for my client.

And I couldn't.

You'd think I'd never served twenty in the Navy.

Never been a Senior Chief Petty Officer.

Never gave a tough order.

Go figure.

Maybe I was waiting to see if she called? Passive aggressive. Wanted her to have to reach out – again.

If she didn't call, then maybe she'd finally comprehended, "We're done."

I'd never see two G's for past expenses.

I'd still be up eight G's for a little over two weeks work.

Fair enough

I embraced that outcome.

I pulled the oar up and let the skiff drift as the wakes of other craft nudged us here and there, often turning us in a slowly rotating circle. Watched Zip dart side to side in the skiff. Peaceful and quiet and all smiles – spelled Z-I-P – from my vantage point.

Life was good. My pulse dropped twenty per minute. Maybe more.

~ + ~

I had my cell phone with me in the skiff in a waterproof pouch about the same size as the tobacco pouch that lived in my grandfather's front pocket. At 6:52 PM my phone played "Bad to the Bone," the ring tone I gave to Candice. I unzipped the pouch and verified the caller ID: Candice's icon lit up – err, trashed the screen, her number listed in white on black.

I didn't want to answer.

I looked over at Zip. He spun around. And around. Fish were jumping.

I answered – ask my psychologist why.

"Evening, Ms. Franklin."

"Yes it almost is, Mr. Trench. And where are you?"

"Home."

"Did you get my note?"

"I did."

Silence for a good minute.

Candice spoke first, her harsh tone louder with each word, "Then. Tell. Me. Why. You. Are. Not. Here."

I did not reply. Her tone was a far cry from the apologetic one in the card.

"Mr. Trench!"

"Ms. Franklin, I had work to do. I did not reply, did not confirm your request, so most people would figure I was not coming – "

"I most certainly deserve the courtesy of formal declination. You are in my employ and –"

"Then how is it I am in the hole two thousand for last –"

"You have not produced."

"Have a great evening. I sure intend to."

I tapped Z10, ending the call, and turned to Zip.

"Hey, boy. Can I join your world? A dog's world? The one I'm in is not having a good day."

He yipped and skip-jumped up into my lap, just about sending us over the side.

Chapter 8
– Tuesday morning

"Did you go to dinner?" said Lynnette as I walked around the waiting area couch. She had female drama written all over her face.

"None-ya," I said adding the smallest of smiles as I arrived at her desk.

"Rude Woman got to you?"

"I didn't say that."

"You're not standing up straight like you almost always do."

Lynnette had become more and more supportive of my business over the two years she'd staffed the front desk. But that morning it felt like she had crossed over from business casual, efficient and cordial, to "involved in Nate's life."

"You taking psychology and counseling at San Jac?" I said.

"U of H."

I straightened. "I was kidding. Didn't know you were in college."

"And just what do you think I do with my evenings and weekends?"

"Partied. You're young."

"Changing the subject is not on this morning's agenda. Nate, seriously, you don't ever talk about your feelings. That's not healthy. It'll kill you."

"You're really going to U of H?"

"No, I'm not. I went through over two years of counseling, a year's worth before Von finally died and the whole year and a half after – weekly. Sometimes twice in one week – enough to qualify me to be Shrink to the Governor."

I didn't know what to say. I didn't respond right away, then punted to humor.

"Some think our governor needs one."

"Silly," she said, head shaking gently, growing a smile.

Who was that woman rising, coming out from behind her desk, her head lilted to the right?

"Lynnette, I've always thought you travelled with a fairly even keel. I would never have guessed, you know, problems."

"That's because counseling works. Just takes more time for some than others. Von died four years ago, you know."

The Executive Office Suites receptionist clamped my arms down with a big hug. When she didn't release me right away, I said so quietly I wasn't sure she heard me, "Glad it worked for you." It took me a few seconds to realize she was not letting go without demonstrated encouragement. I gave her a dose with a very deep breath, expanding my chest measurement by four inches. Her hands popped loose.

Then I shoulder-hugged her back.

Lynnette appeared to have turned the wheel, steered a new course, nudging our association through a sharp turn toward relationship-land.

I stepped back, let a smile grow on my face for just a moment as we made direct eye contact, then turned and headed on down the hall to the safety of my office.

~ + ~

Candice Faith Pence Franklin had not bombed my house overnight, had not been waiting outside my front door that morning, had not sunk my skiff or small boat, and had not shot at me as I drove up to my office.

Still, I felt the weight of the whole Feds vs Client mess on my shoulders as I pulled up the blinds on my office window. How could I do right by a woman who was refusing to pay me but still expected results – *and* comply with the directives of Agent Torville of the United States Secret Service who had basically threatened to lock the door and lose the key?

I hoped the day would not bring more roses.

I set about finishing my final report to her, being careful to include all information I had accumulated prior to her discontinuing payment. I avoided going any further by drawing conclusions or recommending future actions on her behalf as I was no longer in her employ.

My butt was still sore from the ass-chewin' I'd received the week before from islandgenius and I had no intentions of listening to another, so I wasn't about to call and add yellow roses to the mix – but I probably needed third-party review of my report to make sure I didn't sound like a drill sergeant.

Walk-in traffic turned out to be a bit slow for a Tuesday morning, usually my busiest day, so I was done with reports and wondering what to do for lunch when Allison called on the Z10.

I was truly surprised.

I'd seen Allison the Thursday before. Not a happy time. I'd kicked her out of the office – actually refused to let her in while she and Lynnette fought for control of my office door. They wrestled while the caravan of black Fed Ford Explorers drove towards my office, with Spring Franklin on the phone giving me updates.

I picked up the Z10, tapped and said, "Is this the banker that's giving away money?"

"Yes. I printed some more this morning. Stack here on my right's got your name on it, Handsome."

"You really still want to give me some?"

"Of course, I will always have a soft spot in my heart for veterans."

For a second I wondered if the veteran thing was the real reason she'd been my more-than-cooperative banker for five years. Another second and I recognized it for what it was: banker b.s. – I'd heard similar stuff in the Nav.

"Good to know you're not mad at me," I said.

"How could I do that? Only way I get mad at you is if you delinquent on a loan – and then I'd figure how to refinance your ass out of that hole."

I could smell a lunch invitation coming so I trumped her.

"So, what time is lunch?"

"Oh. My. Gosh. Is the man in the demand of the federal government available for such trivial activities as lunch?"

"Where?"

"Cuisine of India; twelve forty-five. Can do?"

One of my favorite restaurants.

"Sure, Gorgeous. Meet you there."

"Flattery will get you another half a point off your interest."

I was glad Allison had called. One less call I needed to make to mend fences from the week before. Except... Lynnette had been so into me a couple hours earlier, I wondered if she'd started keeping my social calendar. Luckily she did the noon-to-one lunch thing and I'd be heading to Cuisine of India while she was out.

~ + ~

Another walk-in customer. Had her smiling in about half an hour. It still wasn't noon.

I was fussing about my office, tidying up after helping a nice grandmother learn where to reach her second cousin on her father's side, when I heard a commotion from down the hall.

Would I hear it again?

I did.

Was it familiar? My door was shut... as it had been the morning before.

I voted in the affirmative: very familiar.

The third commotion came in another minute. It sounded... off — I mean different. I was sure the noise was different. Just not sure what made it different.

I changed my mind. The commotions on that Tuesday just before lunch were unique.

Chapter 9
— Tuesday morning

Lynnette's knock.

"Yes," I said, trying to sound casual. Sure I was.

The door popped open. Lynnette smiled, stepped back as Spring literally sprung into my office, standing in front of my desk in a blink.

"I'm sorry, Nate," said Lynnette. "She's crazy. Says she works for you."

"No problem," I said.

Lynnette had a quizzical look on her face as she closed the door behind her.

"No? You think 'no problem,' Mr. T?" said Spring the Intruder.

"What are you doing here?"

"You are sohhhhhhhhhh in trouble."

Spring Elizabeth Franklin was the younger of two children raised by Candice Faith Pence Franklin, a high school senior, about to graduate in a few weeks. She'd inserted herself in my investigation of her dad, although it took her three tries to actually show up.

"Why aren't you at school?"

"Y. O. U."

"What the hell? Sit down."

"Can't stay long."

"School be the reason?"

"I don't have one."

Have you ever argued with a senior in high

school who's already turned eighteen and is coasting to her graduation ceremony? Hers was three weeks off.

"So you're my trouble," I said.

"No. Not me. You, dummy."

Spring and I had known each other just over two weeks. I hadn't seen her since Saturday, a whole three days. What the hell did she want? I hadn't promised her anything.

"What gives?" I said.

"Why don't you ask me who's the angriest bitch in Harris county?"

Now that was a clue.

"Your mother," I said.

"Exactly."

"What? You think this is news, so you're here to clue me in?"

"Yes."

"And protect me."

"That, too."

"Sit down."

"Not yet."

"Why not?"

"Be right back."

~ + ~

"I'm back."

Spring had returned in five minutes or so, a bit less wired but still as intense as only she could be.

"Bathroom up to your expectations?" I said.

"You are in sohhhh much trouble."

"You said that. Shut the door. Sit."

Spring looked at the two identical chrome-framed straight-back chairs from Sam's before deciding on the one on my left, closer to the window. She landed, ceremoniously, and looked at me with clear amusement."

"You had to go and get greedy," she said.

"Not me."

"Mom's telling anyone that will listen she gave you five thousand dollars and you gave her excuses."

Somebody's arithmetic was squirrelly. I had received ten grand, in Franklins, for the first two weeks, plus expenses for week one. Her mom owed me the third week retainer – another five G's – and the prior week's expenses, another two or so.

I decided the best way to handle Spring's question was to change the subject.

"Have you tailed her yet?"

That froze her. Spring had maintained for over a week that her mother was seeing a lover. Said she would tail her. Spring had a high opinion of her abilities as a sleuth so I alternately tried to talk her out of tailing her mother and challenged her to get it done and settle the matter.

"Not yet," she said, her head shaking. "She's so pissed."

"Such language."

I'd heard similar from Spring. Worse from her BFF, Jocelyn. Spring wasn't much about protocol. Couldn't even begin to spell *decorum*. Like when she showed up at midnight at my place. Without permission. Unscheduled. Uninvited.

Most days Spring Franklin walked around looking young and sweet. Her body was on the thin side, five four and a half, with darkish rusty red hair and gem-quality green eyes that transfixed those who crossed her path.

She was truly sweet and caring, close to overly emotional as is common in teenage girls – but, with the flip of a hidden switch, loony as the craziest teenager you've ever met.

"Mom's pissed," said Spring, "no other way to describe it."

"You gonna tell me what about?"

"I just did."

"The money?"

"Well, sorta. That's what she's saying."

"To everybody."

"That'll listen. It's more like she's mad you haven't caught my Dad. All's she's got for her money is excuses."

"You said that. She tell you I told her it could take until August to figure things out? Cases like this drag on 'cause one or both sinners is usually very good at their craft."

"Just sayin'."

"You forgetting she came to me to find out how your dad was skimming from the restaurants?"

"Now don't say that," said Spring, her bravado weakening. "I'm not. I'm ... updating you. Yeah, that's it. Keeping you posted."

"Early last week your mother had swung full around to wanting me to find *infidelity*."

Spring's head dipped, turned a bunch of slow "no way" twists back and forth.

"I know you think it's all the other way around," I said, "but you haven't got soap on your mom."

She did not reply.

"So where you been?" I said, sounding a bit harsh.
"Busy with school."
"Liar." More harsh.

Chapter 10
– Tuesday

Spring and I chased around the issues for a good fifteen minutes before my watch slapped me.

I was almost late for lunch with Allison.

"Look, I gotta go. You gonna tail your mom or not?"

"How about you tell her the truth?" said Spring, heading toward a yell.

"Not an option. Secret Service said no."

"Since when you worried about them?"

"You forget tailing three or four black Ford Explorers last week?"

"Okay."

"Gotta keep the lid on. I tell your mom, she stomps on your dad. Feds put you and me away and your dad owes thousands in back taxes."

"Okay. Okay."

"So what's your problem with tailing your mom? Your idea, remember?"

"Go ahead, put me in jail."

That was major. Was there something more?

"Spring, what's really going on? Can we get down with this? That what you all say now, right?"

"What if she catches me?"

"Following?"

Spring crossed her legs, tried to get comfortable in the chair. "Yes."

"You're the one who said you'd never be caught doing the tail thing."

"I'm tired of listening to her like I'm sympathetic."

There! That was it. The problem.

Spring's mom was her flesh and blood. Ben Franklin was of the step-dad variety, having married Candice after two years of being a widower with young son, Drake, by then off at U.T. Austin.

Problem was simple: Spring felt much closer, more loved by Ben Franklin than she did her mother.

"But she's your mom so —"

"I'm conflicted, dammit."

"You're not the only one. What's Jocelyn say?"

"Not much."

"Not much?"

"Found a guy."

"Over the weekend?"

"Pretty much."

"Cuttin' down on girls' nights out?"

Jocelyn had finished her high school courses back in January and spent most of the spring working at Sonic. An athletic six-three, dressed in shorts and tank tops, tattoos painting most of long her arms, Jocelyn looked like a world-class delinquent. She wasn't. Jocelyn had been the one to get sense inside Spring's head when Spring showed up at my house at midnight, demanding to talk to me about her worries about her mother and dad. After some "weeping and gnashing of teeth" moderated by Jocelyn, they both joined my investigation of Ben Franklin.

Our secret.

Spring hadn't replied so I said, "I'm right. Aren't I?"

"Get out."

"Okay, I will," I said. "Lunch time. You get on down the road, the one to school, Bay Area Boulevard. Remember it? Now... would be good."

"Yeah, sure. Right. I'm there."

She probably wouldn't do much in class. My hope was she'd be distracted from her mother's drama, if only for a short while.

~ + ~

El Camino Real traffic cleared up just for me. I was five minutes early. Allison was smart to pick twelve forty-five. The first lunch wave began leaving at twelve thirty making room for us and shortening the line by a quarter to one. Otherwise, the wait at Cuisine of India was usually twenty minutes just to get seated for the lunch buffet.

Allison showed up just as I was being shown to our table. She had always had an effect on me, a vibe I couldn't ignore that became even stronger after she shed the gray business suit when she changed banks this time. Her new employer's representative showed up in a black wide-belted pink sleeveless dress – and a lot taller. I pulled her chair out, shocked I thought of doing that. I didn't date much. Didn't pick up any niceties in the Nav.

We placed our drink orders, looked over at the buffet – no line. She pushed her chair out just as I reached for it, was first in line, and handed me my plate, which I nearly dropped.

"You'll have your hands full, Mr. Net, so I'll get my own chair when we sit back down. But thank you. Old-fashioned guys like you are... rare," came with a wide and bright smile.

I let her have her way – like I could do otherwise – and stayed clear of business when we sat back down – until she put her fork down.

"Mr. Net, I know you'll transfer your accounts."

I couldn't hold back a smile. Busted.

"I'm curious, though, as to whether you need to upgrade your level of service. I know what you're paying, of course, and my new programs have a good chance of costing you less. So, how's Trenchcoat doing? Any bump up in business now that Clear Lake has begun an upswing in its recovery from the NASA shuttle layoffs?"

I remember not wanting to mention Candice and the Franklins. That gig clouded my picture of the rest of my business. Chasing around and planting listening devices had set me behind in my regular analytical tasks. I wasn't always in the office and at least half the folks who dropped by when I was gone never came back, at least that was Lynnette's take on things.

I said, "Been pretty consistent that last twelve months or so. Much higher level than three years ago, last eighteen months, for sure."

"Okay, last report on you I saw at old bank was...."

She spoke jargon and I tried not to be caught checking her out instead of listening. Tough job for an old salt. I'd been stationed on shore my whole career, sent out to sea from time to time for a week or two off and on, but nothing ever crossed my desk like Allison Wilson, banker extraordinaire. No one ever talked me into doing more paperwork without a fight – except Allison Wilson.

Yup, when she finished the jargon and said What Do You Think? I agreed to switch my accounts.

After she picked up the check, I walked Allison to her car where she gave me a long hug I'm sure was not in her bank's marketing plan. She waved profusely from an open window as she drove off to the tune of fabulous car speakers.

Resuming my usual life, I was off to Office Depot where they had my rubber bands in stock, as did HEB my liter bottles of club soda and organic corn chips.

Chapter 11
– Tuesday

"So how was lunch?" said Lynnette.

She had never asked me about my lunch. Always asked about my work, the job, but never lunch. Not for two whole years.

Sometimes she talked about her job. As far as I knew, Lynnette didn't have any kids and her family all lived up north. Didn't seem to have a hobby. What else was there to talk about but our j-o-b-s – the only thing we had in common?

"Okay, I guess," I said, not wanting to bring Allison to her attention since the two of them had waged war the Thursday before.

"Just okay?"

"Well, sure. What's up. Somebody leave me a bomb while I was gone?"

"No. Just some more paperwork. She forgot to give you this packet at lunch."

A thick nine-by-twelve envelope in shocking purple appeared in Lynnette's hand – with the logo of Allison's new bank.

Busted.

I'm sure I didn't reply right away, eventually muttering "Umm, thanks."

"Oh, and you had two drop-bys. Said they'd be back. I don't think they will."

I retrieved the folder from her fingers.

Lynnette answered the phone.

"Thanks," I mouthed, tipping my head as if

to doff a hat.

As I meandered down the hall to my office, I wondered why I felt "busted." It didn't make sense. She was just the office receptionist, right?

Allison lit my hormones from day one. That was fact. I didn't know what Lynnette did, exactly, except work for me in an indirect way. It *was* good to have her around as she had always been efficient and polite, unlike the first two Executive Suites front desk employees who'd been more concerned with their makeup.

It was around that time – The Franklins – that Lynnette seemed to become genuinely interested in my success.

So why would I feel confused? I went to lunch with my banker. Ran errands. Returned. Greeted my "office staff."

Got busted.

What was up with that?

~ + ~

One of the two drop-bys *did* come back right after a regular customer left, a paralegal from an attorney's office.

"Sit down, Mr. Monroe. How can I help you?"

"My son. He left ten years ago. Can you find him?"

"I do pretty good at finding folks. He may be a couple thousand miles away, but at least you'll know where."

"I am sure he is not nearby."

"Okay, let's get started."

I pulled my services menu sheet out of my top left drawer and went over it with him before completing my on-screen search parameters data entry fields.

While the computers searched the databases at the pricey online service, I excused myself and checked the two texts Lynnette had sent me during that time.

Both read the same: Your employee is waiting to see you.

Spring.

Hell, she'd left barely three hours earlier. I had sent her to school. What the hell was she doing back at my office. It sure wasn't "our office."

I texted back, "Send her home. School's out."

My computer screen came alive and I reviewed the results with Mr. Monroe.

I had a text notification chime back in two minutes; ignored it.

Another moment, Z10 rang.

I tapped it to voice mail.

"I'm sorry Mr. Monroe. It's usually –"

"No need to worry. I would be concerned if you didn't have callers."

What a nice guy.

On screen three of his search output, we scrolled to a line that struck Mr. Monroe hard.

"Sir, is something wrong?"

"No. Not wrong. Sad. Very sad."

I stopped scrolling, waited for him to continue, afraid to ask another question and raise his evidently painful realization to center stage.

My phone rang again. I tapped to voice mail.

"May I have a copy of all that you have assembled?"

"Certainly. Do you want a printed copy or

the data saved to a CD you can take with you? I can also print to PDF and email it to you"

He seemed to hesitate, so I said, "I can copy it to a flash drive or perhaps your phone also."

"My phone? You can?"

"Let me see your phone, please."

He handed over a Galaxy S II.

"No problem," I said.

I showed him that the charging jack hookup spot was also a port for file access and confirmed I had a USB to Micro cable.

He seemed a bit less nervous through the whole process but had a determined energy about his walk while I accompanied him out to reception.

After engaging in a firm handshake and sharing smiles with Mr. Monroe, I turned toward the couch and gave Spring the look she had coming.

Satisfied that I had successfully used non-verbal communication to convey my message, I did another company-commander-impressing about face and left reception for my office, giving a gentle nod to Lynnette as I passed by.

Chapter 12
– Tuesday

A knock came at my office door five minutes later, firm yet tentative in rhythm – not Lynnette's.

I waited for a second knock.

It came.

I said, "Yes," as loud and gruff as I could.

The knob turned, door eased open, and Spring's head appeared fostering a weak smile.

"Hey," she said.

"What do you want?"

"Need to report in."

"You were not given a case or a file or a task on or to which any report is or was requested, much less required. Dismissed."

I turned to my main monitor, keyed a few dozen strokes.

Spring stayed at the door.

I said, "And close the door."

I continued working, ignoring her presence until the door closed maybe five minutes later.

I did a knee jerk kind of a twist of my head toward the door when the lock clicked. It was in fact closed and Spring was not hiding behind vacant air.

"Setting boundaries" the psychologist called it when the ex and I did the required pre-divorce counseling in Corpus Christi.

No fun, but then the alternative ain't much

of a ratings grabber, either.

~ + ~

I got on the Golden Gumshoes' site and entered chat, hoping to find islandgenius holding court.

He was.

lakesleuth > you heading out to lunch?

islandgenius > before lunch hour is over today. what you get suckered into now?

lakesleuth > nothing new; same old shit; client's daughter was in office this a.m. ranting about mom-client ranting

islandgenius > I thought you said she was going out of town celebrating

lakesleuth > not until June; May is tomorrow; she told recept here that she works for me

islandgenius > now you're into business liability shit. deep shit

lakesleuth > oh, that, too; need slam dunk out of this mess

islandgenius > update me. refresh mess's current status.

lakesleuth > k; can't tail Ben Franklin; can't tell Candice Franklin I can't tail Ben; their daughter Spring likes step-dad Ben better and thinks mom is one having affair, not dad; Candice pissed, refuses to pay last week expenses or this week retainer.

islandgenius > any good points? prior checks clear?

lakesleuth > she paid cash; Franklins, remember?

islandgenius > u tell feds you can't not do job?

Chuck Emerson

    lakesleuth > tried to get that in last Thurs; wasn't an option

    islandgenius > you have contact phone for fed – name was Turnbuckle ?

    lakesleuth > Torville, secret service; no number; not even email

    islandgenius > call his bluff

    lakesleuth > wtf – how?

    islandgenius > just do it. u a gumshoe or not?

    I had a bit of trouble formulating an answer. Finally, I typed

    lakesleuth > easy for god on island to say; impossible here on mainland

    [[islandgenius exit chat]]

    ~ + ~

    I went home early, for another outing on the skiff with Zip.

    Amazing what paddling around in a skiff with man's best friend can do for the psyche.

    Zip convinced me to face up to agent Torville of the U. S. Secret Service.

Chapter 13
– Wednesday morning

I arrived at Trenchcoat Wednesday morning, hardtack stuck in my craw, chewing on the major roadblock to confronting Torville. It had not changed from what I told islandgenius: Torville had not left me so much as his business card. No phone number. No fax. No email. No snail mail.

Could I call Washington?

I could.

I did.

"We do not connect the public directly with our agents. If you will enter your information and question on our dedicated web page, you may receive a response in one to two weeks. Agent availability is not represented or guaranteed."

The only way I was sure to get his attention was the way I got it in the first place: visit the house on Helm Street, the one Ben Franklin visited.

Would they lock me up and throw away the key? Torville had said it was off limits, just like Ben himself.

Maybe I could get one of the local Constables to go with me. Needed a witness.

No way. A dream.

What would I say to the constable, anyway? "... so you see, officer, this young man stole my

$800 touring bicycle off the rack on my car while I was using the ATM at Walgreens. I chased him in my car but he got into this house – it's garage – over on Helm street and shut the door – the garage's – before I could latch onto him and I figured I'd better get you guys to go with me before I knock on the door."

Sure. Yeah, the constable would believe me. I weighed over two hundred at five-ten. Not exactly bicycling profile.

So, I could invite Allison?

Her figure would distract. The Feds would open the door to see what she wanted, right?

How about Candice herself? But then who would be in charge, never mind exposing the truth. Couldn't risk that.

Zip? Naw. I didn't want to scar him at such a young age.

Lynnette? Oh, sure, it was in her job description.

My answer came by the office shortly after nine.

~ + ~

"Heya, Trench," followed the opening of my door but not following any knock. Or call from Lynnette.

My head jerked away from the monitor.

"Jocelyn – I thought you ran off and got married."

"Sprite's jealous she doesn't have a boyfriend."

There before me stood six-feet-three inches of slender athlete, complete with tats the length of both arms. Quite a presence especially since I was sitting down.

She walked over to me – took two strides – gave a knuckle hand shake, then twisted the two chrome chairs to face each other and sat in one nearer the window, putting her feet up on the other.

"Comfortable?" I said.

"Hammies. Don't want 'em to tighten.

I nodded. Seemed reasonable – not that I was ever on the first string.

"What's up?"

"You know Sprite's less than happy."

"And she told you she came by *thrice* yesterday?"

"Not having a boyfriend sends twice as many texts. Okay, triple. What you said."

"So now you're gonna give me that speech where I hire her... again... because it'll make her happy – until she finds true love?"

"Self image thing. Sprite values your opinion like nobody's."

Jocelyn's nick name for Spring was Sprite. They hadn't explained it to me at that point.

"What about your opinions? Spring seems to do what you tell her."

"Rule follower."

"Who? Spring? It ain't you."

"You, Trench. You're the rule follower."

"Rule makers don't think so. Ask the Feds."

"You on Navy retire gig. Doin' twenty sounds like toeing the line, the rules."

"See point number one. The makers think I'm out on the frontier. "

"What-ever. Sprite's dug a hole."

"That's what you're for."

"I'm her bitch."

I about jumped out of my executive chair.

"What the – "

"Her B.F.F.F. Chill. You're more like the guy up in the clouds."

"Zeus?"

"Shuddup. Bring her on. Don't pay her if you don't want to. Make it a concession job."

I was sure Jocelyn meant "commission" job but how a part-time follow-around tracker could sell anything – except entry into a forbidden land – was just not there.

"Jocelyn."

"Bring her on."

"Jocelyn, I might have something for y-o-u."

"I don't need it."

"Cash money. Remember those Franklins. When you go on at Sonic today?"

"Lunch through early dinner. Why?"

"What time you have to be ready to hop the cars?"

"If I text ahead, maybe late as eleven thirty. Whassup?"

It was nine fifteen.

Chapter 14
– Wednesday

"C'mon, Jocelyn. Hang with me for two hours," I said.

"No dissing or such, Trench, but you not exactly in my tribe."

"Look. It's simple. I have a sort of an errand to run and I need a witness, someone with me, standing there where she can hear and watch closely. Remember what she sees and hears."

"Sounds like a date."

"Not even."

"Errand?"

"Would a Franklin do for two hours?"

"Money not the problem. You the problem. What's the gig?"

"Visit your favorite house on Helm Street."

"Get out." She popped her feet off the other chair, sat bolt upright.

We argued about whether to call Spring or not. I won that point solely on how Spring's presence might make life more miserable for her dad.

~ + ~

Right at nine-thirty I pulled into the driveway of the house that had brought me under the "supervision" of the Feds.

I'd had that house on Helm under surveillance for almost two weeks trying to trace the activities of Benjamin Franklin. I saw a stringy blonde tease Ben Franklin with her fingers, then kiss him on the cheek, standing right in that driveway. I saw him enter the front door more than once.

Spring and Candice had seen him enter the front door, too.

I turned off the engine and instructed Jocelyn to stay close. We'd knock on the door but weren't going inside, even if invited. If I were tackled, she was to run like hell. I didn't lock the Forester and handed her the keys. Jocelyn knew the area from the night she and Spring conducted their own spy mission.

The front door opened six inches just as I reached for the knocker.

"You're trespassing, sir," came from inside. The voice was a man's and new to me. He sounded my size but younger. A lot younger. Probably never smoked. "Get off the premises. You're not invited and not wanted."

The door closed, a firm closing. Not a slam. Sounded more like an airlock on Star Trek the Next Generation. It was mostly the compression of the weather stripping and the click of the lock.

I looked over my shoulder at Jocelyn.

Before I could say anything, she used her long arm to reach past me and put her knuckles to the wood. She rapped three times so hard it hurt to hear it.

We waited.

And waited.

Ten minutes. Okay, maybe, five.

Then I heard tires on the asphalt of Helm, not a busy street. I turned and saw a black Fed Ford Explorer ease by, the kind that had caravanned with two or three others to my office six days before.

A minute or so later the front door opened again, that time maybe a foot. I could see inside the house a bit – if you call seeing dark "seeing."

"What do you think you're doing?" said a voice from the dark.

I said, "Looking for Agent Torville."

"Look elsewhere. He ain't here."

The door shut. Quietly. Firmly. Two lock clicks that time.

The voice had sounded different. A man still, another non-smoker, but different.

I pondered.

Jocelyn did not.

Her knuckles gave pain to the door once more.

We didn't wait – we didn't have to.

The door popped open a good two feet, still black as night inside.

"Look miss tattooed calendar girl basketball player," said a deeper voice, louder yet clear, "you got no good sense messing around here."

"Say what you mean," said Jocelyn, sounding like worry was not something she was familiar with.

"As I told your dad here –"

"Trench?" said Jocelyn as she stepped in front of me. "He ain't my dad and you ain't heard the point. Torville. Agent Torville. Where's his butt?"

"Leave and take Trench with you."

"Not on the menu – "

The door slammed shut. Quite a thump. Two clicks.

A few seconds later I heard tires screech on the concrete driveway.

I did a military about-face. My navy boot camp commander would have been proud. A black Ford Explorer, just like the ones that had caravanned to my office the Thursday before, just like the one that had passed by a few minutes earlier, had parked next to my Subaru Forester. I couldn't tell if the Ford monster held one agent or a whole squad, the windows were tinted so dark.

"Heya, Trench, what's next?" said Jocelyn. "We've delivered a message. That Torville guy will hear about it, wherever he is."

Good point.

I turned back around and said, "I'm thinking we hang here five more minutes, just to be a pain."

"I think you just lost that option."

"Why?"

"Turn around."

Chapter 15
– Wednesday morning

The driveway Explorer's twin eased up Helm street and stopped directly behind the Forester.

Given my Forester's severe weight disadvantage, t-boning the government vehicle out of the way was not an option. I could drive over some flower bed brick borders and bushes, on through the lawn, though. That of course assumed the Feds didn't shoot out my tires – or me.

Click. Click. The door behind us opened again.

"You get to stay now," said a squirrelly voice that had to be Torville.

"We can take a hint," I said, still surveying the driveway.

"You were told to leave. You disobeyed orders. Now you get to stay."

"Torville, you get trumped?"

"Overruled."

"You told me you were in charge," I said as I turned to meet Torville's eyes but saw only dark shadows.

"There's more than one command involv – never mind."

"Let's go," said Jocelyn.

I said, "I'm not sure that's gonna – ouch!"

Jocelyn had backhanded me across the top of my shoulder with the same knuckles she'd used on the door.

"Trench, you think they're going to arrest us in broad daylight?"

"What?"

"I count four phone cams across the street, inside the houses. Then there's a man walking his dog, phone in hand, and the young chick across the street who just ran by in her designer spandex, phone in a wrap cradle."

"You're saying what?"

"If the Feds take us inside, the neighbors will go viral. They'll post the plates online and call Channel 11. It's daylight this time – most of these folks are home, retired. Here's their chance to get interviewed for the five o'clock news."

As I twisted around toward the street, a Harris County Constable's car pulled up directly in front of the house.

"Now we're really toast," I said. "Feds got the locals in on this."

"Wrong again. That's my cousin. The Forester. Move."

"What the –"

She waved at the Constable, pointed at me and the Forester, then handed me the keys. "Move."

I hopped in the Forester, turned the ignition key while calculating the maneuvers to get across the lawn. Jocelyn landed and I locked the doors but knew that wouldn't help much. I expected the commandos to burst from the nearer Explorer and surround us.

But nobody got out of the Explorer next to us.

Jocelyn poked my ribs, pointed behind me. I

looked.

The Constable's Impala was inching down Helm. It stopped a couple car lengths down the street, still at the curb.

The second Explorer advanced to where the Constable had been. Looked like clear sailing behind us.

My granddad always said, "Never look a gift horse in the mouth," so I put the four cylinder's transmission in reverse, squealed out of the driveway through a hard turn, goosed the turbo and got us the hell out of Dodge.

~ + ~

"Okay, Jocelyn," I said as we turned down El Camino Real toward my office, "anyone following?"

"You know I got your back."

"You ain't looking that way."

"Why you think I got sun visor down – checkin' my eye shadow?"

Had I ever seen her with eye shadow? No way I remembered. I didn't look at her that way. "How about the side view?"

"You dissing me, Trench."

"Not doin' that. Just making sure. And, hey, your cousin's a constable?"

"Harris County."

"Yes, this is Harris County. What does he know?"

"She's knows enough."

"She?"

"She."

Okay, so I really couldn't see inside the Impala either.

I said, "Where-when-how-why did you get

your cousin the constable in on our visit to Helm?"

"You needed some leverage."

"Leverage is a good thing."

I waited for her to continue. She didn't.

"Jocelyn, you didn't know about my trip to Helm until you were in my office. You were at my side after that. No phone calls. No smoke signals."

"You see me tapping my phone?"

I was so old school. I thought she was playing a video game – Gameboy anybody?

"Crap," I said. "You texted him and he came running?"

"*She's* based at the constable's station right behind the library."

The Freeman library was about six winding blocks from Helm.

"That doesn't explain *why* she came running."

"Had a chat with her Sunday; family picnic."

"Dammit, Jocelyn, you and Spring swore you'd keep all this to yourselves."

"Spring swore. I said I'd keep Spring on a short chain."

I was too hyper to remember the finer details of that week-old conversation. I let it go and tried for detent during our start-stop travel through the traffic-light-hurry-up-and-wait that was El Camino Real.

Jocelyn needed to get to work.

~ + ~

My Z10 rang just as I pulled into my office parking lot.

Number blocked.

Not sure why I didn't let it go to voice mail that time. I should have. Again, ask my psychologist.

"Trenchcoat," I said.

"You are one lucky bastard," said a voice, half-human at best.

"Identify yourself. Caller ID's blocked, asshole."

Jocelyn put a "T" made with her two hands in front of my face. I showed her my right thumb and forefinger microns apart.

"Who says I have to?" said the cyber mutated voice.

"I'll terminate the connection if you don't."

"Go ahead. I'll have your service terminated."

"Stuff it," was my parting sentiment as I disconnected the call.

I did a knuckle handshake with Jocelyn and she got out of the Forester.

I waited just long enough to make sure her car started, then pulled right back out of my parking lot and headed for the ATM that was on the way to the Cricket dealer. A pre-paid throw away phone, purchased with cash, was the new order of the day.

Chapter 16
– Wednesday afternoon

I returned to my office just in time to see Lynnette's Ford Focus make a turn on down the block. I'd missed her. Would she understand? And why did I care if she did?

She'd left three notes in my office mail slot.

Four walk-ins had waited at least twenty minutes each. One had left a note to call, another summed up the other two's communications to Lynnette: I was unprofessional.

Were Candice Franklin and the Feds going to be the ruin of my little cyber investigator gig? I was nothing if I didn't have a good reputation.

~ + ~

Why did I return to my office?

I sat there kicking around that very issue for quite a while.

Hell, why did I go get the anonymous phone if I was going to sit like a duck in a known and frequented location?

I needed to synchronize my notebook computer with my main desktop. Right. That was it.

Not.

Minutes after I got on the internet, the NSA would know where I was. Why? I was sure they already had a queue installed.

The other ping pong ball in my head was Torville.

Why hadn't I talked to him when I had the chance, when he came to the door?

I figured that out two hours later, driving on FM 2094 on the other side of the lake, pulling into the Home Depot lot: that last guy at the house on Helm wasn't Torville.

How'd I know? Gut feelings. Some folks got insight / intuition / vibe-o-meters. Whatever. I had my guts. I was so sure, I was willing to take bets that the voice Jocelyn and I heard was generated by the same type of software or device that called me on the telephone.

I didn't see Torville – or the other two agents at the door. Just heard Voices from the Shadows.

Might have been just one door-opening humanoid using three settings on a synthesizer, a voice scrambler.

So I had done the right thing by getting out of there, even as they amassed their army. And what was up with that? Why didn't their Explorers block my path? Did a local constable truly endanger their secrecy?

I was sure I'd done the right thing buying the throw-away phone. I *felt* it. I did not *know* why. I just went with my gut.

What was the Next Right Thing?

I wasn't exactly sure.

Okay, I had no clue.

Except, I decided to remain in my office until Lynnette returned from lunch at one. I wanted to explain enough to where she'd be able to fend off the throngs of clients that fell upon my executive suite every afternoon. Well, many afternoons.

Why not tell the girl who was sitting in Lynnette's desk right then? The property manager rotated girls from their upstairs office so the continuity of service and job knowledge was shoddy at best during lunch. Did I really want my landlord knowing I was having so much fun.

Definitely not.

~ + ~

"Nate, why didn't you call me on my cell?" said Lynnette when I answered the Z10. She'd called from the Executive Suites phone.

And sounded disappointed.

I got up from my desk, said into the phone as I headed down the hall, "Thought that was for emergencies. Didn't want to interrupt your lunch."

"Or at least text?"

More disappointment. I searched for something intelligent and meaningful to say.

Seemed like forever before I said, as I reached her desk, "Seemed impersonal to do that."

"I'll tell you what's impersonal." Her voice had climbed an octave.

I stopped in front of her desk, nodded, tried to look confused. It wasn't difficult -- I was.

"Okay," I said, "go ahead."

"A funeral," she said as she stood, a deeply serious look on her face. She took a couple steps to the side of her desk as if she were considering coming around from behind it. Would she remain behind her desk or come out and swat me like I was a misbehaving four-year-old? Maybe she would hug me, afraid she'd never see me again?

She began swaying, slowly, transferring her weight from one foot to the other. Was Lynnette Schnable deciding whether to stick her neck out, announce an emotional investment in Nathan Edward Trench or not?

"Hey," I said, trying for soft and comforting, "I didn't want to trouble you, either way. I got crazy stuff going on, worse maybe than last week."

"Continue."

"You know, I guess I figured it was more professional if I told you in person."

Just then a client of the insurance agent at the other end of the hall approached Lynnette's desk.

Lynnette escorted the woman the first ten feet down the hall, then returned to her desk. Stopped. Stood flat still. The disappoint was still there.

She opened her mouth, took a quick but deep breath, said, "Wasn't what you left to do this morning a bit dangerous?"

What in the hell gave her that idea?

"What gave you – "

"The look in your eyes," Nate. "How fast you were walking. The teenager hustling along with you."

Oh, she was in deep.

I said, "I gotta go."

"You were going to tell me – update me. What happened?"

I'd said I didn't call because I wanted to tell her in person. She had just called me on that, so I retracted that first step out the door.

"Okay," I said. "Here goes." I told Lynnette my big client was still stirring embers and had set some dynamics to smoldering. I left out all names, except for the ones she already knew, and the Alphabet Soups, except for the Secret Service.

"Is. It. Dangerous?"

"Not exactly."

"Worst case, what happens?"

"I could get arrested by the Feds. They might hide the key for a while."

She shook her head like the mother of a four year old who'd gone and done what she told him not to, like run on ice.

"Okay, Nate. Thank you. You're busy. Get on out of here. Do what you have to." Lynnette sat down and began shuffling things on her desk, no longer looking at me.

I walked back to my office to put my stuff together. I hoped she at least felt my sense of urgency was true.

When I passed by her desk on my way out, Lynnette looked up before I could think of something witty to say.

She said, "When will I hear from you?"

My heart did a thud. New to me. Lynnette's words told me she was still working on forming a relationship.

"Soon," I said. "*Real soon*, I hope."

"Before five?"

I looked back over my shoulder. She had me in her crosshairs.

She held up her cell phone, said, "What's my number?"

I pulled the Z10 out of my back pocket.

"You're in my contacts."

"Text me to make sure."

I waved and pulled out the Z10.

Lynnette had crossed from courteous to involved.

Had I?

Chapter 17
– Wednesday afternoon

Out in the parking lot after I was done texting Lynnette, I feigned checking the Forester's tires. Got a good look around for large black vehicles.

None.

Got in. Started the turbo four-banger.

Shifted the automatic to drive.

Released the hand brake.

Checked all three mirrors.

Shifted the automatic back to park.

Shut the engine off.

I was so stupid.

My having a pre-paid/throw-away phone did no good. As soon as I called Candice Franklin or her daughter, Spring, or Jocelyn or probably even my office, the Feds would have the new number.

Monitoring by computer. No need to have a federal agent obtain a warrant to listen to the line all day, not since the Patriot Act. Warrant waived. Software reports when contact/connection is made, records it, turning the conversation into zeroes and ones.

Then I woke up.

I started the Forester again and drove back to Cricket.

Purchased three more phones.

~ + ~

Collateral Franklins

I made a run by Ben Franklin's restaurant on Hwy. 3, Charlie's Steak, Seafood and Spirits. Yup. His fire-engine-red Dodge Charger was parked for all to see. I was clear to visit my client.

~ + ~

"Is this an in-person report or an interruption, Mr. Trench?"

Candice Franklin's greeting had all the warmth of a nor'easter as she stared at me through the screen of her home's side door. The one by the driveway.

"May I come in?"

"Have you found Mr. Franklin's lover?"

I stood still for a moment, then said, "No. I don't think – "

"State your purpose."

No love nest address, no leverage.

I said, "I've got a pretty good idea I'm being watched; at least listened to. Be better to discuss inside."

"And why is that, Mr. Trench?"

"Directional microphones even without lasers can hear a conversation at quite a distance, far enough to go undetected – "

"Why are you here?"

"Protecting my client."

"So you say."

"Look, if I'm being watched, being tracked, then any communication with you is also monitored. Cell phone communications can be intercepted, my location tracked. Oh, I can take the battery out, sure, but then I can't use it." I pulled one of the new Crickets out of my back pocket and continued, "Since you might want to contact me or decide to pay back expenses and this week's retainer –"

"Never."

She stepped back into shadows.

I watched the door close. Nice weatherproofing whoosh.

I couldn't have handled that more poorly in the fourth grade.

Maybe that would do it, though. Case closed. Off a rusty hook.

I walked back to the Forester, considering where I'd go next. Spring wasn't home – well, her car wasn't, anyway, and asking her mother for her whereabouts wasn't in the playbook.

Jocelyn would take a chili-cheese dog and a coke. And Jocelyn could then take Cricket number three to Spring. I'd think about delivering the fourth phone to Lynnette.

I keyed the other three phone numbers into all four phones while at a car wash on NASA. The Feds couldn't see me and the building was built with metal trusses and corrugated metal shell, so it had enough iron and tin around to cancel electronic surveillance.

~ + ~

When I walked back into the reception area of the Executive Suites, I noticed four women had populated the sofa and two stuffed chairs. Unusual. I glanced to Lynnette who responded with a nod in the direction of a late-twenties looker in a constable's uniform. She had one of the chairs.

Oh shit. Was it?
No.
Yes.

As I stepped around in front of the uniformed constable, she looked up and stood. Tall. Very tall. Taller than Jocelyn. Maybe six-five. Stronger, for sure.

I said, "You're the cousin of a friend of mine, I'm guessing?"

"Spot on, Mr. Trench. I'm Heather Carey."

"Right. Ahh -- shall we go back to my office? You want anything to drink?"

"Can't have my usual right now. I 'm on a short break. Water, yes. That would be great."

"Got you covered, Mr. Trench," said Lynnette, behind me.

"C'mon. I'm just down the hall."

I smiled in Lynnette's direction but she was staring at her monitor, typing feverishly.

Chapter 18
– Wednesday afternoon

"Please have a seat, Ms. Carey. Glad you stopped by."

"I sit too much," she said as she walked over to the window and looked out, like everyone else that month. "Nice courtyard."

I dropped into my executive chair hoping Captain Kirk would have Scotty beam me up in six seconds. I had wanted to talk to her, ask her a few questions – eventually. I was still working on what all of the questions needed to be. And the possibility my Z10's service could be cut off had risen in my consciousness on the drive back. My law firm customers used the Z10, not the office number – which was forwarded to the Z10 after hours, anyway.

"I got the office for the view," I said. A lie. It was the only one available.

She looked out the window, left and right, up and down, turning her head a bit too fast to really examine anything.

"Mr. Trench," she said as she turned back to me, "I'm here as a cousin of Jocelyn's, her friend, not as a constable. Are you good with that?"

"Sure. How can I help you?"

"That's the tricky part."

My gut locked up. Something in her tone. Dark. Brooding. Conflicted?

"How so?"

"Jocelyn tells me you once worked for NSA."

There it was: name; rank; serial number, please, sir.

"Not exactly. Naval Security Group. Senior Chief Petty Officer, Communications Technician, E-8. Retired over five years ago. You want the rest, it's in my file, my service record."

"Your file....," she said as she padded over, dropped what looked like a clutch purse or a credential wallet on my desk, and sat in the Sam's chair to my right.

"My file? What about my file?"

"I am looking out for Jocelyn's best interests. We straight on this?"

What had that got to do with my service record?

"Sure. You got Jocelyn – and me – out of real bind this morning. I was fixin' to call you and say – "

"This morning you were fixin' to disappear."

I didn't want to discuss my and the Feds relationship, at least not with the local constabulary. I told Jocelyn – and Spring – what they needed to know. I figured the constabulary needed to know even less.

"What about my file?"

Her scrunched forehead told me that she didn't appreciate my not commenting on her statement.

"I checked you out with Texas on Monday."

"I don't have any outstanding wants or warrants or speeding tickets."

"You don't. True."

"No complaints on my P.I. license."

I hoped Candice Franklin hadn't filed one.

"No, you're clean as a whistle."

"And you did all this because...?"

"My cousin is family. You've had her out chasing around in the middle of the night."

"Spring's idea. Jocelyn went along. They went out after I told them not to."

"Both barely eighteen."

"Spring has been very demanding – convincing. She shoved her help down my throat. When I refuse, she goes and does stuff anyway. She's safer when I'm involved. Without Jocelyn, Spring would be totally unsupervisable."

Ms. Carey scrunched some more, said, "So there's your file."

What was it with her and my service record?

"Feds lose it?" I said, joking to deflect any fear on my part.

"In effect, that's what's happened."

I stopped breathing – well, it seemed like it.

"What the hell?" I said.

"Your file is... locked."

Ms. Carey's news was a harsh gut check of the bladder variety.

"I'm going to trust you not to touch my keyboard or mouse."

I excused myself with a nod, and headed out down the hall, leaving the door open. With all the fun that morning, I hadn't answered nature's call.

~ + ~

I splashed water in my face, hoping to clear my head, still wondering what the hell Constable Heather Carey was doing in my federal file. How did she get authorization? Constables in Clear

Lake City work for the Harris County Sheriff, not the FBI. Had she lifted my Social Security number from my P.I. license? She could probably get to that. Was she a decoy, a spy working for Torville? Hell, if that was the deal, she had access to everything – and I was toast.

By the time I was halfway back to my office, I was tight as an old-fashioned pressure cooker, whistle blowing. Sure Constable Carey was Jocelyn's cousin and *for sure* Ms. Carey's arrival up on Helm Street earlier was most fortuitous.

I reentered my office with a gentle smile masking my exploding cranium. The Golden Gumshoes had stressed not showing emotions like the private eyes on television. But what did they know about crazy rednecks working for the Feds?

~ + ~

"You okay, Mr. Trench?"

I hadn't even arrived at my desk when Carey said that. Lynnette hadn't said anything when I walked by her desk on the way back. Smiled. A nice one.

"I'm not sure, Officer Carey. I'm not sure."

I dropped in my executive chair, said, "My file – you were saying the key is missing?"

"You sure you're okay?"

"Enough!" I said, loud and coarse. "What the hell were you doing in my Federal file?"

There. I'd done it. Slapped my morning's savior up side the head.

Great job, Trench.

Why did I lose it? Ask my psychologist.

Chapter 19
– Wednesday afternoon

Ms. Carey kinda dead-panned me for a moment, then said, "I'd be angry, too. I'm sorry to tell you but I figured you were better off knowing."

Apologies are not necessarily connected to reality; don't always address the truth.

Jocelyn was eighteen and feisty. No way would she sit quiet if I came down on her like that. She'd be up on her feet, in my face in a tenth of a second. Spring would fly out the door.

But Jocelyn's cousin hadn't moved a muscle. What was she up to? Only a decoy could be so calm. Or had they started putting Constables through extensive anger management classes?

"Apology is still not information," I said, keeping my tone coarse.

"True. Very true."

"And?" I said, more coarse.

"What I say now does not leave this room."

"Oh, great. I'm hearing about what sounds like a security breach of my service record and you're telling me what you say can't leave my office. No deal."

Ms. Carey remained seated, outwardly calm except for her scrunched forehead.

"Okay," she said, shifting in the Sam's chair. "Jocelyn says you're a straight shooter, just a bit short on social skills so – "

"What the – "

"So I'll get down with this. I'm not really a constable."

Bingo!

"Figures. Damn sure figures," I said. "You a Fed, too?"

"Yes -- but not like you think."

"How do I think?"

"Oh, maybe you think I'm another Secret Service field agent – or CIA."

"You sound too smart to work for Torville."

Heather Carey fought a smile, said after a bit, "He's one of the better field agents, actually"

"You *are* working for the Feds. For Torville. Gotta be."

"Yes to the first. No to the second, sir."

"You're not with Torville. Who then?"

She rose and stepped to the window, at the end near her chair, and my desk. Turned back around in a few seconds, said, "How up to date are you on Alphabet soup?"

"Better than most."

"Okay, what does NCS mean, to you?"

"Let's see. Must be new. Since I got out, anyway. How about, ummmm, Naval Cryptographic Service? National Corruption Squad? Naval Cartography Service."

She popped a short laugh, then said, "Good try. "It's actually -- "

"N.C.I.S., like on television?"

"No. No it's not. Television is screwing with Alphabet Soup. That is a Navy department. You really have no idea?"

"You have no answer, either."

"N.C.S. National Clandestine Service."

"Aren't they all."

She let go a slow nod. "Sure. To a point."

"Okay, which can does this one come out of?"

"Can?"

"Yeah, like Chicken Noodle Soup is probably Campbell's, but could be Progresso, or Healthy Choice maybe."

She let go a small smile. "You gotta know everything, don't you?"

"Gotta."

"Central Intelligence Agency."

"So you *do* work for Torville!"

"No, I sorta keep tabs on Torville."

"You're his supervisor?"

"No. Doesn't work that way."

"How *does* it work?" I said, still coarse. I couldn't remember being that pushy or coarse in years.

I got up. Walked over to my 2.5-gallon jug of spring water. Opened the spigot. Filled a glass. Chugged it. Returned to my desk. Dropped in the executive chair.

I was tired of the Feds rules. They shoot, I stand still and absorb the bullet. Her bosses or Torville's or somebody's had been messing with me and my client work for over two weeks.

Constable N.C.S. still hadn't said anything.

"Ms. Carey. How. Does. It. Work? How do *you* work, Cousin?"

She rapped her knuckles on the window ledge, said, "Look, I'm here concerning *my* cousin. I've told you too much already."

"Your cousin doesn't exactly fall under my supervision – I guess, kind of like you and

Torville. Got a mind of her own."

"It's not that way."

"What *way* is it?"

With one step she was back in front of my desk.

I said, looking her straight in the eye, "What about my file? My file, Agent Carey?"

She picked up her clutch, turned. Two steps, a turn of the knob and she was out the door.

Scotty couldn't have beamed her up any faster.

Chapter 20
– Wednesday afternoon

I shut my office door, sat down and shuffled the three messages Lynnette had left me, trying to calm down and get a perspective on non-Constable Carey's part in the puppeteer's game the Feds were playing. It wasn't the least bit entertaining.

Just as I opened the screen of my Z10 to key in the number of the woman who wanted me to call her, Lynnette rang me.

She said one of the less-than-happy folks from the morning had returned – and Spring was back. Whom did I want to see? If both, in what order?

Spring couldn't stay out of the drama for even twenty-four hours.

"Tell Spring Franklin to go back to school. Can you escort the potential client to me, so I won't give Spring an opportunity to – "

My office door popped open.

Spring.

"Get the hell back to school."

She stopped a yard short of my desk.

"You got a possum biting your ankle or what?" she said.

"Just you. Get back to school."

"I'm a senior. You have that memorized?"

"What of it?"

"Our schedule – mine anyway – is a bit

flexible."

"You're a loose-tongued liar and a piss-poor truth teller."

"My grandmother would wash you mouth out with soap."

"Get out."

"Jocelyn says your phone died. I can't get it to ring or anything. I'm guessing you got disconnected."

Shit.

She was worried. They both were.

Had the foul electronic-voiced caller actually cut my service? I looked more carefully at the Z10 I had just used.

The input screen was fine. The icons that show bars and data service were fine. Had he blocked certain phones?

"Spring, when was this?"

"Half hour. Longer for Jocelyn."

"Can you call me – now?"

"No. Watch."

Her phone appeared out of nowhere, her thumb moving faster than a sewing machine needle.

We listened. Ring. Ring. Ring. Silence. Then a clunk.

"Lynnette – the receptionist – just called me."

"Jocelyn called me and said this was serious. She couldn't get out of work. You get to deal with me. You try dialing Jocelyn."

I did. No rings. The call didn't go much past the touch tones.

"Damn, Spring. Damn you two. Why adopt me?"

"Get out."

I wanted to shift into deep thinking mode, but was feeling very unsettled and had trouble getting there. My wholly-controlled cyber world of five-plus years was coming undone because of one angry woman who liked to pay in cash -- sometimes.

"I guess the Feds can do whatever," said Spring. "That guy, in the news, a couple months back, the one that released stuff says the government is logging our phone calls? This is that."

The Feds had cut me off from my away team.

I opened the sack from Cricket.

"Here, take this. I have another for Jocelyn. You want to take it to her?"

She rolled it around in her hand. "Is this one of those old walkie-talkies?"

"No it's a cell phone that does voice and text only."

"Oh," she said as she flipped open the phone. "You paid cash, like the dealers."

"You watch too much TV."

"I have about forty-five minutes before I have to reappear so I will do the drop."

"Jocelyn or the drugs."

I was kidding.

"Both."

I froze. My breath held.

From nowhere Spring's hand arced around until her small fingers swatted the top of my buzz cut.

"Mr. T., you so need our help."

"You say that a lot."

"I don't do drugs. I'm too creative and crazy

to need them. Jocelyn neither."

"I've put the other phones in the contacts."

She flipped her thumb around some more then said, "I see that. Who is 'L' ?"

Did I want to tell her?

"Oh, wait," said Spring. "The 'L' that works out front? C'mon. What's going on? Mr. Trench have a girlfriend or she 'working' for you nights?"

Spring's smile was way, way too big.

"She may help out from time to time."

"You sure she is down and good with all this?"

"She wants to be."

"She seems nice. Maybe too nice. This detective stuff is not for the weak."

"What do you know about weak?"

"I tail my mom 'cause I'm weak?"

"Good point."

Chapter 21
– Wednesday

I gave Spring the third Cricket for Jocelyn before escorting my big client's daughter to the front desk, shaking her hand as if she were a client, and then turning to apologize to my potential customer. I must have been persuasive as she allowed me to show her to my office.

Trenchcoat Investigations exhibited normal operations until about four-thirty when I escorted my last new customer to the front desk.

I lingered.

I wanted to chat with Lynnette.

I wanted to ask her if she'd do a little work for me on the side. It wasn't really all that difficult. Well, unless you consider asking someone's help in dealing with the Federal government a big deal, a difficult endeavor, a wise activity.

I just didn't want to approach her, ask for her time in a way where she would think my purpose was really of an interpersonal, get-to-know-you-better nature. I couldn't deal with that most good weeks, I had been single so long.

Was it fair for me to ask that of the group receptionist at an Executive Suite?

Sure, I had the Gumshoes for backup out of town – hell they were for out of state. Gumshoes didn't want to compete with other members on their home ground.

I had no close friend, no formal business associate, not even a random sidekick like Spenser's Hawk, Cole's Joe Pike, or Bolitar's Win Lockwood, III.

"Nate?"

I jumped. Lynnette had pulled the cord and returned me from outer space.

"Hey," I said, "you... umm... have a good day?"

"I have two answers for that question – actually I'm not sure which is the answer. Yet."

Her smile was warm and hinted that "yet" had me in the equation.

"Well, you've seen some of mine. Wanna go get some coffee?"

Had I said that? I was more surprised than the hint of puzzlement on Lynnette face.

"You sure you wouldn't prefer something stronger?"

"Well, you can get a latte with an extra shot – oh, you mean alcohol."

Dumb Nate.

"Coffee's fine."

I was glad she said that.

"Good. I can take you over – is the Starbuck's on Bay Area okay for you?"

"Well, it is or even IHOP. I eat there for dinner sometimes."

"Okay, I'll close up right at five and we'll – "

"I can't go right away."

My heart sunk or something. How the hell did I know.

"Nate, don't get nervous. I have just one little errand to run first."

How could she tell?

"Sure," I said. "What time?"

"Let's make it right at six."

With that much time, I wondered if she was thinking of running to purchase a greeting card.

"IHOP?" I said.

She turned on a great smile. "Yes."

I nodded and walked back to my office.

Women. Where did they hide the instructions?

~ + ~

The IHOP was less than five minutes from my office. I had post-initial-interview work to complete for two of the patient folks who had returned that afternoon, so I tried to stay busy at my desk but my mind kept dragging me away.

I had been guessing about Lynnette, guessing she had been hinting she wanted more to do with me than take messages. And I'd entertained the idea positively before that Wednesday morning, all right, *before* the Feds made a play, before my phone was taken over.

I had never intended to stay single after my divorce from my daughter

's mother. I'd dated a bit, especially down in Corpus Christi, but my job with the Naval Security Group had assisted in breaking off at least two relationships.

Gals dated me because they knew I had a steady job and thought I wasn't a go-out-to-sea-for-six-months sailor. Later the shit would hit the fan when I went out on two- to five-week temporary assignments. Not only was I sent on short notice, I couldn't tell anyone where I was going or when I'd be back. Heck, I usually didn't know when I'd be back.

Unreasonable women, you're thinking, what with modern communication, the troops in Afghanistan and such could use the Internet to stay in touch with significant members of their lives. You just couldn't do that from work spaces that were often off limits to those without high level security clearances. Loose lips sink ships.

After moving to southeastern Houston, I had worked so hard on getting Trenchcoat Investigations off the ground, I'd neglected making any purely social contacts. I was where I was because of water and a survey that showed an open market for what I wanted to do. I'd never been a joiner, never a member of a dance or social club, wasn't much on church going either.

I tried the civic clubs but didn't mesh somehow.

I used my "free time" to remodel the small waterfront fixer-upper home I'd bought in Seabrook. Maybe I should change "remodeling" for something like, "making the house fit to live in." Yes, it had been a post-market-collapse repo.

Would it be a good idea for me to venture myself forward as an "as is" sale to Lynnette?

Full disclosure.

Chapter 22
– Wednesday early evening

"Hey, what'll you have?" I said as Lynnette arrived and scooted into the other side of the booth before I could stand up. "Is this booth okay?"

She smiled but I wasn't sure if she turned a true shade of pink because the lights in the forty-year-old IHOP cast a yellow hue that was great for taking a few years off female customers but hid the details us analytical types lived on.

"Aren't we doing coffee?" she said.

"Anything you want – that they serve here."

She raised an eyebrow. "I didn't know you were so playful."

"Only when I'm nervous."

Had I said that? Yup. I remember. Clearly, even to this day.

"Have fun with the menu," I said. "Could take a half hour to read."

She shook her head. "Know it well. I told you."

"How are you – how are you fixed for time?" I said.

"One question at a time, Nate. Which one would you like me to answer first?"

"How – how are you?"

"Which really means?"

"Huh."

"Oh, I'm sorry. You're not a player?"

"I suck at musical instruments."
"Not the meaning I intended."
I said nothing.

Lynnette looked at me for a good fifteen seconds before resuming her travel through the menu.

In another five minutes, she'd talked me into sharing the Appetizer Sampler. I ordered coffee – decaf. She had water.

After the waitress went off to place our order, I asked the question she still hadn't answered.

"How are you for time?"
"Oh, darn you, Nate."
Female speak.
"Did I say something wrong?"
"Just tell me why you wanted to meet."
Strike three.
"Sure. Ummm, you might have been wondering what all's been going on."
"Me? I'm not nosey."

She sure had seemed to be lately, at least when it came to me.

"You remember the Feds who were in the office last Thursday?"

Playfulness left her eyes. "Yes."
"Well, I went to visit them this morning."
"With the tall teenager."
"Yes. Jocelyn."
"Go on."

Lynnette was more or less stone-faced as she listened while I told her about our drive up to the Helm Street house.

When I'd paused at the part where Jocelyn and I arrive back in the office parking lot, she said, "So you got back out of there and you're not arrested or anything."

"True. There – "

"Oh, I'm so glad. I was afraid you were going to tell me you had to turn yourself in this evening."

The woman had a vivid imagination – or did she watch too much television – or did she care for me, about me?

"No. Nothing like that."

"So, you've told me about your escapade. Was that all you wanted to tell me?"

"No. I – "

My Z10 rang.

Number blocked.

"Damnit," I said, loud enough for Lynnette to lurch back in her seat.

"What?" she said.

I held up a finger.

"Trenchcoat."

"You still doing that lucky bastard thing, I see," said the half-human voice from earlier. "Hanging with another girl, you old fox, you."

"What scare tactic you playing now, asshole?"

"For me to know and you to find out – or not."

Somehow the mutation of the human voice by the electronics seemed to echo like Vincent Price's voice in those old horror movies.

"Who are you?" I said. "Who do you work for?"

"See above."

"See what?"

"Same answer, ass-hole."

I waited a good ten seconds, said, "You having fun with your little toy momma bought you for your birth – "

"No getting personal. This is business. You enjoying your new phone service?"

How the hell did he find out about the Cricket phones? Or had he?

"New?" I said.

"Well, not all new. The new *features*."

Ah. he'd meant the Z10 restrictions.

"The ones that keep me from calling my friends?"

"Friends? That what you call the girls you're pimping for?"

Enough. I hung up.

Chapter 23
– Wednesday early evening

"What, Nate? You look like you're about to explode or – "

"Yes."

"Well, I just – "

"Give me a minute."

I sat still working on lowering my heart rate but it took less than a minute for the new Cricket to ring.

Jocelyn on the ID.

"I'm busy. Call you back."

"Hey, Trench. No problem. You were so cool. Had to call, give you the highest five."

What was she talking about? My mind locked up in thought, analysis paralysis. Too many options to hold in place in my mind.

"You there?" said Jocelyn.

"Yes. Wait a second."

"Lynnette, I think I need to take this outside."

"No you don't." She reached across the table.

I pulled back. Damn. I was right. She'd gone over the line.

"You don't understand," I said.

"I understand that someone I care about is – "

"Don't. Might get yourself hurt."

I tossed a twenty on the table, nodded with "sorry" on my face, and hurried outside. With any luck, the wind would be calm and I'd be able to talk with my gang of Thugettes.

~ + ~

Mother nature was kind to me. Not.

I got in the Forester to get out of the stiff breeze. Checked to see if Jocelyn was still on the line.

"You there?"

"Yo, Trench."

"Yo, yourself. What was I cool about?"

"The phone."

"What, you like the piece of junk Cricket?"

"No. Regular call."

"I didn't call you."

"You were talking to some weird dude. Like a video game voice for Darth Vader."

"I didn't call you."

Of that much I was sure.

"What are you sayin' ?"

"What are *you* saying?"

She stopped at that.

"Jocelyn, why don't you take it from the top?"

"You mean start from the beginning?"

"Your personal cell phone rang."

"Sure."

"Then what?"

"It slipped when I was bringing it to my ear."

"What did I say?"

"It slipped so you were already saying stuff."

"Like what?"

"Scare tactic asshole."

"Right. Did you hear the other side?"

"The other guy, or machine, whatever. Sure."

The Feds had upped the ante.

"So you were like listening in on a conversation."

"Thought so."

"Didn't that seem strange to you? Hearing both sides, I mean."

"You're the geek. I figured you were cluing me in."

Darn. Damn. Nice piece of technology.

The Cricket beeped in my ear.

Call waiting.

"Hold still, Jocelyn."

"Spring, you there?"

"You by yourself?"

"ON other line with Jocelyn."

"She ignored my call."

"Which way did you call her."

"Cell. Duh."

"Hers or the new one I gave you for her?"

"Oh, right. The new one."

"Why are you calling?"

"Heard you on a call – both of you. Other guy sounded like Darth Vader."

"Same as Jocelyn, sounds like."

"Oh, well – "

"Hold on."

I returned to Jocelyn, told her about Spring, cautioning them to only use the Crickets, not call each other's cells, then gave her instructions to meet me and Spring immediately on FM 646, east of I-45, at a car wash that was more a karaoke bar than anything. Then I got back on with Spring and she agreed to head on down there as well.

I had plugged the Cricket into my cigarette lighter charger and was sitting back trying to calm down when the rap at my driver's window sent my pulse to max and my knee against the steering wheel.

Lynnette.

Should I roll down the window or get out?

She took care of that decision.

The door opened and she stayed back so I got out of the Forester.

Chapter 24
— Wednesday late

"You're off the phone."

"Yeah, maybe five minutes. Thinking what to do," I said as I got far enough away from the Forester so I could shut the door. "Did the twenty cover the bill."

"I left my driver's license."

Why would she do that?

"You – why do they need your license?"

"You... really don't know?" she said, a small smile sneaking out.

"Well – no. No, I don't."

"So they'd hold the table and keep the bill open until I determined whether or not you were coming back in."

Damn. I wasn't sure how long I'd been on the phone – or off of it for that matter. The parking lot was still mostly empty, the sun was still in the west, and the wind had died down. I did know I needed to be getting down to FM 646.

"You waited for me...."

"I did."

"I'm not good at all this, Lynnette."

"I can see that. How old are you?"

I just smiled.

"Nate, I have sat down the hall from you for over two years. Except for the crazy banker, I don't think you've even had a lunch date much less a dark date."

"Dark date? What – "

"The kind where you go pick up the girl after dark and take her to a movie, or dinner, or dancing. Night time stuff. It's dark out."

She had clearly crossed over the line.

"Okay. Look, Lynnette, you're a darn nice girl. A woman, I mean. But nice the way girls use to be."

"Thank you. Please go on."

I went to stressed mode for the second, no, the third time that day. Things were supposed to start getting easier each week on Wednesdays, right?

"How old am I? You already know I got you by ten years."

"Just checking. Mom says guys finally grow up in their forties."

More stress.

"I think it would be better if I went to the meeting I just scheduled. They'll beat me there.

"It's now?"

"In fifteen minutes, just north of Dickinson."

She kinda kicked the tarmac a time or two like she was thinking, then said, drawing closer, I guessed wanting to make sure I could hear her with the wind and all, "Can I help?"

Stressed to the max.

I grabbed hold of door handle and popped it open.

"I'm sure you could and I'm not gonna involve you in this. You deserve fun, not tension."

Her head dropped down a bit and her shoulders probably dropped too.

"Look, Lynnette, I kinda need to get past all this stuff that's related to the Franklin case. I'm not myself, you know, socially. I have noticed your interest and caring and all that – I think. I do like it. I want to welcome it. But...."

I paused.

Then, "Right now, I've just got to go take care of business. If I don't, well, I won't be any fun for a long time."

She stepped back, turned and walked at what looked like her regular pace towards the front door of the IHOP.

~ + ~

As I entered the NASA bypass, I thought of the last girl I truly loved, my daughter Kara. She would pop in my mind at the most wistful of moments, like when Lynnette walked back inside back then.

Kara had died ten years before at the age of eight. A full-size SUV tire had rolled right over her in one of those freak accidents that can happen when you have lots of kids getting out of class at the end of the day at an elementary school.

She was a sweetheart. It tore my heart when her mother moved them to Florida after our divorce. Corpus Christi, Texas, was a long way from Lake Okeechobee.

Kara usually visited me when I needed a hug. Love her, always.

~ + ~

Did I want another sweetheart?

Lynnette – if she continued to speak to me – had no children that I knew of and was still young enough to have one or two, having just turned thirty-four. I'd heard the docs didn't fight women in their mid thirties so much by then about having kids.

But maybe Lynnette had wanted only me? Didn't want kids. Did I want another child?

Maybe she'd just changed her mind back at the IHOP!

I was stressed out. Not a good time to entertain life-changing plans – so why was I?

As I exited the bypass to get on the south feeder for I-45, Iccurred to me that I had sent Spring and Jocelyn to a bar. The car wash part was closed after dark, so that left only the bar and they were eighteen. Twenty-one to drink in Texas.

I got on the Cricket to Jocelyn, rerouted them to Panera Bread where we'd met the week before.

Yeah, I was stressed out.

It was just as I exited to FM 646 that I remembered to look in my rear view and side mirrors for a tail.

Can you spell dark Ford Explorer. Maybe two.

I went on past the curly turn to FM 646, straight on down the feeder to Dickinson and FM 517.

Only one of the two followed me. One too many.

I got on the Cricket and told Jocelyn to sit tight and I would let the two of them know where to go as soon as I was sure I had dumped my tail.

Or had I a passenger?

Had the Feds been tailing me and I'd not done a good job of scouting my surroundings?

Or maybe they'd installed a transmitter that afternoon. Candice Franklin had put one on the Forester. Why not the Feds?

My detection equipment was at my home in Seabrook. I had to run.

Chapter 25
– Wednesday late

I ended up in an unincorporated area called Bacliff. After taking so many quick turns, I wasn't sure where I was until FM 2004 dumped me on the Emmett Lowry. I took that to Hwy 146 and then back north toward Bacliff when Spring called the Cricket.

"Hey, Mr. T., where you hiding?"

"San Leon heading toward Bacliff. You gals okay?"

"Been a long time since you sent us to Panera. Need you to come pick up the tab. My card's maxed."

I heard some shuffling and then Jocelyn's deeper voice.

"You desert us or what?"

"No. Course not."

"You could update folks."

"You're right. You're right. I've been watching for tails, driving in areas I'm not familiar with – at night."

Should we still meet up?

Yes.

But where? Where to meet?

Bacliff was a long way in time from south League City and Panera Bread where I'd sent Spring and Jocelyn.

The light turned red at FM 517 and I stopped.

"How about Chili's in Kemah," I said.

"Mr. T.," said Spring, "you have us all the way over here at I-45. You paying my gas bill tonight?"

She had a point.

I glanced in my rear-view mirror and saw a very dark Ford Explorer four cars back in outside lane. I was next to the turn lane. I'd have missed him but a big tractor-trailer rig had come up behind him.

I contemplated turning quickly, using the Forester's turbo when the light changed.

And then I accepted I had a transmitter. The Forester was bugged. There was no way the Feds could have followed me all the way. FM 2004 gets little traffic at night.

"Spring, you and Jocelyn go home. Both of you keep these phones powered on. I'll be in touch."

"Mr. T., I can't just jump right back out of the house in two hours. Mom will go nuts."

"Go over to Jocelyn's."

"Mom'll still go nuts. Remember Jocelyn's got an apartment."

"I can't meet you guys. I think the Forester has a beacon."

She giggled, then said, "You mean like the one Mom had me put underneath?"

"Exactly. You and Jocelyn figure out where to go for two hours. I've got to get this monkey off my back."

I disconnected. The light changed. I quickly reached the speed limit and changed lanes to be four cars ahead of my tail. If he wanted to get closer, he'd have to change lanes, where I'd see him again in my side view mirror

~ + ~

I exited Hwy 146 just north of the Kemah Bridge at Toddville Road and snuck into the driveway of a friend of mine who lived around a curve. I parked in his blind driveway. Waited twenty-five minutes.

Nothing.

I headed on home, fully expecting Explorers to be parked down the street.

I wasn't disappointed. But I was.

I expected two Ford Explorers. Saw only one when I arrived. I expected to be blocked in my driveway, like almost happened up on Helm. The one Explorer remained three houses down the street. I expected a rude phone call from the Feds, Mr. Technology Voice, at least. Nothing.

I let Zip in.

Just as I opened the refrigerator, the Candice ring tone throttled the Z10.

I let it go to voice mail.

She didn't leave a message.

Chapter 26
– Wednesday late

I got some food in me and such, then went to the garage and scanned the Forester.

Different location. Better equipment.

The Feds' device was half the size of the one Candice had Spring place underneath the Forester. Half. And coal black like the underside.

Finding it had been a piece of cake. My equipment beeped louder and louder the closer I brought the wand to the source. I had to be patient, moving the wand ever so slowly underneath the small SUV because that sort of device might not transmit a ping but every thirty seconds.

I thought about the transmitter while I put my equipment back in the garage safe, deciding to let the little bug maintain its perch.

Time to call the Thugettes.

"This better be good, Trench."

"Hey, Jocelyn, where are you guys?" I'd called Spring's Cricket.

"My place."

"Spring tell her mom?"

"You serious?"

"Never mind. I've got an Explorer outside."

"You cut their tires?"

She sounded serious.

A tempting idea.

"No. Not... yet."

"You do that and call us back."

The connection dropped.

I thought of calling <u>islandgenius</u> in Hawaii since his clock was so far behind mine, then thought better of it. He'd been less than helpful the last two calls.

A text came in on the Cricket ten minutes later, that time from Jocelyn's.

J: cut tires yet?

I answered,

T: no
J: we told you
T: thought I in charge of investigation
J: you think 2 much
T: ...
J: you sooooo need our help
T: seriously?
J: w/o my cuz, you be in jail.
T: not so sure on that one
J: you say
T: yes I say

She didn't reply right away so I left both phones on the kitchen counter and went into the garage. I found my night goggles right where they were supposed to be and shut off the garage's internal lighting so I could put the night goggles on, get them and me adjusted to the dark. Then I grabbed my halogen portable work light out of its charger and took the side door outside to see who was in the Explorer.

~ + ~

The year before I had mounted a powerful floodlight above the door but I did not turn it on. I left the flood over wide garage door off too. After locking the side door's deadbolt with a key,

I duck walked to the corner of the garage to take a peek down the street.

The Explorer was there but it had moved up, two houses down, not three. Seemed strange. Maybe it was an intimidation game. Inch up on me, one driveway at a time.

I turned up the night vision hoping to count bodies inside the SUV. No soap. I wondered if the Feds had specified mirror glass on all Alphabet Soup vehicles....

I walked all the way around my house, duck walked through the side gate and across the side lawn to my neighbor's house, out of sight of the Explorer. Once I got to the front corner of their stucco two-story, I stuck my neck out and inspected the Explorer again. It hadn't moved but still no vision inside the SUV.

I duck stepped back and stood up. Should I follow my earlier anger and walk right up to the Explorer, demand an audience? Maybe if I had backup? Without it, the Feds could whisk me off to never never land and no one would know for sure.

I went over several ways I could arrive at the Explorer, including going around the next two houses and coming up on the SUV from behind. Nothing seemed to overcome my basic fears. I was a sit-at-a-desk geek at heart, mind, and soul, big enough so guys in the service didn't mess with me but kind of heart and shy of soul. My business was walk-ins. I helped them -- they left with a smile on their face. A geek desk jockey. Being an on-the-street Sam Spade or Elvis Cole or Spenser was a whole 'nother world, one in which I had little practice. No gumshoe, shoe-leather wearing internship was required to get the Private Investigator license in Texas.

I just about shit my pants when a hand landed on my shoulder, pulling me back a foot or so, and a voice said, "Mr. Trench, you need to remain silent and step back."

I recognized the contralto from that morning, Jocelyn's cousin, Constable Heather Carey, or Agent Carey, depending on which story you believed.

I said, "I am going to – "

She clamped my mouth with a gloved hand and pulled me back a couple more steps before saying, in not much more than a whisper, "You are in deep trouble and we need to get into your backyard as soon as possible. Lead the way."

I felt no hard object in my back, no Sig Sauer, no night stick.

Just instructions from a woman, taller than I but not near as heavy.

In the dark. No one around.

I complied.
Why did I comply?
Ask my shrink.

Chapter 27
– Wednesday late evening

I walked onto my patio but she shoved me into the yard.

"Your house is bugged."

I took off the night vision glasses, hoping she'd see the anger in my eyes, said, "You sped out of my office this afternoon faster than Wile E. Coyote. Now you're telling me what to do in the middle of the night. What the – "

"You can't hide."

"I wasn't hiding from you."

"You can't hide from the Feds."

"You're a Fed, then. Truth? Or government spin cycle."

She shook her head like a second grade teacher would to a student who claimed his dog had eaten his homework.

"Come inside," I said and turned.

The gloved hand again restricted my movement.

"Your house is bugged, remember?"

"So what! You're the one doing the bugging."

"No, I'm not."

"You're a Fed."

"Not that kind."

"Same C.I.A."

She placed both hands on my shoulders, looked down at me a good five seconds. I guess she was encouraging me to listen.

"Trench, the National Clandestine Service exercises oversight functions over C.I.A. operations *for* the Director of the C.I.A. We are independent of his operatives, both in hierarchy and in mission."

"You testifying before a Senate committee or what here – "

"Sorry," she said, taking a step closer. "You need to get out of your house."

"You driving me somewhere?"

"Your small car is disabled?"

"No. But one of your transmitters has hitched a ride."

"How do you know?"

"I'm good. So what now?"

She hesitated.

I said, "I'm going into the garage and taking the device off my Forester. What are you driving?"

She sorta ducked her chin, then said, "The Explorer outside, two houses down. The one you were spying on."

"Why did you move up a house? Hell, why didn't you just come in?"

"I'm right where I parked."

"When?"

"Under a half hour ago. Took a while to reconnoiter and approach your property."

What the hell?

"Was there another Explorer when you parked?"

"No. Why?"

I just really didn't want to believe her. The whole damn Fed thing was as screwy as diet ice cream with calorie-free chocolate swirls.

"How would you like a transmitter on your Fedmobile?"

"It already has one."

"Well, why don't you call your ops office and ask them whose C.I.A. Explorer was out there, one house further away, until just before you arrived?"

"What good is that going to do?"

"Keep you busy while I give swimming lessons to the transmitter."

I unlocked the garage, removed the little black bastard from the Forester, walked down my back yard to the boat canal and tossed it three docks down. I had half a notion to drop Constable Carey in with it as she watched me.

I did not.

Instead, just before I reached the patio on my way back from the slam dunk, I got my nose in her face, said, "What are you going to do now?"

When she didn't respond, I said, "Then why did you come here? How did you know I'd be here?"

Constable Carey darted to my left, walking at a rapid pace.

"Not so fast!"

I caught up to her at the side gate. Stepped around her and blocked the gate.

"Heather or whatever your name really is, you high tailed it out of my office not twelve hours ago."

She said nothing, stood like a statue.

"You show up here after dark and act like you're saving me."

She remained still stiff as a board, quiet as falling snow.

"Start talking or I'm going to call Torville."

"He won't talk to you."

"He can hear voice mail and read texts with your name in them."

"You don't have his phone number, much less his cell."

Point well taken.

She tried to walk off but I grabbed her shoulder. Carey twisted out from under my grip, took off running toward the other side of my house.

I let her go. Maybe she'd go see *her shrink* in the morning. She certainly needed it more that I did.

~ + ~

When I walked back inside the house, Zip jumped three feet off the floor and landed all four on my gut. I'd never had him do that. I guessed he was worried.

I let him out and opened a beer.

Sat in front of the mind eraser, my forty-some-odd flat screen. I think there was another playoff game on. Who was playing? Visitor and Home.

My peace and quiet didn't last long.

Chapter 28
– Wednesday very late

Just before midnight, the Z10 cackled with Candice's ring.

Woke me up.

I'd fallen asleep on the recliner.

The ring didn't wake me up so much as Zip licking my face.

I let the rings go to voice mail.

Crawled out of the recliner, petted Zip behind the ear for a sec, then headed for the bathroom.

No voice mail.

I came back into the den and looked around.

Neat enough. Nobody'd see it, anyway.

Headed off to bed.

Candice again.

Ignored again.

Pulled the sheet back.

No voice mail.

Got in bed.

Was about gone when the Cricket rang.

Spring's ring.

Problem: I'd left Cricket in kitchen along with the Z10.

Had I set a notification sound for voice mail on the Cricket?

Probably not.

Got back up, almost tripped over Zip, and headed back down the hall.

Message, Spring's voice:

"Mr. T. Mr. T. You gotta be there. I found him. I found him. Call me. Call me. Call me."

I don't recall whether it was the excitement in her voice that shook me back to one hundred percent awake or my frustration with her not explaining which "him" she meant. Her dad?

I punched two keys.

Phone rang.

"Mr. T. !"

"Spring, this better be good."

"I told you I would. I told you I'd do it."

I let the air damp her enthusiasm for a few moments.

"Who him did you find?"

"Mom's. Mom's. Mom's."

"Alright already. Start from the top."

"I am at the top of my game. My tracking game."

"Awesome, Spring. Awesome," I said, using the most overused positive adjective in the English language at that time. "Tell me how you found him, where he is, where your mom figures in all this."

"He's in Deer Park. Near Pasadena Freeway and Center."

That put him a good half hour away from Seabrook, even longer during rush hour, the plants emptying out shifts and such.

"Spring, where are you now?"

"Down the street."

"From where?"

"From him."

"Where is your mom?"

"Inside."

"Inside... *his* house?"

"Yes. Isn't this exciting!"

The Z10 announced Candice once again.

I wondered.

"Are you sure you weren't seen?"

"No way."

"Jocelyn there, with you?"

"More like nearby. What's that noise?"

"Your mother."

"How can she be there? She's here."

The Z10 finally quit ringing.

"That was her ring on my cell."

"Oh, right. Why would she call?"

" I dunno. Third or fourth try. She's not leaving messages. How long have you been there?"

"Maybe twenty minutes. Maybe less. Maybe more."

I always loved drawing conclusions from imprecise information.

"Okay, from the beginning – you and Jocelyn's last phone call with me – what happened?"

Chapter 29
– Wednesday very late

Spring talked about being bored and her and Jocelyn deciding to go see what her mom was up to.

And how when they got near her house, her mom was pulling out of the driveway, so they followed her – in Jocelyn's father's car, which would have been new to Candice.

They almost lost sight of Candice on Red Bluff Rd., having to give her a long lead with sparse traffic late in the evening. They drove right by *his* house almost missing her mom's car entering the double garage.

How did they know it was *his* house? The not-so-tall white-haired-but-not-bald guy that directed Candice inside.

Spring wasn't sure if he had a lot of tools or junk, the only light in the garage being the small bulb in the opener motor cabinet near the ceiling. And that was also why the pics didn't come out worth a darn using a telephoto at night.

Jocelyn took the phone from Spring at that point and gave me hell for not telling them I was home or wherever.

"Jocelyn, you sent me a surprise after lunch and I was going to wait until the morning to talk about it, so back off."

"We are doing your dirty work and you tell

me to back off? No respect."

"I have lots of respect for y'all's initiative. I don't care much for your telling your cousin everything that's going on."

"What? Not seen her since we left the house – on Helm."

"How about telephone or text or email, in person or electronic?"

"No text. No phone. No tweet. No Facebook. You seen her?"

"No Instagram coded photo?"

"No respect. I'm outta here."

The line went dead.

I watched Sports Center.

Five minutes later or so, Spring said, "Hey, what do we do?"

"With what?"

"Mr. T., I found him, now what?"

"No photos, right?"

"No."

"Not even of your mom's car going into the garage? It's a double wide. single door?"

"Well, yeah, it is and, yeah we did, but his license plate's in a shadow so we're thinking that's not good and we were driving down the street so a couple of the shots were kinda jiggled."

"So you have a pic of both cars in the garage?"

"Yes. Would be better in court with the plate, then?"

"Yes."

"So we leave now, maybe?"

"Stay. She can't remain there all night without your noticing she's not at home."

"Maybe not. I'm usually asleep when she gets up."

And that reminded me I didn't know, exactly, what Candice had called about.

"You've got to stay and get the photo when she leaves, when they open the garage again. What kind of car?"

"Adult car. Big."

"Who made it?"

"Can we move closer?"

"That's up to Jocelyn."

"Sure."

Spring was growing up. I guessed she had just learned that it takes more than one little Ah-Hah to catch a thief or liar.

"Gotta go," I said. "I'll be in touch."

"Mr. T. !"

"Okay, you can call me when you get the license plate with your mom standing nearby or in her car."

"Wait !"

I was pretty sure it was Jocelyn.

I waited. Maybe fifteen seconds.

"Umm, Trench."

"Yes."

"Sprite says you want us to stay."

"If she wants to really nail her mother."

"Okay, tell *me* what needs to be in the photo."

"Hey, a divorce lawyer would love to see a photo with the house garage door open, the guy, Spring's mom at the wheel with the window down and his license plate clear as glass."

"Like Court TV."

I'd never seen the show. Sounded good.

Chuck Emerson

"Yeah. That would do it."

Chapter 30
– Thursday early morning

"She's leaving!"

Five-thirty A.M. Said so on alarm clock. Cricket had rung.

I got up. Pulled the drape back. Outside looked in at me.

Dawn's early light wasn't much for photo taking, even if Jocelyn had brought her darn good digital SLR with her.

"She's leaving! They're both leaving."

"Okay, Spring. I heard you. Calm it down a notch. Where's Jocelyn?"

"Taking pics."

"Can you read the license plate?"

"Don't have the binocs."

"Ask Jocelyn."

"She's out of the car, down behind some bushes. I'm back three houses. All I can see... he's waving or something, garage door closing, getting in his car."

"Okay, well, call me back when Jocelyn and you are mobile."

"Want me to tail Mom?"

"Then you'd leave Jocelyn stranded."

I had managed maybe four hours' sleep. I could work on that. Just couldn't do it often.

When I placed the Cricket on the night stand, I noticed the Z10 blinking green. I picked it up. Woke up the screen. A text had come in an hour earlier.

From Candice:

CFPF: "Decided to meet. Need discuss our relationship. Things."

Such clarity at four thirty in the morning.

Did her lover work at a plant and go on shift at 6:00 A.M.?

I couldn't decide to reply.

I couldn't decide *not* to reply.

Decided I could wait at least an hour. A man could sleep until 6:30 or 7:00.

Which I tried; reset the alarm.

Couldn't.

Spring called again.

"We're in car. Coming over."

Man, I hadn't even ....

"Can't this wait?"

"I found him. That was our deal."

I had yet to dream up how knowing who Candice was screwing instead of her husband would help me get rid of the Feds.

"Go eat breakfast. Come over after."

"You should cook."

And then I remembered –

"Don't come here. Will explain. Go to – where are you, anyway?"

"Was in Deer Park, remember?"

"Okay, that Denny's we did before. 146 and Fairmont."

"That's not the direction we're driving. On Space Center."

"Take a left."

I hung up and put on a pot of coffee before I hit the shower.

~ + ~

Candice texted me while I was in the shower.

Of course.

Didn't notice until pouring coffee, about to leave.

CFPF: Coffee Oasis at 9:30.

I laughed.

Sipped.

Might could actually arrive on time from La Porte Denny's.

I waited until I was at a light on 146 before confirming.

~ + ~

"Don't get up," I said, tossing my tired ass into the booth.

"Here's the car," said Spring.

She stuck the SLR's view screen in my face.

I needed glasses to even read the numbers.

"Jocelyn, what is the license plate number?"

"I think it's from Virginia."

Seemed I remembered Langley was in Virginia.

"Email it to me. Be right back."

"You can't leave us," said Spring, sounding a bit nervous.

"My tablet's in the car."

"I'll pull the SD card out of the camera," said Jocelyn.

~ + ~

The 8Gb file displayed nicely on my Galaxy Tab 10. The license plate on what turned out to be a Chevrolet Impala had come out very clear despite using the telephoto in the dawn light. Virginia's plates were just as dull as the new black-on-white Texas plates just adopted.

Something about the pretty ones were too difficult to read if the car was pulling away from a robbery. I wondered who I could call to get the plate traced. The Golden Gumshoes must have somebody near D.C. Had to be Gumshoes in Virginia.

I explained what I was thinking to the Thugettes.

"You did good work, gals."

They looked at each other like, "oh, sure."

"Okay, did either of you see them kissing?"

Two heads turned in the negative.

"Holding hands? Long hug? Blowing kisses?"

Heads shaking like I was silly.

"Even if she is having an affair," I said "we can't know from just one sighting."

"She stayed overnight," said Spring.

"Five-six hours? Is that overnight? Really. If they're having an affair?"

"You can get it on good in six.... " Jocelyn stopped in mid sentence.

"I doubt the Virginia plates belong to a local lover," I said. "They most likely were plotting your demise, Spring," only half kidding.

"That car could be a plant," said Spring. "Traded plates with somebody at the Intercontinental."

"Sure. It's possible."

"Whatever, Trench," said Jocelyn. "What's on your mind?"

"Okay, look, the Feds, Secret Service, whichever could have so much invested in the situation with Benjamin Franklin that they are now corrupting your mother.

"Why?"

"Me. She hired me. I get under their skin. The Feds don't like it."

"Would having a Fed for a boyfriend explain all that cash?" said Spring.

"It might. Your mother meeting at odd hours with a Federal Agent could definitely explain the bills she had being fully circulated. Fed agent just drops by the Federal Reserve and requisitions used bills that are scheduled to be burned."

"That works but I can't see Mom ever talking to a Fed. I mean she is so anti-government and thinks herself so squeaky clean – "

"Which she probably ain't," said Jocelyn.

"Okay, Spring, look," I said. "Don't you think once it became clear that your dad is involved with the Feds that your mom might agree to cooperate as well?"

"I'll go home. Make her share."

"Maybe that's not the best idea. She grounded you. She's beat you home, will be able to tell you didn't spend the night. Could kick you out permanently."

"And you're not moving in with me," said Jocelyn, her grin growing wider when Spring punched her in the shoulder. "Gotta put you on some weight training. And protein bars. You seriously lack muscle, girlfriend."

Chapter 31
– Thursday

I was embarrassed to be on time for Candice's rendezvous at Coffee Oasis. She had settled in near the back (the street front window wall), sat sipping her coffee, her face calm yet pale. The Candice I'd called a client for two weeks never appeared calm and never looked pale. She might no longer be calling the shots. Probably had co-opted to the Feds and shut down.

Under their supervision, she had to perform. She'd be monitored. Watched. Her handler might be at the out-of-place dark suit and black tie at the end of the coffee bar near the front door reading the New York Times.

I walked slowly, taking stock of the customers seated at the mahogany tables, ignoring the ones standing in line to order. I couldn't read folks from behind very well.

As I approached her table, I wondered what the Feds had on Candice Faith Pence Franklin. Probably something to do with money. Had to be. They wouldn't tell her about Ben. That would bring on the wrath of Godzilla's Sister on all of them. Maybe they knew where she got the fully-circulated Franklins.

"Good morning, Mrs. Franklin."

"Candice. You men never listen. Candice. Call me Candice. Now. Sit. Down."

"Would you like another coffee?"

"Sit. Down. I've ordered yours."

I clicked my heels and sat to her left, my back to the coffee beans, eyes on the front door suit.

"Now, Mr. Trench, I – "

"Nate."

She shook her head as if clearing cobwebs. Had I interrupted a speech prepared courtesy of the Secret Service?

"I've been thinking," she said, brushing back hair that had looked just fine where it was.

"Yes. Please go on."

"Well, perhaps we just drifted out of sync."

Interesting concept and an unusually geeky word for her to be using. I could hardly wait for her answer as I replied, "How so?"

"You were working, yes, and I wasn't being very, well...."

"Candice?"

"I'm here to end our relationship."

I wanted to jump up and cheer! Instead, I cast my lot with sedate and withdrawn.

I said "I see" as dull and quiet as I knew how.

"You have made several points. I did expect results rather quickly. I guess I thought the amount I was paying you would motivate you beyond human capacity."

"I see."

"And I do owe you expenses...."

"Go on, please."

"Is there an amount with which you would consider the matter completed and closed on good terms?"

"You have the billing for the expenses for last week. I really haven't run up new ones." I categorized the Crickets as survival gear. "So, I guess the question would be this past weekend I spent writing your report. And my efforts on Monday when you *visited*."

"Oh, that. Of course. Let me see."

See took out an envelope and pen and scribbled numbers on the back for a couple of minutes.

"Okay... Nate. Five thousand a week is seven hundred a day. Saturday, Sunday, Monday would be twenty-one hundred. Then adding in your expenses, let's call it an even five thousand. Do you agree?"

The Feds had really stomped on her.

"Would that be in cash, again?"

"Yes, I can put that together – today. And... you would consider that 'paid in full,' then."

"I believe I can live with that."

"Yes, well, how about this afternoon. Here. Say three-thirty?"

I was about to say yes, hiding the ultimate in joy, when my stomach fell through the floor, alerting me to the truth.

The payoff was too easy. Too damn easy. No fight in her. Even if she'd agreed, I should have felt some hatred or loathing for me or the process – or the Feds. I didn't. It was like she'd taken too much Lexapro that morning. No energy in her voice, no bitchiness in her attitude. Sexy had definitely gone fishing.

But there had to be more going on. There had to be a real big reason. The United States Secret Service had definitely come to roost on

Candice Faith Pence Franklin. What did they use for the hammer?

Or – was I being set up!

Would the Feds record the whole transaction in digital and then use it to arrest me on tax evasion? Lock the door? Throw away the Patriot Act key?

"Ms. Franklin – Candice. I'll be on the other side of I-45 this afternoon. Could you get over to Friendswood, maybe four, four-thirty?"

She appeared to wake up out of daze, said, "I am not sure. I'll have to call you."

And the plot thickened!

And I so wanted my money.

And I had to forget the big bucks.

I wanted my life as I had known it a month earlier and there was no dollar amount that I'd trade for that.

Chapter 32
– Thursday

At the office the first order of business was to walk in and check Lynnette's temperature. I gathered my courage and resolution as I turned the corner to the Executive Suites waiting area.

Lynnette was not at her desk. No one was.

I checked the coffee. Half a pot, less the cup I poured myself. Somebody had made it.

Bathroom break? I fumbled around a bit too long in my message cubby hole, to no avail. Thought of leaving her a note but I didn't want anyone else to see a "cordial" note.

At my desk with the computer system up and running, the first order of business was to use the traditional resources for license plate numbers. I had four, two by subscription.

No such plate number in Virginia.

Right.

I got on Golden Gumshoes and posted my need.

No immediate response.

And no, contrary to novels, movies, or on TV, I did not have a Good Buddy at the Houston P.D. or Harris County Sherriff, or Texas Rangers to look things up for me in exchange for lunch, dinner, or drinks. The only one "nearby" was Jocelyn's cousin, but if she really did work for N.C.S., she would most likely give me incorrect

Collateral Franklins

information on the plate *and* report me to her supervisor. I couldn't chance it and she'd never given me her number or business card anyway.

I did other things, like realize I hadn't charged either phone.

And I had not heard or felt the text message Lynnette had sent shortly after my arrival:

LS: Glad you're still alive

At least she was still speaking to me – well, texting.

The Z10 lit up with Lynnette's office phone number.

"Mr. Trench, are you available?"

Was she flirting? If I had customer waiting, she would usually say something like, "Ms. Robertson is here to see you."

"Yes. Yes, of course. Who's looking at you?"

"Two teenagers."

Damn. Spring and Jocelyn.

"Do I have a choice?"

"Just checking. I'll send them down. I think they know the way."

~ + ~

"Was it a Fed? Was it?" said Spring, one foot in the door.

"Don't know yet. What you want? I might actually need to take care of paying customers this morning. Did you see your mother?"

"She wasn't there when I got back. Guess she made it to see you?"

I had told them.

"Have you seen her today?"

"She has," said Jocelyn as she closed my office door. "Old lady looked her age for once.

No spring in her coils. Definitely fading fast."

"What do you say, Spring?"

"Pretty much."

I told them to sit down and hush for a minute while I checked on the Golden Gumshoes' Bulletin Board.

Three members wished me good luck.

I looked to Jocelyn.

"Tell me about your cousin, Heather."

"Almost old enough to be my aunt."

"Number?"

"Thirty-two, or about there."

"How long you known her? Her life history. All ya got."

"She moved down here maybe three years ago. I really didn't know I had an 'older' cousin until then. Nice enough. In great shape. Does a mean slam with the volley ball thing. Mostly beach."

"That all?"

"How much you want?"

"All you got."

"You paying me? Ain't savin' your ass from jail enough?"

Of course it was, but I had no time left for Mr. Nice Guy.

"You recall we still have a Fed problem? You two have throw-away phones, why?"

"Tell him, Jocelyn."

It took intermittent prodding to amass very little data on Heather Carey. Jocelyn really didn't know much.

Heather Carey was a Constable for Harris County, Texas, stationed for the last six-plus months at the Clear Lake station, behind the

Freeman Library. Jocelyn had known about Heather for those three years, but had not had contact more than once or twice a year at family functions around Thanksgiving. The volley ball info was by reputation. Jocelyn had never seen Heather play. Jocelyn had lettered two years in high school basketball and said the volleyball team was where the school put the slow-of-foot basketball players. Evidently that didn't apply to Ms. Carey.

Then Spring said, "Why don't you ask Heather to check on the Virginia plate?"

"Yes, Trench, why you not doin' that?"

I didn't want to go there.

"Trench, I'll text her now."

"Don't!"

Chapter 33
– Thursday

Jocelyn looked at me like I was the dumbest fast food worker on the planet, said, "And your great thinking reason?"

"She visited me here at the office yesterday and again at home late evening."

Jocelyn lurched back in her chair. Spring jumped out of hers.

"Easy, both of you," I said.

"Why didn't you tell us?" said Spring

"I did mention it to Jocelyn here."

"You didn't tell me?" said Spring.

"Wait," I said. "This could turn Jerry Springer in a minute. Spring, sit down."

"Yah, but – "

"No buts, Spring. I currently don't trust Heather Carey."

I let that settle down in the dust for a minute, then said, "Ms. Carey won't answer many of my questions about her job description. She seems to be involved in more than just local peacemaking. When I figure it out, Spring I'll tell Jocelyn and she can tell you."

"You're saying my cuz is not with us?"

"Jocelyn, we're going to let it work itself out a bit. Now I'm going to look up the license plate search one more time. Sit still."

The Z10 rang.

Lynnette. Executive Suites number.

Collateral Franklins

I didn't answer.
I popped up the Gumshoes again.
Nothing.
"You two get on out of here. I bet you've got to get to work, Jocelyn. How 'bout you take Spring to Lake on your way?"

~ + ~

I called Lynnette on the front desk number.
"Hey, you busy?"
"You're gonna be. There's a paying customer waiting."
"Anyone you recognize."
"No thank goodness. You travel in a fast crowd."

I wasn't sure if she was kidding or airing a point of incompatibility.

"You bringing her back or should I go up?"
"Gentleman. Name of Baumgartner." She spelled it out. "I'll send him back."
"You free for lunch?"
"Ummm, short notice. Let me check."

Was that a flirt or a cold shoulder?

Women. You never knew, especially if you were Nathan Edward Trench.

~ + ~

Baumgartner turned out to be the executor of his brother's estate and had been referred by a very small law firm that didn't have a referral department that billed. He was very relieved to learn how much lower my hourly and package fees were.

The problem was more of geography. His brother had fathered four children over the years, three different wives in four states. Yes, that doesn't make sense. The exes hadn't moved but one of the children had. A bit cumbersome but a piece of cake compared to Candice Franklin – and family.

I wondered if I took some of Candice's cash and hired an Internet S.E.O. company, I could get so many folks coming in the office, I'd have to hire Lynnette full time. Search Engine Optimization was slippery. You had to be the consummate geek – never leaving the office for meals, working five monitors eighteen hours per day – to sit all day tweaking web pages.

~ + ~

The morning ended up easy and profitable as two more folks came by the office looking for lost cousins and such. Then the Large Consulting Law Firm (they called me with requests for their clients, billed for them) and two past customers called with more tasks that I could do as I had time. No rush.

Then, just as I was going to shut down the computers for lunch – yes, Lynnette had agreed at the end of one of her "you have a customer" alerts – I got a number-blocked call on the Z10 again.

"Trenchcoat Investigations," I said, acting dumb. "Good morning."

"Mr. Trench?"

"Mr. Technology Voice."

"You having a slow morning?"

"No. Been brisk. Busy since breakfast."

"Oh, you're counting the coffee shop."

"Weren't you there? That was work."

"By our metrics – I have the report in front of me – your phone traffic is down perhaps forty percent."

"If you say so."

"Well, I do and was wondering how you would explain this."

"Do you have metrics going back at least three months?"

He didn't reply.

"I didn't think so. If you did, you would learn that my traffic varies widely. I had six jobs off one phone call this morning, in fact." Thank you Large Consulting Law Firm.

"You would say that. One call does appear to have been rather lengthy."

"I keep telling them to email me the info but they call. Anyway, you know who call me. You go figure it out."

"Just a minute."

"No minute available. Time for lunch. Have a morbid afternoon – and see a doctor. Your voice is definitely not working within standard variances. Good bye."

I was proud of myself, my handling of that call, giving myself a pat on the back as I walked to Lynnette's desk to take her to lunch.

"Oh, we had some fun this morning," said Lynnette.

"Just now, actually."

"Well, may your lunch be even better. Where are we going?"

"Lady's choice."

"Nate, please. I'm a girl. Working on being a woman. My grandmother was a *lady*."

Lady's choice, no?

Chapter 34
– Thursday lunch time

Lynnette's smile was more radiant than I'd seen in months as we walked out to the Forester, chatting about I don't remember what. Was I distracted by her smile? You tell me.

I opened the front passenger door for her and she smiled wider. I walked around the back of my small SUV so she couldn't see how giddy I was – imagine, a retired Senior Chief Petty Officer giddy.

"I have to see you" flew on the wings of a screech.

I stopped moving halfway inside the Forester, looked at Lynnette.

She gave me a hand wag and a nod. Too nice. Too patient.

"Be right back," I said, wondering as I walked over to Candice's driver's side what ever happened to the egotistic self-assured country-club tennis woman – and hoping she'd lower her voice instead of shattering windows.

I held up my hands palms open and shoulder height as I looked into Candice's eyes.

"Ms. Franklin, I – "

"Candice. Please. Now of all times."

"We met this morning and things sounded within limits, so I am going – "

She shook her head left and right like an angered, passive-aggressive four-year-old.

"Deal's off."

"Fine" was all I could think of. "I'm going to lunch."

"You can't. It's not safe."

She was suckering me with the big guns.

"I'm going. Call me and I'll let it go to voice mail. Leave a message explaining why the deal's off and why it's not safe to go to lunch. I think it records up to three minutes."

I turned to my right to walk around behind her.

Candice screeched and babbled and drew a crowd – well, some folks stopped walking.

I held my hands way above my head and shook them just before entering the Forrester. I'm not sure if the folks thought I was waving or showing them I didn't have a gun.

Lynnette put a hand on mine as I shifted the automatic into drive with the console lever.

"She's married, right?"

I stomped the brake, I laughed so hard. Must have looked even more unusual to those still frozen in the parking lot.

~ + ~

"Does she pay you well?" was the first thing I now remember Lynnette saying as we drove to Thai Spice, a restaurant with lots of tasty dishes and more-than-reasonable prices. I know she said some caring things after she took her hand off mine while I used both hands to turn onto El Camino Real. I know she did. I was just too discombobulated to absorb it all, scared feelings overriding aural recall.

Candice had flipped.

I had walked.

I'd never see the money.
Did I care?
Yes.
No.
Yes, money is money.

No, if I could be guaranteed not to have to deal with her or the Feds ever again, then the money wouldn't matter. If she fired me *for real*, then I'd be off the hook with her which meant I would have no gripe with the Feds. I'd never need to stalk Ben Franklin again.

But what the hell did "Deal's off" and "It's not safe" mean? She had said the deal was good to go three hours earlier at Coffee Oasis.

And Technology Voice had sounded less menacing than usual not a half hour earlier.

I heard something.

Somebody had asked me a question.

Lynnette.

She was sitting in the passenger seat, remember, dummy.

I was so zoned out – or was I actually locked down?

I shot her a quick nod but waited to speak until we stopped at one of the seven traffic lights between our – my office and the restaurant.

"Lynnette," I said, keeping my foot on the brake while I turned half way toward her, fighting the seat belt, "in retrospect, she paid me too much at the beginning and now she probably can't pay me enough to stick around."

"You look like someone just took your Oreo Cookie, Little Boy."

I let out a sigh. My shoulders dropped. I didn't want to but I was too tired to fight it. My self-protection from the female species, my wall, had crumbled.

"One question," I said as I noticed the car beside us moving.

"Darn. Only one?" said Lynnette, a pixie-like tone in her voice.

"Sounds like Barbie's riding with me to lunch."

We both laughed and just as well. The light named red caught us again.

"Nate?"

"Yes."

"What's the question?"

I flipped to *afraid to ask it*. How had I lost my nerve? Or maybe I'd gained a bit of strength back, afforded a few moments rest in slow-moving traffic.

"Ummmm. Let's get some food in us first."

She backhanded my shoulder.

"Do you play a lot of tennis?" I said.

"Never touch the stuff."

Chapter 35
– Thursday lunch time

Cricket chirped in my left front pocket. I had to twist sideways in the booth to get it out. Lynnette gave me a head shake like you'd give a sainted aunt at eighty.

Spring.

"What?" I said, hoping the displeasure in my voice reached Spring's cranial space but wasn't so strong that it jolted Lynnette.

"He's leaving! He's leaving!"

What the hell?

"Who's leaving – leaving where?"

"The guy. The Impala. In Deer Park."

"What the hell are you doing up there?"

"Well...."

"Hold on."

I dropped the phone from my ear and looked over at Lynnette. She caught my movement and raised her eyes from the menu.

I said, "You may recall the smaller of the two high school students who were by this morning?"

"Nate, at this point, I have her phone number memorized – just kidding."

"I need to deal with this. I can go outside, if you want?"

"Worry about yourself, your business. If you go outside you can yell louder. How about that?"

Made sense.

I nodded with a smile and mouthed "Thank you," before saying to Spring, "Where are you?" as I got up.

"Deer Park, like I said."

"Are you moving – in your car. Any car?"

"Just caught a traffic light."

"You following the Impala?"

"Well, I was."

"What do you mean?"

"He made the light."

"Figures. By the way, your mother's gone nuts."

"Uh, yeah. Already there, years ago."

"You label it. She just showed up at the office in a convertible, wanted me to bust up my lunch plans. Your mother met me for coffee *less than three hours ago*."

"Sure. You told us."

"Wait. How did you get out of school?"

"I had all this perfect attendance. I can skip. I still have way enough to get out of jail free."

Could I believe her? Probably. Did I? Not really.

I said, "Why follow this guy? Why not your mom?"

"You know those tracking devices?"

Not again.

"The ones you mom had you put on your dad's Charger and my Forester?"

"Yes."

"What about them?"

"The one from the Forester is on hers."

"The convertible?"

A short silence, then Spring said, "No, that's not hers. You did say convertible."

"Three strikes, you're out. She's running around in a Solara or something with the top down."

"Crap. White?"

"Yeah."

"That's a Lexus I.S. Wait a minute."

"For what? You're talking and driving again."

"Bluetooth. Light now green. Wait."

Her being stuck in a turn lane reminded me of two weeks before when I tried to follow Ben Franklin's stringy blonde driving a Buick from the Helm house.

Spring came back on the phone four, maybe five minutes later.

"Okay, I checked the tracker app on my phone. The Lexus four-door, Mom's car, is inside the loop near Montrose. She's swapped cars with a friend. Does it all the time."

I recalled Candice saying she had stalked Ben's visits to the Helm house using a friends dull car.

"Okay, well, I'm guessing you've lost that Impala."

No reply.

"Spring, you've lost it?"

"Yeah. Okay, looks like maybe."

"You going back to Lake?"

"Not on your – "

"I didn't think so. Go home and – "

"No way."

"Let. Me. Finish."

"Yes, sir."

Chapter 36
– Thursday lunch time

"Okay, Spring, go home and see if she's there. If not – wait. When she borrows cars how does she get hers back?"

"Sometimes they come here. Sometimes she goes there. I think they're all engaged in some deception or trickery. I'd bet this one brings it back to our house. Usually does."

That didn't leave much time.

"Okay. Go home. Leave a window open a bit near the driveway so you can hear her pull up."

"And?"

"Look around for stuff that ain't usual."

"Like what?"

I realized I was being stupid.

"You've gone through your mother's stuff already, huh."

A short silence, then, "Couple times. I need to understand what's going on with my parents."

"And you're still figuring the bad guy is your mom, not your step-dad."

"He's my dad. Remember the other one died very young."

I did.

"Okay," I said, "how recent you gone through stuff?"

"Oh, a week, maybe."

"Do it again, as much as you can before she gets home. Especially look for notes on pads and stuff."

"Why? What's up?"

"If I knew that I wouldn't need you to look."

"Get off."

"Your mother was one kind of different, strange shut down kind of personality, this morning for coffee, *and* then a crazed Jerry Springer guest type just now. You get that?"

Another silence, some road noise, a turn signal clicker....

Then, "I guess she's finally toast."

"We'll do what's best for both your folks. Agreed?"

"Yeah. Not sure how that can happen. The Feds are doing something and, according to Jocelyn, they're bustin' loose."

"Something's different. I've been getting those artificial voice calls again – like twice a day."

Why had I told her that? Dumb shit.

"Did you record 'em? Love to hear."

That wasn't going to happen. Would be that much more stress in her head. The gals played tough, even Spring, but there was no need to add fodder to her teenage nightmares.

"Go home," I said. "Let me know what you find. Unless it's an emergency, give me about forty-five minutes of peace. You got that?"

"Yeah, sure. Hot date?"

"None of your business. Bye."

I jabbed the Cricket and walked back inside Thai Spice, gave a smile to Lynnette.

"Thanks for your patience," I said. "With any luck, neither of us will have to deal with a telephone."

"I ordered you the yellow curry."

"How did you know I like – "

"Waitress ordered for you. A party of eight came in while you were outside. She took ours before they could order."

"Great."

"This your favorite restaurant, Nate?" she said as she spun the long spoon in her ice tea.

I kinda winked, said, "Busted."

~ + ~

I tried eight ways from heaven to open up a casual yet kinda warm fuzzy conversation with Lynnette.

I began by asking her if she had a nickname she preferred.

"No. No I don't."

"You've really never had a nickname."

"Nate, yes, and, no, not one I'd ever care to hear again."

Sounded a bit angered.

"Sorry. Don't want to dredge up old barnacles."

She dipped her head briefly, looked me square in the eye, said, "It's not you, Nate. It's me."

"You seem fine," I said, fumbling around my mind for what to say next.

"It's still me."

"You've been best thing ever happened to that office. Stayed that way for two years."

"You only see me at work – never mind. I've looked forward to lunch with you for... months." Pink briefly painted her cheeks.

"I just got up the nerve. Don't date much. Not even lunch."

Chapter 37
— Thursday lunch time

"Oh, now, it's okay now, Nate. I know about Allison, and your other girlfriends. You're entitled. "

Lynnette was laughing inside. I could see it.

"Allison. I'll tell you about Allison. She buys me lunch twice. At the second one, she switches me to her new bank."

"Every year maybe?"

"Seems like it. But never mind. I don't date much. I met my daughter's mother just out of high school, a friend of a cousin, female variety. I guess we both figured we should be married, so we got married in six months. Six months after that we figured I couldn't afford a family working for K-Mart's auto department, so I enlisted and then she followed me around, living in dependent housing where I was stationed, taking part-time jobs at the Navy Exchange and stuff like that."

"You weren't on ships? Navy, not on ships?"

"No. I was more a support function."

"A radioman or something?"

Oh, she did not know how that would start a fire among the ranks.

"No. I was a Communications Technician."

"Sounds like a radioman. You hadn't said much about it. Like a secret life."

"It was, mostly."

"I've been working for you people in the suites for two years and I see you every day. In a way I know you better in many ways than I knew my poor gone husband when I married him."

"I, ahh, well, I'm me. Haven't dated. Get chased a couple times a year by older women who want me to improve on their standard of living."

"Now, coming from you, Nate, that's mostly rude."

"It's a Navy thing. When you're out on the town in the service, stateside or over seas, there's always some gals, groupies, figuring they can have a husband and a home and health insurance but not have to put up with the guy but four months of the year. That's stateside. If you're shore duty overseas, they work real hard to catch you, usually working in a bar that just happens to be right outside the gate. They hook a guy, automatically get moved out of poverty to the States, get to be United States citizen, rights to half a guy's pension. Dump him ten, twelve years later. Send for their relatives. They are very convincing. Seen it, too often."

"They do that? In the movies it's always so romantic. The blending of different cultures."

"Oh, you should see them. Nothing cultural about it. It's all about biz."

"Maybe not. I'll take your word for it." She squirmed a bit and the food came.

After we had our plates and utensils organized, I dug my fork into the fixins while saying, "I can take you down to Corpus and watch. It's kinda comical. Really."

"Never mind. Like your vibes, I guess. I

mean you seem like a good guy, a decent human being – most of the time. You sound angry about that overseas stuff."

"Thank you. And you've not seen *me* outside the office, chasing around for Candice Franklin. That's pretty much crazy stuff. Or kicking around the house, taking my dog out on the boat or the skiff. That's a simple life. It's all kinda boring to most of the women I've met here. I don't even dance. Got me a satellite dish and a refrigerator. That's about it."

She laughed. "Until this Franklin woman showed up three weeks ago, you were a stay-at-home."

"Call it that if you want."

"How many sports channels you have?"

"Don't know the total. I can keep up with any sport any time I want to, I guess. How's your Pad Thai?"

"Delicious. It's not hot - spicy."

"I find it light, also."

"Girls in the building complain about Thai food, say it's too hot. This is almost sweet but not like the sweet-sour Chinese thing. Not sugary. Thanks for taking me here."

As I was letting a smile leak out, but looking at my curry, the Z10 chirped.

I really didn't want to take the call. Only person using the office line would be a new client, the Technology Voice, or Candice. A guy had a right to be out to lunch.

I looked up at Lynnette. She met my eyes.

"I'm letting it go to voice mail."

"You go right ahead take care of business."

I had been taking care of business – the

things I wanted to learn about Lynnette at lunch. Where was I? The Z10 quit chirping.

I had been – giving her a Navy orientation. What the heck for? I was giving information. Hadn't got an ounce. I went to fix that.

"Lynnette, I want to – "

The Z10 chimed a voice mail.

"Check it, Nate. It could be new business."

Was she too good to be true?

Or, was she truly chasing me, kinda like desperate? Receptionists didn't make much in Clear Lake, not like inside the Loop. Maybe she was running out of life insurance money.

"Tell me about where you grew up?" I said. "I think you're from Kansas, something about magic slippers."

"You are silly for an older guy – I'm sorry. You're not old to me. Just kinda, ummm, folksy."

She didn't think I was old but called me that? I didn't know what to make of it so I didn't say anything.

Chapter 38
– Thursday lunch time

"Nate, I grew up in Missouri. East side of Kansas. Up the road from Houston far enough to have ugly cold winters, but not dusty like those folks in the oil patch. My dear Von brought us down here to get in with the oil companies. Well, he did and I landed one good paying job inside the Loop, but I quit. That drive was going to put me on blood pressure medication, at least that's what my doctor said."

"Yeah, I know a lot of the folks in Clear Lake and Friendswood seem to favor staying within – "

The Z10 rang again.
I ignored it.

"So, I can understand you," I said. "I figure one day I'd be out of business what with the access you can get to stuff all by yourself on the Internet these days – except for the fact that I'm local to folks who still want to have someone hold their hand with these searches."

"Well, the owners of this building play the drive into town as part of their benefits package – of which there is none. They incorporate each building as a separate business."

"I didn't know that. I – "
The Z10 chimed a voice mail.
"Nate, don't you think you ought to answer?"
I really liked her for her attitude about my

business, but I wanted to learn about her.

"I don't think. I'm feeling good while in the midst of this crazy Franklin case. You did that for me, so I want to keep the moment as long as I can."

Lynnette did the pink cheeks thing, again.

Then I heard a ringing from under the table. It was actually Lynnette's cell phone screaming to get out of the dungeon that was her purse. Never did get those purses that were as large as a good old-fashioned briefcase.

"So," I said, "you do have a boyfriend."

She frowned.

I laughed.

"Answer it," I said. "Go ahead."

She pulled out the phone and looked at the screen.

"It's the office. Hello?"

"Yes, Phyllis."

I looked outside, at the sky. Loved the active clouds in the Houston area.

"Wait a second. Maybe I can find him. I think he has another number. Maybe I have it. I'm gonna put you on hold."

Lynnette looked at me with a runaway freight train eyes.

"Nate, that Franklin woman is raising hell like she did on Monday morning. Demands we contact you using the secret number the company has on file."

Just then the Cricket rang.

I looked at the screen. Spring.

"Lynnette, put that call on hold or mute."

"Spring, what's up?"

"Mom. She's lost it."

"That's what I'm guessing. Whatcha got?"

"She's calling me saying I know how to get hold of you."

"I thought you said she had no – "

"She didn't. Doesn't. "

"What she do then?"

"Kept on screaming but it was like she was talking to somebody else."

"Maybe the receptionist at my office?"

"Well, sure. In an office area. There's an echo."

"Okay, well thanks for the heads up. Is she still on your regular cell."

"I think so. I muted it. Want me to listen in for a minute?"

"No. Search the house. We know where she is so you've got at least fifteen minutes more to play sleuth."

"Good idea!"

I ended the Cricket call, looked to Lynnette who had taken her phone from her ear, said, "Is Phyllis still alive?"

"They went back and forth, Phyllis and the Franklin woman, for maybe thirty seconds, then it disconnected."

"Call her back."

Chapter 39
– Thursday afternoon

"Phyllis? – no. Hi, Angela. Sorry. How are – " Lynnette was cut off.

"Well, is she okay, though?"

"Okay, hang on. Gonna put you on hold for a sec."

"Nate, the Franklin woman just left. Phyllis is in the bathroom – crying, Angela thinks."

I remember wanting to say something cute, like, "Oh, good, we can finish our lunch." Somehow I managed to say, instead, "Gotta get Phyllis some flowers or something. Does she like that or chocolate more. Do you know?"

"Angela says that a Constable came by looking for you. That spooked Candice and she ran out."

"Would I be clairvoyant if I assumed the constable's last name was Carey?"

"You mean psychic?"

"Okay, probably psychotic. Did she give you a name?"

Lynnette tapped her phone, said, "Is the constable still there?"

"Left a hand-written note? What on? Did she sign it?"

"Nate, she can't read it. Cursive. Has a phone number."

"What's that?"

While Lynnette got the phone number, I

debated which phone to use to call Constable Carey. Yeah, I was sure it was her. She hadn't harassed me in over twelve hours.

If I called on Z10, it would compromise Carey with the very people she was purportedly supervising. If I called her on the Cricket, it would compromise not only me but also Spring and Jocelyn.

Did I dare ask Lynnette to call Carey on her cell?

"Here," said Lynnette, handing me a grocery receipt, handwriting very tidy, but purple ink.

"Thanks," I said and reached out for our waitress as she came by with two hands full of dirty dishes.

"Sorry, we don't need the check yet – Lynnette, think about dessert – but do you know if there's a pay phone around here anywhere?"

The slender and short Thai gal showed confusion on her face, said, "I ask manager," and walked on by.

"Nate, what are you thinking?"

"The woman constable yesterday?"

"Yeah, tall, slender, ready for war."

"That's her. She's Jocelyn's cousin."

"Jocelyn...?"

"The tall one of the duo with Spring."

"Oh, right. How is that – I mean, is it good or bad?"

"I have been sorting through that for a whole day. I don't know. Jocelyn is fine. Her cousin is really a distant relative."

"I have bunches of those. Like them where they are – up north!"

I had always wondered how, exactly,

Lynnette had decided to stay in Houston. Was the cold weather back home enough?

The oh so very very tall and husky waiter-manager appeared at our side, said, "You looking for pay phone, right?"

"Yes. You know of one?"

"Across street, down block, on wall outside auto parts store."

I had a vague recollection of one being there.

"It faces the side street?"

"Yes."

"Thank you!"

I turned to Lynnette.

"What did you decide on for dessert?"

"Nate, you seem to, after almost two years, kinda like me...."

I flinched, said, "Enough to buy lunch, at least."

"Funny man. Funny."

I didn't say anything.

"If you like me the way I am, keep me away from desserts and ice cream and cake and pizza parlors. I can eat a half gallon of Breyer's in one movie."

"Okay. Got ya. Let's enjoy the rest of this and then go find that phone on the wall."

Chapter 40
– Thursday afternoon

The pay phone looked like it hadn't had a connection in twenty years. Weather had faded its enamel and heavy blunt objects had dented its casing. I picked up the receiver and was pleasantly surprised by the old-time friend, the loud dial tone.

I punched ten square stainless steel buttons on the keypad and waited.

"Harris County Constable Carey. How may I help you?"

"Hello, Heather."

I purposely didn't identify myself, wanting to see what kind of a reaction I would get, assuming the pay phone had popped up as "unassigned" or "unavailable" on her screen.

"Caller, is this an emergency?"

"Not sure."

"I must have your name, location, and driver's license number to proceed any further."

"I must have your mission statement," I said, wondering what a Fed would call it.

"Your information in three seconds or call terminates."

I counted to three in my head.

Dial tone.

Bingo!

Turnabout with the Feds. Fair play.

I hated always being the one having to guess

what was going on.

Lynnette remarked about the difference. "For such a short phone call, you have a very large smile."

I steered the Forester back out on Bay Area Blvd.

"Lynnette, allow me some small amount of enjoyment with this."

"Absolutely, Darling."

She said what?

She said what?

"Nate?"

Her again.

"Nate?"

I felt a fingernail in my right bicep.

"Sorry. Was thinking about the phone call." Okay, I lied. I didn't know what I knew.

"And so short."

"Good enough. Heard tone of voice. Noted answering protocol. Been trying to decide who she usually works for."

"Sure," she said as we got stuck at Hwy. 3. I didn't think she understood but was being nice.

"And you said Candice Franklin left the office."

"Yes, and you're returning me to work eight minutes late, I'll bet."

"But – oh, sorry."

"Just kidding."

I felt her entire hand on my shoulder, giving it a squeeze combined with gentle nudges. My tummy flipped a couple times, heart rate spiked, and then I imagined Candice lurking nearby, waiting to pounce when the Forester entered the parking lot. That image turned my tummy into a square knot.

Just before I turned in, I said, "Hey, could you look around, tell me if you see a four-door white Lexus sedan, a 430, I think, or a two-door Lexus convertible, white again?"

"You thinking of trading this in?" said Lynnette with a slight giggle.

"You remember the convertible, just before lunch. I know you do. The other is the car she was driving the first time she came by the office."

As I came to a stop in an empty section of the parking lot, Lynnette said, "Weren't you having trouble with black Explorers last week?"

"Yeah. Today I'm looking for white."

"I don't see white but I do see a black Explorer to your left."

I looked, said, as I looked in the rearview mirror, "And one coming in behind. Fasten your seat belt. Wait. Get out. No need for you to get involved."

"I've been trying to get involved with you for months."

She said what?

She said what?

"Out," I said. "That's an order."

"Yes, no, sir," said Lynnette as she popped open the door. After she shut the door, I locked it and was about to hit the gas when I heard a pounding on the passenger door.

Lynnette.

I pressed the electric button to lower the window.

"What?"

"Do your problem Explorers have Schlitterbahn plates on front?"

What the hell?

I looked in the rear view mirror. Couldn't see the plate because of the angle, but did sense something else was different.

"Nate?"

"I'm thinking."

What was wrong with the picture in my rearview mirror? What didn't feel right. I had no data. But I had clear data. The Explorer had stopped in the next aisle, second row.

"I got it. Relax, Lynnette – well a little, anyway."

I could see through the windshield. A kid was sitting in the passenger seat, barely able to see over the dash.

I looked for the first Explorer.

"Lynnette, do you see the first one?"

"Where?"

"The one you saw first."

She reached a hand over and unlocked the door and got in.

"Nate, I don't see it."

"Could you see inside?"

"I don't know. It was a good ways away."

"Was it coming toward us?"

"No. It was parked in front of the back door of the building."

I didn't see it then.

"Which way was it facing?"

"It was pointed at the side street and the passenger door was on the curb."

"Let's look all the way around the car. You get that half, front to rear."

"Nothing but the one that's behind us, sorta, in the next parking row," said Lynnette.
"Good. Let's get out."
"You're sure?"
At that point I couldn't swear which way is up. Safe? Indeterminate , at best.

Chapter 41
– Thursday afternoon

We went in the building and debriefed Angela. Phyllis had gone home. Lynnette was only a few minutes late. I'd been a tenant "forever" by executive suite standards so Angela, who was technically the property manager for that building said not to worry. She handed me the note Candice had left but it didn't add anything to what Lynnette had already relayed to me. I recognized the phone number as Candice's cell, and excused myself to my office where I called Spring on the Cricket.

"Hey, your mom ought to be getting there."
"I wouldn't know."
"What?"
"I left. She called me like eight times demanding your private phone number. She's lost it."
"You said that . Why so, now?"
"I've never heard her so insecure, so desperate."
"How so?"
"I mean, when was the last time you ever heard her say please *once*, never mind four times in a row?"
"Good point. Very good. Where are you?"
"Space Center Houston."
"Why?"
"It's a personal matter."

I couldn't resist saying, "Public bathroom."
"No, you turd."
"Okay, so you're not going back to school."
"Not today."
"And where you spending the night?"
"Damn. I haven't even thought of that."
"Well, Jocelyn's would be the place. The Feds have to be working mine, got it all bugged and scanned maybe."
"You waited to tell me, why?"
"I'm telling you now. Both of you stay away from Seabrook, my place in particular. Hear me?"
"Yes, Grandpa."
"What?"
"I'm outta here, Mr. T."
And she hung up.

Had to be a boyfriend.
Or. Wait. What about "him," the guy in Deer Park. Had she attached the other tracking module?
I got out the Cricket.
Punched speed dial two.
"Can't talk now."
"That's why I'm calling. What's up? Who you with?"
"Can't... gotta go."
The line went dead.

I had four walk-ins that afternoon and tried to chat up <u>islandgenius</u> but he was not online and didn't get back to me.
Lynnette gave me four smiles – they accompanied the customers she brought on back

– plus one when I left before she got off, on purpose.

I had way too much churning through my head to have any true sense of what was churning through my guts.

Lynnette was definitely sharper than she had let on for two years, yet if that evaluation was correct, how could she stand such a simple job? Wasn't she bored? Couldn't she get more money doing almost anything else? Then again it didn't seem she'd been left destitute by her deceased husband.

But hey, she drove a gray four-door Focus, an older one at that. Well, maybe she wasn't into cars, didn't drive long distances back to Missouri or live far from the Executive Suites.

Or, had her plan all along been to meet some up-and-coming entrepreneur and latch onto his coattails. If I remembered correctly, she said she had never worked outside of a couple internships connected with a junior college where she earned an A.B.A. She'd married shortly thereafter and had never actually lived on her own.

On the way home I remembered that Lynnette had talked about a hunk of life insurance dear old Von had left for her. Not millions but enough for her not to worry. No kids, so there was that. She was way too young to qualify for the Social Security Survivor benefit.

Maybe she was frugal and just biding her time until she could get over his death. Was two years enough? I wondered if I should investigate that on the internet or have a chat with the counselors upstairs in my building.

I turned onto my street in Seabrook, early for a change. It was still bright out and Zip would finally get some quality time from me after three days of little attention. And I would get the unconditional love I needed – definitely a dog person. Did Lynnette like dogs?

There was not a single vehicle of any kind parked on my street. A few in driveways, as you'd expect.

Chapter 42
– Thursday evening

It took me a lot longer than I expected to get everything settled inside the house – like trying to get all the laundry sorted and a load into the washer – so Zip and I didn't get out in Sailor's Skiff until the light was failing.

No problem really. Most owners left lanterns on at their docks along the canals so I never felt like I was in the dark of night or anything. And dogs see better than humans at night, right? It was warm and more like late May so the dimming light made it seem cooler.

We had gone all the way down the wide channel into Clear Lake in the skiff, just 'cause it was easier and simpler – and I hadn't done the spring cleanup on my boat, Cyber Sailor. Zip did his usual scouting, hopping from one side or end to the other to inspect new things that reached his ears and nose.

Sunset was just before 8:00 PM, CDT, according to the wunderground.com folks, yet we were still piddling around doing not much of anything well after that when I figured we needed to get back into the channel and on up to home.

I was so relaxed and comfortable as we headed back that I didn't notice two guys on the NASA Pkwy. bridge over the channel outlet near the Lakewood Yacht Club. They made their presence known when their two Maglites, on pinpoint, trashed my eyes, just before we reached the bridge.

"What the hell," I said, shielding my eyes.

Zip yipped a couple times, not understanding.

"You need to get out of your dingy," said an old voice that had smoked too many cigarettes. I thought, European.

"What the hell for?" I said, loud enough to make my irritation clear.

Zip barked, but he sounded nervous.

"You prefer bullets, Mr. Trench?"

My name. My name. Dammit. He knew it. I was pissed.

"I prefer bullets to what, drowning?" I said. "I don't see any hardware."

He turned his Maglite to his other hand for a second. It had to be a revolver, the barrel was so long.

"You understand now, I think," he said. "We all know there's lots of sand here. You can probably walk up the bank. Your dog swims, no?"

"Then what's your point? Why should I bother?"

Zip let loose a series of hard barks.

"You hush your dog or we do it for you. It would be permanent."

"Yeah, and I'll hunt you till the day I die," I said, as loud as I could, hoping someone was out for a walk or had a window open at the townhomes nearby. "Why the hell do I matter to you? You want the skiff? I doubt it."

"You're correct, Mr. Trench."

The skiff had begun to drift back toward Clear Lake. I wondered if that could help. "You think I carry a roll of hundreds in my pocket when I come out here?"

"That's two strikes," said another voice, younger, foreign born English speaker, not South American, and definitely a non-smoker.

"Hey, I got the first one right."

Zip barked twice and I pulled him to me.

"That was not an answer," said the first voice.

"So, I've got one more chance before – before you blow up my boat?"

"Just listen," said the first voice, the old smokey one. "My man has a message for you."

I said nothing, holding Zip and stroking his back.

The younger one said, "First, run that little dingy back up here. It's impolite to shout."

"It's impolite to shine – "

Both lights hit me with a little wider beam in the face. Zip just about jumped out of my grasp. They must have been using five-cells. Damn bright.

"Do not interrupt," said the older one.

"Right," I said.

"Bring the dingy up here, under this bridge," said the younger man.

I did as instructed, paddling a bit slower than usual for some reason. Keeping Zip settled at that point turned out to be more of a problem than the drift.

"Okay, Mr. Trench," said the older man.

It still pissed me off. How did they know my name? Who did they work for?

Not a couple of thugs. Not with knowing my name. Were they Feds? Not if there really were just two of them. I was scared but I was leaning more towards pissed. I'd be carrying the Sig in a waterproof holster next outing.

"Go ahead," I said, hoping I'd not shown surprise in my tone.

"You can stay in your little dingy if you do what we ask," said the younger.

"And that is?"

"You are to leave well enough alone."

"What's that supposed to mean?"

"You have put your nose where it is not wanted. Is not needed. Is not safe for anyone."

"I have lots of cases. Which one?"

"Oh, please, Senior Chief Trench," said the older one, "you have no real cases. You can know which one to vacate. One for one, you understand?"

They wanted me off Candice Franklin's gig. I really liked the idea but not at gunpoint.

"You guys Feds? Secret Service? DEA? CIA? ICE? What?"

"See, you are sticking your nose in," said the older. "This must stop."

I heard a quiet splash followed immediately by a soft thhupp. Had to be a bullet entering the water beside Sailor's Skiff. Didn't come from the long barrel I had seen. That sound was an average semi-automatic, a silencer on the end.

"Got your message," I said. "Will you make sure Ms. Franklin gets it as well?"

"Your last activity in this matter shall be to fire her, in person, with class," said the younger man.

"I did, this morning."

"The agreement was misunderstood. Try again in the morning – wait. Do not try. Get the job done, Chief Petty Officer Trench. Over and done by noon. We'll be checking on things."

"Sure. Piece of cake."

"Use lots of frosting," said the younger. "And chocolate cake. Women like chocolate."

"Good night," said the older one.

Their flashlights went out.

I could sorta see two dark figures passing down the guardrail, their backs to me. One was taller than the other. Which was the older, I had no idea.

I let loose of Zip and he chased 'round and 'round in the skiff, almost tossing us overboard.

Never in the years I had lived in the area did I think of NASA Pkwy. as a deserted street after dark, but it had been. No one passed by on foot. No one piloted a boat past us. No one walked out on their balcony at the townhomes to ask what was going on, why the two spots of light were shining on a lone soul in a skiff. If they did, they didn't alert me.

I kept the skiff near the bridge for ten minutes hoping someone would come forth. Didn't happen.

Chapter 43
– Thursday evening

I poured some more dog chow into Zip's bowl before collapsing into my recliner. Once there, I had a fight with the remote. It wanted me on pay channels and I never went there.

Then the Cricket rang.

Where was it?

Another ring.

Kitchen.

I dumped myself out of the recliner, suddenly remembering I hadn't heard back from Spring. Was that her on the phone?

Jocelyn.

"What's the haps, tall one," I said.

"You did not say that, Trench. That is so old school."

"Whassup?"

"Same song."

"Well, why'd you call?"

"Spring."

"How so?"

"You talk with her?"

"Not since just after lunch."

"Would be after I have."

I walked out the patio door, hoping my backyard wasn't bugged

"Damn, Jocelyn. She doesn't answer her Cricket?"

"Negative."

"Okay. I talked to Spring on phone after lunch. She had lost the tail on the guy she'd connected to her mother.W as at Space Center Houston. Said it was private. Had been home before that, looking through house for hints to her mother's change in behavior – which is much worse now."

"What happened? You met Candice for coffee, you said."

"That went great. She agreed to pay my incurred expenses and half-a-week's retainer and then terminate our business relationship."

"So where's your problem, Trench?"

By then I'd reached the bulkhead of my dock.

"She showed up at my office parking lot as I was about to drive off to lunch. She went nuts, saying the deal was off and it wasn't safe to go to lunch. Things like that. Screeching the whole time."

"And you told her what?"

"That I was going to lunch."

"Out in the parking lot."

"Yes."

I filled Jocelyn in on the rest of it, leaving out the part about the skiff and getting shot at. She said she'd go nosing around, see if Spring was hanging with a guy or what.

As I walked back up to the house, I realized I was wide awake all over again, my nerves jumping. I tried to figure out who was on first and whether I dare call Candice that late. I only had until noon the next day to divorce us – again.

And just who were those guys on the bridge?

And who did they work for?

~ + ~

I had scribbled notes on a legal pad while watching SportsCenter indirectly for about forty-five minutes when pounding arrived at my front door. I thought the pound-knock sounded familiar but waited for an encore.

It came again about a minute later, sounding not quite as familiar but at least I didn't hear "We know you're in there" or "Open Up – Police."

I decided the third time would be the charm but it never came.

About three minutes later, the patio's sliding glass door opened and Jocelyn came in.

"You can't say I didn't knock," she said.

"You could text just before you arrive."

"Wrong. You are so wrong. They can track 'em all. Text can be read near its point of origin, just sayin'."

"On that same point," I said, and waved Jocelyn over to me.

I placed the legal pad on the couch, a pillow over it, then slowly tore off a page. Yeah, I figured the bugs were very sensitive.

I wrote a note and handed to Jocelyn. "Remember we weren't going to meet here because we figured my house is bugged? Let's move this chat out back." Handed it to her.

I unlocked my larger safe, the one in the garage, and retrieved my all-purpose scanner. I had to find out if my backyard was being swept (constant scan for electromagnetic emissions). The ugly red box could detect electronic transmissions at all commercial and ham frequencies, decoding many of the more common ones, and was sensitive enough to pick up random leakage from equipment not properly shielded. The scanner was close to illegal as far as what it could do with the police bands.

Out in the back yard, while Jocelyn sent a Frisbee the length of the yard for Zip to chase and return, I worked my scanner, first up and down the middle, then the entire perimeter. No active devices, just a little ship to ship.

We could talk.

I motioned to Jocelyn and took us half way to the bulkhead before saying, "And whom did you see outside in front violating my point of origin?"

"Not sure. There's one of those old Oldsmobiles, Alero or something, two-three houses down. That's different. Not seen it before."

I guessed it belonged to a college student, come home in need of funds. Lots of Baby Boomers lived on my block.

"What you know about Spring?"

"More than you."

"Be a pain, why don't you. Tell me."

"I know this: she's not home; she's not at that guy's she was thinking of dating; she's definitely not at Space Center Houston – it closes at five."

"Has Spring just up and disappeared before?"

"All teenagers do that."

"Spring doesn't' seem like the type."

"Dunno. Not since we've been BFFs, truth be real."

"How long's that?"
"Sophomore year, just before Christmas."
"How do you know she's not home?"
"Went over there."
"Drive by, knock on door, what?"
"Circled block, three times."
"No car?"
"No car."

I guessed she had done the same at the non-boyfriend's.

"Mom's car?"
"In driveway."
"Could Spring's be in the garage?"
"Never. Not allowed. Slow oil leak."
"And you've called her, texted her?"
"Yes."
"Both phones."
"Trench you are about to find out how high I can kick."
"Sure. Show me that at Spring's house."
"What the – "
"We're going to visit her grouchy, crazy mother."

Chapter 44
– Thursday late

She'd done such a good job with her fist up on Helm, I had Jocelyn do the honors on the Franklins' side door, the one right off the driveway.

Her first rap didn't bring a response. Go figure: lights on in four windows as we drove up.

I held Jocelyn back. Waited.

Just as I was about to give the okay for knock two, the door burst open.

"It's you!" said Candice, her fuchsia robe flashing Wilma Flintstone pajamas. "And what are you doing out this late?" She bopped the side of Jocelyn's head with the back of her hand. "Up to no good, no doubt."

Candice took a step back, shook her head, and slammed the door.

Jocelyn did what Jocelyn does: she grabbed the knob, twisted, laid a shoulder into the door. It flew wide open, breaking something when the door hit a counter.

Inside we plunged, greeted by the same highly pitched voice that had intended to disrupt my lunch with Lynnette.

"What you two doing here at the same time? Get out of my house."

"Ms. Franklin," I said, grabbing Jocelyn by the arm. "We're looking for Spring."

"What do you mean, 'we'? Get out."

"Ma'am, Spring hasn't been Spring today," said Jocelyn.

"Not for months, you skinny car hop. For months she hasn't been the same. It's your fault. Get out, I said. Get out!"

A look flashed across Candice's face as she glanced behind us, a look like none I'd seen to that point, a cross between embarrassed and guilty-as-charged.

I spun around, figuring on Spring.

Not even close.

That was my official introduction to Benjamin Ivan Franklin, the man the Feds told me to stay clear of. Would he remember me from the day, almost three weeks before, when I had eaten lunch at his restaurant on Hwy. 3, Charlie's Steak, Seafood, and Spirits?

"Hiya, Jocelyn," said Ben. "This your dad?"

"Naw, Franklin," said Jocelyn, giving him a knuckle shake. "He's the uncle type."

Damn she was good.

"Ben Franklin. Restaurateur," he said, reaching an open hand.

"Get out, all of you!" said Candice.

"Candy, you wanna tell me what's with all your screaming?" said Ben. "I could hear you out in the street, windows up."

Candy. Now that was news.

Candice did a cumbersome turn-around, then charged down a hall or something, her robe chasing after her.

"Mr. Uncle," said Jocelyn, "how 'bout you give me a ride back to *my* ride?"

"Sure," I said turning back to Ben Franklin. "See you another time?"

"Yeah. Sure," said Franklin and he stepped to Jocelyn and gave her a shoulder hug.

She seemed okay with it.

I nodded and we left.

Out in the driveway, after the door had closed behind us, Jocelyn said, "You get a better idea of what Spring deals with here?"

I had.

"I hear you."

That evening erased my evaluation of Candice Faith Pence Franklin as a cold-hearted yet intelligent, ultra self confident, conniving, money-hungry aggressive socialite bitch.

As I put the key in the Forester, it struck me that she was the first casualty of the Feds' activity with her husband, part of what the CIA described in their summary reports as *collateral damage*. Just one of those "things" that "happens" in the course of their work for which the Feds don't seem to accept responsibility or suffer remorse. *The country, National Security, et cetera.*

How about Ben? Was he next or already crazy but hiding it better? He did owe taxes from before his marriage to Candice so the Feds owned a good piece of his time. Did they own his mind yet?

~ + ~

I was more worried than ever about my young "associate," so I drove the Forester around the corner and parked.

Jocelyn and I chatted, tried to figure out where else to look for Spring. We came up with zero, nada, zip, so, depressed and angry, I drove us back to my place.

And that solved the problem – at first.

How, you ask?

Spring's car was in my driveway. Locked. No visible damage. Hood a bit warm.

She'd blocked my path into the side of the garage reserved for the Forester, so I was sure it was her who parked it.

"Bet she's in back," said Jocelyn.

We ran around the house.

She wasn't.

And the skiff was gone.

Chapter 45
– Thursday late

We chased around in circles out back for maybe fifteen minutes before finally going inside. We had been tired before we arrived at my place and it became clear we weren't thinking very well at that point anyway.

"Do you think Spring's mom will out me now with her dad?" I said, retrieving a Guinness Stout from my refrigerator.

"Not saying. Can't say. Woman's mostly what you old folks call a cannon – a loose cannon. That's it."

"You're probably right. I'm sitting here stupid. I didn't see it coming."

"She waved the bucks and you *got* stupid."

I turned around from the kitchen counter to give Jocelyn a frown just in time to watch her jump and land sideways on the couch. At least she hadn't taken my recliner.

I descended into my recliner a couple minutes later, deciding that the new version of Candice Faith Pence Franklin, Candy, would probably tell her husband about me. Might leave out many important details, but, yeah, she'd use me for an invisibility cloak.

I also concluded that the conniving bitch version, Candice, would only not tell her husband about me if I'd delivered on either objective: found proof he was screwing around or skimming big bucks. I had proof of neither and knew the powerful version of Candice was a figment of my imagination.

Or did she used to be that way.

"Jocelyn."

"Be me, Jocelyn."

"You've known Spring about two-and-a-half years."

"Like I told you."

"Right. Was her mom as much of a cannon back then or has she gotten worse – or did she suddenly change?"

"Not sure," said Jocelyn. "I like didn't spend much time at her place. No fun. Sprite was usually at my folks with me or we were out. Without permission. Without them knowing."

"You're saying Spring's a practiced liar?"

"Not so much. Just a teenager like me. We do thing 'cause we do things."

I'd often thought the "do things 'cause we do things" applied to the female of the species, regardless of age. I let her statement land on the coffee table without comment.

Jocelyn still wanted to talk, said, "The guy she was at Space Center with," she said.

"What?"

"You said she was with a guy at Space Center Houston."

"No. That was your guess. I was guessing she had picked up the tail on the guy her mom went to visit."

"Shit," said Jocelyn.

"What?"

"Took her back to school. Said she'd stay off that."

"Well, you know Spring better than I ever will. You actually surprised?"

"Sprite's really good people. Just needs other people. Needs to shine."

"How so?"

"Duh. You just saw why tonight."

I had.

From our very first encounter – Spring called me – I got it that she was a much-conflicted young lady. Very sincere and caring, yet severely conflicted about liking her step-dad, Ben, more than her natural parent, Candice. She wanted everyone to be happy. Most teenagers were much more selfish.

I said, "I bet she thinks she's so damn smart she – "

"Can work her way out of anything."

"She any good at using the skiff?"

"We never did small boats. Just rich kids birthday parties. Hired pilots."

"Rich kids? Spring ain't exactly needy."

"Dad Ben does good," said Spring. "Mom spends it on or at the country club. Lookin' like she's gonna go cougar on some young stud."

"Don't tell me – never mind. Where would Spring take a skiff?"

"Dunno. Said never done one. You got just the small docking channels and the one long one. We can go look. Leave her a 'dumb shit' note on car."

"Better yet. You stay. I'll go take Cyber Sailor out. I'll have Zip. He can smell friends."

~ + ~

I didn't have much of an adventure.

Oh, yes, I did.

I went out the sliding glass door, my mind churning a thousand bits of information a second, and walked toward my dock in the light of the neighbors' safety floods.

Yeah, I was stressed.

When I reached the dock, I set about putting out in Sailor's Skiff.

I was almost ready to paddle when I realized that I was *in Sailor' Skiff*, that it was back – and so must be Spring.

Yeah, I was stressed.

But, where was Spring?

Who else but Spring would take out the skiff?

Well, how about the Feds? They'd played old TV show reruns for me when I installed wireless audio transmitters on the windows of what turned out to be their project control house on Helm, so maybe they were messing with me. But why would they return it? Where did they or he go after returning it?

Or it could have been the employer of those two guys on the bridge. Yeah, they would know where I lived. If they did, they wouldn't return it. They'd just put a bullet hole through the bottom and watch it sink.

Which took me back to Spring. Where. Was. She?

~ + ~

I decided that Spring might not have been the one to take the skiff out. With all the eccentric "players" in the game that was my life that day, I had to go back to black-and-white, bare knuckles investigating.

So I walked around my house to the

driveway.

Spring's car.
Was still there.
Hood no longer warm.
Doors still locked.
Needed a flashlight to look inside.
Garage locked. Keys to the Forester, two flashlights, on kitchen counter.
Rang my own front doorbell.
Front door opened.
Spring.

Chapter 46
– Thursday late

"What the hell – where were you?"

"Sound like my Mom."

"Crap. Maybe some people care whether the planet loses a Spring or not."

She turned and stomped back into the den. I followed, closing the door a bit more forcefully than usual.

Jocelyn on couch with feet on coffee table, smartass grin on her face.

"Yo, Trench. Look what the cat dragged in."

"That's how she got in?"

"No," said Jocelyn. "Was in the garage. I went out there, thinkin' we didn't check."

"Damn," I said. How stupid was it to overlook the garage with its large cabinets – two of them big enough for Spring to fit inside and close the door.

"No worries," said Jocelyn. "She's just moody. Didn't eat."

"Okay, well, I don't cook much and – "

It hit me. Spring was in the house the whole time.

The skiff came back all on its own.

No.

No way.

"Shit," I said. "All doors locked?"

"You doubt us?" said Jocelyn.

"What? What?" said Spring. "What's going

on?"

"In a minute," I said. "Right now, get clear of windows, any spot in line of sight to a window. If the window can see you, so can the bullet."

I don't know to this day where or how I thought of that, of an ambush or invasion or an automatic rifle peppering my home. Today, it seems more like I was losing it. Back then, though, I was sitting on a short trigger because I had been spooked by electronic surveillance, spooked by lack of privacy, spooked by not knowing all the forces working against me.

Who did those two guys on the bridge belong to?

Was Torville the only Fed after my ass – our asses?

Was Candice Franklin coming down off her Lexapro or whatever was her prescribed mood altering and control chemical, or was she really going nuts for the same reason I was heading that way?

~ + ~

The den bordered two bedrooms and the garage but the flat screen could be seen at an angle though the high kitchen window over the sink. If we'd been in a movie, the bad guys would shatter that first, dramatic effect and all. Except a flower bed rested outside beneath that kitchen window. A bad guy would have to be over six feet tall to see inside, with a four-inch drop off the house slab to the patio and another two or three inches of bed dug out.

Except – I had two stepstools and five heavy wooden patio chairs outside.

Damn.

Double damn.

I keyed 911.

"Harris County Emergency. What is the nature of your emergency?"

"Suspected home invasion."

"Suspected, how, sir?"

In ten minutes I couldn't quite convince the operator or her supervisor that we were at risk. They also repeated questions as to reasons for Spring and Jocelyn being at my place that late.

I had Spring scream as I hung up while the operator's supervisor was in mid sentence, figuring that would bring them out, two eighteen-year-olds in the house and all. Dramatic effect.

~ + ~

We each had found a safe spot out of the line of sight of the window. Unfortunately that did not include my recliner which would invite target practice at the back of my head. I sat on the ledge in front of the fireplace that I never lit.

With me off the telephone, the air became more and more electric with tension, the three of us not liking the Feng Shui one bit, twisting and fidgeting right where we sat.

"So, Spring," I said after five minutes or so of silent tension, "how about you tell me and your BFF here what went down all afternoon, starting from when you were at Space Center Houston and I called?"

"Private. Like I told you."

"Oh, stuff it, Sprite," said Jocelyn.

I waited. Watched.

"Like, it had something to do with Mom or that guy she spent last night with, if that's what you're asking."

"Yes, asking that," I said. "And I'm wondering about whom you were with – could be a setup."

"I'm no dummy," said Spring. "I've had boyfriends before."

"Let me guess. Fifteen years older. Early thirties."

"Damn you."

Jocelyn struggled to hold back a laugh, then gave in, saying, "I'm sorry. I'm sorry. Not. You are so not middle age material."

"Wait," I said. "I'm middle age. He's just a cradle robber."

"Damn you," said Spring as she flung a pillow across the room, missing Jocelyn but taking out my framed honorable discharge.

"Easy, now," I said. "You're still not up front with the info. Ya gotta deal, Spring. Now would be very good."

"Get down with it," said Jocelyn.

"Oh, go down on yourself," said Spring.

Had she said that?

Chapter 47
– Thursday late

The girls were obviously on edge, their inner tension leaking out in behaviors much out of character from what I'd seen since I met them – had it been three weeks?

Less.

Two.

First encounter: Spring had called, asked to meet, and then not showed up at Coffee Oasis two Thursdays back. I hadn't met with her in person until she showed up on the third try on Saturday evening, at Denny's by Baybrook Mall – and then ran out. Jocelyn had not entered the picture until the following Tuesday evening when both had shown up at my house uninvited, not too far from midnight.

On that Thursday evening when we hid from the kitchen window, we all got to where we couldn't stand the silence and ended up going round and round with the terse, dark, and oblique remarks for what seemed like hours – until the door bell rang.

I figured the cops.

The girls just jumped.

"Sit still. Sit safe. I'll answer it."

"Do you have your Kevlar vest on?" said Spring.

"Don't own one. Never did. I'm a geek."

"You were hired to do the foot leather thing,

gumshoe," said Jocelyn, a bit of incredulity in her tone.

"Yeah. Yeah. Sit still."

I looked out the peep hole.

Nothing.

I checked the porch light switch beside the door.

Up.

I leaned against the door and peered out the peephole again, expecting light on the front porch again.

No light. Dark.

"Who's there?" I said, as loud as I could without coughing.

Thump. My head recoiled from the door, taking me with it.

Thud. Thump.

"Who the hell are you?"

From outside, a muffled, "Trench, back away from the door. We're coming in."

Had to be Agent Torville.

"I'll unlock it."

I turned the dead bolt and the doorknob button as quick as I could, flung the door towards me and jumped back.

Short and stocky Torville sauntered in like he owned the place.

"Hey, Trench. Enjoyed listening to y'all chat. Got boring so thought I'd come in. You got any coffee?"

"Not this late, you asshole."

"Easy now. I didn't use the beam on your door. Could have busted it down, cost you a small bundle, no?"

"What do you want?"

"Is this the Fed A-Gent?" said Jocelyn.

"So this is the mouth," said Torville.

Turning to Spring, pointing a very short but thick index finger, he said, "You, Short Shit. We have words or I cuff you. In just a minute."

He stepped toward Jocelyn who untwisted her legs and stood before Torville reached her.

Torville backed up, trying to make direct eye contact.

"You having trouble with your eyes, Short Shit?" said Jocelyn.

"How 'bout you rest your eyes on these," he said, flopping open his credentials wallet.

"I see pretty printed stuff. In plastic. Wallet smells though."

"You don't respect your country's Secret Service and its agents?"

"I respect – or not – people. That's p-e-o-p-l-e. Right now I have you classified as ass-hole. Step back, Dudley the Short."

Torville reached his hand back to side of his neck and brought forward a microphone tube. "Send in Phillips. Have one to take downtown."

"Cancel that," I said, loud as hell, moving forward and ripping the voice tube off Torville's head. "You've got questions to answer," I said, spinning him around by his shoulder. "Sit. Down. Now."

Torville began laughing and that turned out to be a mistake.

Jocelyn dove, tackled him, slamming his back on the coffee table, the back of Torville's head catching the edge.

He went limp.

"I think we're in trouble," said Spring.

"We're in trouble. We're in trouble."

~ + ~

At that point I recall a couple of Seabrook uniforms barging in, followed maybe half a minute later by two EMS techs with at least two Feds on their heels insisting we all clear the scene.

Things got really messy when I think two or maybe three more Feds joined the melee, Jocelyn giving them the most lip and physical resistance.

It took a while to sort everything out. Okay, an hour.

But, hey. No shots were fired. No one was arrested -- the Feds didn't want to explain the reason for their presence at my place. The girls were eighteen so I stayed out of jail.

And it turned out the EMS guys were handy. They woke Torville up with some old fashioned smelling salts, I think. Then, after twenty minutes of prodding and electronic leads clamped to his body, determined that he would have a hell of a headache for a couple of days. He refused a visit to an emergency room, although they strongly recommend it.

And no shots were fired through any windows.

Chapter 48
– Friday morning

I got about four hours sleep, waking up with the two thugs on the NASA Pkwy. bridge front and center on my mind. Nobody had ever pulled a gun on me.

While making coffee, my brain tried to tie the thugs to the Feds. It worked hard, thinking about this and supposing that, all the way through frying some eggs, without discovering a connection that would tie a red ribbon around a lead steel box.

As I ate the eggs, my mind tried to tie the thugs to Constable–Agent Heather Carey's operation.

No cigar.

Something was really rotten in Clear Lake, that was clear. What I couldn't figure out was why the situation had landed like pigeon shit on my collar.

I was clean. Never did a drug deal with the Mafia, the Italian one or any of those indigenous to Mexico. Never dealt under the table. I had taken cash – from Candice Franklin. Those C-notes were promptly deposited in my business account.

I'd done business with and provided my service to good folks who needed to find a deadbeat dad or a missing cousin or a former employee.

Even taking a long, hot shower that morning didn't erase the two thugs from my mind – nor bring the faces into focus. All I had were silhouettes and they were questionable, a trench coat here, a forties mobster hat there – maybe.

When I guided the first pass of my triple-bladed Schick, I came up with a connection for the bridge thugs: Technology Voice.

I'd first thought he was part of the Feds harassment, but there seemed no firm indication of that.

Technology Voice had arrived before Heather Carey. He could have been the voice at the Helm street house, the agent in the dark shadows. Except. He called at times that meshed with the Feds activities, yes, and Carey's it seemed. But didn't *consistently* link up with the actions of the Feds. Ditto Heather Carey. And, since there was no coincidental link between Technology Voice and the thugs... Well, hell, if there was no coincidental activity then that made the connection.

Yeah, I was going in circles grasping at straws in the second row of the merry-go-round.

And, as I rinsed the razor after the final pass, I thought of Lynnette. Damn. Had I blown it there? Had I inferred – promised, even worse – I'd call her yesterday evening? After kicking around the question while I got dressed, I finally reconciled the situation: the look Lynnette gave me when I walked into the Executive Suites waiting room would tell me if I had blown it.

All I had to do was drive the Forrester to work.

Was it in the garage? Spring had blocked me. When she left, did I open the garage door and move it?

I went in the garage. No Forester.

I pushed the fob and opened the garage door.

Forester had been hiding outside in the driveway.

Outside. Tampered with, I bet.

I brought it in.

Scanned.

Three transmitters.

Three?

Three. The one that I found the day before, plus another much like it and a third, completely different one of older design.

Were the Seabrook police now following me along with the Feds? Their budget was smaller so they'd be likely to purchase older technology to save funds. I mean, heck, how many folks did the Seabrook P.D. need to track in a given year? Nice town. Nice people.

The drama, the stress, the chaos had begun when I sold out for five G's a week – and that cash flow had only lasted two weeks. Meanwhile the chaos had ramped higher and higher on a case where the Feds had ordered me to do nothing.

I debated whether to call Candice and see which one of her personalities answered the phone. Could that agreement we had at Coffee Oasis the morning before be reinstated and executed, formally ending her contract for my services – and pay off my expenses? If nothing else, I would have a clear conscience following Agent Torville's orders.

Should I contract for an ultra-high-tech call-tracking service to trace Technology Voice the next time he – or she – called?

Should I contact Heather Carey and get her to out her operation?

Should I take Lynnette to lunch again and explain exactly what had been going on with Candice and Heather Carey and the Feds?

Should I call and tell the girls, Spring and Jocelyn, to come by my office so I could formally detach them from my operations? They didn't need the stress. They had young lives to live, which came with their own dramas. And they didn't need criminal files opened in their names.

I'd pay them some money, maybe five hundred apiece, to show my appreciation for their past support. Yeah, that was a plan. I'd do that.

Except I had to get the nerve to get in the Forester and drive to my office.

It was already 8:45 AM.

I'd be a half hour late.

In five years, I'd never been more than five minutes late.

What would Lynnette think of me?

Chapter 49
– Friday

I flipped the turn signal on the Forester as I cheated towards the right and west, ready to enter the NASA Pkwy. in Seabrook as soon as the turning traffic from Hwy. 146 cleared. I was about to push the gas when the Z10 sounded the zap that told me I had a text message.

Should I look down?

I looked left.

Time to hit the gas.

The Forester's turbo kicked in and I merged into traffic that would not have been there had I gotten out of bed and headed off to work on time.

The text reminder zapped.

I got the green light at Repsdorph. No texting while driving.

I got the green light at Bayou View. On any other day that would be amazing. On that Friday morning, I'd had enough amazement the night before. All I wanted was to see who was contacting me.

I got my wish at Kirby. Red light. Four cars in front.

I pulled the Z10 out of the cup holder and looked.

Lynnette.

She had texted, "Are you alive? Just wanted you to know somebody noticed you weren't here.

Hope you didn't break a leg – literally. Four customers waiting."

Four customers?

Four?

That was a good number for any complete morning or afternoon. Four before nine? Had to be more Feds. Had to be.

I looked up. The light was still red – no it wasn't.

I gunned the Forester.

I was the fifth vehicle to cross Kirby and the Z10 zapped again.

The traffic signal at Lakeview was green, of course.

Went on past Space Center Blvd., all the way to St. John's before the Forester caught red. By then the Z10 had reminded me twice more.

I thumbed on the screen, looked.

"J. K." was shown in a small text window.

Kidding. Just kidding. So, no customers. I didn't know whether to laugh or get pissed. She had shown me her playful side. I decided Lynnette was still talking to me.

~ + ~

"No, Jocelyn," I said, "ain't heard nothing from the Feds or Seabrook cops."

She had stopped by mid morning on her way to work at Sonic, checking to see if I'd been arrested or if there was a warrant out for her arrest after the melee at my place the night before.

"I told you, there's no way Torville is going to press charges – he'd be the laughing stock of his department or division or whatever it is. We'd be on TV, in the Houston Chronicle, and maybe even go viral on Twitter. No way would his career survive such a public fiasco. The Secret Service would ship him to Guam or somewhere outside the loop, something Torville's ego could not endure.

"Now you got a choice, Jocelyn. Sit down or get out of here. Your bouncing around between the door and the window is driving me nuts."

"Sorry, Trench. Don't mean to bust up your morning."

"You're apologizing? Please, sit down. I'll get Lynnette to take our picture."

"Back off the warm fuzzy stuff."

"You're tough but you're still a girl."

"Nuh uh."

"Sure. We could post the pic on Facebook. Get votes."

Like I'd ever done that. Didn't have a personal FB account. Trenchcoat Investigations had a page which nobody visited. That was it. Trenchcoat also had a regular web page and that worked just fine in funneling customers to me who could use my service, didn't want to drive inside the Loop, and for whom I had sufficient assets.

"Not on the book. Don't do social," she said. "Don't want to be on the book downtown neither."

She was referring to Harris Country criminal records.

"Go sling some burgers, then," I said. "I got work to do."

"Whassup with Spring's mom?"

I had sensed from day one that Jocelyn didn't care much for Candice Franklin so I was surprised she asked.

"I ain't heard from her."

"Ain't got the cojones to call her?"

What the hell?

"You do Spanish?" I said.

"Enough. You gonna call?"

I rolled my chair back from the desk and stretched my legs.

"I sure want to. Sure don't know what would work. Was hoping to hear from Spring. Her mom could be in an asylum by now for all we know."

"She's mean. She's edgy. She's selfish. She lives for drama. She's not for-certain crazy. Female loony crazy. Sure. Especially first thing in the morning."

"You would know."

"That's why Spring gets my respect."

"I got that. Yesterday. Now how about showing me some of that respect and gettin' on off to Sonic?"

"It's too early."

"Lobby out by Lynnette is nice and quiet."

She popped up, nodded with almost a smile, and was out the door in her usual two steps.

I rolled my chair back up to my desk and wondered what college would take a chance on a raw female athlete. Even a junior college. Thought I'd ask Spring about the grades and such, then remembered that Jocelyn had graduated after the fall semester. Spring took the whole senior year, would graduate in a couple weeks.

Chapter 50
– Friday

Ten or fifteen minutes after Jocelyn left, the Z10 thrummed.

Blocked call.

I let it go. Wasn't in the mood for the Technology Voice dude or dudette, whatever the electronically modified caller had to say.

I'd brought my electronics scanner to the office and swept it before I sat down to work. It was clear that Torville and his buddies had been listening to everything the girls and I said just before they entered my home the night before.

I wasn't going to have that at the office.

Then the Z10 rang with the Executive Suites' office ring. Lynnette said she was busy so I went down the hall to escort a new client back to my office. She had heard about me from a member of her bridge club. Seems I had found a second cousin for her good friend.

It was a pleasant visit – her getting out and meeting the world and all.

Finding third cousins wasn't exactly difficult. The problem escalated, however, if my client wasn't sure of the legal first name and believed the last name had changed when the cousin was put up for adoption. As she left I sent her an email with the link to the flowchart and checklist I'd devised to help clients organize their thoughts and relatives.

It was nearly lunch and I was about to saunter down the hall and see what was up with Lynnette when another blocked caller buzzed on the Z10. I had a few minutes so I answered.

"Trenchcoat Investigations. Good morning."

"You going to take a nap for lunch?"

Technology Voice. The strange echo that had made the prior Technology Voice calls creepy was missing, though.

"And whom might I be speaking with?" I said.

"Your buddy."

"My technology buddy?"

"If you wish."

"What have you got to say for yourself today?" I laughed, going for sarcastic.

"In reading the mid-day reports, I was at first convinced the agents had padded their reports. But, the second incident overnight – I am truly in awe. Lots of assaults. A Fed down and out on his back. Nobody gets arrested. You are amazing. You got the gift of gab or something. Maybe you ought to be a political speech writer."

"Okay. You didn't call me just to pour compliments all over the data stream."

"Correct. You're a smart one, every now and then."

"So, why did you call?"

"Forgive me. I figured you deserved some courtesy."

"And?"

"I'm letting you know I will be dropping by your office this afternoon."

The connection went dead.

~ + ~

"Lynnette."

"Yes?"

"Thanks for joining me for lunch. Sincerely."

"It's only an hour."

What did she mean? I didn't know if she was kidding or stating fact.

I guess she saw confusion on my face. "Just kidding, Nate. I love Longhorn's food and I'm hoping you'll laugh, take a deep breath and relax."

"What would you like?"

"You."

What did that mean? Was she kidding again?

"No, I mean to eat," I said, my voice sounding kinda strangled.

"You pick. You're buying."

I did not know how to date. Not then. Not in high school.

I did not know how to read even the kind woman in front of me, someone who's direct and polite at work and whose daytime life I'd been around and interacted with for two years.

"How about you decide," I said. "I didn't get much sleep. That's a good excuse, right?"

"Can you spell romance?"

"Well, sure."

That got an eye flutter, then some pink in her cheeks.

I'd surprised myself, especially when I'd gone right past her saying, "You."

"Lynnette, I'm really missing some points here."

"True. How do you like your steak?"

"Medium. Medium to rare. 'Pink' is what I usually say."

"I like mine bleeding red. Rivulets."

Was she serious?

"I, ahh – "

"Just *kidding*!"

She could read my face. Read me. I couldn't read her face, her tone. She was showing me new material – looks and tones. I liked them. Just didn't know which way to go when. Maybe I was nervous because I liked her more than I had revealed to myself. I didn't want to say anything "wrong," wanted her to like me, yet wanted to tell her more about Trenchcoat. Probably figured that once she knew what she was getting into, she'd catch the midnight train for Dallas.

Chapter 51
– Friday

After the waiter had our order – well, after Lynnette gave the waiter our order – I said, "Can I tell you some serious stuff for a bit. Might take me a while and I'll probably start and stop."

"What are your saying?"

"Well, just let me talk until I'm finished."

"Why didn't you say so? Sure."

I talked round and round about the Franklins and the Feds and Technology Voice, not so much the two girls. Lynnette had met them – and Candice, actually, but maybe not the real Candice. Had I even met the real Candice Faith Pence Franklin? Anyway, I told the story but left out blow-by-blow type descriptions of things like the rumble the night before.

I talked a bit about Kara, my divorce and her death, and how I still missed her. Lynnette asked how she died and I told her about the SUV tire but froze for what seemed like an hour after I said "tire," but it could only have been a few seconds. Lynnette didn't say anything. She did nod here and there, gave me some smiles, but mostly let me talk. That in itself was a new experience for me.

And then I talked about the Feds and how my life was at that point inches from total destruction should Torville or his boss decide I was to be dealt with. Again, I left out a lot of

Collateral Franklins

highly confrontational stuff, like the night before and the NASA Pkwy. bridge thugs.

"Okay, I'm done. You can ask questions if you want."

"Yes. Where is our food?"

I looked around, said, "This place is full. Were we the last to be seated?"

"Very observant, Nate. I was surprised we only waited a couple minutes for a table."

"Guess they all got here at eight minutes after twelve."

She laughed, said, "I do have one major question."

"Okay, shoot."

"Why did you tell me all that?"

~ + ~

The steaks and baked potatoes arrived right after Lynnette's meaty question. They were good and we talked about silly customers of mine and others and the goofy things they do while they're waiting in the reception area at the Executive Suites.

I had my debit card out and said to our waiter seconds after he arrived with the check, "Here ya go. Gotta get back to work. Can you bump us up a little in line?"

"Yes, sir." And he was gone.

"Nate, you going to answer my one big question?"

"Oh, the 'why did I tell you all that' question?"

"Yes. Hurry. The waiter will be back."

"Well, up until lately, my life, my work, didn't have much danger in it. Things were pretty simple and predictable, especially off work. Now, well, here you are and we are and, well, things are crazy."

"You suppose I've noticed?"

"Sure. But there's more."

"There's always more, Nate. Always."

~ + ~

Outside, just before we got to the Forester, Lynnette grabbed my bicep, stopped me, turned me around, said, "Nate, it's taken me more than a couple years at Executive Suites knowing you to entertain the thought that I could maybe hang around with a new guy. Von died four years ago last month. We were married almost twelve years. All those years of counseling. But now, it seems you're the guy."

I didn't say anything. Stunned, mostly.

"Nate, I'm surprised and I'm not. I didn't work at this. Let's just see what happens."

I nodded, opened the door for her, and drove us back without checking my rear view mirror every twenty seconds.

Lynnette said, just as I pulled in the parking lot, "What's on tap for this afternoon?"

"I guess we'll see what comes in the office."

"That's not quite the truth, is it? You've got something on your mind, Nathaniel Trench."

"Okay. Yeah. That Technology Voice guy."

"Yes?"

"He said he'd be dropping by this afternoon."

"What does he look like?"

"Hell, I don't know. With that mass of electronics, he could be a midget female."

Chapter 52
– Friday afternoon

A middle-aged new blonde named Monica, one of the MSWs from the counseling office on the third floor, came by around one thirty and asked if I could help them out.

"We're having trouble determining if our client has multiple personalities or if her ex is truly a criminal out on bail with a history of violence."

That didn't track for me but they'd always been helpful.

"I thought you folks could get to court records and stuff."

"We are a social service agency, but to get information like that, we have to engage the Attorney General's office. Takes lots of time or a criminal act on the part of her ex that generates a police report."

"And your client might not survive the criminal act."

"Exactly. Can you help?"

"You can't get Texas records?"

"If we understand her correctly, he is wanted in Louisiana."

She had a file folder in her lap so I said, "Let me see what you have."

While I chased around public records in Louisiana, Oklahoma, Arkansas, Texas, and New Mexico, just to make sure, Monica texted somebody. Seemed non stop. I could have searched the whole country but that would have taken much more time.

While waiting for a couple of reports to generate, I said, "Were you all able to help Mr. Worthington?"

"Who is he?"

"I brought him up on Monday."

Monica gave me a blank stare.

"You have a confidentiality patient thing?"

"You could say that, Mr. Trench."

"Okay, well, here comes the first page of your report. Your client is or was married to a very bad boy," I said while scanning a summary. "If this isn't enough, I'm guessing he's had a couple other names. Take time to check."

"Oh, thank you Mr. Trench. Thank you so very very much."

"It's okay, you all are the good guys. I'll have a couple more pages in – "

Z10 rang.

Lynnette. Executive Suites phone.

"Heya. What's up?" I said.

"She's. She's. She's here."

"Who?"

"The Voice you mentioned. Well, I think it is. She says you're expecting her. You said it could be a woman, all the technology and stuff."

"You've never seen her before?"

"No. Hurry. She looks less than happy to wait."

"Can you walk her down – wait. Don't. Monica and I are finishing up. Be down in five."

~ + ~

I urged Monica around the corner to

Lynnette's desk and told her one more time that I was happy to help out.

"Mr. Trench, you've improved the life of this woman so much. Thank you."

"Tell your boss I like cherry pie best of all."

"What?"

"Never mind. Looks like I have a client waiting."

I turned to Lynnette who nodded toward the back couch where a woman sat, her back to me and head down. I moved around the two oversized chairs and saw she could have played linebacker for the Bears even when Butkus was holding court. Her briefcase was open in her lap and she appeared to be typing in it.

"Excuse me, you're waiting to see Nate Trench, Trenchcoat – "

"Oh, I know what you look like. Go stand over there a minute. I have to finish this communiqué. Don't stand behind me, either."

Her voice gave me the chills, like back in school when the chalk would turn hard on the chalkboard and screech like the dickens.

I padded over to Lynnette, making faces until she saw one.

"You think that's the Voice, Nate?"

"It could be. The attitude fits."

"You want me to call the cops – never mind. They're here – she's a cop, huh."

"No telling. She could be with the Russian Consulate."

"Well, she's not a greeter at Wally World, that's for sure."

" Ice woman," I said, trying to shore up my outer wall. "Sorry to put this stress in your life.

That's what I was trying to tell you at – "

"Shush. You're fine. I knew. I've got a pretty good idea what I might be getting into. Why are you over here?"

"Orders. She's typing something in a briefcase computer. Literally. Ordered me to not stand behind her, so I am."

"Can she type standing up? Turn around."

The woman had risen and was assembling her gear: briefcase, oversize purse, and walking stick. Walking stick? Yeah, that's what it was. She skip shuffled towards us, putting one foot forward, then the stick, black with a short curl at the top like an old tree branch, then brought the other foot forward. Must have blown out a knee on a third-and-one.

"Which way," she said, her voice filling the waiting room. She would have rattled windows if there'd been any.

"Over here to the left," I said, gently swinging my arm as a maitre d' would at a French restaurant.

I fell in behind her as we took the turn down the hall to Trenchcoat Investigations.

"May I get you something? Water? Coffee?"

"There's time for that later."

"Let me get the door." I rushed ahead and turned the knob.

"You didn't have it locked?"

"I was just down the hall. Nobody – "

"We're going to have to train you more than I thought."

Train me?

Chapter 53
– Friday afternoon

My visitor dumped her stuff in the near chair, propped the walking stick against my desk, walking over to the far end of the window without it. No limp. No shuffle. She didn't need it.

I was about to sit in my big, high-backed executive chair when she said, "Aren't you going to lock the door?"

"Why would I? You could shoot me. Who are you?"

She just stared.

"Was that you who called me on the phone about three hours ago?"

"You must get lots of calls. Whom do you mean?"

"Technology Voice."

She smiled, believe it or not, and said, "That's me."

My brain skipped a beat before I mentally bopped myself upside the head. I had just fallen for an old trick. She had set me up to give her the correct answer to the very question I had asked.

"Who do you work for?"

"Many."

"Right now, dammit. Today. Who you dragging that cane around for?"

"Oh, we need not become heated and bluster profanity, sir."

"You're here saying I'm expecting you."

"You were. Someone."

"Well, I did allow for Technology Voice being a female instead of the cold electronic man of steel."

"Good for you. Now lock the door."

"Don't see the need."

"I'll show you need."

She walked back over to her briefcase, which she promptly placed on my desk, pushing my inbox practically off the back edge. From inside she withdrew what looked like a twelve-inch replica of an old V-2 rocket, except the nose cone could be screwed off. How could I tell? She unscrewed it revealing a small satellite dish which began rotating on the rocket's axis. Looked like radar dish from a Buck Rogers set.

"This humble device, Mr. Trench, blocks all electronic listening devices, scanners, what-have-you."

"So why lock the door?"

"Sometimes this electronics blocking makes eavesdroppers angry. We want them to stay outside your office, no?"

"Who do you work for?"

"That's a secret. You're used to those, now aren't you."

"Who do you work for, today?"

"Let's just say I'm stepping in for Heather Carey."

"What? Who does she work for?"

I had wondered where Carey had gone. Was Jocelyn's aunt a plant, a spy who had failed to bring home the goods – or had she been called away on a more critical matter?

"Not a question you should expect answered, Mr. Trench. You don't have the need to know."

"I am quite familiar with N.T.K., Ms. – what the hell is your name – today?"

She choacked off a laugh, returned to the window, but at my end, and spoke to those gathered outside, "Give me a name and we'll use that."

I refused by being silent. She wasn't looking my way as it was.

"Mr. Trench, a name."

I remained silent.

"You are not affording me the proper amount of respect."

Not a word did I utter.

She turned from the window and stepped to the empty chair, said, "Sit down."

I remained beside my chair. Not in it.

She sat down – more like landed – but barely fit in the chair. I wondered how she had managed to not hurt herself on the chair arms. She put a shit-eating grin on her face and watched me for a good three minutes.

I was thinking at the time that our stare down might last the rest of the afternoon but the door popped open, preventing that.

Torville.

"Trench, who is this?"

I wondered why Lynnette hadn't called to warn me of Torville's arrival.

"You don't know?" I said.

Torville gave a loud bark that I think was supposed to be a laugh, said, "Ma'am, I need you to – " Right then he had spotted the V-2.

"Trench, what is this? A toy? Mattel goes to

Mars?"

"Ask her. She brought it."

"Okay. Enough. Ma'am, you need to leave," said Torville as he flashed his creds. "I am on official business and you must leave."

She shook her head.

"Get up, Ma'am. Now."

She shook her head. Reached toward her briefcase.

Torville walked behind her, grabbed her shoulder, said, raising his voice, "Evans, get in here with agent Willows. Need a removal."

"Ma'am, this is your last chance to leave *with* your briefcase – it's hers Trench?"

"She walked in with it," I said.

"Last chance," said Torville. "Once my two agents arrive, they will escort you to a vehicle and take you downtown for processing under federal law."

She shrugged and twisted Torville's hand off her, then reached toward the briefcase again.

Torville stepped around the chair, slapped her arm away from the briefcase.

Somehow the woman retrieved the cane with her left hand, added her right, and swung-punched at Torville, landing the handle on the side of his head.

The Secret Service agent folded onto the floor like an emptied pillow case, lights out for the second time in less than twenty-four hours.

Sometimes you're just better off staying in bed.

Chapter 54
– Friday afternoon

The large woman looked at Torville's limp suit, then stood, put the cane down, and rummaged around in the accordion top of her briefcase. A wallet similar to Torville's credentials appeared.

"Nathan Edward Trench?"

"Yes."

"Here are my credentials. I trust you will find them in order," she said as she reached toward me.

INTERPOL. Ingrid Scholl.

About then agent Evans arrived, automatic drawn, with a woman in dark suit much like his, also with her automatic drawn. Agent Willows no doubt.

"Oh, shit," said agent Evans, the junior agent who had brought me and Torville water or coffee or something the first time his boss had visited my office eight days before. "What happened to Torville. Willows – "

"Hold it, Evans," I said. "You might want to look at these before you take another step."

I took three steps around the side my desk ever so slowly with both hands held high, trembling just a little inside. For all I knew, Evans or Willows could be a hair triggers.

Evans was a lot taller than me and had no problem extracting the creds while agent

Willows tried to watch me and agent Scholl, her automatic still drawn.

"Oh, shit," said Evans. "She's INTERPOL."

"What do we do with Torville?" said Willows.

"Check him out. I'll cover you. Trench, step back behind your desk. Remain standing. Scholl, please be seated until I have backup."

"He's got a pulse but out cold, I guess," said Willows.

Evans touched something behind his ear, said, "Call the medics. Yes, just like last night."

~ + ~

Evans placed a cell phone call to his AIC and kept Scholl in my office saying he needed her to be cleared by Torville's supervisor. The EMS folks showed up just in time for Torville to roll over by himself. He wasn't the most cooperative patient and I was damn sure his head hurt even worse than it had at my place. That cane was heavy.

Maybe half an hour after Torville's arrival, I got a ring from Lynnette on the Suites line.

"Hey. What's up."

"You still having a party down there?"

"Not exactly. Are we too loud?"

"She's here."

"What? I've got two women in here – three counting one of the EMS team."

"She. The big client she."

"Damn. Tell her I can't see her today."

"She told me I've got thirty more seconds or she'll go on down the hall by herself."

"I'll be right out."

"Sorry guys, I've got a client in the waiting

room."

"No," said Torville, his voice a bit high and scratchy.

"You guys mind," I said. "I need to tell Torville something in private."

Torville was on his back and I wanted to whisper in his ear but his charges were having none of it and Scholl did not look pleased either.

"Okay, Torville, they won't let me talk to you in private so I'm going to say one word and see if you get my meaning."

"What-ever."

"Candice."

That brought a knee jump followed by the waving of a hand and, "Let him go. I'll vouch. Get right back, Trench or I'll...."

"Agent Torville is not in control of his faculties," said Evans. "Stay where you are."

I said, "I'm afraid your mission will be compromised."

"You're a private dick, nothing more. Stand over behind your desk like a good little boy and — "

"Damn!" said Willows in response to the door crashing into her from behind.

"Federal officers," said Evans, his eyes and automatic locked on Candice Franklin. "Put your hands up and turn around, slowly."

Candice didn't know what to make of my crowded office and just stood there, a glassy look in her eyes.

As Willows reached for Candice, two Webster police officers entered.

You can guess what happened after that.

Two clusters in fifteen hours, Nate Trench

right in the middle of both.

I wanted to sit down but didn't dare move, waited for a chance to ask permission. Put nervous armed law enforcement folks from three different jurisdictions in a one-room office, you get the potential of escalating chaos, with bullets shot at close range most often finding a target.

Chapter 55
– Friday evening

I'd figured a cocktail or two might give a soft landing to one hell of a day – and I wanted to chat with Lynnette in a relaxed environment.

"So how did you get them to let Mrs. Franklin leave?" said Lynnette, her left hand massaging the back of my neck as I drove us up to the Davenport Lounge on Clear Lake City Blvd. The massage made it difficult to change lanes. I'd never had a woman do that massage thing. I didn't want her to stop but I didn't want to appear submissive. A guy thing.

"I'm not real sure," I said. "She was such a b-i-t-c-h that I think they were glad just to ship her out and let a rookie go interview her tomorrow. If they hadn't I was going to call upstairs and get a counselor. And thanks for calling the cops."

"I tried to get Mrs. Franklin to stay put but failed again."

"No problem. She's more than a handful and you're not mean enough to tackle her."

"You so sure of that?"

"Well, yes, I guess. You're nice. She's psychotic."

Lynnette took her hand away from my neck, said, "I was psychotic when Von died. For weeks, months. Maybe a year before and after."

"I can imagine that but would not have guessed so. You seem a defined personality. Like you're pretty much together and know who you are."

"Now you're really stretching."

"Okay, I like you a lot. Will that work?"

"For now."

We both laughed.

"You going to make a left turn."

"Oh yeah."

I looked back into the mirror, then got in the specially designed lane on El Camino Real and made the left turn at the next change of the light.

~ + ~

"Nate, you know the part where you think I'm so nice and I kinda challenged you?" said Lynnette as she fiddled with her napkin at the Davenport Lounge.

"Oh, in the Forester on the way up here?"

"Yes."

"Okay, what? You're still gonna tell me you're not?"

"Von and I were married for nearly twelve years."

"Right. I remember."

"When he died, my whole life died. We did everything together, including watch television."

"You never had any kids?"

"We tried. And we tried. That's how I started out as a stay-at-home. We wanted children right away, even before I was twenty."

"What happened?"

"Our internal chemistry didn't match. Something like that."

"Sad. Very sad. You ever figure out exactly what was wrong?"

"I think I did but I didn't say anything to

Von. He was a great guy. Worked hard. Treated me well. Very well."

"You try to adopt?"

Lynnette turned away for a moment. Looked like she might have been holding back tears, didn't want me to see.

"I – we – we wanted one of our own, first," she said as she turned to pick up her cosmopolitan and stare at it.

"How about we change the subject?" I said.

"Yes. Probably ought to take me back to my car, in a minute."

"Did I say something wrong?"

"No it's me. I thought I was ready to talk about all this to a stranger. You're not a stranger, exactly. I guess I just need a bit more counseling."

"Counseling?"

"Yes. For two years after Von died. I went twice a week the first year. I was going weekly until right after Valentine's, two years ago. I figured I need to be ready to step out on my own, even if I wasn't a hundred percent ready."

"That's when you started dating?"

"Well, when I first tried. Went to dinner twice."

Sounded like all was not fully cleansed in the land of Lynnette.

"You're fine," I said, hoping to sound perky. "Nobody worth a darn on the inside is built like a battleship."

"Thanks, Nate, and please take me home – to my car."

~ + ~

I drove kinda slow on my way back to

Seabrook, partly because I was tired and partly because I wanted to make more sense out of the day. The Feds and INTERPOL had taken me for quite a ride. And I was sad that Lynnette wasn't quite as ready to head on down the road as she had thought, making my reflexes a bit slower than usual, endorphins running loose all over the place, and my mind distracted by the myriad of thoughts and feelings.

First off was that pompous Scholl woman, the INTERPOL agent. I wondered if either myself or the Secret Service agents, Evans and Willows, much less the Webster police, could figure out if the credentials Ingrid Scholl presented were valid. Forged documents, drivers licenses, credentials, and the like were easily obtained in Houston. And why not? Four million people is a large enough market to support a vibrant underground economy, especially with the shipping industry being the USA's fourth largest.

And what did she think she was going to train me for? And how did an INTERPOL agent qualify to stand in for a Harris County Constable-CIA agent by the name of Heather Carey?

I wondered if Torville and company had managed to sequester Scholl downtown.

Second, what had Torville wanted? Why had he come by my office? Was he going to chew me out for the night before – maybe punch me out? Why had he come by my house the night before, anyway? And was he actually the Technology Voice who had told me he'd be by my office? He did come by. Dammit he did.

I had done a damn good job of leaving Ben

Franklin alone and if they hadn't queered the deal with Candice, I'd been free and clear of my obligations to her as well.

Third, who was that guy Spring was with at Space Center Houston?

Fourth, I still wanted to know what Torville had Ben Franklin doing and why.

Fifth, I still wondered where Candice got all those used Franklins.

~ + ~

When I got home I took care of Zip, then found the remote and collapsed into my recliner. The NBA playoff game had just started. Don't ask me which one. During the first pair of free throws, I remembered I still had a major problem. After about forty-five minutes in the recliner, I managed to get up and scan my house for foreign electronics equipment. I found five units and rendered them toast. The equipment I used to toast their circuits remains patented to this day and still comes with sticker shock.

Back in my recliner I watched a good part of the second game – I think. I remember waking up around two, still in my recliner, the talking heads still babbling away on the LCD TV, and Zip needing to go outside for a bit.

I know I found my bed because I woke up there.

Chapter 56
– Saturday

News that it was nine in the morning came too soon. Spring and Jocelyn were the messengers, one calling my cell and the other texting saying they were at the front door and wondering if I had lost my hearing.

I put on some shorts and an old t-shirt and opened the front door, saying, "Hope you're not here for breakfast."

"Who eats breakfast?" said Jocelyn, giving me a knuckle handshake as she walked in behind Spring who seemed sullen and avoided eye contact when she walked by.

"What's up?" I said as I walked past them to the kitchen to make coffee.

Neither answered.

"You two deaf?"

"Soon," said Jocelyn.

I got the water in the tank, filter and coffee in the basket, and turned the drip coffee maker on, then wondered if we'd all be better at Classic Café.

"Spring, you with us?"

"She's got a lot on her mind," said Jocelyn.

"What time do you got to work?"

"I've got the late shift this evening. Saturday night date night cancelled."

I said. "Either of you drinking coffee this morning?"

"Just Mom," said Spring.

"Your mom's drinking coffee?" I said, turning to look at Spring. "Is she outside in a car or something?"

"Sprite's just giving a report," said Jocelyn.

"She's my Mom!" said Spring.

And I knew what was up: Down in the dumps, with Spring.

"Okay, you want to talk about it or you figuring on sulking all day? You could be standing by her right now, you know."

Spring fidgeted, recrossed one leg under her on the couch, looked past me out the kitchen window, it looked like.

"Sprite got kicked out."

"I did not."

"True," said Jocelyn. "Your mom told you to leave."

"Just for this morning. A while. She wanted space."

"Whoa," I said. "How about I get a timeline of events?"

Spring switched legs around again, said, "The coffee done yet?"

"You get a cup when you talk," I said.

"Sprite, let go. This man's been good to you and – "

"He got Mom arrested."

"Oh, so now it's drama versus drama," I said.

Both girls looked at me with confusion across their brows.

"Look," I said, "your mother was not arrested. She was questioned. In an empty office in the Executive Suites, a few doors down from mine."

"Naw," said Spring.

"Yaw," I said. "When they figured out she just happened to drop by, they let her go."

"She said they weren't very nice."

"Sprite, your mom says that all the time. And she's always pushing. She's even rude to Lynnette," I said.

Spring put the sullen face back on. Repositioned, sitting on both legs.

I figured she was back on her loyalty swing, motivated by genes and our civilization to be loyal to her mother, her true feelings liking her step dad, Ben Franklin, more. Which was the original reason she contacted me. In the two weeks I'd known her, she appeared to vacillate daily on the issue.

"Jocelyn, you got any suggestions."

"Here's what she told me, okay?"

"Go ahead," I said, looking straight at Spring who was looking at the fireplace.

"So, Mrs. Franklin gets home like at seven this morning and isn't happy Spring's not there so she calls me. I of course lie and Spring up and splits my place for home."

"This is usually an everyday thing, I'm guessing."

"Pretty much," says Jocelyn. "Spring doesn't cook and her mother doesn't want to, so it's like a daily war. You know, who's for dinner?"

"Okay, so how about what happened next – is that what sent Spring down in the dungeon?"

"She hasn't said. Probably it's all of it."

"All of what?" I said.

"Back off the gas pedal, Trench. I'm tellin' ya."

Collateral Franklins

And I did and Jocelyn did.

"When Spring got home, her mother wanted to know where she'd been. Nothing new there. Spring asked her mother where she'd been – Spring didn't know about the commotion at your office at that point. Candice didn't take kindly to being questioned and grounded Spring who promptly stormed out of the house, only to forget her purse. She had her car keys, but not her clutch, her driver's license, credit cards, cash, or cell phone.

"Spring went to a neighbor's and borrowed their phone. I picked her up. We went cruising. What are Friday nights for, after all?"

"I've rescued your butt 'nough times!" said Spring.

"Okay," said Jocelyn. "Anyway, at one-thirty this morning, I took Spring by her house where she used the secret key on the side porch to get inside. That set off the invader alarms and woke her mother who was drunk as a soggy dunked donut, even after sleeping a couple hours.

"The fight that ensued is now a blur in Spring's mind and a total war in Candice's hangover filtered recollection this morning. Anyway, Spring was grounded for the remainder of May. Twenty-eight days. And all of June, another thirty."

"So, Spring's grounded. How did she manage to get here?" I said.

"Same way she got out of the house before she had a car."

I had been dumb. "Little" Spring at five-four could crawl out a lot of home windows.

"So, it's Jocelyn's taxi and counseling

service," I said, shaking my head.
 "Pretty much."

Chapter 57
– Saturday

"Well, gals, I had fully intended to sleep all morning. Since you two have prevented that, I'm going to launch Cyber Sailor with my best friend – you've met Zip – and get away from all the drama."

"But that's not why I'm here," said Spring.

"You're not here, Jocelyn?" I said.

"Push come shove, I'm always there."

I had no doubt that was the case.

"Mr. T., you gotta help!"

Spring had returned to proactive mode.

"I have been nothing but the managing uncle in your family for three weeks now. Even non-union folks gets days off. This is mine."

Spring crawled off the couch and was in my face before I could take another sip of coffee.

"This is real important."

"You said that in the first phone conversation we had. Then you didn't show up at Coffee Oasis."

"This is worse. Same thing but worse."

"And then you called again and didn't show up at Franca's."

"I know you now. You can do stuff."

Now what could that be?

"Jocelyn," I said, "you not tell me the whole story?"

"I told you Spring's story."

"What's that supposed to mean?" I said.

Spring spun around. Kicked my ottoman hard enough to move it a full foot.

"What?" I said.

"Dad left."

~ + ~

"Why are we sitting here?" said Jocelyn. "It's getting warm."

I did not reply. It was maybe eleven thirty.

"Tell me again," said Jocelyn. "Why are we here?"

I shook my head ever so slowly as I turned to her.

"Like I said twelve times already, I want to see what Ben Franklin does today."

"It's Saturday. He works his tail off," said Spring.

Nobody said anything for a good five minutes and then Jocelyn said, "Hey, Trench."

"What?"

"After our last visit up to Helm Street, might be a good bet Ben is being shadowed even now at his restaurants."

"That's why we're in your car and parked in the lot next door."

"Even, then, it's not like we don't look weird. Two chicks and an old dude in an oil burner."

"Fits right in with Webster. We'll rent a limo when he goes to the one in Clear Lake Shores," I said, stifling a laugh.

"Get out," said Spring.

"Weren't you supposed to not track him any more?" said Jocelyn.

"After two raids on my property – office and home – I don't think much of our Secret Service

Collateral Franklins

friends."

"Secret Service?" said Spring. "I thought they guarded the Prez."

"Our version of the S. S. has been given responsibilities outside the presidency."

"Like what?"

"Like currency," I said. "Been responsible for that since right around the Civil War."

"W.T.F.?" said Spring.

"United States Treasury. Money. Fort Knox. Counterfeiters. Stuff like that. The dollar is the currency for the United States. Britain has the pound sterling. Europe has the euro."

"Spring slept through that class," said Jocelyn.

Spring poked her friend in the ribs.

I saw Ben Franklin exit the restaurant.

"Chill out. Ben approaches."

"Why is Dad standing next to the Charger?"

"What?" said Jocelyn.

"He's not getting in."

"Showing off his hot red wheels to a chick we can't see," said Jocelyn.

I wanted to turn around and take a swing at them – playfully. What a pair.

"I'm guessing he's meeting someone," I said.

"Why do you say that?" said Spring.

"He walked out. Left his home."

"Actually, he never came home, " said Spring

"You said he left."

"Well, Mom put it that way, I guess."

"What's he going to do for clothes? Did he call your mom?"

"I'm not sure. He has three or four shirts and a couple pair of pants at each restaurant. Spills and business meetings and stuff," said Spring.

"He's got a cot at each one, too?"

"No."

"You think maybe he's staying at Helm?" said Jocelyn.

Spring bopped her buddy with a backhand to the shoulder. "He's not that much a part of the Feds. Take it back."

"I take it where I want it."

"Back off. Both of you."

"Now you sound like a parent," said Spring.

"He just Trench," said Jocelyn.

I twisted around and said, "Look, Spring, you drug me into this. Then you dragged Jocelyn with you. If you don't like what I'm doin', then by all means walk."

"Hey, Trench, she's just – "

"And quit bailing her out, Jocelyn. Graduation's in a few weeks. Act like it. From here on out you are in charge of the rest of your *own* life."

"Definitely parent mode," said Spring.

I straightened back around in my seat, looked at the parking lot.

No red Dodge Charger.

I looked left. Nothing.

I looked right. Bingo. He had just turned west from Hwy. 3 onto the NASA Pkwy., into Webster proper.

"Fasten your seatbelts," I said.

"Won't catch him," said Spring.

Whose side was she on, anyway?

Chapter 58
– Saturday

Spring spoke true. The abundance of Webster traffic lights and their religiously enforced speed limits combined to hold me blocks behind.

I thought I saw Ben turn south onto Kobayashi, but we did not find him. We checked his restaurant near there but the sports bar was barely kicking and no red Charger. Later I kicked my ass for not going inside and looking around, asking for the manger and such. Ben had fooled me once before at that very sports bar. He'd left out the back without my knowing and returned, walking right in the front door.

And I got no support from the peanut gallery, aka, my Thugettes.

"You willing to accept another, what they call course of action, Trench?" said Jocelyn, as I pulled into Mario's Pizza.

"The current course of action is lunch. Anyone object to a salad?"

"This is pizza," said Spring.

"I'm with my girl," said Jocelyn.

"I'm with my diet – sorta. Let's eat and see what we come up with."

"You gonna try to steer us a certain way?" said Jocelyn.

"Mostly just keep you out of jail."

~ + ~

The service was a little slow being Saturday and pizza the menu, so it took about twenty minutes for the Canadian bacon pineapple mushroom pizza to arrive. In the meantime, I'd grabbed a small side salad and demolished it. .

I'd taken one bite when Jocelyn said, "You need to scoot over in the booth."

"What?"

"Gonna be another party joining us."

"I didn't invite anyone."

"I sorta didn't either."

"Jocelyn, you're starting to sound like Spring."

"Heya," said Spring.

Jocelyn looked up from her Cricket, said, "Well, maybe you can play the gentleman thing."

"Sure. Provided you tell me who."

Jocelyn gave me a strange smile and a something tapped me on the shoulder.

"What the – "

Heather Carey, dressed in running shorts and a tank top, looked me in the eye, said, "Mind if I sit across from my cousin?"

"Mind if you tell me what you're doing here?"

"Supporting my cousin and her best friend."

"And that would need improving how?"

"Trench, let her in," said Jocelyn.

"You know an Ingrid Scholl?" I said, still sitting, but by then turned out.

Carey looked over at Jocelyn then back at me, wrinkles for the first time around her lips and nose. "You, ahh, met her?"

I shook my head in disbelief, slid out of the booth, and went to find our waitress.

~ + ~

"You'll have silverware and a plate shortly," I said as I slid back in.

"Thanks, Trench. You can be a gentle guy after all," said Jocelyn.

"So, you knew we would be eating lunch here?" I said looking at Carey's right ear.

She turned toward me with a smile, then back to look at Jocelyn. "Your show."

"Trench," said Jocelyn, like it was a question.

"What's up?"

"Meet your different course of action."

"I don't think so. A higher up dropped by my office and said she was stepping in for your cousin, Ms. Carey here."

"What? Who. That's bullshit," said Heather Carey, loud enough to pause the activities in our remote section of Mario's pizza. It took a good ten seconds before the rest of the area resumed talking.

"Take it up with her."

"You can't be serious. What is this *person's* name?"

"You already have it."

"I do not. You and I haven't – " She stopped mid sentence, looked back to Jocelyn, then to Spring, and then twisted to look me dead in the eye. "Wait. You're saying *Ingrid Scholl* replaced me."

"Stepped in – that's how she put it."

"I, ummm, ahhh, can't really discuss that situation."

"Oh, great, you really work for INTERPOL too?"

Carey's frown grew more grotesque before she uttered, "INTERPOL?"

"After saying no to my requests for quite some time, Scholl handed over a creds wallet, like the Feds do, right after she clunked Torville. INTERPOL is what's on the documents."

"INTERPOL?"

"Evans with Torville's team honored it, too."

"He would," said Carey. Looked like she meant to keep her internal reactor's thoughts to herself. A frown sent her eyebrows lower.

"Look, you can just get the hell out of here if you think I'm going to put up with 'need to know' and 'unauthorized' and such crap."

She scooted a bit farther away in the booth, struggled with her frown while she sat back, looking towards Jocelyn and Spring but I didn't think she was actually looking at them.

"You two – three want to tell me what's cookin' here?" said Spring.

"Sprite, just sit back, let my cousin work this out."

"Oh, prairie patties, Jocelyn, you don't know either, huh."

"Spring," I said, "be kind toward your buddy. In the *need-to-know* world, most times nobody has a clear picture of the entire event or mission. They just work off of 'orders are orders' and like that. It's designed that way."

Chapter 59
– Saturday afternoon

"Now, Ms. Carey, I'd like – "

"Stuff it, Trench. I want to know about Ingrid Scholl."

"Call her. She acts like she knows you. I sure don't."

We went back and forth with similar discord for a good five minutes, mixed in between the Thugettes begging for another pizza because they'd had to share and water and tea refills and excitable diners near us.

"So, Ms. Carey, I – "

"Knock it off, Trench," said Jocelyn. "Call her Heather. She's family."

"Jocelyn," said Heather, "I prefer my last name in professional situations."

"Nothing professional the way you two are mouthing off," said Jocelyn.

"It is entertaining," said Spring. "At least it's not my folks going at it."

That was the first I'd heard of the Franklins engaging in verbal war.

"Ms. Carey, how do you explain the INTERPOL creds?"

She looked at me with half a snarl, glanced over to Jocelyn whose hand was out flat doing the "calm down" motion, then back to me before saying, "Crap."

I didn't exactly wait for her to continue. I

just didn't think of a response.

"Trench, look," said Carey and stopped.

Jocelyn gave her cousin a "thumbs up."

"Okay. Okay. Okay. Here's the deal. There is no Ingrid Scholl."

"I met her."

"Oh, she's got creds alright. But they're not hers."

"What?"

"I'm sorry. What you're getting is S.O.P. for appeasing an interviewee who doubts the credibility of the agent's purpose."

"What?"

"The senior INTERPOL agents – and they will deny this – carry a set of credentials that is not their own. Since the CIA agents were killed because of that web site that gave out their names, most international police type folks go around on an 'invented' passport for a secondary persona. The most common is 'Ingrid Scholl.' She probably used that because she figured you'd be looking for me and would want to know if she was for real. It was her way of tipping me off when you came to question me about her."

"So you really don't know the woman."

"No."

"So you don't know why she was in my office."

"Correct."

"So what are you doing here today?"

"Jocelyn wants me to help out. I want to make sure she's safe."

"You have no official function – like you said at my office."

"Not really. You're not my case. I have no

true role in Agent Torville's operation."

"But you know about him."

"We were briefed that he and others were here and to give them a wide berth."

"When you say 'we,' are you speaking as a true Constable of Harris County or are you speaking as an agent for NCS?"

She looked straight at me, said, "Yes."

I looked at her, said nothing for a good minute.

~ + ~

I was getting nowhere – and I was getting pissed.

I was powerless against the Feds – but they were closer to a known quantity than some strange foreign agent who did office drop-ins for kicks.

And I was fed up with Technology Voice who seemed to call around the time other things are going on.

"Okay... Heather. How do you think you can help us?"

"Might be able to help you with research."

I doubted she'd get me a pipeline to the stuff I couldn't get but decided to play along for a while.

"Accepted. How about accompanying me on house calls up on Helm Street?"

"I'm not sure I could even do the Constable drive by like I did. Torville and his group should know who I am at this point."

"Will he learn that you are truly a Harris County Constable or will he learn that you work for NCS?"

"Hey, wow," said Spring. "Like on TV?"

"That's N.C.I.S.," I said.

"She's different," said Jocelyn. "Superwoman."

"Not in this lifetime, Cuz."

"Okay, Cuz. Whichever," I said. "What does Torville know?"

"If he checks me out, he gets a Harris County Constable."

"Guaranteed?"

"I'm afraid in this life they're – "

"No guarantees," I said, cutting her off. "In the service, guys promised to *be there*. To have your back. To make sure. With civilians, it's like nobody accepts responsibility for anything or anyone."

"You okay, Trench?" said Spring.

I was not okay but having Spring ask it was like getting to eat icing off the spoon.

"Sure," I said, lying all the way. "I lived in that other world for twenty years. Some things just come as a surprise."

"And I will do more than I should," said Heather Carey. "That's the best I can do. I'm really wondering what that INTERPOL woman told you. If she's out taking my place, well, I'm going to be chatting with Langley here in a bit."

"Beats you being alone, Trench," said Jocelyn.

"Hey, we know you're the only one that's sane around here, Mr. T." said Spring

I'd just been schooled.

Chapter 60
– Saturday afternoon

"Nate – may I call you that?" said Heather Carey.
"No problem. You're Heather. Go on."
"Deal. Is there something specific you want me to check right now?"
"Lots of details. I'll have to write you a list."
"Okay, anything that's not a detail you want to talk about?"
"I'm a list guy. Twenty years in Navy, we did lots of reports."
"Okay, well, then help me out a minute."
"Shoot."
"Tell me about the INTERPOL woman."
"You're not going to like my description."
"Get out," said Jocelyn, slapping the table.
"Hey, just don't want to offend," I said.
"Go on," said Heather.
"She has to weigh two fifty. And could be that old."
"Wait, Nate. How tall is she?"
Did she have heels on?"
"I'd say, no heels, maybe five-five. Shoes she had on were like boots but with a real short shaft – short top. Heel like ropers, maybe an inch, maybe a bit more.
"And you're saying two fifty seriously?"
"Played high school and service football of one kind or another. She was as big around as

some of our short offensive linemen."

"Okay. Give me more, like accent, hair color, you know."

"Accent, maybe a bit of Sweden or Norway in there. Black hair. Near coal black but not glossy. No shine to it."

"Anything remarkable."

"Oh, like the cane she didn't need?"

"How so?"

I explained how Scholl had labored down the hall to my office but didn't need the walking stick in my office, moving smoothly around the room several times without it. Couldn't use it when she left. The Feds held it as evidence.

"Okay, Nate," said Heather, "guess her age."

"Hmmm. At first, with the cane, maybe mid sixties. Without it, around my office, the way she took out Torville, held her ground with Evans and the rest of the Feds, I'd say mid fifties."

"Could she have been a guy?"

I was so not ready for that. The stringy blonde with Ben Franklin was enough incorrect perception for me for the rest of the year.

"I don't look at folks that way. I'm a cyber investigator. Have a lot to learn when it comes to evaluating folks, you know, instantly critiquing their appearance, mannerisms, gait. I do sometimes get a vibe. Hers was coarse as an iron file."

"No problem. I just have to figure out who she is for my own safety."

"I hear that," I said. "You're carrying, right?"

In Texas, if you're a civilian, you take a few classes, you can carry a gun. We call it Concealed Handgun License.

"Not officially. I'm off the clock."

"It's in the car, I bet," said Jocelyn.

"Easy, Cuz."

"Heather, what else you want to know?" I said.

"I'll text you."

"Jocelyn, did you *already* give her the Crickets?"

"Not yours."

"What's yours, Heather, and I'll text you first."

~ + ~

"What are we up to now, boss man," said Jocelyn.

We were back in Jocelyn's car with her driving, me in the passenger seat. "How about we go looking for pretty red cars up on Helm?"

"Mr. T!"

"Sprite, chill," said Jocelyn.

"Look, we are now well fed and Constable-Agent Carey – Heather is going to work with us. We need to start figuring out why who is which what."

"What he said," said Spring.

"Okay, but let me and Sprite sneak around the corner," said Jocelyn. "No sense driving this piece of junk by there. My car will get put in their database."

Jocelyn had a very good point.

"Okay, and I'll check some things while I wait."

"Can't do squat with the Cricket," said Spring.

"I have the Z10 with me."

"You are giving out your location," said

Jocelyn. "Turn feature off."

"I did, two weeks ago."

"Good stuff. You do know, Trench, those aren't selling very well."

"The Crickets?" I said, knowing better.

"The Blackberry Zebra elephant."

"You back off, now, you hear?"

"Excellent hearing here," said Jocelyn.

"But can you listen?" I said, laughing a bit softer than I wanted to.

"No comment," said Spring.

"What she said," said Jocelyn.

"Then it's settled. You two are empowered to organize a search party for the purposes of locating and identifying a red Dodge Charger and whereabouts of its usual operator."

"Be nice if we could see him pulling shirts on hangers out of the back seat," said Spring who then broke down in tears.

Chapter 61
– Saturday afternoon

Jocelyn had parked under a large old tree a couple blocks away, the shade matching the color of her junker and keeping things cool inside. It all made it more difficult for folks to see me from a distance. And it gave me a chance to take out the yellow legal pad page where I'd written down what was bothering me the most. I needed to add to the list. Three items became nine.

1. Who did those two guys on the bridge belong to?

2. Was Torville the only Fed after my ass – our asses?

3. Was Candice Franklin coming down off her Lexapro or whatever was her prescribed mood altering and control chemical, or was she really going nuts for the same reason I was heading that way – lack of certainty?

4. Who was masquerading as Ingrid Scholl – and why? INTERPOL?

5. Who was really Technology Voice?

6. Who was the guy Spring had the daytime date with at Space Center Houston – I figured he was somebody's operative, but whose?

7. Did I need to closely monitor Heather Carey? Was she really a National Clandestine Service operative masquerading as a Harris Country Constable?

8. Had the Feds permanently trashed Candice & Ben Franklins marriage?

9. Other than the Thugettes, who could I trust – Lynnette? I really didn't know who she was "after work" but I wanted to be able to trust her.

I sat there thinking there had to be a way for my vast research resources to help me answer these nine questions. Some, anyway. If my electronic resources didn't work, it would be gumshoe to the max for Nate Trench.

~ + ~

The list's growing from three to nine points had helped clear my head a little. It also told me I was an idiot to sit defenseless in an relic of a car in the shade, so I began the old check all mirror routine, one every fifteen seconds.

Thugettes returned in half an hour.

"He's there – well, not any more," said Spring as she plopped in the back seat.

"What?" I said.

"Charger is parked in driveway. He just left in one of those black Explorers, the ones with the windows tinted so dark you can't see in."

"You okay, Spring?"

"I guess."

"No she's not," said Jocelyn as she landed in the driver's seat. "She lies."

"Stuff it," said Spring.

"Okay, which one of you is going to give me a professional report."

"What's that?" said Spring. "You haven't told – "

"You're the one who wanted to be a gumshoe, a detective. I need information supplied along a timeline."

"Yeah, okay, Jocelyn, you tell him."

And Jocelyn did. Seems they were gone longer than I realized. Mark me down for non-professional action on that one.

When they got close enough on Helm to watch the house, Ben was fiddling around with something in the Charger's trunk while parked in the driveway. The Charger was still in the driveway but Ben had gone in and out of the house at least five times, continuing to mess with things in his trunk, not really carrying much in or out.

"You really have no idea what he was doing?" I said.

"Can't say for sure," said Jocelyn. "I worked the telephoto lens and still couldn't figure out what he had in his hands. Small boxes, mostly."

"How small? Shoebox? Guess."

"Shoebox but not as long. Maybe a third shorter. No clue on inside."

"Couldn't see any labels or manufacturers logos?"

"Nope."

"I don't know Mr. T.," said Spring. "Just didn't make any sense."

"Okay, Spring, did you get a sense of how he felt as you watched him? He's your dad. Did he look the least bit nervous, walk faster than usual, that sort of thing?"

"Walking straight, no limps, no looking around. Not in a big hurry. Just working like the machine he can be. Well, he walks fast a lot of times, leaving in the morning. Not fast just now but focused – yeah, that's it. He looked genuinely focused on whatever he was doing."

"And he left without the Charger?"

"Yeah, this Explorer pulled up next to the mailbox and Dad hopped in."

"Wasn't carrying anything."

"Not big if he was. Maybe in his pockets. He was in a windbreaker. We were across the street and down a couple houses. The Explorer blocked his getting in the car."

I wondered if the Feds knew the gals were out there and had a little fun at our expense.

"Okay," I said. So we know where the Charger is. We don't know where Ben is but he has to come back to get the Charger."

"But the Explorer can take him. A taxi like deal, maybe," said Jocelyn.

"Why did we want to know?" said Spring. "I mean, I want to know, but Mr. T., you wanted to follow him around. He walked, like I said."

"Cards on the table, Trench," said Jocelyn. "What's going on in that head of yours?"

"Can you and I discuss this later?" I said.

"No. That's without me," said Spring.

True.

"Go ahead, Trench. She can handle it."

"Let's get out of here before we're noticed," I said. "I'll explain as we go. Head back to my place."

Chapter 62
– Saturday afternoon

"Okay," I said as Jocelyn turned down Space Center Blvd. "Tell me why Ben Franklin left – didn't come home."

"Mom's nuts. He's dumping her."

"Sprite, maybe your mother ran him off or told him to not come home?"

"Naw. No. No. No."

"That all you got, Trench?" said Jocelyn.

"Or maybe," I said, "he feels she needs some space right now so he's giving her the house and he'll go rent an apartment."

"No. Not his style," said Spring. "He likes work and done."

"You mean, sit down, talk, iron out, get it settled?"

"That. Yes, that."

"What if your dad knows something about the Feds thing that we don't, and your mother doesn't either."

"Well, duh," said Jocelyn.

"Right," I said. "So maybe it means deeper involvement on his part and wants to spare your mother that stress?"

"No," said Spring. "Mom said the marriage is over and done with."

"Okay, then how about this: what he knows is coming down the pipeline with the Feds is something that would put you and your mom in great jeopardy, so he's schemed up a way to insulate her as much as humanly possible from the dangers he sees just down the road?"

"You said same thing twice," said Jocelyn.

"Wait," said Spring. "He dumps her so the Feds or such think he doesn't care any more?"

"I'm thinking that's a possible explanation," I said.

"Might work on Mom. You think they'd actually believe he'd divorce me?"

"Nerds would see you're adopted and not grasp how close you are to Ben Franklin."

"Ain't fair. Ain't fair. Ain't fair."

"Trench," said Jocelyn, "what could be so bad that Ben feels he needs to bail on his family?"

"That's what I'm – we're going to find out."

"How?"

"First off, I'm going to text your cousin."

I let them watch as I entered these four messages separately in the text window.

> Something big coming down on Helm street with Torville?

> Ben Franklin over there today. Ben Franklin moving out of home.

> Ben picked up from Helm by black Explorer. Charger remained.

> See what NCS will tell you. Thanks. Nate.

~ + ~

"Done. Now I have question for Spring."

"She's not here," said Spring.

"Just do it," said Jocelyn.

"Okay," I said, "I want the entire story on the other afternoon with the guy at Space Center

Houston."

"No you don't."

"Just do it."

I didn't say a word. We were two blocks from my place by then. We'd get her talking once we were inside my house.

"Can't hear you," said Jocelyn as she pulled into my driveway.

"Okay, let's all go in – "

Z10 rang.

Blocked.

"This is Nate Trench."

"You have a driver now, I see," said Technology Voice in a lower tone than the last two or three calls.

Chapter 63
– Saturday afternoon

I buried the face of the Z10 against my gut, put a finger across my lips making sure both of them saw me, said, "Wait here."

I popped open the car door as I brought the Z10 back to my face, said, "Well, hello there High Tech One."

"I trust your driver has delivered you safely to your destination."

I wanted to ask him-her-it whether him-her-it had made the acquaintance of Ingrid Scholl, but I didn't.

"You know where I am, I'm sure," I said as worked my key in the front door's deadbolt. "How do I look?"

"Let's quit the chit chat. You need to lower your profile."

I crossed the den into the kitchen, heading for a drink of water.

"I have done that."

"Not by my measuring stick," said Technology Voice.

"Buy a new one."

"A bit rude today, aren't you."

"You got a name? High Tech One's a bit long."

"Rude. Most rude. You must reform."

"You're the one using an electronically modified voice. Talk about rude!"

"Security protocol. We value that."

"We? Who's 'we'?"

"You know well organizations' security protocols."

The Thugettes were always great at following instructions to the letter, so it was no surprise to learn that one of them had caused the noise behind me.

I turned around.

"Sounds like the badgering and harassment protocol from this end of the line. I'll pass."

The Thugettes' eyes resembled those of scared little girls as I pointed at the Z10 and threw it the bird.

"Not a good idea."

Jocelyn tiptoed into the kitchen and gave me a major knuckle handshake.

"What's a good idea?" I said.

"Complete retreat," said Technology Voice. " No involvement."

"With whom?"

"You know the case."

"Look High Tech One, we have a situation here where I think I've severely reduced my profile and you think I haven't. Only way I can understand that is you give me your measuring stick, graduations on it and all. Drop it by my office sometime next week. I'm there eight-thirty to noon, one to five. Can't reach common ground if we can't orient ourselves around common measurements."

My mind juggled a bingo machine's worth of jumping balls as to the true identify of Technology Voice. Hell, he-she-it hadn't ever given a name to use on the hassle-threat calls.

"You. Must. Try. Harder," said Technology Voice.

I did not respond.

"You there. Hear this: You. Have. Four. Hours. To. Demonstrate. Your. Complete. Cooperation."

"Can you hear me loud and clear, like we used to say in the Navy?"

"I can. You. Are. Not. Hearing. Us. Me."

"Well, hear this," I said, motioning to the Thugettes over to me. "Are you listening?"

"Losing. Patience. I lose patience, you lose life."

I wrote *laugh loud* on a note pad, showed Spring and Jocelyn, then held up one finger, said "Now"; two fingers, said, "Hear"; three fingers, we laughed our asses off beside the Z10 for a good fifteen, maybe twenty seconds, until I looked at the Z10 and realized the call had disconnected.

Back then I wasn't sure my jubilant choir had been the right course of action against Technology Voice. I felt better afterwards and the laughing choir cheered up Spring. I figured the moment deserved a toast, so I handed each Thugette a chocolate-coated vanilla Haagen-Daas bar from my freezer.

~ + ~

A short while later we walked down to the bulkhead. The girls played with Zip. I carried my special sensor equipment and ran tests. The machine showed no electronic activity. I guessed that at least one tormentor had secured a visual vantage point or installed video surveillance. I doubted their software was so sophisticated they could read lips at distance.

I joined the girls and Zip for a while, then called Spring over for a chat.

"Okay, who was the guy at Space Center Houston? What was the deal? What's his deal. Now, Spring."

She threw the Frisbee in the water. Zip dove after it. Had I forgotten to tell them not to do that?

"You don't give up, Mr. T. Can't a girl have a private life? Seriously."

"I am serious. Damn serious. So are the clandestine operations surrounding your family these days. Any tall, dark, and handsome that's *new* on the scene with you is suspect. Could 'a' been hired to cozy up to you, over time turning casual conversation into data, intelligence: our movements; our plans.

"So, out with it. From the time I left you gals at Denny's in La Porte. "

"What if I was the one using someone's information?"

"How would you know who to get information *from*?"

"He works for NASA."

"What's that got to do with your family?"

"Everything around here deals with NASA–JSC."

"Space Center Houston is a not-for-profit educational tourist operation. Johnson Space Center trains astronauts, among other things."

"What's the hap? They're all tied together."

"Looks like it on the map, huh."

"It is. They are. We went on the tram over to

JSC and got a tour. I memorized a lot of things."

"Did you get the part about JSC being government?"

"So?"

"Space Center Houston isn't."

"Then how did we get to go in there?"

"Government cooperates with civilian enterprise, like giving the Texas to the San Jacinto Monument."

"You mean the battleship? The one at the park?"

"Yes. Going on a tour onboard the Texas is real close to touring NASA. The federal government makes facilities – ships; installations – available to locals, cities, non-profits, with the idea both will benefit from improved public relations. You don't get to see the good stuff or the truly new stuff. They keep the secrets behind lots of locked doors. Use guards who carry guns."

Spring looked enlightened, her eyes opening wider. Then her smile turned upside down and the sparkle left her eyes.

I hated to do it, but I ran her through the drill, starting with, of course, "Where did you meet him?" Hammered her every single step of the way.

The guy was four years older, a fairly recent graduate of Sam Houston State, the cousin of one of Spring's classmates. He did work at the JSC but had only been there four months. She was vague as to how and where they met. The rest seemed simple and innocent, more a diversion from her problems, bolstered by the flimsy rationale that she was doing something to help her parents' cause.

We had bigger fish to fry and I gave Spring back to Zip.

Chapter 64
– Saturday afternoon

My attention shifted to Ingrid Scholl. Why Scholl? The Z10 chimed, its screen displaying the number on the business card Scholl gave me during the police and Secret Service on-site investigation of Torville's second injury. A very flimsy business card. Didn't say INTERPOL, either. I asked about that. She looked at me like it was the dumbest question she'd heard in years.

"Good afternoon, Agent Scholl."

"Inspector Scholl. You Americans!"

"You called?"

"It is time I train you."

"To do what, may I ask?"

I was so trying to be polite, unlike most Americans.

"This is not a secure phone line, is it?"

"No. A cell phone."

"Then I cannot discuss the purpose of what I have mentioned."

Going for a news anchor tone, I said, "And you would be wise to not disclose the meeting time or location."

"You Americans and your joking."

"Perhaps you can drop by the site of our last encounter. Between one and five on Monday afternoon would work for me."

She hung up.

I wondered.

Of all nine problems on my list, I knew least about that woman. This guaranteed a large degree of insecurity, which is a sugar-coated word for *fear*.

~ + ~

Was it safe to separate from the Thugettes for the rest of the weekend? Spring's situation at home was tenuous. She'd been grounded but hadn't been home all day. I'd never been briefed on Jocelyn's home life or arrangements – she'd had her own apartment for a couple months but where was it? Jocelyn didn't reach out for help continually as her running mate did, so I had not pursued Jocelyn's accommodations.

Maybe Jocelyn's would be the ideal place for Spring to disappear? But what would Spring's absence from home do to a by-then very fragile Candice Faith Pence Franklin?

If Spring and Jocelyn were sequestered, what respite could late Saturday afternoon afford me?

Torville could be back at my doorstep at any time. So could Technology Voice and his/her crew. And my guts told me there was a third operator messing with my life.

I couldn't stay home because the enemy(ies) could hear every word said, every basketball game listened to, every opening and shutting of the refrigerator.

Maybe what I should do was disable all the electronic surveillance in and around my home. I had used it to send false information and we'd slam-dunked Technology Voice, but both tactics most likely would not work again.

Debugging my home would take forever if I did it alone.

I'd need help.

I made a decision: the Thugettes weren't leaving just yet.

~ + ~

I received another phone call just after the Thugettes left. They'd been invaluable in finding the nooks and crannies and pinholes where the seven electronic devices had been installed.

Z10 screen said, Number Not Available. Well, that beat blocked or none.

"Nate Trench, at your service," I said, happy to take a call inside my home again.

"Are you busy, Mr. Trench?" came over the air waves with a thick South American accent. Why was it familiar to me?

"Depends, sir. How may I help you?"

"We need to talk."

Now that was close to Mexican Mafia.

"May I ask who's calling me?"

"Adrian Portofino, at your service."

"Thank you, Mr. Portofino. And what might be the nature of your business?"

"Correct, Mr. Trench. That is the subject of our meeting. How soon can you be ready?"

I thought a minute, realized I was dumb tired and needed a couple days off.

"Tuesday afternoon would be good for me, sir."

A pause, a gargling deep breath by a heavy smoker, then, "Mr. Trench, perhaps I am not making myself clear. Are you busy? Yes or no."

"Depends."

"Ah, yes. Again you say this. The matter is

one of urgency – to all concerned, sir."

"And how am I concerned?"

"You will need to join us and learn, Mr. Trench."

"Us?" I said, figuring I was in for a committee.

"One other gentleman. You have spoken with us before."

I remembered the accent. One of the guys who gave me a message from the bridge.

"I loaned out my vest – last week."

"Please explain. What is vest to do with meeting?"

"Kevlar vest. Supposed to stop bullets. You still got that silencer?"

"You Americans, try polite insults. Understand you live now because we let you live. For now."

I didn't respond. I remember not responding quite clearly. Maybe it was because my heart had stopped beating?

"Are you listening, Mr. Trench?"

I got some words out after maybe ten seconds, saying, "I can hear you."

"Good. You meet us. Outriggers. Eleven thirty this night. Downstairs bar."

"Hey, that's kinda late. You must know I haven't had much sleep lately."

"Please, sir. This also rings as insult."

"How will I know you? It was kinda dark last time I – "

"It will be dark again, no?" He laughed, shorts bursts, a couple three of them – like Vincent Price.

I had such a knot in my stomach, I couldn't

breathe.

The South American, Central American nee Mexican accent coughed as if to clear a smoker's throat, said, "We will make ourselves known."

I searched for a smart-ass comeback.

"Oh," he said, a couple of my heartbeats later, "and come alone."

~ + ~

I needed in-person, real-time help. I had just a few hours to recruit some. But whom? Could I trust them?

Seabrook police?

They were already tired of me after the rumble the night before. Lots of paperwork went with that event. Besides, Torville probably monitored their communications.

Lynnette?

Maybe I could trust her but she was so not familiar with the world's underbelly. Hell, I wasn't much better. So no help there, really. Besides, even though I did not know if we could become a true and lasting couple, I wanted the option of finding out.

Spring and Jocelyn?

They had amazing courage, but I liked them too much to further endanger their lives. Hopefully they would be so tired, they'd be asleep before eleven for once.

Golden Gumshoes?

Those members anxious to help were located out of my service area. Local investigators didn't want to aid their competition and were probably as allergic to bullets as I was. The overwhelming majority were very smart, intuitive, and analytical, not expert marksmen.

Friends?

I had many happy acquaintances among the Houston, Seabrook, and League City police forces plus the Harris and Galveston county sheriffs departments. But no true friends, allies, or sidekicks like you read about in most detective fiction.

FBI, ICE, Texas Rangers?

Yeah, sure.

I needed mean, deadly help.

No, I wasn't a member of Hell's Angels.

A true law enforcement officer, familiar with the national, maybe international scope of things, a veteran of some years not afraid of a fight – that's what I needed.

I turned on the flat screen, clicked the sports listings.

NBA had a triple header going.

I grabbed an Alaskan amber from the refrigerator and dropped into the recliner. Hoped something would occur to me before it got dark.

Chapter 65
– Saturday evening

Things got damn boring even though the NBA was good – the commentators were always the good ones during the playoffs – but I'd had so much interaction with people over that week, so much stress, I had no cheer left to put into the game.

Zip tried to cheer me up from time to time, usually during commercials, the new name for basketball times-out. It was truly amazing how a dog could know when a commercial was on – or was he just really into me?

The second game of the triple header began and I still hadn't solved my demons. I needed to belly up to the fact that I had no way to guarantee my safety if I showed up at Outriggers alone.

It was a popular place so the two thugs wouldn't off me right there. The downstairs bar was open on three sides, people coming and going all the time, so you wouldn't notice someone being *escorted* from the premises unless they were with you. The actual Outriggers restaurant was upstairs, the downstairs a converted flood space and right on the water, docks on two sides. Another way for the two thugs to operate. Many folks took their boats to dinner instead of fighting traffic.

I was on my way to the refrigerator for a

third beer when a text came in from Jocelyn on the Cricket.

> u ok dude?

I eagerly tapped:

> 4 sure; you gals?
> got popcorn – 3 dvds – good 2 go
> NBA here
> u speak / cuz?

Cuz? Cousin. Heather Carey. Constable Heather Carey. NCS agent Heather Carey. Had I spoken with her?

What an idiot was holding that Cricket at my house in Seabrook.

> no. will contact now. later gals.
> ☺

I scrolled contacts and tapped Carey's number.

"Trench, you know what time it is?"

"Serious time."

"It's not for most. What's up? I'm on a date."

I explained.

She interrupted repeatedly, sprinkling a variety of expletives – what did her date think – as I told my tale.

I was about to apologize and just fade into the night when she surprised me.

"I'm in. Hulk dinner date is too close to boring to live long. Where are you?"

"Home. Meet me at Seabrook's Classic Café. Can you make it by ten? I'll go early, get us a table."

"Think so. I'll try my best. This is your safe phone, text and voice, right?"

"Yes."

~ + ~

Before I left early for the Classic Café, I checked Zip's water, the doors, and the windows, then entered the garage from the kitchen. The overhead light didn't come on when I tapped the hardwired switch that operated the garage door opener but I didn't realize it until I pulled the kitchen door shut behind me. A couple of bruisers came out of nowhere and tackled me to the cement floor. I twisted trying to get free but lightning bolts in my left elbow shot with such voltage I almost passed out. A guy my size is not used to being overpowered so easily. They had to be professionals.

Within seconds I had a mouth full of handkerchief, a watch cap over my head, and duct tape wrapped around ankles and wrists, arms behind me. Six pairs of hands lifted and carried me horizontally a short distance outside to a vehicle that drove up just as my own garage door closed behind us.

What itched like hard carpet brushed my arms and legs – I was wearing shorts – as I was laid down rather gently considering the brute force available. Had to be the back of an SUV. I wasn't in the trunk of a car – the surface I lay on was perfectly flat and regular car doors near me opened and shut; three of them.

The ride seemed long but I couldn't be sure. I'd never bounced through Houston traffic on my side.

My captors had not said a single word during my abduction and did not say a single word until they arrived at my destination.

Four car doors opened and closed but my door was left alone. This brought on what I now know to call a "panic attack." I started counting one-thousand-one, one-thousand-two, hoping to rein in my imagination.

Maybe ten minutes later the vehicle door next to me opened and I was gently guided out and stood up, held there while the duct tape around my ankles was removed, tearing a good bit of leg hair with it. My left elbow was still tender.

"Al baño, Patrón?" said a voice that went along with the Spanish.

"Si. Afuera," said another man.

Had the two thugs double-crossed me? Got a couple of their buddies and moved up our meeting time?

Maybe it was the Feds, but Spanish didn't sound like Feds to me. But, hey, why not? Lots of folks in Texas spoke fluent Spanish.

In maybe a minute I was inside a noisy room that smelled like showers at the YMCA or a public pool. My watch cap and gag were removed but all I could see were walls covered with a three-shades of tan bathroom tiles and two men wearing watch caps with holes for their eyes. Both were taller than me and two suit coat sizes larger. One brought out a pair of scissors and cut the duct tape on my wrists, then told me in English to empty my pockets into a small bucket before pointing me towards the facilities.

I took a leak and washed my hands but didn't look for a way out. Unlike the detectives in the movies, I wasn't any good at climbing out of windows, didn't run very fast, and didn't know any martial arts. Hell, I was a geek and they hadn't let me bring my keyboard with me so I couldn't smack them with it. Besides, folks organized enough to have four guys bring me in would not leave doors open.

A short while later I was escorted to a couch which had waterproof covering and had been cleaned recently. Maybe the old Naugahyde. No stains, no severely depressed cushions, it was right at home in a club house next to what was outside. Looking through an eight-by-ten-foot window before I sat down, I saw an Olympic size private swimming pool. It was quite a sight in the dark of night, lit up by underwater lights, its iridescent green hue near that of the waters I'd seen off the coast of Jamaica.

The two watch caps left me to my thoughts and I was alone for several minutes, maybe ten.

Then Agent Torville walked in.

Chapter 66
— Saturday evening

Torville's appearance from a side door touched a white hot electrode to my nervous system, like I'd just grabbed a two-twenty-volt wire and been thrown off. It took me a minute to get my breath back. Torville fiddled with some papers at a mahogany lectern to the left of the large window and didn't seem to notice.

When my breathing slowed, I said, "You playing both sides?"

"I'm disappointed in you, Nate. You're not going to inquire as to my health?"

A hundred smart Navy-learned retorts entered my mind. I went easy on him.

"How's your head?" I said, perky, cheery.

"I'll live."

"Too bad."

"Mr. Trench... Sorry to bring you out so late."

"Must I believe you?"

"Such bias. I've just apologized for taking your time without permission."

"A soft spin. Not valid, but, hey, what spins are?"

"Hostility will get you another ride on a hard surface."

"So you wanted my undivided attention. Well, you've got it, spending a good chunk of United States tax dollars on overtime to haul me out wherever we are – or are you working both sides? Whose money brought me here? Which is where?"

"Fresno. Not California."

"Texas. South of Pearland. Located a skip near here. Whose side are you on?"

"For a geek making so-so bucks, you're posturing like James Bond."

"Sorry. Don't know the man." Okay, literally, the truth.

"Now a comedian."

He walked over and sat on the arm of the next couch.

"Trench, why don't you just shut up?"

"Free country – well, it used to be."

"Dammit, asshole. You forget I can lock you up with the Patriot Act and a key. Send your adopted daughters to reform school for operating a meth lab."

"Not thinking they do any of that, actually, Agent Torville."

"We'd bring our own."

"Of course."

"So tell me why you're such a smartass tonight. You almost looked scared last time."

That was a hard question. I *was* surprised with my devil-may-care-attitude. I was scared deep down inside but my anger was far more powerful that evening.

"Because you could have killed me and you haven't," I said. "Because you could have locked me up and you haven't. Because you've gone to great lengths to bring me out here and have my undivided attention."

"Anything else?"

"Because you haven't physically assaulted me. Your crew was very agile except for the ribs. No bruises, no broken teeth. Just an abduction. I'm sitting here on a comfortable sofa, not even handcuffed."

"If handcuffs are your thing, I'd be happy to oblige. Could even chain you to the sofa frame.

Then it hit me. "This is *off the record*, isn't it, Torville?"

He gave me a "you're a stupid fool" look as he rose from the other sofa's arm and walked at a leisurely pace over to the large window and stood beside the lectern.

"Okay, Trench. I know it's late."

"You said that already."

"How's this?"

Torville pulled something the dimensions of a Zippo lighter out of his pocket and tapped it twice with his thumb.

The huge window behind him flashed solid white, then a video appeared, me and Jocelyn outside the Helm Street house, audio and all, taken evidently from the eave to the right of the front door back on Wednesday morning. The sound was ugly but the video was crisp, 720p at least, maybe 1080.

Torville raised his hand towards the screen, then did the thumb tap again. The screen went white.

"Now do I have your attention?"

By then I was so pumped up with my own bravado, I no longer feared for my life or incarceration.

"My attention is a given. My cooperation, probably not."

"You just keep think that. Here's the deal."

He waved the Zippo at the screen again. Maybe twenty photos of me driving around town rotated across on a carousel.

"Nathan Edward Trench, you've stepped right into the middle of a secret government operation."

"You Feds tell that to everybody."

"Dammit, Trench. This is serious. Shut up and listen."

I gave him a smile to rival the Cheshire Cat's.

"We want you to stay clear of Benjamin Franklin."

I kept smiling.

"We need you to stay clear of Mr. Franklin because we have nearly two years invested in an international sting operation, the scope of which would make a darn good Jason Bourne movie. You like those?"

Had he not read my file? I'd worked in intelligence for over twenty years. It had all been international since the Cold War.

I kept smiling.

"Now, Trench, in return for your cooperation, we'll not lock you up."

"Cut to new information."

"You ungrateful bastard."

"You can't lock me up. I've got too many live witnesses. You gonna put them away, too? Jail two eighteen-year-olds. Threaten their parents? You think Candice Franklin is goofy now, go ahead, abduct the daughter and make it look like 'teenager abducted just before graduation.'"

"Watch this."

Torville played with the Zippo again, a bit

longer it seemed. More little taps with his thumb.

The white screen showed three live video feeds, one in HD color from inside the Franklin house where Candice was watching TV and smoking a cigarette – smoking?

Another feed showed my den in greenish nightscope. *What the hell?* I'd just debugged the place.

The third was a split shot, my front and back yards, both telephoto shots evidenced by the grainy black and white. Zip was playing with his thirty foot chain, tossing it up in the air only to have the extreme length to come into play.

Those faded and a new video rotated onto the screen: Spring and Jocelyn sprawled out on the carpeted floor of what had to be Jocelyn's apartment, a huge bowl of popcorn between them, laughing and kicking at each other. The HD color just made it worse.

Chapter 67
– Saturday evening

"You got video of the other side?" I said. "You want to impress me, show me that."

Torville rolled the controller over and over in his fingers, a "you got to be the dumbest guy I've ever met" look on his face.

"I mean," I said, "this demo is impressive but it has nothing to do with anything that's illegal, you asshole."

Yeah, I was really pissed.

Not true.

I was really scared, scared for the gals. The Thugettes needed to be assured of an open life ahead of them.

"You really want to make a big deal out of this," said Torville. "That's it, isn't it? What, you want on Nightline? Sixty Minutes? Maybe the evening news. Is that what you're shooting for, you damn idiot geek?"

I worked my way out of the couch, stood, a major glare on my face.

Torville held out his unoccupied hand, palm wide facing me. "Sorry. Okay, I can't show you the other side. You know that."

"You're showing me your designer audiovisual setup. What else did taxpayers buy you last Christmas?"

"Sit down, swine."

"I *have* backed away from Ben Franklin," I

said, dropping down on the couch.

The temptation to squash the little shit, knowing I could do it one-handed, was too great to allow my emotions any leverage. The couch wasn't easy to climb out of, the cushion having slowly sagged under my weight, so he'd have a running start if I tried to jump up and go at him.

"You watched him today," said Torville.

"You trashed my life twice since I agreed to back off both the Franklins. I had to see if anything had changed. Be nice if Spring Franklin had parents alive and in one piece so they can attend her high school graduation."

"Okay. Okay."

I know that's what he said. I remember it clearly but I didn't believe it carried any sincerity at the time. Wanted to. Didn't.

"Trench, you have some kind of guardian angel, some kind of I don't know what."

"NSA told you to make sure you didn't kill me. I'm recallable for another five years, aren't I?"

Torville looked surprised.

"Don't bullshit me any more. My clearance is expensive. Training takes way too long."

He clicked the screen off and the night view returned. I wondered it there really was a pool outside.

"Tell me what you want," he said. "What is it?

"What does it matter? You don't f-in' care. Show here is nice but you don't care. Not about anything but Secret Service Agent Torville."

"What do you want to stay out of our way?"

"Let's talk about you."

Torville laughed. Some would have called it a guffaw.

"Yes, you," I said. "What does agent Torville want."

He swung his hand like he wanted to throw the Zippo-sized controller through the big glass window.

"Torville – wait, you have a first name. What is it?"

"Should have read my creds more carefully."

"Next time, leave them out there for more than two seconds."

"I'll be right back."

I watched Torville exit through the side door, the one he'd entered through when I was enamored by the view.

~ + ~

"Thanks for waiting," said Torville as he entered from behind me, that time from the same area I had. I wondered if he'd just needed to use the john.

"So, what's your name."

"Please, Trench."

"What do you want?"

He looked at me like he was still constipated.

"Torville, what do you want out of all this."

I knew what I wanted his answer to be. Something so very obvious, I couldn't believe I hadn't thought of it before. Something I could "trade."

"You crazy? Stupid? All agents want to get their man. Their job done well, in as little time as possible."

"So why you've been spending two years on this?"

"It's. A. Very. Big. Deal."
"I'm listening."
"I. Can't. Tell. You."
"Oh, bullshit."

Torville spun around like a newly turned top, looked for something to throw or kick it looked like, slammed his fist against the frame around the window.

"Dammit, Trench!" said Torville.

"Easy, now Walter," came over ceiling speakers. Female voice. Youngish; not a smoker. A bit of an echo.

"Gretchen, can't you stay out of this?"

Chapter 68
– Saturday evening

The side door Torville had used earlier opened and a cross-looking tallish, medium build woman just past middle age strolled past me. Dressed to the nines, her stride told me she would take on anything.

"Nate Trench, my boss, Gretchen Longstreet."

I pushed to stand up, but she waved me back down, came over and sat at the other end of my couch, hand outstretched.

"You want to come to work for us?" she said, her handshake firm.

I had to shake my head. Too many additional variables for one Saturday.

"Umm, no," I said. "I want you folks to quit being territorial. I want you folks to get a job done and not treat me like an idiot."

"You have an impeccable record and a top rating. Still, the old need to know thing. It's worse, much more restrictive since the Patriot Act. There's a lot they won't even tell me."

"Tell that to Snowden."

"Yes, well, we view Edward Snowden as a traitor and a fugitive, but forgive Walter. He takes his job very seriously. He would have locked you up but those same NSA folks that Snowden doesn't like would have none of that."

"Right." Did I believe her?

"So, what can we do to make this all work for you, Mr. Nathaniel Trench?"

Right then I saw two scenarios. One, Gretchen Longsteet was working good cop, bad cop on me. The other was the answer to the thugs.

"Nate," I said. "Not Nathaniel. Nate. Just Nate."

"Okay, and please call me Gretchen."

"Oh, crap," said Torville, spinning on his heels. "Is this a – "

"Stand still, Walter," said Gretchen. "I've got this. Go ahead, Nate."

"Okay," I said. "How about you give me an outline of the purpose of the mission or project that you've saddled Ben Franklin on. I won't tell a soul, his daughter and wife included."

Torville threw another imaginary object through the window glass. "I told you this was a waste of time."

"I'm not sure it is, Walter. Let's give him something."

"No."

"Yes."

Torville threw a third imaginary object into the glass.

"Walter, give him a level two summary."

"But I don't – "

"I'm in charge. My ass. Give it to him; use some of the visual in the library."

I wondered what level two was. I didn't want to sit through an overview that was so broad you could read about it in a typo-strewn Wikipedia page.

"Let's see if my verbal summary will be

enough."

"Very well."

"Listen up, Trench. Here goes."

Torville pulled some papers out of his back pocket, flipped through them a minute, then said, "Forgive me if this sounds a bit stiff. Have several updates. Don't have time to redraft."

"I did twenty for Uncle. I'm used to it."

"Fine," said Torville. "Benjamin Ivan Franklin owes back taxes for profits of a holding company that he was a fifty percent partner in before he met and married Candice. They sold the company – a catering business – and his partner supposedly said he had taken care of their last and final tax return. Item one: the partner had not done any of the work nor made a tentative payment. The partner died in a car wreck a week or two after the sale of their interest in the assets of the firm had closed. Ben was none the wiser yet remains fully liable under partnership laws of Texas and the Internal Revenue Code."

Spring had told me true about her dad's story. One minute an airhead, the next a crack news reporter. What a crazy kid.

Torville continued, "It took the IRS many years to get around to Ben. That is not unusual. The penalties and interest were by then more than the original tax. Instead of putting a lien on all of Ben assets – which would most likely have ruined his credit with his suppliers and bankers and thus bankrupted his business, making him unable to pay in any case – Mr. Franklin agreed to work with us as part of a global thrust, Project Charade. He would help to defeat terrorist

Collateral Franklins

attempts to bring money into this country in support of terrorist by flipping local businesses. They buy 'em, hold 'em a year. Sell them at first cash price comes along. Clean money in hand."

Torville motioned the Zippo toward the screen and the night reappeared.

"So, my *investigator*, in return for his full cooperation, Ben is to be forgiven back taxes and penalties et cetera."

"Great movie plot," I said. "Please go on."

"This is no movie. This is ensuring safety of our citizens. We have adjusted electronic data supporting reports of his bank accounts, financial transactions, Texas franchise tax returns, unemployment insurance filings, and insurance coverages in this regard as far as they appear in any computer or publicly filed record of his business."

"So you're the ones skimming!" I said.

"What are you talking about?" said Torville

"When Candice hired me she wanted me to figure out how Ben has been skimming money from the restaurants – and where he's putting it."

"Walter, you never told me about this," said Gretchen. "You have a recording on file. Where's the report?"

"We don't have any ahhh recordings of her first two or three meetings with Mr. Trench," he said, ducking his head, rearranging the pages in his hands.

"I see," said Gretchen.

Torville coughed to clear his throat, said, "Shall I continue?"

"Yes. Yes," I said. "Movie's just getting

interesting."

"Slam the trash talk," said Torville.

"Continue with the level two, Walter," said Gretchen.

"Yes. Our efforts would show public views of ever-declining revenue and profit for his businesses, restaurants owned by Shrimp-Steak, Inc., a Texas corporation. This was to lure investors who were more interested in laundering money through purchase and sale of tangible assets than they were in making a profit. Such operations look for businesses in enough trouble to where the business owner needs a buyer bad and would not ask questions and just cash the check. The first actual adjustment became active to Dunn and Bradstreet, et cetera, some fifteen months ago."

"Tell him the public profile part," said Gretchen.

"Okay," said Torville, setting the pages on the lectern. "As part of Project Charade, Ben was to be seen in public being shown affection by a stringy-haired, short-skirted blonde, often at a private residence and at his restaurants at all hours of the day, giving the appearance of an illicit relationship, an affair."

"That's why Candice wanted me to find the lover! I thought I'd been the only one to see that little one-act play. Up close that gent is garish. That stringy blond is really a guy, right?"

"Yes. Yes," said Gretchen.

"What about the skimming?" said Torville.

"By the end of the second week," I said, "Candice didn't seem to care about the money."

"Okay, thank you, Walter," said Gretchen as

she turned to me on the couch. "Can we have your cooperation... now?"

"Better than that. I'm going to do you guys a big favor."

"How? Tell me more," she said.

"I am going to isolate one of your targets for you."

Chapter 69
– Saturday evening

"Gretchen, he's just blowing smoke," said Torville, a short while later. "The only clandestine meeting Trench ever had was with a hooker in Singapore."

"We need to hurry," I said. "Might need five, maybe ten of your men to be safe."

"Nobody's going any – "

"Hold on, Walter," said Gretchen Longstreet. "Hear him out. The audio on your installation inside his place failed this afternoon. We don't know what Nate's been up to recently."

"Nonsense. He sits and plays on Facebook all day when he's not watching basketball. He's not really a detective anyway."

"Call him an analyst. We do ours. Now stuff it."

Turning to me, Gretchen said, "Where are we needing to go and why?"

"Seabrook. Classic Café. I'll tell you on the way. I have an operative waiting for me. She'll think I've died if we don't get there soon. Someone you might even know."

"This is really getting thick," said Torville.

"Move it," said Longstreet.

~ + ~

They surprised me with a helicopter but it was still almost thirty minutes before we arrived at the Classic Café, even using a helicopter, which we had to land several blocks away.

It was a very nervous Heather Carey I found sitting in a back corner of the Classic Cafe munching on French fries. She didn't know there was a landing pad in Seabrook either.

"We gotta go, Heather."

"Sit down. Tell me what's going on."

"Don't have time. C'mon. One of your charges is outside waiting for us."

"My what?"

We had less than an hour to deploy everyone, like I was doing the organizing. Gretchen Longstreet ran ops and Torville sat in the control center van, stationed around the block in a parking lot for a fresh seafood market wholesaler. Heather Carey became an extra, a back stop of sorts, assigned as sidekick to a sniper who was to watch exit routes should the team not apprehend the thugs for some reason. There were two road routes out of Outriggers and you could watch both from one location. Carey and new sniper friend were laid out in the keel of shallow boat parked in a trailer nearby, holding position until Torville called them to action.

I had the hard part.

I got to walk into Outriggers and act like I was scared shitless, but have extreme confidence inside. Sure, part one was a no brainer. Part two was out of my league. I had qualified on a small rifle in Navy boot camp and on the service .45 monster, but not done much shooting except to get my Concealed Carry Permit after I had my investigator's license. I did have a Kevlar vest on, courtesy of Uncle Sam. If I'd had my way, I'd have worn a Kevlar jump suit with only my face unprotected. I didn't care about the heat.

The easy part was sipping a Fat Tire with my elbow propped on the bar, one foot on the bar rail, watching some of the dinner crowd go up the stairs while the boat Barbies, heading ever deeper into the land of intoxication, tried to walk downstairs without falling.

The band was twenty-five feet from me and pretty good. The dancers, well, they were enjoying themselves.

~ + ~

Eleven thirty came and went with me out there naked except for my cell phone. Longstreet had ruled out my carrying anything but my car keys. She feared the thugs would have a gadget that could read the electronic impulses of an ear bud system, plus detect metal like guns and bullets. I had a buzz cut anyway. Two agents with supercardiod directional mikes stationed in shadows outside the bar itself would attempt to listen in. Their effectiveness depended on how loud the crowd was, the breezes off Galveston Bay, and visual contact with our mouths. An agent seated up next to the band gave me hand signals from time to time. It felt good to know I was not alone.

Eleven forty-five brought a party of ten or fifteen people into the lower bar. I couldn't get a good read on the group. All sorts of shapes and sizes. I was just looking for one or two guys that looked out of place in a waterside bar or who resembled the tall-slender, short-stocky image I had of the two guys on the NASA bridge. I wished the rendezvous would hurry up, fearing the deep shit I'd be in if no one showed.

I got my wish five minutes later.

A hand on my shoulder, then, "I need your cell phone." A woman's voice.

"What the hell," I said. Something about the voice pierced the din into my deeper cranial functions. I tried to turn around.

"Don't turn around. You won't live to tell your girlfriend about tonight."

"What girlfriend? Who are you?"

"C'mon. Every guy thinks he has a girlfriend. Your cell phone. Now."

"Right front pants pocket," I said.

"Cute. Get it out. Slowly. Put it on the bar.

"Who are you?"

"You could say I'm the boss of the two guys you met boating."

"Boating?"

Evans told me I was to play dumb. Drag things out.

"On a small bridge. On NASA road, looking down."

"That so?"

"Mr. Portofino spoke with you this afternoon."

I had my meeting.

Chapter 70
– Saturday night

"Okay, you're here," I said. "We're supposed to talk. I like to make eye – "

"I'm so sorry," she said, poking me in the side with something hard while stumbling against me and landing her other hand on my shoulder like she was a drunken old friend. The Kevlar blocked my usual skin sensitivity so I didn't know if the poke was a gun barrel or a finger or the handle of a dinner fork. "I don't like to look people in the eye. They're all so pitiful."

She didn't say anything about how firm my torso was so I figured gun.

"Your voice matches your attitude, lady." My bravado with Torville had remained somehow.

"Listen. Now."

"I'm listening."

"I have a message for you."

"Wait," I said, figuring she wouldn't shoot me right there, two people directly behind her chatting last time I looked and one sitting next to me. He was sober.

"You're. Not. In. Charge," she said, her voice much lower.

"Your voice. We've met." I twisted around expecting the huge INTERPOL agent. I got someone Candice would play tennis with at the country club. The agent's sun dress was unremarkable and she couldn't have been over one-thirty-five. Right voice. Right unhappy face, although younger makeup.

I glanced at her feet. The poke increased two fold.

"Ouch. Back off."

Why didn't she want me to see she was wearing running shoes.

"Confused?" she said. "I should shoot you. Nobody will hear. Now turn back. You're ugly."

The ugly attitude was INTERPOL's.

"No soap," I said, loud so others could hear.

"Quiet down, asshole."

"No confusion here. I know you, Ms. Scholl, was it? We ought to patent that diet of yours. Ouch!"

She'd kneed me in the nuts, twisted me half around. Did anyone see it? Sure. Sure they did. It was midnight.

"Turn back, you Kevlar pig, or I drive my bony knee into your balls again."

I almost lost the sandwich I'd grabbed while waiting. Did the Kevlar make me think I was Spenser or something?

"You deaf, fat boy? Turn the fuck around."

She bounced my nuts with her free fist. Would the Feds rescue me or should I take the dance outside?

"So, fat boy, where are your buddies?"

"Who? What?"

"Drop the bullshit. You wouldn't be this brave if you didn't have backup."

"I only have one and he's a she."

"Where?"

"In the parking lot, next to the dumpster." Sounded reasonable.

"Good, then we're going to take a walk, visit your friend."

"What happened to your message."

"Oh, I'm sure you'll get it, eventually. You can't be that stupid."

"Gotta pay my tab. Don't want to attract attention."

She slid a twenty out of somewhere, tossed it on the counter, and placed my Fat Tire bottle on top.

"Move. Anything funny and I'll plant a slug in the hole in your vest."

"What hole?"

"The one where your head is."

~ + ~

We were walking outside, side by side through a fairly dark spot, Scholl's arm on my shoulder like she was a drunk needing some balance, when she separated from me, lunging forward while someone the size and technique of a pro middle linebacker tackled me to the left, near the building and down to the gravel lot. The thugs?

I groaned.

Heard Scholl cuss, then yell what sounded like a cussword in a Slavic tongue.

A pop – a gunshot; small caliber.

"Clear," said a guy near where I guessed Scholl had gone.

The weight that had taken me to the ground rolled off.

"Here, I'll help you up. You okay?" It was Evans.

"What the hell's going – "

"Probably offed herself. It's a cultural thing.

Their ops are like the Kamikazes in World War Two. Never talk."

"What the hell happened?"

"What do you mean? You okay?"

"Yah." I pushed myself into a sitting position. "She was right beside me, then you took me down?"

"I took you down to your left after agent Melcher took her straight down forward. Didn't want you in on the fight."

I reached out my hand.

"Thanks, Evans. Good work. I owe you one."

"Just my job. I don't get to tackle folks much any more. It's kinda fun."

"Played college?"

"Rugby."

Those rugby guys are nuts.

"Don't we like need to take cover," I said. "Her backups will be on us any second."

"No problem."

"Okay, where? What did you say?" I said, standing up, slowly.

"C'mon. We need to get you to the van."

"The van. We going to hide there?"

"I think AIC wants to debrief," said Evans.

"Was the woman the other agent tackled, was she the one you wanted to get?"

"Think so, at least high up enough to trash their ops here for months."

He swung a high five at me but I just nicked his hand in the dim light.

"Sorry. Didn't see that coming."

"Let's go."

"Was it all worth it?" I said, speaking mostly to myself. Evans didn't say anything.

We walked for a bit and came around a big motor home.

Evans stopped at the back side door, said, "They're waiting for you in here."

"About the backups. Can you tell me anything?"

"Sure. I'm sorry. I didn't answer you."

"Do I need to look over my shoulder for the rest of my life?"

"No," he said, letting out what must have been the approved Secret Service short laugh. "Let's see, we took down two Venezuelan nationals, one over behind that dumpster we just walked by."

"Venezuelan. Huh. Guess my ear is off. One taller, the other heavier?"

"Maybe so. We can check. The other guy was back around the other side from here, near the water, behind the band."

"And that's it? She didn't have more?"

"Yes. Two Taliban, we think. We subdued them without gunfire, around by the seafood market. They're not talking so far."

"Anybody hurt? All these people. All these drunks."

"No explosives. We fired two shots. She offed herself. Collateral damage zero. Agent took down the guy on the other side with twenty-two to the head while the band played Hot Legs and you were getting your nuts crunched. Nobody heard the shot. Our hilltop sniper took out the dumpster guy when he brought up his long barrel to take you down just before I tackled you."

My heart skipped a beat. Stomach clenched.

Dizzy became my first name.

Evans grabbed my arm, steadied me.

After I guess a minute, I said, "I was this close to toast?" holding my thumb and index finger together up near my face.

"Not a chance," said Evans, his smile one you could believe even in the dim light.

I returned his smile as best I could as I slowly nodded before taking his hand and shaking it with all the vigor I had left in me.

"Later, Mr. Trench," said Evans and he was gone.

As I turned toward the huge motor home, my mind argued with Evans' one statement, "Collateral damage zero." He wasn't counting Ben and Candice Franklin. And he wasn't counting Spring, or Jocelyn.

I pivoted and leaned my back against the motor home, smiling, thinking Spring would be totally pissed she'd missed the action that evening. Gretchen Longstreet would probably tell me I couldn't tell anybody else what had just happened. I didn't give a rat's ass. Spring and Jocelyn needed to be debriefed just like me.

I turned back around, reached for the door, knocked, muttered, "The Feds better think it's time to give Ben Franklin back to his family."

THE END

Appendix

ALPHABET SOUP

Ingredients

AFSS	Air Force Security Service
ASA	Army Security Agency
ATF	Alcohol, Tobacco, Firearms & Explosives
CIA	Central Intelligence Agency
DARPA	Defense Advanced Research Projects Agcy.
DHS	Department of Homeland Security
DIA	Defense Intelligence Agency
FBI	Federal Bureau of Investigation
ICE	Immigration & Customs Enforcement
INTERPOL	International Criminal Police Organization
NCS	National Clandestine Service
NSA	National Security Agency
NSG	Naval Security Group

Recipes

FISA	Foreign Intelligence Surveillance Act
PAT	Patriot Act

Resources

Electronic Frontier Foundation
https://www.eff.org/nsa-spying/timeline

Made in the USA
Charleston, SC
27 July 2014

Love + Joy
to Yours!!
Be Blessed
12-12-2022

This book is a gift to

Ms. Emmy Lou Ducray

From

Deborah

Date

12-12-2022

"Psalm 91"

A SEASON OF *Hope*

Christian art gifts

Originally published by Christelike Uitgewersmaatskappy
under the title *'n Seisoen van hoop*

© 2011

English edition
© 2011 Published by Christian Art Gifts, Inc.

First edition 2022

Translated by San-Mari Mills

Cover designed by Christian Art Gifts

Images used under license from Shutterstock.com

Devotions written by Solly Ozrovech

Unless otherwise indicated, all Scripture quotations are taken from the *Holy Bible*, New Living Translation, copyright © 1996, 2004, 2007 by Tyndale House Publishers, Carol Stream, Illinois 60188. All rights reserved.

Scripture quotations marked NIV are taken from the *Holy Bible*, New International Version® NIV®. Copyright © 1973, 1978, 1984 by International Bible Society. Used by permission of Zondervan Publishing House. All rights reserved.

Set in 13 on 15 pt Adobe Garamond Pro
by Christian Art Publishers

Printed in China

ISBN 978-1-63952-084-8

© All rights reserved. No part of this book may be reproduced in any form without permission in writing from the publisher, except in the case of brief quotations in critical articles or reviews.

22 23 24 25 26 27 28 29 30 31 – 10 9 8 7 6 5 4 3 2 1

I lovingly dedicate this book
to all my cherished readers.

Foreword

John Payne said, "Nobody who knows the open ocean will set sail on a ship without an anchor, even if it is the most modern and famous vessel. Unforeseen events might arise when the anchor will be the only hope for the people aboard; not the captain or the crew, not the equipment, the compass or the wheel – but the anchor!"

Hope has always been a Christian virtue and despair has long been a deadly sin. If it were not for hope, we would all have had broken hearts. Therefore, hang on to Hope, for if you lose it, you lose everything.

In 1 Corinthians 13:7 Paul states that "love never gives up, never loses faith, is always hopeful, and endures through every circumstance." What oxygen is to the lungs, hope is to the soul – without that we die within.

God offers us hope out of His love!
Soli Deo Gloria.

January

Praise the LORD;
praise God our Savior!
For each day He
carries us in His arms.
           PSALM 68:19

The journey of a
thousand miles begins
with a single step.
~ CONFUCIUS ~

Almighty Creator God:
We are pilgrims at the start of a new and unknown year,
taking our first hesitant steps on an untraveled road.
We thank You that You know the road
and every obstacle along the way;
that You want to be our Leader and Guide
and show us the way to the eternal Father's house.
Help us to take Your hand in faith
and to follow You unconditionally.
We thank You that You will be in the future
just as You were in the past;
that You will lead the way through all our tomorrows
with the same love as yesterday and the day before.
Thank You that nothing and nobody can snatch us from Your
hand, even if we stray from You in stubborn willfulness.
Grant that we will begin and end this year with faith in You;
that nothing will steal our joy and peace in You.
We want to venture onto the road ahead
with the courage and faith of mature Christians.
Lord Jesus, we want to follow in Your footsteps;
footsteps of service, love and sacrifice.
We pray this in the name above all names:
Jesus our Lord.
Amen.

Read Hebrews 11:1-6

This I Believe

Faith is the confidence that what we hope for will actually happen; it gives us assurance about things we cannot see (Heb. 11:1).

The first verse of Hebrews 11 is the essence of the chapter, but try to make time to read all forty verses. You are introduced to a gallery of heroes of the faith who impacted their times as well as the following centuries. In verse six the writer says that it is impossible to please God, to do His will, if you don't believe. God's will is for us all to be saved: for this reason He sent His Son to this sin-torn world.

Faith as such cannot save you; neither baptism nor Holy Communion, church membership or devout parents. Only Jesus Christ can save you, "There is salvation in no one else! God has given no other name under heaven by which we must be saved" (Acts 4:12). Faith is the unsteady hand I hold out to God to accept the salvation that Jesus Christ brought about, and make it my own.

> Faith is seeing with the eyes of the heart.
> ALEXANDER MACLAREN

In the American musical *Paint Your Wagon,* the rugged Lee Marvin sings the song, "They Call the Wind Maria". One line goes, "I am so lost, not even God can find me." That is simply not true. No one is so lost that God can't grab hold of the shaking hand held out to him, lift him from the grime of sin and place him on the firm Rock, Jesus Christ. Jesus Himself said, "Anything is possible if a person believes" (Mark 9:23).

I believe, Lord! Please help me in my unbelief. Amen.

Read Matthew 25:14-30

Work Ennobles Us

The master said, "Well done, my good and faithful servant. You have been faithful in handling this small amount, so now I will give you many more responsibilities. Let's celebrate together!" (Matt. 25:23).

Christ tells this parable to illustrate how people can use their God-given talents either to ennoble or impoverish their lives. God is the origin of all work and creation. He created the earth and everything in it. In this way He placed His godly stamp of approval on the nobility of work. We find God's universal command on work in Exodus 20:9, "You have six days each week for your ordinary work."

When we obey God's instructions about work, the result is ennobling work ethics, pride in our work, and job satisfaction. All work is ennobling because it gives us inner wealth as we meet God's purpose for our lives: Washing, ironing and keeping house; the work of artists, poets and composers; surgeons, preachers or professional athletes; studying or teaching; all of this is creative work.

Millet's famous painting *The Angelus* (church bell) is his tribute to honest, ennobling work. Two simple laborers are standing in a potato field after a long day's work; the woman is joining her hands up close to her face, her head bowed, silently praying. The man is crumpling his hat in his calloused hands. The church bell has called everybody to prayer. The last rays of the setting sun form a halo around the two laborers and the wheelbarrow in which the tools of their trade are seen. In this way the artist portrays the message that every piece of honest labor finds its way to God as a perfect prayer while it ennobles humankind.

> Thank God – every morning when you get up – that you have something to do which must be done.
> CHARLES KINGSLEY

Creator God, grant that I will do my task in such a way that I will grow spiritually all the time and be ennobled, to better serve and glorify You. Amen.

Read Philippians 3:10-16

Even Higher

I press on to reach the end of the race and receive the heavenly prize for which God, through Christ Jesus, is calling us (Phil. 3:14).

One of the most powerful driving forces in the world is an ideal. It might be for good or evil, but it is always powerful. Our world is widely blessed by people who, driven by their ideals, reached new heights with scientific and technological discoveries.

> Ah, but a man's reach should exceed his grasp, or what's a heaven for?
> ROBERT BROWNING

Just think of a world without electricity, television or computers – all a result of the power of ideals. Watt noticed how steam lifted a kettle's lid, and the result is power that makes industries work by steam energy. Franklin watched lightning flash and his ideal was to harness this power. Morse's ideal was for a message to be carried by air, and thanks to his Morse Code, a ship can call for help from any place on the wide oceans. Ideals drive people to strive even higher – also on a spiritual level.

Frank Dicksee gave one of his most inspiring paintings the title *Ideals*. It portrays a young man climbing a steep hill. With a determined display of power he makes it to an almost out-of-reach peak. His upturned eyes sparkle with the fire of inspiration, and with eager arms outstretched he reaches for a Figure in the clouds above him. But after rising from the earth, this Figure goes on to heaven, indicating to the young man that he must follow and conquer through effort and strife. It is an image of a young Christian, striving higher and higher in search of the prize God is calling him for.

Lord, my God and Father, keep the ideals in my heart burning. Give me the grace to discern between noble ideals and those that separate me from You. Amen.

January 3

Read Luke 15:11-20

Dead-end Street

"The young man became so hungry that even the pods he was feeding the pigs looked good to him. But no one gave him anything" (Luke 15:16).

This parable tells the story of a young man who left home and ended up in a dead-end street. His motive? Self-love. He rebelled against his parents' rules and saw himself as an independent adult.

> Some often repent, yet never reform; they resemble a man traveling on a dangerous path, who frequently starts and stops, but never turns back.
> BONNELL THORNTON

What he didn't realize was that true freedom is found only within laws; outside the law there is no freedom or happiness. He traveled to a distant country of decadence and materialism. His father must have found it very painful to see him take off like that, but he was wise enough not to try to hold him back against his will. When the young man had nothing left and the country was in the throes of a severe famine, he ended up looking after pigs: a true dead end!

The wise and sensible thing to do when you end up in a dead-end street is to turn around. This is what repentance means. In *Robinson Crusoe,* Crusoe ran away from home. All he wanted was to go to sea. He was shipwrecked on his first journey and barely survived. He saw how wrong he had been, but he was afraid and ashamed to go back home because he thought his friends would make fun of him.

People are not ashamed to sin, but they are ashamed to repent and confess. Free yourself from a dead-end street: turn around and mend your ways!

Lord Jesus, You are the Way to eternal life. Keep me on the right track and help me not to end up in a dead-end street. Amen.

Read Psalm 119:99-105

Where Are You Going?

I have refused to walk on any evil path, so that I may remain obedient to Your word (Ps. 119:101).

We must stay on the main road of God's grace so that we don't lose our way and end up on the wrong path. The road to take is clearly indicated in God's Word and the psalmist gives wise advice when he says, "How can a young person stay pure? By obeying Your Word" (Ps. 119:9). Paul says in Philippians 3:16, "But we must hold on to the progress we have already made." The prayer of our heart must always be, "Show me the right path, O LORD; point out the road for me to follow" (Ps. 25:4). Then we will know where we are headed and we will reach the final destination that God has prepared for us.

There is a Christian legend that tells how, during the bloody persecution of the early Christians in Rome, Peter was fleeing the city along the Via Appia. There he saw a vision of Jesus in front of him, asking, "Peter, *quo vadis*?" (where are you going?). He replied that he was fleeing so that he could survive to preach the Gospel. Christ said that He would then go to Rome Himself to die a second time. Peter stopped in his tracks, turned back and testified powerfully, encouraging the Christians in Rome.

> There is a time when we must firmly choose the course which we will follow or the endless drift of events will make the decision for us.
> HERBERT V. PROCHNOW

Legend has it that he was crucified upside down on his own request. He felt that he was not worthy of dying like his Master.

Heavenly God and Father, teach me through Your Spirit, the path You want me to walk. Thank You that Christ is my Guide on this path. Amen.

January 5

Read James 4:13-17

God Willing

What you ought to say is, "If the Lord wants us to, we will live and do this or that" (James 4:15).

The uncertainty of the future is summed up in this Scripture verse. The wise writer of the book of Proverbs also said, "Don't brag about tomorrow, since you don't know what the day will bring" (Prov. 27:1).

The uncertainty of the future is no reason for fear or inactivity, but an opportunity to realize our complete dependence on God. The true believer will always keep this in mind when making his plans. This does not mean that we become paralyzed into total inactivity, but that we should put all our plans in God's loving hands, and always remember that they must be within His holy will. The future is not in our hands and no one dare be so arrogant as to think that he can decide about it without God.

> God is more interested in your future and your relationships than you are.
> BILLY GRAHAM

Jesus told a parable about a prosperous man whose fertile farm produced fine crops. He decided to tear down his barns and build bigger ones in which he would store his grain and possessions, and said to himself, "You have enough stored away for years to come. Now take it easy! Eat, drink, and be merry!" (Luke 12:19). But that same night God took his life from him and he could take nothing of all his hoarded treasures on his eternal journey (see Luke 12:13-21).

Never plan for the future without consulting God.

Everlasting God, You control the future just like You controlled the past. Help me not to try plan my future without You. Amen.

Read Psalm 103:8-13

God's Favor

The LORD is compassionate and merciful; slow to get angry and filled with unfailing love (Ps. 103:8).

Take note that all the good things the Lord does for us are favors. He is under no obligation to give us anything and we deserve nothing of what He does for us. There will be a radical change in our approach to life if we get into the habit of thinking about the gracious favor and goodness of God every day, and thank Him for it. Each day we will become aware of all the undeserved blessings He pours out onto us.

God's favor lifts your spirits, because it is impossible to live in thankfulness and still be depressed. Thanksgiving and praise must remain an important component of your daily life, because recalling God's gracious wonders in your life makes you grow spiritually. It helps you deal with trials and tribulation and to walk the Lord's road with joyful gratitude.

> Gratitude is not only the greatest of all virtues, but the parent of all the others.
> MARCUS CICERO

A little girl once said to her father that she would like to count the stars. "Sure, my child, count the stars," her father said. After a while the little girl said, "Wow, Daddy, I never knew there were so many." Sometimes I also feel like saying, "Heavenly Father, I'm going to count Your favors." And quickly I must confess, "Father, I never knew there were so many!"

Lord my God, Your loving-kindness is overwhelming. I stand before You in thankful amazement at all the favors You bestow on me. Amen.

Read Isaiah 30:12-18

Make Haste Slowly

The Sovereign LORD, the Holy One of Israel, says, "Only in returning to Me and resting in Me will you be saved. In quietness and confidence is your strength. But you would have none of it" (Isa. 30:15).

There is a well-proven expression: More haste, less speed. In this chapter God warned the people of Judah not to be hasty in turning to Egypt and other countries for help, because they would not be able to help them. Judah had to wait on the Lord calmly, in quietness and trust. No hasty negotiations or panicky action would speed up or delay God's overall plan. Salvation is from God alone.

> One needs occasionally to stand aside from the hum and rush of human interests and passions to hear the voice of God.
> ANNA J. COOPER

Because He saved us, we must wait on Him, quietly trusting Him to give us the strength to overcome the problems on our path in life. We can merely thank God for His timely help.

Like Israel, we have a choice between salvation and ruin. If we repent and find peace in God, we will be saved. All the terms used in today's text indicate full confidence in God's strength. We must forget about our own foolish plans and rely on God. If we make the right choice, God will have mercy on us and do only good things for us.

Lord Jesus, teach me through the Holy Spirit, not to be hurried in making decisions, but to wait for You to open doors. Stand by me in weak moments when I make rash decisions. Amen.

Read Judges 16:15-18

To the Point of Revulsion

She tormented him with her nagging day after day until he was sick to death of it (Judg. 16:16).

Delilah played a cold and calculated game with Samson. She pretended to love him while she only wanted to use him to her own advantage. She kept on and on, trying to get him to tell her the secret of his strength so that she could betray him. Samson was deceived by Delilah because he wanted to believe her lies. He couldn't see Delilah for who she really was. One should decide what kind of person one wants to fall in love with before desire takes over. Make sure if the person's character and faith in God are just as attractive as the physical appearance. Personality, temperament and determination to overcome problems should be just as pleasant as kisses. Be patient with yourself and your relationship. Don't allow constant nagging to force you to give in. It is one of the mightiest weapons in Satan's armory.

Legend has it that the trees once revolted against the ax and came to an agreement never to provide the ax with wood for a handle. However, the ax attended the conference of the trees and because of his never-ending nagging, the trees decided to provide him with wood for a handle, on condition that he would only chop down smaller and alien trees. The minute that he had a handle he started chopping down trees fast and furiously; first the big ones and then the small ones. He spared none. Watch out for evil – it is always accompanied by nagging which eventually drives you to despair. Satan never stops trying.

> Better shun
> the bait than struggle
> in the snare.
> JOHN DRYDEN

Savior and Master, without Your grace and support I will never win the battle against evil. Help me to stand firm and never give in. Amen.

Read Colossians 3:1-4

Reach New Heights

Think about the things of heaven, not the things of earth (Col. 3:2).

We are in the world, but not of the world. We all belong to God through Christ's death and resurrection and are secure in Him. Through our baptism we started living in Christ as new people. We are now united with Christ and the things of Christ, and the insignificant and temporary things of the world are not of primary importance to us anymore. Paul does not want us to isolate ourselves from the world and meditate on eternity all the time. We must reach for a higher spiritual life and growth. To Christians, Christ is their life and this dominates their thoughts and fills their lives. Everything is now evaluated in the light of the cross and all earthly things are seen in their true perspective.

There is a legend about snails that arranged a race one day. This event was widely advertised and snails came from neighboring meadows to watch and take part. A crowd of snails gathered down by the brook where the track was set out. There they waved banners and shouted when the contestants took off. Their speed was breathtaking: a full eight meters per hour! Never before had such speeds been recorded. In five hours' time the athletes started reaching the winning post in "rapid" succession. It was the most important event of the year on the snail calendar. The winner was rewarded with a parsley leaf.

We may be in the world, but we must never get too comfortable here. Always aim to achieve, grow and reach new heights.

> If the ladder is not leaning against the right wall, every step we take just gets us to the wrong place faster.
> STEPHEN R. COVEY

Holy Spirit, teach me to maintain a good balance between being a human in the world and also a child of God. Grant that I will regularly sail out to deep waters, and reach new heights. Amen.

Read Romans 7:15-24

A Battle with Self

I have discovered this principle of life – that when I want to do what is right, I inevitably do what is wrong (Rom. 7:21).

Here we read about the battle between the ego and the alter ego. In all of us there is this conflict in our minds between right and wrong, good and bad. We aren't able to obey the laws of God in our own strength and without the Spirit of God. The more we try to keep to the law, the more we become torn, tragic beings, caught up in a dead existence. Certain things about humanity become clear: Mere knowledge of the law provides no solution. Merely admitting that the law is good doesn't mean that you will manage to obey it. On the contrary, your failed efforts make you all the more aware of how deep you have sunk into your sinful existence.

> When sin is your burden, Christ will be your delight.
> THOMAS WATSON

It is only then that you are ready to hear about God's salvation that He made possible for you through Jesus Christ. Only then can Christ and the Holy Spirit rule in your life.

God told Saul to destroy the Amalekites. Saul thought he knew better than God and allowed some of them to escape. Years later Saul lay on the battlefield of Gilboa and said to his armor bearer, "Take your sword and kill me before these pagan Philistines come to run me through and taunt and torture me" (1 Sam. 31:4). One of the Amalekites stripped Saul's body of his armor and took his crown (see 2 Sam. 1:10). This is the cycle of sin if we make a compromise with it. One day it returns and finds that we are weak and robs us of our crown and honor. Allow God to rule over you before it is too late.

Father, You know me better than I know myself. I put myself in Your hands and beg that You reform me to Your glory. Amen.

January 11

Read Acts 1:1-8

Be a Witness

"But you will receive power when the Holy Spirit comes upon you. And you will be My witnesses, telling people about Me everywhere – in Jerusalem, throughout Judea, in Samaria, and to the ends of the earth" (Acts 1:8).

Jesus told His disciples that they would in future be the defenders of the faith. The power of the Holy Spirit made them Jesus' witnesses: first in Jerusalem, then in Samaria and also to the ends of the earth. To be a witness or protector of the faith, you must have unshakable faith in your own heart. Your life must confirm your testimony and you must tell others about your faith.

> We are all missionaries ... Wherever we go, we either bring people nearer to Christ, or we repel them from Christ.
> ERIC LIDDELL

Two brothers grew up in the same home. One was a good religious boy. The other was the black sheep of the family, a drug addict and alcoholic. One afternoon, the good brother came out of the house just as the bad brother came staggering through the garden gate. When the good brother walked past the other one, his Bible under his arm, the intoxicated brother asked, "Do you believe what is written in that Bible?" "Of course," he replied. "Do you believe that God can save all people?" "Of course," he answered again. "Do you believe that God can save a bad guy like me?" "Of course," repeated the irritated brother. "My dear brother," continued the drunk, "you and I have been living under the same roof for twenty-two years, and you have never told me this. If I were you, and you were me, I would have crawled on my knees on pieces of broken bottles across the breadth of England to go and tell you this. And you never told me."

I beg You, Lord Jesus, that You will help me to be a faithful defender of the faith and in this way help build Your kingdom. Amen.

Read Psalm 130:1-8

From the Depths of Despair

From the depths of despair, O Lord, I call for Your help. Hear my cry, O Lord. Pay attention to my prayer (Ps. 130:1-2).

Most people find themselves in the depths of despair at some time or another. It might be because of sin and feelings of guilt; sorrow or loss; disappointment or failure. But what counts is not *if* we find ourselves in the dark hole, but *how* we handle our circumstances when we land in there.

For those who don't know God, there is little hope of deliverance. At least God's children have good prospects in all circumstances. In their darkest moments they can say, "I am counting on the Lord. I have put my hope in His word. I long for the Lord more than sentries long for the dawn" (vv. 5-6). It is about calling out to God in the depths of our despair. Only He is almighty and able to change our situation for the better. For this reason we never give up, because we are sure that the bright day of God's grace follows the darkest night. Hope is the fulfillment of the believer's deepest longing and expectations.

> It is impossible to despair when you remember that your Helper is omnipotent.
> — Jeremy Taylor

One story goes that Satan was notified by an angel of God that God was going to take all the temptations that Satan used away from him, except for one. "Which one is that?" Satan asked. "Depression," the angel answered. Then Satan roared with laughter, "Well done! With this one temptation I will snare them all."

Only those who know the way to God in the depths of their despair will survive.

Loving Lord Jesus, thank You that I have free access to God through You; that I may call on Him for help in the depths of my despair. I praise and thank You for this. Amen.

Read Hebrews 11:1-6

Have Faith in God

And it is impossible to please God without faith. Anyone who wants to come to Him must believe that God exists and that He rewards those who sincerely seek Him (Heb. 11:6).

What is faith and why is it an unavoidable condition for our salvation? Faith is the weak hand I hold out to accept the salvation that Jesus made possible, and make it my own. There are no other conditions, but this one cannot be evaded. God wants all people to be saved, but only faith in Jesus Christ can save us.

Nobody has sunk too deep in the swamp of sin that God cannot find him, grip that shaking hand that is held out to Him, pull him out of the swamp of sin and place him on the steadfast Rock, Jesus Christ! But you must have faith in God.

> Since no man is excluded from calling upon God, the gate of salvation is open to all. There is nothing else to hinder us from entering, but our own unbelief.
> —JOHN CALVIN

When you go on a train journey, the conductor will get to your compartment at some stage. He is only interested in one thing. He will not inquire about your family or your bank account; he isn't interested in your status in society, or your sporting achievements. All he will say is, "Ticket please!"

On our journey to eternity, the ticket we will be asked for is, "Do you have faith?" This is an inevitable truth.

Holy Spirit of God, You who work faith in us, help me, in all circumstances, to cling firmly to my faith in God, through Jesus Christ alone. Amen.

Read Hebrews 9:11-14

All the More Reason

Just think how much more the blood of Christ will purify our consciences from sinful deeds so that we can worship the living God. For by the power of the eternal Spirit, Christ offered Himself to God as a perfect sacrifice for our sins (Heb. 9:14).

Some people have a major problem with their conscience. They feel they have to do something to purify themselves in order to be acceptable to God; usually by keeping to a set of rules and regulations.

However, these things don't purify anybody's heart; at best they just bring about outer purification. Only the blood of the Lamb can clear your conscience, free you from death and enable you to live your life in God's service. If you are struggling with a guilty conscience, it gives you so much more reason to know and believe that Christ sets your conscience free and gives you peace of mind. It is not unpleasant or difficult to arrange our lives the way God wants. The Holy Spirit changes our natural disposition so that we wish more and more to submit to God's will (see Phil. 2:13). There is no better reason for experiencing true Christian joy. This is why we must serve God all the more with joy and thanksgiving.

> My conscience is captive to the Word of God.
> MARTIN LUTHER

The most important thing in life is to do the right thing. But how do you decide what the right thing is? Your conscience is not enough. Your conscience is like a sailor's compass. It gives him a sense of direction. However, you could not sail the ocean of life, just as a sailor could not cross the Atlantic, with only a compass to guide him. He also needs a map that indicates the route. Without such a map, your conscience can lead you astray. Therefore, we Christians have all the more reason to have Christ in our lives as the Way, the Truth and the Life!

Master, I know my own straying heart and this gives me every reason to hold Your hand. Lead me on the eternal path. Amen.

Read Romans 5:1-5

Not of Our Own Doing

Therefore, since we have been made right in God's sight by faith, we have peace with God because of what Jesus Christ our Lord has done for us (Rom. 5:1).

God's love is so evident in this Scripture verse. When we were helpless, Christ died for us. Thus we were saved, but not by our own doing.

Paul explains that we are all guilty before God and that God justifies us because we believe; we have peace with God; we stand firm in grace and rejoice in the salvation that comes from God.

To be at peace with God means that we are reconciled with Him because Jesus paid the price. Our joy flows from our hope; an expectation that depends on God alone. It gives us the strength to deal with our suffering. Our hope is not a rainbow that disappears as we approach it.

God poured out His love into our hearts. For this reason our expectations for the future will not disappear, but we will depend on God's grace alone.

The block of marble from which Michelangelo chiseled the statue of David in Florence had laid somewhere without serving any purpose until it caught the artist's eye and he saw its possibilities. In his artist's hands it took shape and from the lifeless marble, a work of art emerged. The marble had nothing to do with it. Likewise, Christ uses our lives to create His masterpiece. He makes us God's children.

> Grace is the gift of Christ, who exposes the gulf which separates God and man, and, by exposing it, bridges it.
> KARL BARTH

Father, I bow down before You in deep gratitude because You loved me when I was still a sinner and You saved me through Your unfathomable grace. I praise Your holy name! Amen.

Read 2 Corinthians 8:1-7

So Close, Yet So Far

They even did more than we had hoped, for their first action was to give themselves to the Lord and to us, just as God wanted them to do (2 Cor. 8:5).

Paul praised the Corinthians for the many good things taking place among them. They were cheerful in spite of trouble and hard times, and in spite of poverty they were hospitable and generous. He praised them for their knowledge of God, their ability to minister His Word and on top of that, their unlimited zeal. Paul knew that only one thing made this possible, the fact that they first gave themselves to the Lord.

There are many Christians who live a good life. Their names are written in the membership register of their church, they serve their congregation diligently and wholeheartedly, they do a lot for charity, but something is still lacking. They have not yet surrendered to Christ as an act of faith. This is a sad state of affairs that can only be put right by allowing Christ into your life unconditionally. He is waiting with pierced hands outstretched to receive you, if only you would take the necessary step. Without this, all the other things you do are in vain.

A man caught in a snowstorm put the harness around his own neck in an effort to keep warm, and decided to walk through the snow behind the horses. Eventually he could see his house. Faintly, he saw the glow of the fire in the fireplace. And then – in the face of the violent storm – he stumbled and fell. The horses reached the stable safely. A search party found the dead man in the snow; so close and yet so far.

> Procrastination is the thief of time.
> EDWARD YOUNG

Holy Spirit of God, work in my life so that I will have no doubt about my relationship with Jesus as my Savior and Redeemer. Amen.

Read James 3:5-12

A Slip of the Tongue

No one can tame the tongue. It is restless and evil, full of deadly poison (James 3:8).

James emphasizes the careless use of the tongue. By controlling their tongue, believers can confirm their faith with deeds. The tongue is a fire that, in an unguarded moment, can set alight the whole world and do immense damage through gossip, insults, lies, cursing, perjury, and similar evils.

Only when Christ has taken control of our lives, is the tongue also controlled. Then it is used positively to glorify God and serve our fellow humans. Inconsistency is not allowed in a Christian's life; both fresh and bitter water don't flow from the same fountain, and a fig on a grapevine is an unnatural occurrence. Christ not only purifies our hearts, but also our tongues.

A man who slandered his friend had such a guilty conscience that he went to his pastor for advice to find peace of mind again. "If you want to make peace with your conscience, take a bag full of feathers and put one feather on each doorstep in town," the pastor said. The man did this and went back to the pastor to tell him that he had done his penance. "Not yet," the pastor added. "Now take your bag and go and collect all those feathers again." "But the wind has blown them all away," the man called out, very upset. "Exactly," the pastor replied, "that is the price of abusing the tongue: No matter how hard you try, you can never take back your words."

> If slander be a snake, it is a winged one – it flies as well as creeps.
> DOUGLAS JERROLD

Gracious God and Father, forgive me for the times I have abused my tongue. Let the Holy Spirit help me to always keep my words pure and to serve You with my tongue also. Amen.

Read 1 Kings 19:3-8

Never Despair

Then he went on alone into the wilderness, traveling all day. He sat down under a solitary broom tree and prayed that he might die. "I have had enough, LORD," he said. "Take my life, for I am no better than my ancestors who have already died" (1 Kings 19:4).

Elijah was driven to despair by his fear of the bloodthirsty Jezebel. He went into the desert, hoping to end it all. The hero of Carmel, who could pray fire down from heaven, was now running away from an evil woman. This is how easy it is to fall into despair and forget the power and grace of the Lord.

We all have our moments of disappointment, sorrow and suffering. This is when the child of God should draw from his reserves of faith and refuse to give in or throw in the towel. The writer of the letter to the Hebrews calls on us to do this when he says, "Let us run with endurance the race that God has set before us ... keeping our eyes on Jesus" (Heb. 12:1-2).

> What oxygen is to the lungs, such is hope to the meaning of life.
> EMIL BRUNNER

Many people see Watts's painting *Hope,* as a portrayal of despair. They look at the bent figure, the blindfolded eyes, the lyre, all strings broken except one, and they ask, "Where is the hope in this painting?" Hope is in the heart! The message of this painting is that even this tragic, desperate figure is revived by the blessed touch of Hope. She hears the pure sound of one string and it is caught up in her heart. Despair has no place in God's economy; it cannot dominate the heart. No matter how dark your life may seem at times, the Christian faith will always triumph again.

Almighty God and Father of our Lord Jesus Christ, thank You that I may trust You at all times to be my defense against despair. I praise Your name in gratitude. Amen.

January 19

Read Psalm 40:1-6

In Good Faith

He has given me a new song to sing, a hymn of praise to our God. Many will see what He has done and be amazed. They will put their trust in the L%%RD%% (Ps. 40:3).

The psalmist is in dire straits and places his faith in God, trusting God to help him. He has faith in God's integrity to be true to His promises. Then he witnesses, "Oh, the joys of those who trust the L%%ORD%%" (v. 4). He talks about the way God rescued him and seeks the Lord's help in all good faith because of his trust in God.

> Never be afraid to trust an unknown future to a known God.
> C%%ORRIE TEN%% B%%OOM%%

It is not always easy to wait for God's help, but if we put our trust in Him He lifts us out of the despair that is threatening us, and places us back on firm ground. He makes our steps secure and sturdy again and once more gives us a goal to strive for. This is why Isaiah's words are so meaningful to believers, "Don't be afraid, for I am with you. Don't be discouraged, for I am your God" (Isa. 41:10). When we place our faith in God, we can approach the future as people who have been set free.

Trust always hears the melody of God's faithfulness. One of the most stirring Roman legends is that of the devout Cecelia, whose one consuming passion in life was music. One day when she was playing her instrument, she heard other music from above, much more beautiful and melodious than her own; as if it was coming directly from heaven. She realized that it was heavenly, angelic and sacred. She then stopped playing to listen to this music. Those who accept God in faith, already hear God's heavenly music here on earth.

Your faithfulness, Lord my God, is eternal. Let me not doubt this under any circumstances. Amen.

Read Romans 7:21-8:1

In Truth

I have discovered this principle of life – that when I want to do what is right, I inevitably do what is wrong. Oh, what a miserable person I am! Who will free me from this life that is dominated by sin and death? Thank God! The answer is in Jesus Christ our Lord. So you see how it is: In my mind I really want to obey God's law, but because of my sinful nature I am a slave to sin (Rom. 7:21; 24-25).

If it weren't for Christ, we would already have been condemned according to the law, because we are sinners by nature, who break God's law. But in truth we have been set free because we believe in Christ and because He paid the price for all our sins. We find the condition for this justification in Romans 8: "Therefore, there is now no condemnation for those who are in Christ Jesus, because through Christ Jesus the law of the Spirit who gives life has set you free from the law of sin and death" (Rom. 8:1-2 NIV).

The unsaved person who does not live from the Spirit cannot obey the law of his own accord. The more you try to obey the law without Christ, the more of a tragic and torn person you become, sinking into a miserable, dead existence. Don't stop at the point where you are sobbing your heart out in your misery; accept that you have been saved by Jesus Christ to become God's child.

> The knowledge of sin is the beginning of salvation.
> EPICURUS

Abraham Lincoln issued "The Emancipation Proclamation" that proclaimed the liberation of all slaves. This gave everyone freedom, irrespective of their personal circumstances, their wishes or whether they deserved it or not. Likewise, God grants forgiveness to everyone who accepts salvation in Jesus Christ, irrespective of their position before the law.

Gracious God and Father, thank You that I don't have to be weighed down by the burden of my sins, but that I have been set free by Your love as Jesus is my Redeemer and my Savior. Amen.

Read 2 Corinthians 11:23-30

Boast in Weakness

If I must boast, I would rather boast about the things that show how weak I am (2 Cor. 11:30).

When someone applies for a position, it is customary to present a curriculum vitae, so that the employer is provided details of the applicant's qualifications and a career history. Paul lists impressive qualifications in 2 Corinthians 11. But in conclusion he says that he would rather boast about his weaknesses. He endured pain and faced danger in his work, but rather emphasizes the fact that he was able to do it by the grace of God. All the hardship he mentions confirms how good God is to a weak human being.

If God appoints us in a leadership position or where we have authority, our attitude towards people should be one of compassion, caring and honest service. Everything we do must be to God's glory and honor alone, and not ours.

> We must view humility as one of the most essential things that characterizes true Christianity.
> JONATHAN EDWARDS

Years ago a young lady visited Beethoven's house. She positioned herself at the piano of the great musician and proudly played Beethoven's *Moonlight Sonata*. Then she turned to the elderly caretaker of the house and said, "I gather that many famous people come here." "Yes," the man replied, "Paderewski was here last week." "And did he play the piano?" the lady asked curiously. "No," the old man said, "he said he wasn't worthy of doing it." Listing one's qualifications requires a particular kind of humbleness that rather boasts of weakness than own achievement.

Jesus, let me never boast about the talents or gifts You gave me, but always strive to follow Your example of humility. Amen.

Read John 16:25-33

Take Heart

"I have told you all this so that you may have peace in Me. Here on earth you will have many trials and sorrows. But take heart, because I have overcome the world" (John 16:33).

If life is getting you down and problems multiply day by day, be brave and take heart. To be able to do this you must heed Paul's advice to the Ephesians: "Be strong in the Lord and in His mighty power" (Eph. 6:10). Bear up, because when the night is at its darkest, daybreak is at its closest.

> Whatever you do, you need courage.
> RALPH WALDO EMERSON

Be strong when sorrow becomes part of your life, because everybody is faced with grief at some stage in life. God gave us His Holy Spirit as Comforter. Be brave if you are entangled in a religious struggle. Satan will keep on attacking you and try to rob you of your faith, or sabotage it. Just remember that Christ conquered him and if you are courageous you will be able to defeat him as well. The Word says, "My grace is all you need. My power works best in weakness" (2 Cor. 12:9).

When Constantius, the son of Constantine, succeeded him to the throne, there were many Christians in the emperor's service. Constantius issued a decree in which he demanded that they renounce their Christian faith or lose their positions. A great number willingly renounced their faith in order to keep their posts. However, a number were prepared to lose their jobs for the sake of their faith. When the emperor knew exactly which workers had the courage of their convictions, he gave all those who renounced their faith notice, and appointed Christians in their place. His defense was, "Those who did not have the courage to be faithful to Christ will not be faithful to me either."

Faithful Lord Jesus, give me courage of such quality that I will remain true to You even in the most difficult circumstances. Amen.

Read Revelation 2:8-11

Faithful

"Don't be afraid of what you are about to suffer. The devil will throw some of you into prison to test you. You will suffer for ten days. But if you remain faithful even when facing death, I will give you the crown of life" (Rev. 2:10).

Faithfulness is a highly esteemed Christian virtue. When the monotonous buzz and drudgery of daily life become too much for you, be faithful! Be faithful in the big things, but also in the small things. Be faithful when people watch you, but above all, be faithful when no one except God sees you. Be true to yourself and the noblest things God placed inside you. Be especially faithful to God and the greatest Christian principles of life.

> Faith expects from God what is beyond all expectation.
> ANDREW MURRAY

May we one day hear from His holy mouth, "Well done, My good and faithful servant. You have been faithful in handling this small amount, so now I will give you many more responsibilities. Let's celebrate together!" (Matt. 25:23).

Sir Edward John Poynter painted a masterpiece titled *Faithful unto Death*. The painting depicts a Roman soldier who was on guard when the volcanic eruption hit the town of Pompeii. All around him people are fleeing, terror-stricken, but he remains at his post courageously and faithfully until he is buried by the lava. The soldier is holding his spear firmly. The terror of that horrific moment can be seen in his eyes. Loyalty wrestles with his natural instinct to flee for his life. Alone, but faithful, he dies on duty. If a heathen can do this, how much more should a Christian remain faithful to God in life and, yes, also in death!

In addition to all the other gifts of grace that You grant me, O Master, also grant me the virtue of faithfulness. Amen.

Read Philippians 4:4-9

Joyful

Always be full of joy in the Lord. I say it again – rejoice! (Phil. 4:4).

In times of prosperity and adversity; in the company of friend and foe; whether heaven is covered by ominous storm clouds or the sun softly caresses you; always rejoice in the Lord! Indestructible Christian joy has nothing to do with your circumstances; it is an attitude of the heart, a philosophy of life. With the song of salvation in a heart, life is pure joy.

At midnight Paul and Silas sang songs of praise to God's glory in prison. This is the kind of joy that comes from deep inside of you and is able to overcome any adversity. Remember what we read in Proverbs 15:15, "For the despondent, every day brings trouble; for the happy heart, life is a continual feast."

There is a legend that says after the devil was cast from heaven, he one day crisscrossed the entire universe, looking for someone he could lead astray. On this expedition he met one of the good heavenly angels and the two of them had a long conversation. Before they parted, the heavenly angel asked the devil, "Lucifer, what do you miss most since you left heaven?" A wistful expression appeared on the devil's face and he said, "If you must know, I miss the joy and gladness. I miss the joy in heaven!" If you have never known that joy or if you've lost it somewhere along the way, come to the wellspring of all joy: Jesus Christ.

> I believe God, through His Spirit, grants us love, joy, and peace no matter what is happening in our lives. As Christians, we shouldn't expect our joy to always feel like happiness, but instead recognize joy as inner security – a safeness in our life with Christ.
>
> JILL BRISCOE

In You I find my gladness and joy, Lord Jesus. Thank You that You give me a joy that the world cannot take away. Amen.

Read Colossians 2:20-23

At First Sight

Such regulations indeed have an appearance of wisdom, with their self-imposed worship, their false humility and their harsh treatment of the body, but they lack any value in restraining sensual indulgence (Col. 2:23 NIV).

At first sight many people think that religion is merely obeying laws. However, we cannot reach God by following rules and performing religious actions. Obeying the law does not lead to salvation. The good news is that God bends down to humankind and we may respond to that.

Man-made religions place the emphasis on the person; to the Christian, the emphasis is on Christ's salvation. Although Paul does say that believers should resist sinful desires, this comes as a result of our new life in Christ and not because of it. Our salvation does not depend on our self-discipline or ability to obey rules, but on the power in Jesus' death and resurrection. Then we go beyond the face value of religion to its deepest core truth.

> I find the doing of the will of God leaves me no time for disputing about His plans.
> GEORGE MACDONALD

There is a fable that tells of a crow that very much wanted to be a peacock. So he put beautiful peacock feathers in between his tail feathers, went to land among a group of crows and tried to reign over them on the assumption that he was now a beautiful peacock. But not one of the crows was deceived, because in spite of his borrowed plumes, they knew at face value that he was nothing more or less than a plain crow.

Savior, make me sincere so that You will always know what to expect from me. Also make my face value my inner value. Amen.

Read Joshua 1:1-9

Trust and Obey

"Be strong and courageous, for you are the one who will lead these people to possess all the land I swore to their ancestors I would give them" (Josh. 1:6).

The Lord called Joshua to lead the people of Israel into the Promised Land as Moses' successor. The Lord had a very specific purpose with Joshua. Joshua had already been trained for this task for years.

God reassured him of His help and support in this task. He would give the land to them. Even the borders of the land had already been determined. The command to Joshua was supported by the Lord's assurance that He would be with Joshua and never leave him alone.

> God's work done in God's way never lack God's supplies.
> HUDSON TAYLOR

With this assurance Joshua could act purposefully and without hesitation. He had to hold onto God's instructions and God's law. Only because of his close relationship with the Lord would Joshua be able to perform this task.

All of us are called to serve the Lord for a specific purpose at some or other time. In order to be successful, the same conditions apply to us as to Joshua. If we obey, we can trust God completely for our success in every task He assigns to us.

Doctor Robert Bruce, one of the most dedicated clerics in Scotland, studied Law, but against the wishes of both his parents God called him to the pulpit in Edinburgh. He said, "I would rather walk a kilometer over burning coals than relive those nights I wrestled with God's voice calling me."

Do only Your will Lord, Your will with me. Make me willing and able to do Your will to the best of my ability and to Your glory. Amen.

January 27

Read Acts 17:21-29

Words and Deeds

For as I was walking along I saw your many shrines. And one of your altars had this inscription on it: "To an Unknown God." This God, whom you worship without knowing, is the one I'm telling you about (Acts 17:23).

If you are religious, you are not necessarily a Christian. The people of Athens were religious and had many places of worship, and yet they were not Christian.

Being religious on its own doesn't make you a Christian. For that you need a personal and firsthand meeting with the living Christ. The Holy Spirit must lead you to repentance and rebirth, conversion and spiritual growth. Even confessing your Christianity by mouth doesn't make you Jesus Christ's disciple. You must confirm it day and night with your actions, and not only when you are in church, but also every day where you rub shoulders with the sinful world and have to put your testimony into practice. For this you need God's special grace.

When the statue of George Peabody, a famous Englishman, was unveiled in a busy part of London, the sculptor was asked to say a few words. He simply touched the statue twice and the only words he said were, "There is my speech!" What an example for us as Christians. Our deeds and our words, our dedicated lives must testify to the Savior what we confess.

> If Christ lives in us, controlling our personalities, we will leave glorious marks on the lives we touch. Not because of our lovely characters, but because of His.
> — EUGENIA PRICE

Lord Jesus, let Your Holy Spirit help me to deliver a testimony of intrinsic value every day and in every way You may call me to. Amen.

Read 2 Timothy 3:12-17

Remain Faithful

But you must remain faithful to the things you have been taught. You know they are true, for you know you can trust those who taught you (2 Tim. 3:14).

In today's Scripture passage Paul gives Timothy his last instructions for carrying out his ministry. The first is that he must remain faithful to the things he was taught and firmly believe in them, because much false doctrine is preached and a person can easily stray from the faith. The Scriptures are the guarantee of the authenticity of his faith which has its origin in the Word and is rooted in it. This is always the litmus test that must be passed by each teaching that people want to sell you. Paul says that if Timothy preached that Word, he would gain credibility and his own faith would be strengthened.

We ought to think clearly and soberly if people want to force an unfamiliar faith on us. Yet one sometimes wonders if it is really worthwhile to conscientiously follow the doctrine as it was passed on to us. Paul motivates Timothy to do it. It should also be a warning to us to be wary of every theory the world wants to sell us.

A woman was showing someone her exquisite family silver. As she removed the pieces from the showcase, she apologized because the silver was so tarnished. Her excuse was, "I can't keep the silver shiny, unless I use it." This is equally true of our faith. Out of sight in a Sunday cupboard of the soul, to be taken out only for show, it always requires an excuse. You cannot let your faith shine unless you use it.

> Faith goes up the stairs that love has built and looks out the window which hope has opened.
> CHARLES H. SPURGEON

God of grace and love, I so badly want faith that is acceptable to the world. Keep me to the things Your Word teaches me. Amen.

January 29

Read John 19:28-37

It Is Finished

When Jesus had tasted it [the sour wine], He said, "It is finished!" Then He bowed His head and released His spirit (John 19:30).

Jesus came to fulfill God's plan of salvation. He had to pay the full price for our sins. From a Christian perspective, His death put an end to the complicated sacrifice system because He made atonement for all our sins.

On account of what He accomplished for us, we are now free to approach God because we have been ransomed. All who believe in His death and resurrection can live with God forever and don't have to die because of sin anymore.

The Old Testament prophecies have been fulfilled. The gates of Paradise that slammed shut behind Adam and Eve, opened again in Christ when He called out triumphantly on the cross, "It is finished!" He completed His task for us!

> The blood of Jesus washes away our past and the Name of Jesus opens up our future.
> JESSE DUPLANTIS

When Cecil John Rhodes was on his deathbed, his last words were, "So much to do, so little time." He could not say at the end of his career, like the Master, "I brought glory to You here on earth by completing the work You gave Me to do" (John 17:4). How good the Son of God must have felt to achieve the purpose His Father planned for Him and to bring about the salvation of all people.

Stand by me, dear Master, to faithfully do what You give me and to do it joyfully and with dedication to the end. Amen.

Read John 8:12-20

Jesus Is the Light

Jesus spoke to the people once more and said, "I am the light of the world. If you follow Me, you won't have to walk in darkness, because you will have the light that leads to life" (John 8:12).

Jesus was teaching in the section of the temple known as the Treasury. During the Feast of Tabernacles, candles were lit as a symbol of the pillar of fire that led the people of Israel through the desert. This is why, in this sacred moment, Jesus referred to Himself as the "light of the world". For the nomadic people, the pillar of fire was a symbol of God's presence, protection and guidance. In the same way, Jesus came to make God's presence, protection and guidance visible to the world.

Sin and death bring everlasting darkness. Christ came to the world to bring mankind the hope and the light of eternal life. It cannot be bought, but only accepted as a gift. Jesus gives it only to those who accept Him, those who decide to live as people of the light. Then we can see where we are going and not get caught in the snares of sin. Then we need never again stumble along aimlessly in the dark.

> In darkness there is no choice. It is light that enables us to see the differences between things; and it is Christ who gives us light.
> C. T. WHITMELL

The story is told of a sculptor who had a model of a beautiful cathedral in his workshop. But it was covered in dust. One day a cleaner put a light in the model and the rays shone through the stained glass windows. Everybody stopped to admire its beauty. The light brought about a wonderful metamorphosis. We should also have the Light of the world inside us to display our true beauty.

Guide me every day and every step of my life, O Light of the world! Help my insignificant life to reflect Your holy light and in this way honor You. Amen.

February

*Rejoice in our confident hope.
Be patient in trouble,
and keep on praying.*
   ROMANS 12:12

Forgiveness of sin lies at the heart of Christianity, and yet it remains a dangerous topic to preach on.
~ MARTIN LUTHER ~

Majestic and Almighty God,
we find ourselves caught up in the reality of life once again.
The first month of the year has passed and we are so busy
that we are almost forgetting about You.
We worship You as the King of Life.
Help us to live in such a way that the world will see You in us.
Be with us in the classroom, on the farm,
behind a desk, in the factory and in the workshop.
Make us faithful and obedient to Your will.
Purify our love and let us love You above all else.
We shamefully confess that we neglect
to testify about Your saving grace.
We know that tomorrow is still in Your merciful hands,
and that we do not hope in vain.
Let hope live in our hearts while You walk the road with us.
In Jesus' glorious name.
Amen.

Read Luke 2:8-20

Glory to God in the Highest

Glory to God in the highest heaven, and on earth peace to those on whom His favor rests (Luke 2:14, NIV).

The song of praise that the angels sang to God is an echo of heavenly music, and has inspired composers for more than two thousand years. It is often called the *Gloria* because of the first word of the Latin translation of the angels' song.

Praise to God should also be the starting point in our worship. After all, the purpose of all of creation is to glorify God. In fact, there can be no real worship without praise. Praising God does not necessarily have to be accompanied by song, but must live in the hearts of His children all the time.

A group of monks in France were well-loved for their compassion and good deeds. But no matter how hard they tried, their singing was always a mess at their worship services. One day a traveling monk and renowned singer stayed over at the monastery. They were overjoyed because now they would really be able to sing at their services, and they planned to persuade him to stay with them.

> Praise makes good people better, and bad people worse.
> THOMAS FULLER

But that night an angel appeared to the prior of the monastery and asked, "Why wasn't there any singing in your chapel tonight? We always look forward to the beautiful singing at your services!" "You must be mistaken," the prior called out. "Usually our singing is poor, but tonight a singer with a beautiful voice sang at our service. For the first time in years our music was wonderful." The angel smiled and said softly, "And yet we heard nothing in heaven." Praise to God must rise up from our own hearts to reach heaven.

Praise God for He is good! Praise the Lord, O my soul, forget not one of His merciful deeds. Amen.

Read Galatians 6:11-18

The Victory of the Cross

May I never boast except in the cross of our Lord Jesus Christ, through which the world has been crucified to me, and I to the world (Gal. 6:14, NIV).

To Christians, the cross is a symbol of victory. There are, however, many temptations and viewpoints out there. We are under subtle pressure every day, and indoctrinated from all sides in well-disguised ways to give in to our sinful nature.

There is only one way to escape these destructive influences: by realizing that the old self died with Christ on the cross and that it is not you living now, but Christ living in you (see Gal. 2:20). If you want to be victorious in any other way than the way of the cross, you will fail.

> We do not attach any intrinsic virtue to the Cross; this would be sinful and idolatrous. Our veneration is referred to Him who died upon it.
> JAMES GIBBONS

Only when you lay your life down at the Cross, will the Holy Spirit become Master of your life. Then you will become a new person. Therefore, like Paul, you should not allow anything or anyone to take the place of Christ in your life. What in your life threatens to take the place of the Cross?

A well-known fable contains a deep truth. The empress Helena went to the Holy Land to look for the cross. Excavations were made and three crosses were found. Which one was Jesus' cross? They took a dead body and hanged it on one cross after the other. When the body touched Jesus' cross, it became alive. You and I demonstrate the power of the cross. The best test: It brings the dead back to life.

At the cross, defiled with guilt, at first I trembled. There You saved my soul, and my gift was life! I praise and thank You, Lord. Amen.

Read Lamentations 3:21-27

Where There Is Life, There Is Hope

I say to myself, "The LORD is my portion; therefore I will wait for Him!" (Lam. 3:24, NIV).

This song of praise by Jeremiah represents the central idea of the entire book of Lamentations. The author experienced the Lord's love, grace and compassion in his suffering. For that reason he could appeal to his readers to hope, repent and confess their sins.

The Lord hears prayers of penance and delivers us from suffering. Therefore we must never lose hope as long as we live. To keep hoping in the Lord is the same as asking what His will is. There can be no hope in the Lord if we are not serious about living our lives in line with His will. Only then can we say patiently, even in the shadow of death: As long as there is life, there is hope (see v. 27). Make this your life philosophy from a young age.

Hope is the anchor of the soul. See in your faith's eye a physician standing at a child's bedside as he is wrestling with death. The doctor bows over the sick child, vigilant, patient, devoted. His whole bearing is one of dignity and knowledge. Dawn is breaking; daybreak that is so often present at a sickbed during the critical hour. The mother and father are standing in the shadows of the room. She hides her face to conceal her emotions, and he puts his hand on her shoulder to comfort her. The physician and the parents cling to the unspoken thought: Where there is life, there is hope. And God is the only one to cling to.

> Hope is the struggle of the soul, breaking loose from what is perishable, and attesting her eternity.
> HERMAN MELVILLE

In the darkest moments, O Lord, I will still put my hope in You. Grant that through Your great mercy I am never disappointed. Amen.

Read Ecclesiastes 10:1-3; Proverbs 10:5

A Sound Mind

The heart of the wise inclines to the right, but the heart of the fool to the left (Eccles. 10:2, NIV).

There are people with a sound mind (*compos mentis*) for this world, but their minds are clouded (*non compos mentis*) about eternity.

Some learned stargazers scan the skies through their sophisticated telescopes, and yet they find it difficult to see the Bright Morning Star, Jesus Christ. Some mathematicians, highly skilled in the art of calculating, fail to understand a simple mathematical evangelical fact. Christ said, "What good will it be for someone to gain the whole world, yet forfeit their soul?" (Matt. 16:26). Botanists can tell you all there is to know about every plant species on earth, but they are ignorant about the Rose of Sharon and the Lily of the Valley.

In the year 1870 the Methodists of Indiana in the USA held their annual conference. At this occasion, the president of the college where they came together, said, "I think we live in an exciting age." The moderator then asked him, "What do you see?" "I believe we have reached a time of great inventions. I believe that people will fly like birds in the sky." The moderator replied, "This is heresy. The Bible says the sky is reserved for the flight of angels only." After the conference, the college president, a man called Wright, went home where he was greeted by his two young boys, Wilbur and Orville. The Wright brothers built and flew the first manned airplane. There is a fundamental difference between wisdom and foolishness.

> Common sense in an uncommon degree is what the world calls wisdom.
> SAMUEL TAYLOR

Source of all true wisdom and knowledge, I plead with You for wisdom and knowledge so that I will be able to discern the things that really matter. Amen.

February 4

Read Luke 24:1-7

The Genius Loci

He is not here; He has risen! Remember how He told you, while He was still with you in Galilee. (Luke 24:6, NIV)

When you visit the Garden Tomb in Jerusalem, you experience a very distinctive atmosphere that has an indescribable influence on your spirit: A true *genius loci* (a pervading spirit of the place).

You enter the tomb with deep reverence, you inhale the spirit of the resurrection and after standing there a while, praying, you turn back and walk out into the surrounding garden. And there it is written on the door in big white letters: "He is not here – for He is risen!" While you sit in the garden, you know the undeniable fact: The Savior was here; He is still here as living Lord! You sense an atmosphere you won't experience in any other place in the world. Jesus conquered death here! Here you can make sense of the greatest tragedies in life.

> The great Easter truth is not that we are to live newly after death – that is not the great thing – but that we are to be new here and now by the power of the resurrection.
> PHILLIPS BROOKS

Every year thousands of people climb a mountain peak in the Italian Alps, past the stations of the Via Dolorosa, to gather at a cross high up in the mountain. One tourist noticed a pathway on the other side of the cross and struggled through the dense vegetation. To his greatest surprise, he discovered another sacred place that symbolizes the empty tomb. It was neglected and overgrown. Everyone only gets as far as the cross and experiences the despair and sorrow of it all. Too few move on from the cross to receive the true message of Passover: the message of the empty grave.

Risen Savior, I thank You for the empty tomb and for being alive. Help me to remain in Your sacred presence. Amen.

Read John 21:15-19

Passing with Flying Colors

The third time He said to him, "Simon, son of John, do you love Me?" He said, "Lord, You know all things; You know that I love you." Jesus said, "Feed My sheep" (John 21:17, NIV).

P̲eter was often called into Jesus' exam room to be tested. His impulsive nature resulted in him not always reading the examination papers carefully and then often failing. Like the night Jesus was taken captive and Peter went to Caiaphas' palace to warm his hands at the enemy's fire: He answered the simple question whether he knew Jesus with a "No". It is not surprising that his history of failing tests drove him to tears and made him flee the exam room in shame.

> Witnessing is breaking down the obstacles of self-love in order to show our neighbors Christ, who lives in us.
> PAUL FROST

A few days later Peter was given the chance of doing a supplementary exam. Jesus appeared to His disciples after His resurrection and chose Peter to answer his last and decisive exam question. As he had denied his Master three times, he was asked three times whether he loved Christ. Three times he gave the correct answer: "Lord, You know all things; You know that I love You." Peter left Jesus' examination room triumphantly after passing his test *cum laude*. How are you doing in Christ's examination room?

A despondent and miserable Christian stood outside his church building. "Don't you want to attend our church tonight?" he asked a passerby. The stranger briefly looked at him and answered, "No thanks, I have enough problems of my own." It is not surprising that this Christian did not pass his witnessing examination cum laude.

Loving Master, I so often disappoint You. Enable me, through the Holy Spirit, to pass the test cum laude in future. Amen.

Read Psalm 118:24; Proverbs 6:6-11

Seize the Day!

The LORD has done it this very day; let us rejoice today and be glad (Ps. 118:24, NIV).

The proverb *carpe diem* contains a serious warning to each human being. We can only be successful if we embrace every day that God gives us in His grace. Yesterday is but a memory; tomorrow is just a dream; all we really have is today! Therefore we must make optimal use of it.

Ants don't have a leader, a supervisor or ruler, and yet they do each day what must be done that day: They gather food for the winter ahead. Those who slumber and sleep and fold their hands fall into poverty like someone who has been robbed of everything.

Each day is filled with challenges, but also with a full measure of God's grace. There are a full day's dreams, but also a full day that the Holy Spirit leads us so that we can make those dreams come true – if we use the opportunity! Tennyson said that the heights reached and held by great people were not reached by sudden flights, but while others slept, they toiled upward in the night. They achieved success through perseverance.

Today will come once only, and every day that goes to waste, impoverishes the quality of our lives. This is especially true of our spiritual lives. "Today if you hear His voice, do not harden your hearts" (Heb. 3:7-8).

> Dawn does not come twice to awaken a man.
> ANONYMOUS

Today is given to us by the grace of God, but none of us know if we will still be alive tomorrow. This makes today important for eternity. Some of the decisions you make today, will determine where you will spend eternity. For this reason: *Carpe diem*!

Holy Father, today is such a precious gift from Your hand. Let me realize its worth every day and live to Your glory. Amen.

Read Psalm 71:1-8; Isaiah 49:1

From Beginning to End

Listen to me, you islands; hear this you distant nations: Before I was born the LORD called me; from my mother's womb He has spoken my name (Isa. 49:1, NIV).

How wonderful and comforting it is to know that the Lord knows us from before birth, and loves us. Our names are an extension of our personality. If God knows your name, He also knows all about you: your needs and wants. God knows you even better than your parents. You are unique to Him and He loves you unconditionally.

This also means that the Lord knows about everything we do, and this should motivate us to live pure and right, for His glory. He knows our weaknesses and wants to help us: "If we confess our sins, He is faithful and just and will forgive us our sins and purify us from all unrighteousness" (1 John 1:9).

This truth demands that we know the Lord. A child belongs to his mother and she treats him with love because she knows his every need and provides for him; this is the way it should be between the Lord and us.

An elderly mother was sorely tried and tested by a no-good son. When a neighbor asked her how the son was doing, she answered, "Bad; worse than you could ever imagine." "How can you put up with him?" the neighbor asked. "If he was mine, I would have kicked him out of the house." "Yes," came the reply, "I would also have done it if he was yours. But don't you see; he isn't yours, he's mine." This is the tenderness God feels for each of His children, even before they are born.

> There are three things that only God knows: the beginning of things; the course things will take; and the end of things.
> WELSH PROVERB

Loving Father, the greatness of Your love is beyond my understanding. Let me live in such a way that I am worthy of that love. Amen.

Read Ephesians 5:15-20

Give Thanks to God

Give thanks for everything to God the Father in the name of our Lord Jesus Christ (Eph. 5:20).

Paul describes an approach to life that always leads to unending thankfulness toward God. A saved person is a grateful person and his gratitude finds expression in different ways: There is always a song of praise to God in his heart; a willingness to give thanks to the Lord; excitement and gladness about God's unfathomable love.

We could never thank God enough for saving sinners. If you want to know whether you belong to God, test it against the fountain of gratitude bubbling over from your heart. A song of gratitude must always become a life of gratitude in which the world can see the grace of God in our actions.

> Thou hast given so much to me, give one thing more – a grateful heart.
> — GEORGE HERBERT

When Robinson Crusoe landed on a lonely island after being shipwrecked, he wrote down the good and the bad of his situation in two different columns. Although he was alone on a solitary island, he was still alive while the entire crew of the ship died. He was isolated from other people, but had enough food. He had no clothes, but the climate was so mild that he didn't need clothes. He was without weapons, but there were no wild animals like he saw in Africa. He had no one to talk to, but God was always there.

Therefore, he decided, for every negative situation there was a positive opposite that he could thank God for.

I praise You with gratitude in my heart, Lord my God, for all the good things You do for me. Grant that I will not forget any of them. Amen.

Read Proverbs 14:12-16

Take Note

Only simpletons believe everything they're told! The prudent carefully consider their steps (Proverbs 14:15).

Take careful note: If God is not our first priority, all other things in life become meaningless. Then life becomes nothing more than a struggle to earn enough money for food, clothes and a roof over one's head. Then life is little more than one monotonous day after the other.

> All God expects from you is to do your best at all times.
> ROBERT H. BENSON

But *nota bene,* please note, when God is your first priority, life becomes an adventure. Then even the daily grind gets new meaning, and the most ordinary events become promising. If you have become bored, take a good look at your relationship with God. Your boredom might be caused by the fact that God doesn't top your priority list anymore.

We may look at a massive block of granite and not really take note of the way we're handling it. But diamond polishers will look at it totally different. They put on a pair of special spectacles and nervously take up their instruments to start their delicate task. Please note: We work with diamonds when we work for God, not with granite. Diamonds that must glitter forever in our King's crown.

So we must be very, very careful. We dare not be afraid otherwise we might cause flaws in the diamond. But we must take careful note of the directions laid down for us if we are to achieve success.

Heavenly Father, thank You for trusting me with the work of the kingdom. Let me take careful note of the guidelines You give me in Your Word. Amen.

Read John 8:36; Romans 6:15-23

Perfect Freedom

"So if the Son sets you free, you are truly free" (John 8:36).

A slave has a temporary position in a household without any rights or job security, and could be sold at any time. A son, on the other hand, has vested rights in a family. God's only Son, Jesus can make us God's sons and daughters. He can even make a slave truly free.

The fruit of life in Christ is complete freedom, in direct contrast to the fruit of life in sin. Therefore we must live as people who are free from sin by serving God joyfully. This *ad libitum* (life of freedom) has got nothing to do with licentiousness, but is the highest form of obedience to God. True freedom always obeys God's laws.

Freedom is the only soil in which human thinking grows and develops to its full stature. This is abundantly illustrated by the arts. In the dark ages human imagination and thinking were restrained by religious chains which allowed no freedom of expression. Consequently the arts stagnated and died. Artists were stuck in a groove with endless repetitions of Madonnas and saints.

> God forces no one, for love cannot compel, and God's service is a thing of perfect freedom.
> — HANS DENK

With the Renaissance came freedom. Doors swung open and the people were overwhelmed by glorious wonderment at the world and themselves. Freedom brought the best of the arts to the fore. Likewise, the freedom that Jesus brought must bring the best in us to the fore.

Thank You, Jesus, that Your death gave me freedom. Let me guard the freedom so that it doesn't turn into licentiousness. Amen.

Read Psalm 51:3-14

Confession of Sin

Against You, and You alone, have I sinned; I have done what is evil in Your sight. You will be proved right in what You say, and Your judgment against me is just (Ps. 51:4).

According to 2 Samuel 12, David sincerely regretted his adultery with Bathsheba, and the murder of her husband in an effort to hide his sin. He knew that many people had been affected and hurt by his behavior. Because he had honest remorse, the Lord forgave him. No sin is too big to be forgiven.

Do you perhaps feel that you will never again be able to approach God because you did a terrible thing? He can and will forgive any sin. However, His forgiveness doesn't mean that He will undo the natural consequences of your sin. We see that David's life and that of his family were never the same again (see 2 Sam. 12:1-23). A deep awareness of sin is necessary when we've done wrong before God. Forgiveness is called an act of salvation by the poet and he sings about it in his song of praise (see Ps. 51:16-17). True remorse and genuine awareness of sin, a deep longing for forgiveness, a true desire for renewal and change are the fruits of a real sense of sin.

> "Everyone who sins is a slave of sin."
> JOHN 8:34

An eagle searching for food pounced from the blue sky and caught a huge fish in its claws. Slowly it started rising up in the sky, but the fish was bigger and heavier than he thought. Slowly the eagle rose higher and higher until it seemed to come to a standstill in the air. Still clutching its prey, it began to tumble downwards. The eagle's life ended with its prey still in its clutches. This is an illustration of the hold sin has over us until we are delivered from it by our confession of sin to God.

Gracious God, my sin always looms before me, but I know that You forgive again and again. Forgive me again in Jesus' name. Amen.

Read Romans 1:16-17; Psalm 19:8-12

God's Library Book

For I am not ashamed of this Good News about Christ. It is the power of God at work, saving everyone who believes – the Jew first and also the Gentile (Rom. 1:16).

We can say with confidence that the Bible is a book from God's library. And this book is, in its very being, power from God that leads to salvation for all who believe. If you realize this, you also realize that you can never be ashamed of it, but with holy pride tell one and all about it.

> The Bible is alive, it speaks to me; it has feet, it runs after me; it has hands, it lays hold of me.
> MARTIN LUTHER

The way to become part of the power of the Gospel is by hearing it and believing. Faith in itself does not save you; only Jesus Christ can do that. But faith is the acceptance of Jesus' glorious act of salvation in your own life.

God makes Himself known to us through His creation and through His Word. According to Psalm 19 the Word sets us free, it protects us, makes us wise and brings joy and light into our lives. We find guidelines in it for our pilgrim's journey, not chains that bind us.

In the city of Troy there was a statue of Minerva, called the Palladium. The Trojans believed that it descended from heaven and as long as it stood in its place, the city would not be taken. The Greek, Ulysses, was sent to steal the statue. He succeeded in his mission and took it to the Greek camp. Not long afterwards the city of Troy was conquered. The Bible must have such a place in our world, only a thousand times better. As long as it lives in our hearts and we obey it, we are safe.

Word Incarnate, my Savior and Redeemer, thank You for the Gospel that comes from You and enriches our lives. Amen.

Read Ephesians 5:15-17; Colossians 3:23-25

Time Flies

Make the most of every opportunity in these evil days (Eph. 5:16).

In the Amplified Bible this verse reads as follows: "Making the very most of the time [buying up each opportunity], because the days are evil." Paul here emphasizes the fact that the believer should probe his own life and must use every opportunity to grow spiritually, because time cannot be reversed. This underlines the fact that the influence of sin is enormous. It is still true today and therefore we must set ourselves high standards, act sensibly and make use of every possible opportunity to do good.

> God often gives us, in one fleeting moment, what He has withheld from us for a long time.
> THOMAS À KEMPIS

Knowing what God wants us to do is not good enough; we must act conscientiously and immediately. Our faith must be visible in our actions and we must keep in mind that every moment God grants us is borrowed time, and that we will have to account for it.

Years ago in England, the pastor of a congregation said to himself one rainy night, "I don't think I'll go to church tonight; no one else will turn up." Eventually he did go and saw just one single person in the pews. He almost decided not to preach, but did after all. The boy in the gallery heard the message and gave his life to the Lord. The boy later became a preacher who drew 13,000 people at a time to his services, and led crowds all over the world to Christ. He was Charles Haddon Spurgeon.

Make the most of the time, because it passes so quickly and you can never turn back the clock.

I thank You, Lord my God, for the precious gift of time. Support me in my effort to use it to the best of my ability and not to let it pass unused. Amen.

Read 1 Corinthians 6:15-20

A Healthy Body and Soul

Don't you realize that your body is the temple of the Holy Spirit, who lives in you and was given to you by God? You do not belong to yourself (1 Cor. 6:19).

The fact that Paul cautioned the Corinthians about sexual immorality and prostitution was important in that community, because the temple of the goddess Aphrodite was in Corinth. Sex was part of heathen worship rituals.

Paul told them outright that a Christian must have nothing to do with these sexual perversities. The Christian's body is also part of the body of Christ. The Holy Spirit helps us to make good judgments about these things because body and soul are inseparably linked. We cannot do with our bodies what we please. When we become Jesus' disciples, we are filled with the Holy Spirit and the Spirit lives in us. For this reason both body and soul belong to God and through His strength we are healed. After all, we have been bought at a high price: By Christ's sacrificial blood.

> The soul, like the body, lives by what it feeds on.
> GILBERT HOLLAND

The Nardoo plant in Australia looks a lot like wheat but it doesn't have the nutritious value of corn meal. Strangely enough people who eat it don't get hungry, but they pine away gradually and eventually they die. Likewise, a healthy body housing a sick spirit dies, or the other way around. A healthy body houses a healthy soul.

Creator God, I praise and thank You for the wonderful body You gave me. Let me guard my body and mind as a treasure from Your hand. Amen.

Read Mark 1:23-28

What Wonderful News!

Amazement gripped the audience, and they began to discuss what had happened. "What sort of new teaching is this?" they asked excitedly. "It has such authority! Even evil spirits obey His orders!" (Mark 1:27).

Mark placed great emphasis on Jesus' confrontation with evil spirits to illustrate that He had authority over them. In today's Scripture passage Jesus had just cast an evil spirit out. It is interesting to note that Jesus never needed to cast out evil spirits through impressive rituals. One word spoken by Him was enough to break Satan's power over them and make the Evil One flee.

The people loved seeing the wonderful things the Master did. To them these things were miracles. The authority with which Jesus cast out evil was impressive and amazing, and He was talked about through the entire area of Galilee.

When the Gospel tells us that Jesus walked on the water of the Sea of Galilee, I have no right to say it is contradictory to human reasoning. It might be contradictory to what I have experienced, but my experiences are insignificant and secondary. If I had to dwarf Christianity to my experiences, there would be nothing left of the wonder.

> Jesus was Himself the one convincing and permanent miracle.
> IAN MACLAREN

Christ rises high above my personal experiences. It is wonderful to talk about what He has said and done. It even goes beyond walking on water, because He said, "When you see Me, you are seeing the one who sent Me" (John 12:45). Now that is wonderful news!

I stand in great awe before You, O Lord! I want to tell others about it zealously and with enthusiasm. Amen.

Read John 19:28-37

The Artist's Masterpiece

When Jesus had tasted it [the sour wine], He said, "It is finished!" Then He bowed His head and released His spirit (John 19:30).

Jesus' death on the cross and His triumphant resurrection was the *magnum opus,* the masterpiece of His act of salvation. The human race was separated from God and could only be forgiven if an animal was sacrificed to God as atonement for their sins. This was the only way that people could become pure before God again. Because of repeated sins, they had to repeatedly bring offerings.

> They gave Him a manger for a cradle, a carpenter's bench for a pulpit, thorns for a crown, and a cross for a throne. He took them and made them the very glory of His career.
> W. E. ORCHARD

Jesus' death on the cross, brought a sufficient and final sacrifice. His death put an end to the complicated offering system. On account of what He has done for us, we can now approach God freely and speak to Him like a child to his father. Because of this great work of Christ, everyone who believes in His death and resurrection may live with God, and they do not have to die an eternal death because of their sin.

A Roman soldier said of Christianity, "This system cannot survive because it is based on a catastrophe, a pillory of shame, on the death of its leader!" And yet this is precisely the foundation on which it is built. The once mighty Roman Empire has long been destroyed, but through the *magnum opus* of Jesus Christ, Christianity lives forevermore.

I praise and thank You, Lord Jesus, for Your masterwork with Your crucifixion and resurrection. Help me to live like a child of the resurrection. Amen.

Read Psalm 42:1-11

Never Despair

Why am I discouraged? Why is my heart so sad? I will put my hope in God! I will praise Him again — my Savior and my God! (Ps. 42:11).

The theme of Psalm 42 is that we must hold on to the Lord when despair threatens us. It sometimes happens that the Lord keeps quiet, even if we beg Him for help and desperately seek Him. Such times can easily lead to depression and despair, but the psalmist discovered a solution to the problem. He kept thinking of all the blessings God poured out over his life (see vv. 4-5).

> Courage consists not in blindly overlooking danger, but in seeing it and conquering it.
> JEAN PAUL RICHTER

Then he realized that God was there, even if He remained silent. He knew that he would have reason to praise God again. He also looked at creation, proof of God's love. He knew that even in his misery, he would not be separated from God's love (see vv. 7-8). This made him trust God faithfully and expectantly. Apply these steps if you are overcome with doubt and despair in your life. Hold on to God in all circumstances and sing songs of praise to Him.

The great Baptist pioneer in Germany, Pastor Oncken, suffered much in his youth for the sake of truth and faith, and was often fined and thrown in jail. Once the mayor of Hamburg held up his finger and said, "Do you see this finger? As long as I can move it, I will keep you down." Oncken answered, "Sir, I see your finger, but I also see an Arm that you don't see, and as long as that Arm is stretched out over me, you cannot keep me down." He knew the secret to never give way to despair.

Holy Master, keep me from giving in to despair. Through You there is hope in the darkest times of my life. Amen.

Read John 14:25-31

Go in Peace

"I am leaving you with a gift – peace of mind and heart. And the peace I give is a gift the world cannot give. So don't be troubled or afraid" (John 14:27).

When the Holy Spirit works in your life, you experience deep and lasting peace. The world explains peace as contentment, or the absence of conflict. Real peace, however, is much more: it is sharing in God's blessings and having an intimate and personal relationship with Him. The person who has this peace in his heart doesn't fear the present or the future.

Things like sin, fear, uncertainty, doubt and other emotions constantly create conflict inside our hearts. But the peace Jesus gives works in your heart and life to put an end to all these negative perceptions, so that you can have inner peace instead of conflict. Jesus said He would give us that peace if we would only accept it. Being at peace with God means being at peace with yourself and your fellow human beings. May you also hear Jesus say, "Go in peace," and may you experience it every day.

> Peace is not the absence of war, it is a virtue, a state of mind, a disposition for benevolence, confidence, justice.
> BARUCH DE SPINOZA

In Kensington Gardens in London is a painting of the battlefield of Waterloo after the famous battle. The grass and vegetation were flourishing again. In the painting a lamb was sleeping in the mouth of a dismantled canon. This portrayed a particularly suggestive image. I thought about how the battle between God and the soul started and ended. Instead of the words: "The wages of sin is death!", I heard a voice inside: "Peace I leave with you; My peace I give you." Amidst the ferocious struggle of the soul, I saw the Lamb of God, who took away the sin of the world.

Holy Spirit, help me find and keep the peace of God. Amen.

Read 1 Corinthians 15:54-58

I Came, I Saw, I Conquered

Thank God! He gives us victory over sin and death through our Lord Jesus Christ! (1 Cor. 15:57).

Jesus Christ came to this sin-torn world, saw it and triumphed over it in glory. At first it seemed as if Satan gained a victory in the Garden of Eden, as well as with the death of Christ on the cross. But God transformed what appeared to be victories for people into defeat when He triumphantly rose from the dead (see Col. 2:15; Heb. 2:14-15).

We need not fear death anymore, because death has been defeated and our hope goes beyond the grave. Death was finally conquered in Christ. Sin causes death, and the law clearly outlines what sin is. By paying for our sins with His blood, Christ fulfilled the law. Through His victorious resurrection, the law and sin and death lost their hold over us. Christ came, saw and conquered!

In several paintings of the crucifixion we see a skull at the foot of the cross. This is a symbol of Adam, and expresses the early tradition that Christ was crucified where Adam died. The church father Chrysostom claims: "Some say that Adam died there, and there lieth; Jesus in this place where death had reigned; there also set up the trophy." The legend undoubtedly has something to do with 1 Corinthians 15:22.

> Victory is always preceded by strife; the skipper is tested by the storm; the soldier proves himself on the battlefield.
> —CYPRIAN

Just like everyone dies because of their connection with Adam, everyone will live again in Christ. In Adam's world of sin and death Christ came, saw and conquered.

Christ, thank You that I may share in Your victory by accepting You as my Savior and Redeemer forever and ever. Amen.

A Year of Miracles and Achievements

You crown the year with a bountiful harvest; even the hard pathways overflow with abundance (Ps. 65:11).

It is God who in Jesus Christ makes life good; who makes an ordinary year a wonderful and joyous year. Psalm 65 tells us about the good things He gives us (v. 4): answer to prayer (vv. 2, 5); caring for all people (vv. 2, 5, 8); maintaining the order of creation (vv. 6-7); rain and abundant harvests (vv. 9-10); livestock and ample pastures (vv. 12-13). Everybody and everything are joyful because God did wonderful things for them and crowned the year with His goodness. He made it an *annus mirabilis*, a year of wonders! In this psalm of the harvest, the glory of the Creator God is celebrated and displayed in nature.

> If the only prayer you said in your whole life was, "Thank You," that would suffice.
> MEISTER ECKHART

Nature helps us to understand something of God. We see in nature how generous God is. He gives us so much more than we need or deserve. If we remember that, we will be thankful and share with others what He gives us.

Travelers who pass through the high mountains in the East, tell how guides pile one stone on top of another as they wind their way up the dangerous and narrow paths. They mutter prayers of thanksgiving: Thanks to God for leading and protecting them thus far, and also for a safe return journey. When we experience times of achievement and prosperity, we should also thank God for the miracles in our lives.

God, I thank You for the miracles You perform in my life by Your grace. Amen.

Read 2 Timothy 1:6-12

Victory or Death

For God has not given us a spirit of fear and timidity, but of power, love, and self-discipline (2 Tim. 1:7).

After Paul's arrest Timothy was probably afraid to carry on with his ministry. Paul reminded him that believers should not be surprised by the painful trials they would be subjected to, because these trials would make them partners with Christ in His suffering (see 1 Pet. 4:12-13). The Holy Spirit gives a person the necessary strength to endure this. We know that Timothy took this to heart, even if it meant that he ended up in prison himself (see Heb. 12:23).

> The first step on the way to victory is to recognize the enemy.
> CORRIE TEN BOOM

Paul encouraged believers to persevere, whatever the price. If they would only think about the things the Lord did for them, everything would fall into perspective and they would realize whether they lived or died, nothing could separate them from Christ's love (see Rom. 8:35). Knowing this makes you fearless to listen to the Lord only, at all costs, and fulfill your calling in prayerful dependence on Him.

In the battle of Carioli in the Old Roman Empire, the Romans were on the winning side because of the influence of their passionate leader Caius Marcius. It broke his soldiers' hearts to see him with bleeding wounds. They begged him to fall back to the encampment, but with his characteristic courage he called out, "Winners dare not tire. The crown of life belongs to those who stay faithful till death!" This should also be our philosophy in the service of our Leader.

Lord God, help me through Your Spirit to remain faithful to You, even when those around me lose faith. Amen.

Read 2 Corinthians 8:2-7

Total Surrender

They even did more than we had hoped, for their first action was to give themselves to the Lord and to us, just as God wanted them to do (2 Cor. 8:5).

Paul, who wrote from Macedonia, hoped that the believers of Corinth would be inspired to solve their own problems and be united as believers. The secret of this was total surrender to God in the first, and most important place. The kingdom of God grows through the *in toto* surrender to God; total surrender.

If you love someone with all your heart, it is possible to do things for that person and to give him things. This is what God expects from us if we have surrendered our lives to Him completely. In the Scripture passage we see how various churches worked together to help a small group of believers far away from them. If we have surrendered completely, we will look for ways and means to contribute to a ministry outside our circle. Thus, by complete surrender and obedience, we help the kingdom of God to grow.

The British East India Company said at the beginning of the nineteenth century: "Sending Christian missionaries to our Eastern possessions is the most insane, most expensive and most irresponsible project that has ever been suggested by a mad and half-witted enthusiast." The British lieutenant-general in Bengal said at the end of the nineteen century: "To my mind, the totally surrendered British missionaries did more, and more lasting good things for India than all our other agencies together." People in total surrender make a substantial difference for God in this world.

> We can only learn to know ourselves and do what we can, namely surrender our will and fulfill God's will in us.
> St. Teresa of Avila

Heavenly Father, I will hold nothing back, but do what You ask in total surrender and obedience. Amen.

Read Acts 17:21-28

Faith Not Just Knowledge

His purpose was for nations to seek after God and perhaps feel their way toward Him and find Him – though He is not far from any one of us (Acts 17:27).

Paul found a point of contact at the altars and places of worship to tell the Greeks about the one true God. He used examples they were familiar with to tell them that true Christianity must meet certain requirements. He told them about the resurrection of the living Christ. It was most certainly good news for the Greeks to hear that there is only one God, because they were scared that they would leave out a god when they worship and then get punished.

Paul used their fear to point out to them that only total surrender to Jesus could bring blessings, prosperity and peace. Despite the fact that they were religious, they didn't know the true God. We live in a religious society but not all people are Christians. We must tell them who the true God is and what He did for humankind through His Son. We become true Christians through His salvation and faith in Him.

> Knowledge is a truth that is stored in the brain. Faith is a flame that burns in the heart.
> JOSEPH NEWTON

Martin Luther gave a definition of faith: "There are two kinds of faith: firstly, faith that believes everything about God, which means that it is a kind of knowledge, rather than faith. Secondly, there is a kind of faith in God that means I place my trust in Him completely, surrender myself to Him and believe that He cares for me, and know without a doubt that He will deal with me according to everything that is said of Him. Faith like this, that casts itself on God in life and death, is true Christian faith."

Holy God, let my faith never become something insignificant. Amen.

Read John 4:31-38

A Particular Way of Working

Then Jesus explained: "My nourishment comes from doing the will of God, who sent Me, and from finishing His work" (John 4:34).

Jesus' modus operandi in His mission to the world was to do His Father's will: He would follow His Father's orders. In Palestine, the period from sowing the seed up to the harvest was about four months. While Jesus and His disciples were sitting, watching the citizens of Sychar all dressed in white, Jesus emphasized that His disciples need not wait much longer; the fields were ready for harvest. Their modus operandi must be the same as His: To do the Father's work without delay.

Then the harvester and the Father would rejoice together. All missionary work is the harvest of the seed that the Father and the Son sowed. It is an unbelievable privilege for a believer to follow Jesus' modus operandi, His way of working, and be part of the process.

> The Spirit of Christ is the spirit of missions. The nearer we get to Him, the more intensely missionary we become.
> —HENRY MARTYN

Paul's missionary journeys took him where there was a call for help. David Livingstone said, "God had an only Son, and He was a missionary!" A merchant met a converted cannibal busy reading the Bible and the merchant said to him, "In our country that book is out of date." The cannibal answered, "If it was out of date here, you would have been eaten a long time ago!" The epitaph on the grave of Dr. John Geddie, in Aneityum in the New Hebrides, reads: "When he landed in 1848, there were no Christians here and when he left in 1872, there were no heathens!" He was true to Jesus' modus operandi.

Master, let the modus operandi of my life be to do the Father's work, like You did. Amen.

Read Nehemiah 4:1-8

Nothing Is Achieved without Work

At last the wall was completed to half its height around the entire city, for the people had worked with enthusiasm (Neh. 4:6).

Judah's enemies mocked them and tried to scare them. They claimed that the wall the people of Judah were rebuilding around Jerusalem was useless. Nehemiah found this mocking offensive and blasphemous. The Lord gave them the orders to complete this task. Nehemiah inspired the people of Judah and they carried on with the work. Finally they succeeded in their goal because their hearts were in their work. They proved once again that nothing can be achieved without hard work.

> Work is love made visible.
> KHALIL GIBRAN

These people even carried on working under warlike circumstances to rebuild the walls of Jerusalem. They had to pray while working and work while praying. Whatever the challenges we as Christians face, we must always remember that nothing worthwhile can be achieved without honest work; especially not in the kingdom of God.

A physician once said that when he was a medical student he attended an operation performed by a famous surgeon. For some reason the physician's assistant hadn't turned up and he chose the student to help him save that life. The student didn't have words to describe how proud he was to help this renowned surgeon. With this is mind, Spurgeon said, "I realize that God can save the world without my help, but He asks of me in love to assist Him. I praise and thank Him for the honor and privilege to assist Him and save lives."

Lord, I want to make it my goal to work for You. Let me always see it as an honor and a privilege to work with You. Amen.

Read Acts 15:1-15

Divide and Rule

When they arrived in Jerusalem, Paul and Barnabas were welcomed by the whole church, including the apostles and elders. They reported everything God had done through them. But then some of the believers who belonged to the sect of the Pharisees stood up and insisted, "The Gentile converts must be circumcised and required to follow the law of Moses" (Acts 15:4-5).

Satan is a master of sabotage and one of the most devious plans in his evil armory is to divide and to rule. He spares nothing and no one. If he can cause disagreement and division among the Lord's children, he has achieved his demonic goal. In the early church he played the Jewish Christians off against one another. Paul, Barnabas and other church leaders agreed that although the Old Testament laws were very important, they were not a precondition for salvation.

The law cannot save, only Jesus Christ can save you. The churches of Jerusalem talked about this, and involved all the Christians in the matter. Paul and Barnabas stated their case and an evenly balanced proposal was accepted by all. And so Satan's effort to bring division in the church and to rule, failed.

> Separation from evil is the necessary first principle of communion with Him ... Separation from evil is His principle of unity.
> J.N. DARBY

Sabot is the French term for a wooden shoe worn by factory workers to keep their feet dry on the wet, cold cement floors of the factories where they worked. If the workers wanted undeserved time off, one of them would secretly take off his wooden shoe and force it into the sensitive machinery of the factory. Then the whole factory would come to a standstill and they had time off until the machines had been repaired. That's where the word *sabotage* comes from, and also the connotation that Satan is the greatest saboteur with his "divide and rule" program.

Lord, keep me from bringing division in Your kingdom. Amen.

Read Luke 1:76-80

Light from the Darkness

Because of God's tender mercy, the morning light from heaven is about to break upon us, to give light to those who sit in the darkness and in the shadow of death, and to guide us to the path of peace (Luke 1:78-79).

In the lives of the Lord's children there are often times of darkness, like the darkness the people of Israel experienced in Isaiah's time. They went through an ominous time, but looked forward to a new beginning. A new David would establish the reign of peace that would never end. Isaiah rejoiced, "The people walking in darkness have seen a great light; on those living in the land of deep darkness a light has dawned" (Isa. 9:2, NIV).

God would turn around the fate of His people. The prophet was so sure that there would be light in the darkness that he spoke in the past tense, as if it had already happened. God's promise to Abraham that all the nations would be blessed through him would be fulfilled by the Messiah that would come from Abraham's descendants. Zechariah saw the Baby Jesus as a light for the world; He would be a light to those who accepted and served Him.

Against an escarpment in the Alps near the village Jemi there is a white marble cross with the following inscription on the beam: "Only Jesus brings light!" According to tradition the only daughter from a noble family went mountain climbing one day, fell down a gaping abyss and died. The parents were inconsolable. They couldn't find peace anywhere, until they turned to Jesus Christ. Then they erected the white cross against the rock face to tell the world that in the deepest sorrow and darkness, "Only Jesus brings light!"

> Noticing your darkness is proof that there is a great light.
> RAOUL PRINS

Guide me to walk in Your light so that I can also be a light to the world. Amen.

Read Psalm 124:1-8

Without God Everything Is in Vain

> If the LORD had not been on our side when people attacked us? (Ps. 124:2).

In the midst of mortal danger among hostile people, Israel survived only because they were covered by the protective power of the Lord. This psalm is a psalm of thanksgiving to God for His protective grace, and a confession that proclaims: *Nisi Dominus, Frustra!:* Without God all our efforts would be in vain.

We as New Testament believers can also use this psalm as a confession that God is our refuge and protector. Martin Luther wrote a song based on this psalm that starts with the words: "If God wasn't with us in this time ... " God gives us life and freedom, but outside of His omnipotence and grace there are only frustration and disappointment. To take on something in our own strength, without God's help, usually ends in failure, because without God everything is in vain.

> When You are our strength, it is truly strength, but when we do things in our own strength, it is nothing but weakness.
> AUGUSTINE OF HIPPO

A father and his little boy were working in the garden. The boy was told to throw a pile of stones into a ditch. After a while he called out, "Dad, there's one stone I can't lift. I tried with all my might, but it won't budge. "No, son," the wise father answered, "you didn't try with all your might, because I am here as part of your strength and you didn't ask me to help you." If we do the work the Lord expects us to, we are not only able to do what we can in our own strength, but also in His strength.

God, grant me the grace to always remember that I can do anything through Him who gives me strength, but that without Him everything is in vain. Amen.

February 29

March

*All of us, like sheep,
have strayed away. We have
left God's path to follow our own.
Yet the LORD laid on Him
the sins of us all.*
ISAIAH 53:6

The cross is seen as the saving act of Christ, but even more than this, it is seen as the final place of reconciliation between God and humanity.

CALVIN MILLER

Loving Father God,
because of Your love for us,
You sent Your Son as Sacrifice, Example and Savior.
He had to become the Man of Sorrows
to make the joy of heaven possible for us.
He descended into poverty,
so that we could experience the riches of Your forgiveness.
He shed His godly Majesty,
so that we could become children of the King.
He gave His love unconditionally,
so that we could love others.
Through His life He set the perfect example.
He died a brutal death on the cross,
so that we could have salvation, forgiveness and eternal life.
He triumphantly rose from death,
so that we could be part of His triumphal procession.
Lord Jesus, Man of Sorrows,
make us willing to accept the challenges
of being Your children,
and to live and die as Your faithful witnesses.
Thank You that they who share in Your cross,
also share in Your crown;
that they who suffer with You, will also live with You.
Soli Deo Gloria!
Amen.

Read 1 John 2:14-17

This World Is Fading Away

> And this world is fading away, along with everything that people crave. But anyone who does what pleases God will live forever (1 John 2:17).

Christians are given a serious warning not to love the sinful world or the things of the world. This most certainly doesn't mean that we must withdraw from the world; on the contrary! We are meant to do the Lord's will in the world and pursue eternal things. Christians must steer clear of physical lust, materialism and an obsession with self-glorification.

> Money makes a good servant, but a bad master.
> FRANCIS BACON

If we have the wrong attitude toward our possessions, we might struggle to accept that these things are temporary.

John's conviction that those who obey God will live forever is based on Jesus' life and promises, and His death and resurrection. We get new courage to do God's will if we believe that this evil world will come to an end and God will be everything to everybody (see 1 Cor. 15:28; Matt. 6:19-21).

A widow struggled to make a meager living for herself and her children on a small patch of land. After many years she finally allowed an oil prospector to drill on her property. He struck oil in abundance and the widow started living in luxury. The hidden wealth was always hers and she hadn't realized it.

This is the situation many Christians find themselves in. They possess incredible untapped spiritual wealth. We don't realize how rich we really are, and have not yet started making use of our spiritual capital because we can't let go of the short-lived pleasures of this world.

God, keep me from becoming attached to this temporary world and so detach myself from Christ and eternity. Amen.

Read Acts 1:1-11

Extreme Boundaries

> You will receive power when the Holy Spirit comes upon you. And you will be My witnesses, telling people about Me everywhere – in Jerusalem, throughout Judea, in Samaria, and to the ends of the earth (Acts 1:8).

Thule was the most distant country known to the Romans. Whenever Jesus sent His disciples out from Jerusalem, through Judea and Samaria and to the ends of the earth, his instructions were: *Ultima Thule* – beyond the borders of the known world. In our Scripture verse today we read how the Gospel was spreading in widening circles. It started with the devout Jews in Jerusalem and afterwards spread to Samaria where the first Gentile would accept the Gospel, and finally it would be preached to the ends of the earth. God's Good News has not reached its final destination as long as there are people who have not heard it. Make sure you are involved in spreading God's message to your family or circle of friends, your school or workplace, and wherever God might send you.

A converted clergyman once testified that the credit for his repentance should go to his elderly neighbor. When the neighbor heard this he was surprised because he couldn't remember ever discussing conversion with the man. "No," said the convert, "you never had much to say, but your life changed me. I could listen to all the sermons of preachers and think of counterarguments for all their statements, but I couldn't argue the way you lived."

> The world is far more ready to receive the Gospel than Christians are to hand it out.
> GEORGE W. PETERS

Master, true to Your command, I will witness for You with my words and deeds every day. Grant me the grace to remain true to my intentions. Amen.

Read Matthew 27:20-26

The Voice of the People

Pilate responded, "Then what should I do with Jesus who is called the Messiah?" They shouted back, "Crucify Him!" (Matt. 27:22).

The voice of the people is dynamic and unreliable. At Jesus' Triumphal Entry into Jerusalem the crowds shouted, "Blessings on the one who comes in the name of the LORD! Praise God in highest heaven!" (Matt. 21:9). Then, barely a week later, the same people shouted, "Crucify Him!" Large crowds are easily swayed. The crowd's anger toward Jesus was roused to the extent that even His disciples were afraid of defending Him. In this case the price paid for the instability of the voice of the masses, was the life of an innocent Man. Pilate's indecision led to the crowd taking over the decision. There are few things as dangerous as giving in to the demands of an emotional crowd.

> I choose goodness ... I will go without a dollar before I take a dishonest one. I will be overlooked before I will boast. I will confess before I will accuse. I choose goodness.
> MAX LUCADO

We have a responsibility toward God not to simply become part of a hysterical crowd. We must listen to what God has to say through His Holy Spirit. A man who had a new radio installed, forgot to connect an aerial. There was no way the sound waves could reach the radio. Consequently the radio didn't work properly until the aerial was connected.

It is only when we are connected to Jesus that we can properly understand Him. Through the help of the Holy Spirit we can pick up God's voice, so that we are not just another voice in a hysterical crowd.

Gracious Jesus, help me to always keep in touch with You so that I will be sensitive to Your will. Amen.

Read Luke 15:17-24

I Have Sinned

His son said to him, "Father, I have sinned against both heaven and you, and I am no longer worthy of being called your son" (Luke 15:21).

Some people need to sink to the lowest level in life before they come to their senses and admit that they have sinned. The youngest son's attitude was due to a false perception of what true freedom meant. We still see this today. People often have to land in the worst possible circumstances before they turn to the One who is able to help them.

> A confessed sin is a new virtue that is added to one's character.
> JAMES S. KNOWLES

Are you perhaps trying to live your life the way you want to? Is satisfying your own selfish desires your ultimate happiness? Don't be misled by the false perceptions of the world. Everything that glitters and sounds cheerful does not necessarily bring happiness. Being able to confess in all sincerity to God: "I have sinned" is the point of departure for a new and happy life.

A seventeen-year-old girl ran away from her parents' farm to the big city. According to the girl, her parents were "heartless and old-fashioned". She lived in the big city, but after two months she phoned her parents, "I would rather wash dishes in your kitchen than see my soul starve here in the city. Please send me money to come home." She is back home now and the most exemplary girl in the neighborhood. She says to her friends, "I have had enough of the world. My parents' kitchen looks just like heaven to me." Confessing your sins and starting over again is an experience that renews life.

Savior, every time I remorsefully and shamefully confess my sins before You I pray that You will give me strength to be strong in times of temptation. Amen.

Read 1 Peter 5:8-11

Stand Guard

Stay alert! Watch out for your great enemy, the devil. He prowls around like a roaring lion, looking for someone to devour (1 Pet. 5:8).

In this Scripture passage all believers are called upon to be vigilant and alert, relying on God's promise of His power and grace. The devil is the enemy you must watch out for. In first Peter 2:11 Peter speaks about "sinful desires" that will destroy your life if you yield to them. The way to guard against these enemies is to remain steadfast in your faith and not allow unfair treatment to make you take matters into your own hands. Keep your eyes on Jesus and resist the enemy; then the Evil One will flee from you.

To illustrate the allure of evil, the Greeks created the story of the Sirens; beautiful women portrayed as seductresses. They sang their charming song to sailors who sailed past their island, and tried to lure them to their own destruction. Ulysses filled the ears of His sailors with wax so that they couldn't hear the seductive sounds. He tied himself to the mast with strong rope. He went to all this trouble in an effort to escape the Sirens as they sailed past the island.

As God's children we must always stay close to the Lord and constantly guard against temptation.

> Little by little, with patience and fortitude, and with the help of God, you will sooner overcome temptations than with your own strength and persistence.
> THOMAS À KEMPIS

Savior, I trust in Your power and strength to help me watch and pray in every temptation against powers that threaten to overcome me. Amen.

Read Luke 2:8-14

Jesus, Savior of All

The Savior — yes, the Messiah, the Lord — has been born today in Bethlehem, the city of David! (Luke 2:11).

The greatest event in the history of humankind had just taken place! The Messiah had been born! The Jews had waited many centuries for this and when it finally happened, the great news was shared with the shepherds. The good news of Jesus Christ is that He comes to everybody; even ordinary people. He comes to anyone who is willing to accept Him. Whoever you are and whatever you do, you can have Jesus in your life. Don't think you need exceptional qualities or qualifications. He came to pay the price for our sin and opened the door to God for us. He offers us new life and a new heart and He brings renewal in all areas of life.

> Christ is a jewel more worth than a thousand worlds, as all know who have Him. Get Him, and get all; miss Him and miss all.
> THOMAS BROOKS

Abraham Lincoln was once ill and couldn't grant anyone an interview; not even the most important and renowned people in the country. Then a penniless lady begged so passionately to see the president that one of the guards went to Lincoln and told him about her. "Show her in," were his words. Even if he wouldn't see the most important and mighty who came to pay him homage, he granted this simple lady an audience; she had come to plead for the life of her soldier husband.

Isn't this what Christ does? Angels and saints will be kept away, but yet He is willing to speak to remorseful sinners when they approach Him in their need, because Jesus is the Savior of all!

Savior, thank You that I can boldly come to You with all my troubles because You have a willing ear and a loving heart. Amen.

Read John 19:1-7

Here Is the Man

> Then Jesus came out wearing the crown of thorns and the purple robe. And Pilate said, "Look here is the man!" (John 19:5).

The soldiers not only obeyed their instructions to lash Jesus, but they also mocked Him and punched Him with their fists. They put a crown of thorns on His head and put a royal purple robe on Him to ridicule His claim to kingship. Then Pilate said to the crowds, "Here is the man!" By that he meant that they could all see the accused before them. The leading priests and temple guards stirred up the crowds to insist that Jesus must die.

What does it do to you when you hear these words and see in your mind's eye your Savior standing before Pilate? Deep in your heart you know it was for all our sakes: The crown of thorns, the lashes, the purple robe. And what is your reaction to this: Crucify Him, or crown Him?

> The Cross is a way of life; the way of love meeting all hate with love, and evil with good; all negatives with positives.
> RUFUS MOSELEY

Seeley points out in his essay *Ecce Homo*, that when Jesus called His disciples to Him, He expected only faith from them, not to endorse some or other dogma. Seeing that they only understood later that He would suffer, die and be raised from the dead, the disciples could have had no understanding of reconciliation and the meaning of the resurrection.

We don't find Jesus examining His followers' confession of sin. All He asked was that they would see Him in His stature as Savior and the world's Redeemer. See only Jesus, your Savior.

God, give me grace to see only Jesus, my Savior before me at all times, and to serve Him to the best of my ability and with all my strength. Amen.

March 7

Read 1 John 3:18-24

Deeds, Not Words

Dear children, let's not merely say that we love each other; let us show the truth by our actions (1 John 3:18).

True love requires deeds and not just nice words, because love can only be proved by deeds. We must never think that we know everything. Because it is when we think we know it all, and that no one can teach us anything, that words become more important to us than deeds. It is essential to know what is written in the Word of God. If however, we don't do what it says, it is of no help to us because then it is no more than just words. Thus, doing Bible study and listening to sermons is of no help in itself. Only when we bring our words and actions in line with God's Word, does it serve a purpose.

> Words are, of course, the most powerful drug used by mankind.
> RUDYARD KIPLING

Many Christians often talk about their great plans, lofty ideals and wonderful dreams. They talk much and discuss their good intentions, but do nothing to save people who are dying in sin. Words without deeds are meaningless. Ask God to help you. Speak less and do more.

Lord, give me the strength to work for You, when and wherever You call me. I want to respond with practical deeds and not with idle words. Amen.

Read Mark 8:34-38

An Essential Requirement

"If any of you wants to be My follower, you must turn from your selfish ways, take up your cross, and follow Me" (Mark 8:34).

Mark originally wrote this letter to the Romans, and they knew what it meant to carry a cross. The Roman authorities executed dangerous non-Roman criminals by crucifixion. The condemned also had to carry the crossbar to the place of execution as proof that he subjected himself to Roman authority.

Jesus used the image of the cross to indicate that He should be followed in total surrender. This is an essential requirement for being Jesus' disciple. Christ has nothing against pleasure and He also doesn't want us to bear unnecessary pain. In this Scripture passage He was referring to the courage it takes to follow Him, even if the future looks bleak and we start experiencing difficulties.

Polycarpus, one of the early church fathers and martyrs, was taken captive at the age of eighty-six because he refused to worship an emperor. While he was being led to the stake, the Romans pleaded with him to renounce his faith in Christ and walk away, a free man. Polycarpus answered, "Eighty-six years have I served Him, and He has never done me wrong. How then, can I blaspheme my King and my Savior!" His last words were a prayer of thanksgiving, "I thank You, Lord my God, that I may be a part of the church and cross of Jesus Christ." Then he died. Carrying his cross was essential for him to show his faith in Jesus Christ.

> Carry your cross.
> Don't let your
> cross carry you.
> PHILIP NERI

Christ, if You call me to carry a cross, in whatever form it may be, help me to do it with dignity and joy, to Your glory. Amen.

Read 2 Timothy 4:1-8

I Hope for Better Things

I have fought the good fight, I have finished the race, and I have remained faithful. And now the prize awaits me — the crown of righteousness, which the Lord, the righteous Judge, will give me on the day of His return. And the prize is not just for me but for all who eagerly look forward to His appearing (2 Tim. 4:7-8).

Paul was aware of the fact that his death was close at hand. He had hope for better things, and a firm trust in God that he would receive the victor's crown from His hand. Paul used various images from the athlete's world. Study these verses in faith and they will enable you to fulfill your calling with courage and conviction and with a holy fearlessness, knowing the best is yet to come! Paul says his victor's crown is a life with God. We are told that we will be rewarded for our faith and our deeds (see Matt. 19:29; 2 Cor. 5:10).

In mythology it is told that Bacchus dearly loved Ariadne. On their wedding day he gave her a crown of polished gold, set with diamonds. When she died, he took her crown and threw it high up in the air in despair. Instead of falling, it rose higher and higher up in the air; the gold glittered in the sunlight and the diamonds shone with a heavenly radiance, until they became stars. Today the constellation of Ariadne adorns the skies. Paul had barely died when his crown descended from heaven. Stephen, the martyr, had not yet shut his eyes in death when he already saw the glory of a martyr's crown in Christ's hands. For those who believe in Him and follow Him faithfully, the best is yet to come, "Remain faithful even when facing death, I will give you the crown of life" (Rev. 2:10).

> A true reward is not given or received by people; it is the holy joy of being rewarded by Christ.
> THOMAS À KEMPIS

God, thank You for the wonderful and gracious privilege Your children have of a winner's crown: A life with God. Amen.

Read 2 Corinthians 5:16-21

The Way Things Were

This means that anyone who belongs to Christ has become a new person. The old life is gone; a new life has begun! (2 Cor. 5:17).

When you accept Christ as your Savior and Redeemer, things change because a radical change has taken place in your life. Through Jesus Christ, God brings us back to Him again and reconciles us with Him, by forgiving all our sins and declaring that we have been justified. Everything in our lives changes drastically. If we believe in Christ, we aren't enemies or strangers of God any longer. Because we are reconciled with Him, we enjoy the privilege of encouraging others to believe in Him as well. We want others also undergo this change and for things to never be the same again for them. The relationship between Creator and creation is restored and peace has come again; all this because we were no longer satisfied with the way things were. We live and do differently because Christ entered our lives.

> Conversion is but the first step in the divine life. As long as we live we should more and more be turning from all that is evil and to all that is good.
> — Tyron Edwards

"He has made me new again!" This is what conversion actually means. It is like a beautiful stained-glass window in an elegant church building that has been shattered and broken into pieces. An experienced stained-glass artist comes to pick up all the fragments and takes them away. Then returns with a brand-new window he made by putting all the pieces of the old one together again. Likewise, the Master Artist takes the fragments of our old sinful life and repairs it, turning it into something new and beautiful. God's great task here on earth is fixing broken things.

Savior, thank You for changing me and the way my life was to something far better. Amen.

Read Matthew 26:47-54

Even You, Brutus?

The traitor, Judas, had given them a prearranged signal: "You will know which one to arrest when I greet Him with a kiss" (Matt. 26:48).

Et tu, Brute? Julius Caesar spoke these words when he realized he had been betrayed by his beloved friend, Brutus. This situation can also be applied to Judas's betrayal of Christ. Judas told the temple guards to arrest the man he would greet. It was not an arrest by Roman soldiers and had nothing to do with Roman laws. It was an arrest by spiritual leaders. If Judas at least had the courage to openly point to Jesus, it would have been more acceptable, but to use an intimate greeting as a sign, gives away Judas's inner decay. Jesus could have said to Judas, and rightly so, *"Et tu, Judas? Even you, Judas?"* What about you and me when it comes to confessing His name?

> The devil tempts that he may ruin and destroy; God tests that He may crown.
> ST. AMBROSE

It is said that when Leonardo da Vinci painted *The Last Supper*, he was looking for a model for Jesus. He heard a handsome young man sing in a church choir in a cathedral in London and used him as a model. But he battled to find a model for Judas. He searched for years until he found a drunken hobo lying in a sewage gully next to a pavement. He used this man as a model for Judas. When he saw something familiar about the man's distorted features, he discovered to his dismay that it was the same man he had used years before as a model for Christ. Judas personifies all people with great potential for good, and yet, in spite of this, they allow the capacity for evil to take over. We all have this dual personality; therefore we should watch and pray that we will never betray Jesus as Judas did.

God, keep me from betraying my Savior. Amen.

Read Acts 28:1-10

Pray and Work

As it happened, Publius's father was ill with fever and dysentery. Paul went in and prayed for him, and laying his hands on him, he healed him (Acts 28:8).

Paul was on his way to Rome to defend his faith, and God promised him that he would arrive in Rome safely. Neither shipwreck nor snakebite would thwart God's plan. Paul still had work to do and as long as he prayed, he found the strength to do his God-given task and to perform miracles. Our lives are in God's hands and as long as we pray and do our duty, we can trust Him. Just praying and neglecting our duties is as wrong as just working and never asking God for His support and strength.

The great preacher, Dwight L. Moody, was sailing on his way to America when a fire started on deck. In those days people still had to stand on deck in long rows and hand pails of water from one to the other to extinguish a fire. One person said to Moody, "Shouldn't we rather go down on our knees and have a prayer meeting?" Moody's answer was short and sweet, "We'll pray while passing the water buckets." Prayer and the passing on of water buckets are equally important to put out a fire on board a ship.

> To really pray is to stand to attention before the King and be ready to receive orders from Him.
> — DONALD COGGAN

Holy Spirit, guide me to maintain a healthy balance between prayer and the task assigned to me. Amen.

Glory to God

You are my God, and I will praise You! You are my God, and I will exalt You! Give thanks to the LORD, for He is good! His faithful love endures forever (Ps. 118:28-29).

One of the main themes of the book of Psalms is praise to God as the Creator and Maintainer of creation. To praise Him means noticing His greatness of character and deeds, appreciating this greatness and expressing our appreciation. This is what we call praise.

Three things become clear from this prayer of confession: The Lord is on my side, therefore I need not be afraid; I will not die but live to proclaim the Lord's act of salvation; the Lord disciplines me for my own good. First the psalm confesses God's presence (see vv. 6-7), then salvation (see v. 14) and, in conclusion, rejoices, "You are my God!" This is indeed worth singing songs of praise to God!

Edmond Rostand's play titled *Chantecler*, is about a rooster that secretly believed the sun rose because he crowed. His cynical critics laughed in his face. One morning, dejected and disappointed, he forgot to crow. His critics were quick to point out that the sun rose in spite of the fact that he didn't crow. Courageously, Chantecler answered, "It might be completely true that the sun doesn't rise because of my scratchy voice, but at least it is something I can do, and no one can take the joy of doing it away from me. If I cannot make the sun rise, I have at least raised my voice to greet its arrival joyfully." This is a philosophy that suits Christians well.

> You don't have to be afraid of praising God too much; unlike humans He never gets a big head.
> PAUL DIBBLE

Praiseworthy God, thank You that I may glorify and praise You. May I never forget one of Your kind actions and always remember to thank and praise You for them. Amen.

Read John 14:1-14

The Way, the Truth and the Life

Jesus told him, "I am the way, the truth, and the life. No one can come to the Father except through Me" (John 14:6).

In today's Scripture passage Jesus tells us that He is the only way to the Father's heart. Some people find that the road is too narrow, but that isn't true. The whole world can walk on it if only the world would accept the road.

We must hold on to the fact of salvation that there is a road to the Father. It is the road that Jesus bridged with the cross and because of that, heaven and earth are linked. Jesus says that He is the Way and the Truth and the Life: As the Way, He is our only spiritual path to the Father; as the Truth He is the only one that stands firm as the fulfillment of all God's promises, and as the Life He incorporates us in His godly life so that we may live with Him in the present, and forever. Jesus is not only a signpost. He is the road.

> The way to Jesus is over an old-fashioned hill called Calvary.
> — Gypsy Smith

The old city of Troy had only one entrance. No matter from which direction the traveler approached the city, he couldn't enter legitimately except through one specific entrance.

In the same way, there is only one entrance that leads us into the presence of God: The living Christ.

Eternal God, I praise and thank You for giving us a road to Your Father's heart. Your truth is eternal and unchangeable. You give Me salvation and fulfillment. Amen.

Read Job 1:1-12

In Good Faith

There once was a man named Job who lived in the land of Uz. He was blameless — a man of complete integrity. He feared God and stayed away from evil (Job 1:1).

Job was a man of good reputation. He is called a blameless and sincere man because He feared the Lord, worshiped Him, and obeyed and loved Him. He was also a good man because he stayed away from everything bad. He didn't allow sin into his life and he made sure that he resisted every temptation. To be a truly good person doesn't mean only obeying God's commandments. It also includes all the above-mentioned things. We see in the book of Job how a good man suffered, and this while there didn't even seem to be a good reason for it. Unfortunately our broken world is like this. But the story of Job doesn't end in despair. We see in his life that faith in God was still justified, even when circumstances appeared hopeless. A good reputation that is founded on prosperity or rewards is superficial and empty. True integrity must be built on the certainty that God's purpose with our lives will be achieved.

> Cease from an excessive desire of knowing, for you will find much distraction and delusion in it.
> THOMAS À KEMPIS

Near the Rialto Bridge in Venice is a church. Its front gable looks out over the trade center of the city. An inscription in the gable reads: "Round about this church may the merchant be equitable, the weights just, and may no fraudulent contract be negotiated." Above the words, a simple cross is chiseled into the gable, with the words: "May Your cross O Christ, reflect the true integrity of this place."

If we take these things into account, can it be said of us that we are persons of integrity?

Holy Spirit, stand by me to live a life of integrity and goodness before God to His greater honor and glory. Amen.

Read 1 Corinthians 13:1-13

Let Jealousy Be Absent

Love is patient and kind. Love is not jealous or boastful or proud (1 Cor. 13:4).

The only effective remedy for envy and jealousy is true love. The Corinthians were envious of people with special gifts they did not have. In chapter 13 Paul describes what true love, the greatest gift, really means. Love is more important than all the other spiritual gifts in the church. Not even strong faith or the ability to perform miracles is meaningful if it is not accompanied by love. Love is often confused with lust in our modern society. The love that God radiates, reaches other people, whereas lust is turned inwards and concentrates only on self-satisfaction and envy.

> In jealousy there is more self-love than love.
> FRANÇOIS DE LA ROCHEFOUCAULD

Henri-Frederic Amiel writes in his journal, "Jealousy is a terrible thing. It resembles love, only it is precisely love's contrary. Instead of wishing for the welfare of the object loved, it desires the dependence of that object upon itself, and its own triumph. Love is the forgetfulness of self; jealousy is the most passionate form of egotism, the glorification of a despotic, exacting, and vain ego, which can neither forget nor subordinate itself."

Jesus Christ, infuse me with Your love so that jealousy and envy will be banned from my life. Amen.

Read Philippians 3:12-21

Press On

I press on to reach the end of the race and receive the heavenly prize for which God, through Christ Jesus, is calling us (Phil. 3:14).

After Paul's dramatic conversion, his only goal in life was to know Christ, to follow Him and do everything He called him for. He strained every nerve and sinew to the utmost to achieve this goal. Every believer should have this attitude.

Nothing should make you give up your intention to know Christ and do His will. You must have the dedication of an athlete and renounce everything that can take your mind off Christ; even things that are not necessarily wrong in themselves, but which prevent you from doing your very best. If anything distracts you so that you can't be an effective Christian, let it go. Because Christ made you His child, you must exert yourself to be completely His.

A hunter went out one day to hunt something. For hours he tracked a beautiful eland bull. Then he saw the tracks of a jackal and left the antelope to go after the jackal. He reached a place where he saw a hare's tracks crossing the jackal's, and he decided to track the hare. At dusk he came across the tracks of a mouse and he started following the mouse's tracks. In the end he returned home empty-handed.

> Enthusiasm is the key not only to the achievement of great things but to the accomplishment of anything that is worthwhile.
> SAMUEL GOLDWYN

Without purposeful effort you achieve little in life – especially on a spiritual level.

Lord, give me the strength to exert myself so that I will receive the heavenly prize and be Your follower and servant to the very end. Amen.

Read Matthew 26:47-56

High Stakes

Judas had given them a prearranged signal: "You will know which one to arrest when I greet Him with a kiss" (Matt. 26:48).

Judas decided to take a gamble. And as with any gambler, the winnings far outweigh the cost. In this case the gamble cost Christ His life and also the life of the gambler, Judas. The stakes were high and in the end too high for Judas as he paid with his life.

> The devil invented gambling.
> AUGUSTINE OF HIPPO

William Hogarth's well-known painting depicts a group of men around a gambling table, oblivious of all sound and feeling, caught up in how the dice falls. Some are elated by their winnings, others in the depths of despair because of their losses. The house is burning and the flames are already coming through the roof. The night watchman bursts into the room and warns the gamblers to run for their lives. But they are so engrossed in the game that they do not want to hear or understand, and they perish together with the gambling house. To gamble with life destroys both body and soul.

Savior, strengthen me to stay faithful to You, whatever the price. Amen.

Love Conquers All

Love never gives up, never loses faith, is always hopeful, and endures through every circumstance. Prophecy and speaking in unknown languages and special knowledge will become useless. But love will last forever! (1 Cor. 13:7-8).

God gives us spiritual gifts so that we can encourage, serve and strengthen one another. Thus, spiritual gifts are meant for His church. When the hereafter dawns, we will be made perfect and all of us will be in God's perfect presence. Then spiritual gifts will not exist anymore, because we will need nothing but love. Love is just as immortal as God Himself, because God is love (1 John 4:8). There is no problem that love cannot solve; no tangle that it cannot unravel; no chasm or misunderstanding it cannot bridge. Love always conquers everything, because God always triumphs.

> I have decided to stick with love. Hate is too great a burden to bear.
> MARTIN LUTHER KING JR.

In the magazine *Christian Endeavor World,* Amos Wells wrote an article about a modern bridge built across a wide river. The construction started from both sides and would meet perfectly in the middle. But for some reason, the two parts did not fit perfectly into each other on the last day. There was a two-inch gap and it couldn't be bridged in any way. A telegram was sent to the designer of the bridge and everybody waited for his reply. His answer was short and sweet: "Wait until tomorrow afternoon!" The next day the amazed spectators watched as the warm rays from the sun caused the metal to expand, and section by section it locked together into a solid whole. Love also triumphs at all times, no matter how improbable it might seem to us.

Jesus, how great You are that Your love can overcome everything. I praise You for this. Amen.

Read John 7:32-37

The Water of Life

On the last day, the climax of the festival, Jesus stood and shouted to the crowds, "Anyone who is thirsty may come to Me!" (John 7:37).

Jesus uses the words "living water" in John 4:10 to refer to eternal life. Here it refers to the Holy Spirit. These two things go together, because if you have eternal life, the Holy Spirit works in you. Where the Holy Spirit's presence is accepted, He brings about eternal life. In John 14:16 Jesus teaches us more about the Holy Spirit. On the day of Pentecost He came down on Jesus' followers (see Acts 2) and since then He is at work in all who believe that Jesus is the Savior. The Spirit always existed, but the specific acceptance of the Spirit by all believers only became a reality after Jesus had finished His work on earth.

In Cape Cod on the American coast, there is a strange fountain. It is in a hollow. The hollow is dry except during high tide. Then fresh, sweet, pure drinking water suddenly bubbles up from the bottom. In times of drought many dams and fountains in the region are dry, but this fountain never dries up. It is called the Moon fountain and is as reliable as the tides of the sea.

> Our lives become meaningful and worthwhile when the Holy Spirit takes over.
> STEPHAN O'NEILL

In the same way the Holy Spirit brings life to the barren and dry lives of sinful people. He is indeed "the Water of Life".

Holy Spirit, guide me so that I always keep in touch with You so that my life does not dry out and wither, but that I will live to Your glory. Amen.

Read Psalm 139:1-12

To You Personally

O LORD, You have examined my heart and know everything about me. You know when I sit down or stand up. You know my thoughts even when I'm far away (Ps. 139:1-2).

This psalm speaks personally to every human being, and says that each of us must join the psalmist in singing a song of praise to the Lord because He knows us so well. While we humbly place ourselves before His penetrating eyes we must pray: "Lead me along the path of everlasting life" (v. 24).

The psalmist was most probably an accused in the temple, awaiting the decision of the priest on his guilt or innocence. He argued his case and, like Job, thought about his fate. He came to the conclusion that God is extremely just and thus he sang Him a song of praise. He confessed with gratitude that God was wherever he went and knew everything about him, because God created him. For this reason, God's actions and words toward him were intimate and personal.

> He who offers God a second place, offers Him no place.
> JOHN RUSKIN

What would you make of a container of the purest gold, created by a master, but filled with mud and soot? Would you not say that the contents do not go with the beauty of the bowl and that it shouldn't contain something like that? This is why God speaks to each of us personally. We are inclined to take the beautifully molded container of our lives and fill it with all kinds of bad things. It is when God speaks to us personally, through His Spirit, that we become aware that we have strayed. May God never speak to us in vain.

Father God, let me become quiet before You every day, that I may hear Your personal message for me, and become aware of Your purpose with my life. Amen.

Read John 11:1-11

He Is Sick

This is the Mary who later poured the expensive perfume on the Lord's feet and wiped them with her hair. Her brother, Lazarus, was sick (John 11:2).

Here Christ reveals His life-giving power. Bethany was situated about three kilometers east of Jerusalem on the way to Jericho. Martha and Mary turned to Jesus when their brother became ill. They believed He could help them because they had seen Him perform miracles. The sisters let Jesus know that Lazarus was seriously ill. Jesus did not rush to get to them because He saw an opportunity in the things that were happening: He would make the omnipotence and glory of God known and visible. It was about the glory of the Father and the Son. Lazarus being brought to life again prepares us for Jesus' own resurrection. Like the two sisters, we also often have to wait for the Lord. He has His own schedule to fulfill His Father's plan. To wait means to temper our faith.

> Our Lord has written the promise of resurrection, not in books alone, but in every leaf in springtime.
> MARTIN LUTHER

When a church bell is cast, two molds are prepared: an inside and outside one. They are molded in this way to create the perfect shape between the two of them for the bell. Then the metal is poured in and when it has cooled down, the moulds are broken. But the bell itself remains intact and will soon toll joyful sounds. This is a good image of us arising from sickness and death.

Risen Savior, through Your omnipotence and glory, You give Your children life. I praise Your great name. Amen.

Read 2 Timothy 1:1-11

A Mentor

I am writing to Timothy, my dear son. May God the Father and Christ Jesus our Lord give you grace, mercy, and peace (2 Tim. 1:2).

In this letter that Paul wrote to his spiritual *alumnus* – his former student – he sounded somewhat depressed. The persecution of Christians had become more brutal, and increased in severity under Emperor Nero. Paul was now in an isolated cell in Rome. Not just under house arrest like he was previously. While Paul was awaiting his execution, he wrote his last letter to Timothy to call on him to continue his ministry fearlessly: to fan the flames of the spiritual gift God gave him (see 1:6-7); never to be ashamed of the Gospel or of Paul (see 1:8-18) and to act with authority (see 2:1-3). As mentor, he also gave his last instructions for the ministry: Timothy had to stop people from arguing about words; he must make himself available to God; avoid unholy and foolish talk and the things that threaten a young person's life; he should not become involved in questions that were meant to catch him out. These are wise words of a father to his beloved "child", pupil and student.

> Being a mentor means a work relationship, and to be a facilitator of another's development and growth.
> TED WARD

A mentor is someone who passes truths on to his student. In this rushed century we are inclined to forget this. We need a mentor's help with our reading, thinking and our work. We need someone to help us to see the bigger picture. Someone, who through his experience will pass knowledge and wisdom on to his learners in a way they will understand. Like Jesus taught His disciples.

Lord, thank You for every person in my life who contributes to my spiritual enrichment and growth. Amen.

Read Psalm 131:1-3

A Nurturing Mother

Instead, I have calmed and quieted myself, like a weaned child who no longer cries for its mother's milk (Ps. 131:2).

In this comforting psalm, the psalmist uses the image of a mother and her child to express his relationship with the Lord. The peace of mind the Lord granted him in the past is also his security for the future. His greatest wish is humble trust in God. This can only be achieved by quiet acceptance and not faithless restlessness. He uses the image of a weaned child with his mother. It tells us that God is our nurturing mother (see Isa. 66:7-13). Like a child waits on its mother, Israel – and we – must wait on the Lord.

In the *Christian Herald* the story is told of a woman who was deserted by her husband. In her husband's absence, she had to work her fingers to the bone for seven months to provide for her children and herself. Then she had to go to hospital as her next child was due. Because she didn't have the money to pay the hospital, she sold some of her blood for a blood transfusion another patient needed. She gave birth to her baby without any problems and saved a stranger's life with her blood. "I would have sold more of my blood and would even have given my life if it could put an end to my children's suffering," she said. This reflects Christ's love and this is why Isaiah says, "I will comfort you ... as a mother comforts her child" (Isa. 66:13).

> The God to whom little children say their prayers has a face very much like their mother's.
> — JAMES M. BARRIE

I will rejoice all the time in the love of God through my Savior, who cares for me like a mother and loves me dearly. Amen.

Read Mark 8:1-13

A Sign from Heaven

When He [Jesus] heard this, He sighed deeply in His Spirit and said, "Why do these people keep demanding a miraculous sign? I tell you the truth, I will not give this generation any such sign" (Mark 8:12).

The Pharisees tried to put Jesus' miracles down to luck, chance or evil powers. That is why they wanted to see "a miraculous sign from heaven" which would be proof that Jesus' acts and that which He claimed were genuine, because it would be something that could come from God only. Jesus refused because He knew they wouldn't even be convinced by a sign from heaven. They had already made up their minds not to believe in Him.

A person's heart can become so hard that you cannot even be convinced by facts and evidence from heaven. A sign is actually something that happens as proof of something someone said. The sign must come from heaven to prove that Jesus comes from God.

The Pharisees wanted a sign as an instant solution to their problem, instead of having childlike faith in Jesus' miraculous power. Don't we often do the same?

God is able to perform miracles because everything is possible for Him. Sometimes that which looks like a miracle to us is not a miracle to God. To Him it is simply the implementation of the laws He originally laid down and still maintains.

> I believe in Christianity as I believe that the sun has risen – not only because I see it, but because by it, I see everything else.
> — C. S. Lewis

Lord, You want to give Your children only the best and that is why I trust You unconditionally, because I know that everything is possible to You. Amen.

Read Matthew 27:3-10

A Crime Against Oneself

Then Judas threw the silver coins down in the Temple and went out and hanged himself (Matt. 27:5).

Jesus' traitor would have undone his treachery, but the leaders refused to stop the trial.

Perhaps Judas betrayed Jesus in the first place in an effort to force Him into leading a revolt against Rome. Obviously it didn't work. Whatever his motivation, Judas changed his mind, but too late. It often happens that, at a later stage, we want to undo things we started, but can't. That is why it is so much better to first think of the possible consequences of an action before we do it. Then we won't have to blame ourselves later. In Judas's case it led to suicide.

> Despair is the absolute extreme of self-love. It is reached when a person deliberately turns his back on all help from anyone else in order to taste the rotten luxury of knowing himself to be lost.
>
> THOMAS MERTON

Death is not something one desires. It is not a blessing, but God's curse on sin. Sometimes we long for it in our ignorance. There are people in the world who, overwhelmed by troubles and feelings of guilt, live without God and without hope. Prematurely and violently they then put an end to their miserable lives. But no one is as lost and unhappy as the person who commits suicide. It was the case with Judas because he betrayed Love. For this reason, he also committed a crime against himself in the end.

Master, stand by me so that I will be true to Your principles and hold on to You to the very end. Amen.

Read Psalm 27:1-3; 7-14

Our Father God

Even if my father and mother abandon me, the LORD will hold me close (Ps. 27:10).

In this psalm, the psalmist talks about his unconditional faith in God. It helps him to overcome his fear and loneliness. First he mentions that his trust in the Lord will protect him while he takes shelter in the temple that he loves. Then he twice approaches the Lord for help and every time concludes his cry for help with a pronouncement of trust in God. The song originates from the psalmist's faith in the Lord and therefore he confidently approaches Him with his troubles. We often turn to God when we have a problem. David sought the Lord's help every day. It is shortsighted to only call on God when we are already in trouble. Many of our problems could have been prevented if we put our trust in God's guidance. Even in the absence of earthly parents, God took the place of David's parents and cared for him and lovingly protected him.

> Religion is the first thing and the last thing, and until a man has found God, and been found by God, he begins at no beginning and works to no end.
> H. G. WELLS

We experience problems along the path of life to make us aware of God's parental love and protection. A golfing enthusiast spoke of a very difficult course where golfers must hit the ball across a ditch onto the green. "Why don't they just fill up the ditch?" a friend asked. An elderly lady watched a tennis match and saw how often the ball was hit into the net. "Why don't they just take the net away?" she wanted to know. God uses obstructions and obstacles for us to discover His loving parenthood. If a day comes that all our problems disappear, victory would be rather pointless. Let us praise God for problems and overcome them with joy.

Great God, thank You that You are always there to love me. Amen.

Read Hebrews 1:1-9

In Person

Long ago God spoke many times and in many ways to our ancestors through the prophets. And now in these final days, He has spoken to us through His Son. God promised everything to the Son as an inheritance, and through the Son He created the universe (Heb. 1:1-2).

The writer of the letter to the Hebrews says that in the past God made use of mediators, but now there was intimate communication with God Himself through Jesus Christ. The writer sent this letter, first of all to remind the Hebrews of everything Christ did for them and what He was busy doing at the time.

Secondly, he wrote to tell the Hebrew people how their daily relationship with the Lord should be a testimony to the fact that they must use the path Christ opened for them to the Father. What is new is not that God speaks, but that He is present through His Son. Where He only spoke to people in early times, He now reveals Himself in person.

On occasion, Dr. William Spurgeon of Wales was presenting lectures in one of the cities in Scotland. After the proceedings, a refined elderly gentleman approached him and said, "Dr. Spurgeon, I am pleased to meet you. I am Henry Drummond's father." Spurgeon replied, "Oh, but then I already know you, because I know your son very well!"

> If Jesus Christ is not true God, how could He help us? If He is not true Man, how could He help us?
> DIETRICH BONHOEFFER

How wonderful it is that if we know Jesus Christ well, we also get to know the Father through Him!

Jesus Christ, I praise You that, through You, I get to know the Father better in all His love and grace. Amen.

March 29

Read James 4:2-7

Humble Dependence

He gives us even more grace to stand against such evil desires. As the Scriptures say, "God opposes the proud, but favors the humble" (James 4:6).

James is encouraging people to put the wisdom from God into practice. One of the most important characteristics of this wisdom is humility, and it is found in submitting yourself to God's will. Pride is a blatant declaration that it is below our dignity to submit to God. Only when we acknowledge our own insignificance before God, are we ready to receive God's grace. As long as we rely on our own strength, we think that we can do without God. We must resist Satan and not only try to get away from him. The Lord Jesus has already defeated Satan and in humble dependence on Him we needn't fear Satan any longer. This does not mean that we dare pride ourselves on our own strength, but that we humbly rely on God's strength.

> Pride is the cold mountain peak; humility is the quiet valley.
> ANNE AUSTIN

At an important dinner, hosted by a well-known millionaire who did a lot for social welfare, the conversation turned to prayer. The millionaire claimed that he didn't need prayer and didn't believe in it. He had everything he could ever wish for, and therefore there was no need for him to ask favors; doing this was below him. The rector of a university commented, "There is something you can pray for." "And what might that be?" the rich man asked. The answer was, "You can pray for humility!" No matter how rich we might be, we will only be further enriched by a humble spirit that thanks God for all His grace and goodness.

Jesus Christ, You washed Your disciples' feet; help me to also live in humble thankfulness to You. Amen.

Read Luke 23:13-25

Take a Stand

They kept shouting, "Crucify Him! Crucify Him!" (Luke 23:21).

Pilate wanted to set Jesus free, but the crowds shouted at the top of their voices that He had to be crucified. Pilate wasn't prepared to put his position at risk by allowing a rebellion to develop. It is very difficult to take a stand for what is right if there is a lot at stake. It is easier to see our opponents merely as problems that need to be solved, and not as people who should be treated with respect. If Pilate had been a courageous man, he would have set Jesus free. We must never underestimate the power of group pressure. Risking the rejection of the community is not necessarily the way to go when you have to pass judgment on a person. And don't be surprised if you become an outcast for putting your Christianity into practice. If they could do it to Jesus, why not to you?

> Christians are not men and women who are hoping for salvation, but those who have experienced it.
> M. LLOYD-JONES

At the beginning of the Reformation, Martin van Basel discovered the truth, but he was afraid to proclaim it publically. He wrote on parchment: "O great and gracious Christ, I know that I can be saved only by Your blood; I know Your suffering and love for me. I love You dearly!" Then he hid the parchment under a stone in his cell. It was discovered there a hundred years later. At about the same time he wrote it, Martin Luther discovered the truth in Jesus. He said, "My Lord confessed me in front of the people, I will not shy away from confessing Him before kings." And as well-known as Martin Luther is, so unknown was Martin van Basel.

Lord, guide me to follow Your example and practice my Christianity. Amen.

April

He was oppressed and treated harshly, yet He never said a word. He was led as a lamb to the slaughter. And as a sheep is silent before the shearers, He did not open His mouth.

ISAIAH 53:7

There is perhaps not a phrase in the Bible that is so full of secret truth as is "The blood of Jesus."

CORRIE TEN BOOM

Dear Man of Sorrows,
as we follow You on Your journey to the Cross,
we are overcome by awe and humility
at the unfathomable love You have for us.
Gethsemane, Gabbatha, Golgotha — Your love is revealed all over.
We confess in humility that we have nothing to offer
to pay for a love so great;
no gift or equivalent worthy of Your love.
You were willing to be crucified so that the token of this deed
would force people through all centuries
to kneel at the foot of the cross
and be broken at the realization of Your love.
May this Easter time bring love in our hearts
that reaches deeper than sentiment,
a love that seeks to know Your will and do it.
Grant that the remembrance of Your cross will inspire us anew
to accept the challenge of sin,
and to triumph in Your name.
In the name of our crucified Savior.
Amen.

Read Matthew 6:8-15

Free and Fair Forgiveness

"If you forgive those who sin against you, your heavenly Father will forgive you. But if you refuse to forgive others, your Father will not forgive your sins" (Matt. 6:14-15).

Christ is warning about forgiveness tends to take us by surprise. The forgiveness we receive from God will be proportionate to our forgiveness of others. If we refuse to forgive others, God will refuse to forgive us. Why? Because if we are not prepared to forgive others, we are implying that we don't see ourselves as sinners who need God's forgiveness.

> He that cannot forgive others breaks the bridge over which he must pass himself; for every man has need to be forgiven.
> THOMAS FULLER

God's forgiveness of our sins is not the direct result of our forgiveness of others. Nevertheless, it rests on the principle that we must know the meaning of forgiveness (see Eph. 4:32). How quick would you be to forgive if your own forgiveness is proportionate to the measure that you forgive others? It is easy to ask God's forgiveness, but difficult to forgive others. Every time you ask Him to forgive you, you must ask yourself, "Have I forgiven those who hurt or wronged me?"

A man who knew the great preacher Henry Ward Beecher, tells the story of someone who hated Beecher so much that he said he wouldn't even cross the road to hear him preach. This man later became Beecher's best friend and his reason for his change of heart was simple, "Every time someone wronged Beecher, he would not rest before he had done some good to that person."

Father, forgive my sins and help me to forgive those who hurt me, like You forgive those who sin against You. Amen.

Read Mark 8:34-9:1

Fair Exchange

"Is anything worth more than your soul?" (Mark 8:37).

Many people chase after joy and pleasure all their lives. According to Christ this is not a fair exchange for your soul. Everything we possess or enjoy on earth is relative and temporary. If we work hard just to gain superficial things, we run the risk of discovering in the final analysis that our lives are empty and meaningless.

Follow Jesus and you will discover what it means to live life to the full. This is a fair exchange for all the superficial pleasures and short-lived possessions.

A story is told of a little boy whose hand got stuck in a candy jar. He ran to his father for help and quickly his father discovered that his hand was tightly clenched into a fist inside the jar. "Open up your hand, Son," his father said, "and then your hand will slip out easily." Sobbing, the child complained, "But Daddy, if I open my hand I will have to let go of the candy." The candy was clenched in his fist and he didn't want to let go.

> We can offer up much in the large, but to make sacrifices in the little things is what we are seldom equal to.
> — JOHANN WOLFGANG VON GOETHE

Many people have the same problem. They will have to let the attractive, yet meaningless things in life go, before their heavenly Father can do anything for them. Let go of the candy this world offers you and you will find that the world cannot separate you from God anymore. This is always a fair exchange.

Christ, strengthen me so that I will accept the sacrifices I have to make to get to know You better as a fair exchange. Amen.

Read Mark 5:1-13

Good and Evil

When Jesus climbed out of the boat, a man possessed by an evil spirit came out from a cemetery to meet Him (Mark 5:2).

In the region of the Gerasenes lived Gentiles who were pig farmers. Jesus was reaching out to the Gentiles. The demon-possessed man was so dangerous that he had to live outside the city among the tombs. He was wild and so uncontrollable and strong that he couldn't be tied up – until Jesus tamed him with His words. The evil spirit inside the man didn't want to be tortured, because that meant he would live in perdition forever. The demon-possessed man said his name was Legion, which meant "many". It was obvious that there were many evil spirits in this poor man. But Jesus' omnipotence was demonstrated when He cast the evil spirits from the man and sent them into a nearby herd of pigs. The pigs plunged into the sea where they drowned and the evil spirits were destroyed. This extraordinary man became a powerful witness for Jesus after He had set him free.

> Of two evils choose neither.
> CHARLES H. SPURGEON

Replicas of George Grey Barnard's impressive sculpture can be seen in art museums all over the world. The sculpture portrays two strongmen locked in a life-and-death struggle. The following words of Victor Hugo are carved on the base: "I feel two natures struggling within me." It is an image of our lives where good and evil constantly do battle. This is what Paul is talking about in Romans 7:21, "When I want to do what is right, I inevitably do what is wrong." Who will set us free from our misery? Only Jesus Christ!

Jesus, keep me close to You so that I can be strong in the battle against evil. Amen.

Read Matthew 24:36-51

No Fixed Date

"However, no one knows the day or the hour when these things will happen, not even the angels in heaven or the Son Himself. Only the Father knows" (Matt. 24:36).

It is good that we don't know exactly when Christ will come again. Not knowing forces us to be ready at all times. We live every day of our lives in anticipation, expecting Him back any moment.

> To be ever looking for the Lord's appearing is one of the best helps to a close walk with God.
> J.C. Ryle

If we knew Christ's second coming wouldn't be in our lifetime, the mission of spreading the Gospel might lose its urgency. The new earth is our destination, but now we still have to fulfill our mission here on earth. That is why we must carry on working and that is the reason why Christ didn't give us a fixed date for His second coming.

The Jacobeans of Scotland always greeted each other with the words, "Prince Charles will return!" Eventually Prince Charles did return, but just to bring Scotland misery, defeat, disaster and suffering. Every time we partake in Communion, the followers of the living Christ say, "Until He comes again!" And when He comes again, He will not bring misery and suffering, like Prince Charles, but He will heal all wounds, comfort all hearts, set all prisoners free from sin and dry all tears from our eyes. This is a day we can look forward to and long for, even if we don't know when that day will come.

Dearest Father, I look forward to Jesus' second coming in great anticipation. Help me to do my duty to the best of my ability up until then. Amen.

Read Matthew 2:1-9

Open the Door of Your Heart

Then Herod called for a private meeting with the wise men, and he learned from them the time when the star first appeared (Matt. 2:7).

Herod was afraid that the newborn King would take his throne from him. He didn't understand the meaning of the arrival of the Messiah at all. Jesus didn't want Herod's throne. He wanted to be King of Herod's life and give him eternal life. Because of Herod's mistaken perceptions, he sent for the wise men to question them in secret about the place Jesus was born so that he could go and take His life.

To this day people are afraid that Jesus wants to deprive them of things, while all He wants to do is give them freedom, peace and joy.

William Holman Hunt's famous painting *The Light of the World* is the artist's impression of Christ's approach to the human soul. Christ stands outside a locked door, the hinges rusted because they have fallen into disuse, the door almost overgrown with climbing plants. Darkness is falling and He has a lantern in His hand, while He knocks to be let in. After completing the painting, Hunt showed it to a friend. After studying it in silence for a long while, the friend said it was beautiful, but something was wrong: there was no handle on the door. "That's not a mistake," the artist answered. "The doorknob can only be opened for Christ from the inside."

> It is in silence that God is known, and through mysteries that He declares Himself.
> ROBERT H. BENSON

In this way, each and every one of us must surrender to Christ personally.

Savior, only You give Your children the gifts of grace, peace, and joy. But each and everyone must surrender to You personally. Please guide me in this. Amen.

Read John 19:28-33

He Died for You

When Jesus had tasted it [the sour wine], He said, "It is finished!" Then He bowed His head and released His spirit (John 19:30).

Jesus was the all-sufficient and final offer for the sins of man. In this context the word "finished" means the same as "paid in full". Jesus came to fulfill God's salvation work, to finish it (John 4:34; 14:4). He paid the full price for our sins. Thus, His death, seen from a Christian perspective, put an end to the Old Testament sacrifice system, because He made atonement for all our sins.

Through Jesus' death we can approach God. We are free from the sin that kept us from Him before Christ's death.

A deaf-mute boy wrote on his slate for his teacher to see: "I cannot understand how Jesus alone could die for all people." The teacher thought for a moment, went outside and came back, her apron filled with dead leaves. Then she took the diamond ring from her finger and weighed it up against the leaves. The boy's face brightened up and then he wrote on his slate: "Now I see it. Jesus is a diamond, much more precious than all the dead leaves in the world. That is why He could pay the price for all our sins." Can you say in all sincerity, "He did it for me?"

> Man's strongest instinct is to self-preservation; grace's highest call is to self-sacrifice.
> PAUL FROST

Triune God, only when I remember what Jesus did for me, can I live and work like a saved child. Thank You that You make it possible for me through Jesus. Amen.

April 6

Read Psalm 84:1-13

In the Presence of God

I long, yes, I faint with longing to enter the courts of the LORD. With my whole being, body and soul, I will shout joyfully to the living God (Ps. 84:2).

The psalmist's greatest longing is to be near God. He wants to get away from the rush of life and meet God in solitude.

The believer experiences special and enriching moments in God's presence. When we go to church we are given the opportunity of getting away from the humdrum activities of our everyday life and meditate and pray in silence. There we also find joy in prayer, song, teaching and the fellowship of believers; but mainly by being in God's presence and meeting Him face-to-face.

> The idea is to live all of our lives in the presence of God, under the authority of God, and for the honor and glory of God.
> R. C. SPROUL

A group of eminent scientists sat rooted to the spot as they listened to Michael Faraday deliver a lecture in which he analyzed the nature and character of the magnet. At the conclusion of his lecture, the hall reverberated with ongoing applause. Then the Prince of Wales, who was present, thanked him and again applause raised the roof.

But this was promptly followed by a strange silence – Faraday had disappeared without a trace. He had finished his lecture at the same time that his congregation's weekly prayer meeting started, a gathering he always attended. He quietly slipped out under the enthusiastic applause to spend some time and to pray in the presence of God together with a small group of fellow believers.

Great God, thank You that I can praise You together with my fellow believers. Amen.

Read Colossians 3:1-4

Focus on God

Think about the things of heaven, not the things of earth. For you died to this life, and your real life is hidden with Christ in God (Col. 3:2-3).

A Christian's true home is with Christ. This gives us a whole new perspective on earthly things. If we want to see life from God's perspective, we must fill our thoughts with things Jesus Christ taught us during His earthly ministry.

> I would not give up one moment of heaven for all the riches and treasures of the world, even if it lasts a thousand years.
> — MARTIN LUTHER

We see material things in the right perspective if we look at them from God's vantage point. The more we see life as God sees it, the more we want to live in harmony with Him. We shouldn't become too fond of worldly things. We can only manage this if we keep our eyes and thoughts focused on God. However, at the same time we mustn't only look heavenward and neglect our God-given duties on earth.

A writer says he stopped at a market stall in the street one cold windy day where an old man was selling apples. He made a remark to the old man about the miserable weather. He was quite surprised when a friendly smile spread across the rugged old face and the apple seller answered, "Yes, it's shivery weather; but look up and think of afterwards – just think of it!" The idea of sunny days, budding trees and singing birds comforted him while the icy winter winds cut through him. This might be a cold, pitiless world, but look up to heaven – just think of it!

Holy Trinity, keep my eyes and thoughts focused on You because only then can I live a balanced life. Amen.

Read Matthew 20:20-28

Called to Serve

"Even the Son of Man came not to be served but to serve others and to give His life as a ransom for many" (Matt. 20:28).

Jesus taught the circle of disciples that the most important person in the kingdom of God would be the one who serves others. He put leadership into a new perspective. A true leader has the heart of a servant. Instead of using people, we should follow the example Jesus set us and serve them.

Someone noted down the story of a bedridden boy who spent his dull days in the slums of London. Like a caged animal, he was confined by the four walls of a small room with just one window. But no ray of sunlight ever came through that small window. Both his parents worked during the day and his only companion was gloomy silence without even a glimmer of sunlight. There his little broken body lay, from one bleak and desolate day to the next.

However, an inventive friend noticed that on a cloudless day, the sun shone on the wall opposite the tiny room for an hour or two. He took a cracked mirror and every sunny day, as long as the ray of sunlight shone on the wall, he stood in it with his mirror, and reflected the sunlight onto his friend's bed. In this way, his heart filled with love and compassion, he brought sunshine and joy into a young life robbed of all warmth and joy.

> You have an ego – a consciousness of being an individual! But that doesn't mean that you are to worship yourself, to think constantly of yourself, and to live entirely for self.
> BILLY GRAHAM

Keep me from thinking I am better than others, dear Lord, so that I may play an important role in Your kingdom. Give me a servant's attitude. Amen.

April 9

Read 1 Corinthians 13:1-6

The Greatest of All

If I could speak all the languages of earth and of angels, but didn't love others, I would only be a noisy gong or a clanging cymbal (1 Cor. 13:1).

Love is the highest and greatest of all the spiritual gifts in the church. Even strong faith and the ability to perform miracles would be meaningless if we didn't love others. It is love in our lives that makes our gifts and actions glorify God.

It is true that people receive different gifts, but everybody can and must love. This love however, must not be confused with our normal affection for others. It is more like heaven becoming visible on earth and the work of the Holy Spirit. That is why love is the very best of all virtues.

The father of an excellent cricket player regularly attended his son's matches and sat through the whole match, even though he was blind. Then his father died and he had to play a very important match soon after his father's death. Everyone thought he wouldn't play but he did – and he played with more passion and dedication than ever before.

> The reason for loving God is God Himself and how He should be loved is to love Him without limit.
> BERNARD OF CLAIRVAUX

When a friend asked him why he had played while everybody thought he wouldn't, his answer was simple, "This was the first time my dad saw me play and that's why I wanted to do my very best to reward his love."

Lord Jesus, may Your love for me always be the single most important thing and may I spread that love in the world every day. Amen.

Read Galatians 6:11-18

The Cross of Christ

May I never boast except in the cross of our Lord Jesus Christ, through which the world has been crucified to me, and I to the world (Gal. 6:14 NIV).

There is salvation through the cross because Jesus died on it for the sins of all of mankind. We don't honor the cross, but the Man who died on it and opened up the path to heaven and the loving heart of God. We are again reconciled with God.

In a striking painting by Guido Reni that is displayed in the Vatican, there is a skull at the foot of the cross. It is generally assumed to be Adam's skull. In his writings Chrysostom refers to the legend that Jesus was crucified where Adam was buried, and that with His victory on the cross, Jesus brought life to the place where there was only death. The legend probably originated from the Bible text, "As in Adam all die, so in Christ all will be made alive" (see 1 Cor. 15: 22, NIV).

> The Lord is loving unto man, and swift to pardon, but slow to punish. Let no man therefore despair of his own salvation.
> CYRIL OF ALEXANDRIA

In early works of art, Adam was often portrayed with a goblet in his hand, catching up the blood flowing from the cross. The message to us all is: Salvation comes through the cross.

Crucified and risen Savior, grant that like Paul, I will never boast except in the cross of Jesus. By Your death on the cross, salvation came for me too. Amen.

Read Psalm 147:1-11

To the Greater Glory of God

Praise the LORD! How good to sing praises to our God! How delightful and how fitting! (Ps. 147:1).

We can never sing perfect or complete praises to our God, but through our imperfect and insignificant efforts God's glory is spread on earth.

> A man can no more diminish God's glory by refusing to worship Him, than a lunatic can put out the sun by scribbling the word "darkness" on the walls of his cell.
> C. S. LEWIS

In of one of the great temples in Japan, the worshipers run around a table one hundred times, and every time they have completed a round, they throw a piece of wood into a chest. Once the laborious task is done, the exhausted worshiper goes home, under the impression that he has satisfied his god.

We find this unbelievably foolish and yet unless we go with the definite purpose to worship, to reverently listen to God's voice, humbly bow our proud heads in prayer and sing His praises, heart and soul, we are just as foolish and unfulfilled as the Japanese runner.

In the small church in a rural village the service was coming to an end. Just then the local doctor and a horse breeder arrived to fetch their families. They were still busy making small talk outside the church building when the closing hymn started. Suddenly both were quiet. Then the doctor said, "My friend, there is something about a congregation's songs of praise that makes a person standing outside, feel he should be inside!"

God, You are worthy of worship; may my worship always be in spirit and in truth so that it contributes to Your greater glory. Amen.

Read Psalm 23:1-6

Our Heavenly Host

Surely Your goodness and unfailing love will pursue me all the days of my life, and I will live in the house of the LORD forever (Ps. 23:6).

In the Middle Ages, a host was compelled to protect his guests at all costs. God offers us His protection when we are surrounded by enemies. In the final scene of this psalm we see that the believer will live with God forever. God, the perfect Shepherd and Host, promises to lead and protect us all our lives until we reach His house.

In two contrasting forms of architecture and in two radically different parts of the world, and in two different centuries, architects tried to express the idea of eternity. First an attempt was made in Europe to materialize this abstract concept by massive rocks, as in the pyramids, temples and tombs. These builders of ancient times tried to erect strongholds that would challenge the corrosive and destructive fingers of time, and in this way express human views of the permanent and eternal.

Secondly, the Gothic style of architecture was developed in Western Europe. While the Egyptians tried to portray the eternal with great masses of stone, the modern builders tried to express it by means of tall columns, pillars and arches that reached out to heaven, like human aspirations. By this, thoughts were led away from earthly life to things above.

> He who provides for this life, but takes no care for eternity, is wise for a moment, but a fool forever.
> JOHN TILLOTSON

Dearest Lord, help me never to become so attached to earthly things that I lose sight of You. Let me forever long to dwell in Your eternal home. Amen.

Read Matthew 27:11-14

The Devil's Advocate

"Don't You hear all these charges they are bringing against You?" Pilate demanded (Matt. 27:13).

The Roman Catholic Church uses the term *promoter fidei* (Promoter of the Faith), popularly known as *advocates diabolic* (the devil's advocate) for a church official who is appointed to debate in the Canonization processes against the nominated beatification of a saint. It is this official's responsibility to pick up weak points in the evidence of those who are in favor of the proposed blessing of the *beatis,* the blessed person. It is expected that in this court case of opposing powers, the truth will come out to support the blessed or refuse the canonization.

Pilate took the role of *advocates diabolic* in Jesus' trial on himself when he presented Jesus to the crowds. He asked the people what Jesus had done wrong, but got no reply except for the roaring of the crowd, their voices hoarse with shouting, "Crucify Him! Crucify Him!" At his wife's insistence, Pilate tried to wash his hands of it, but in Jesus' case there was no convenient no-man's-land of indecision. Consequently Pilate failed in his self-imposed task to bring the truth to light and find Jesus innocent. Because Pilate was a weakling in the devil's service, he couldn't give a just verdict and Jesus was taken away to be crucified. In an ironic way he therefore became a true *advocates diabolic*.

> Satan deals with confusion and lies. Put the truth in front of him and he is gone.
> PAUL MATTOCK

Crucified Lord Jesus, let me never be a weakling in my witnessing and deny or betray You. Help me not to be an instrument of the Evil One. Amen.

Read John 1:29-34

The Lamb of God

The next day John saw Jesus coming toward him and said, "Look! The Lamb of God who takes away the sin of the world!" (John 1:29).

In ancient Israel a lamb was sacrificed in the temple every morning and evening for the sins of the people (see Exod. 29:38-42). We read in Isaiah 53:7 that the Messiah, God's Anointed, would be led to the slaughter like a lamb to pay the price for the sins of the world. The sins of the world were washed clean when Jesus died as the Perfect Sacrifice.

This is also the meaning of the Passover Lamb. This is the way in which we received forgiveness for our sins (see 1 Cor. 5:7). The "world" refers to the sins of all of humanity. Jesus, the Lamb, already paid the price for our sins with His death. We can receive forgiveness by confessing our sins before Him and asking Him for forgiveness.

> Jesus Christ is God's everything for man's total need.
> RICHARD HALVERSON

The Jews attached a particular meaning to the lamb. During the period between the Old and New Testaments there were times of great battle in which the Maccabees fought, died, but also conquered. In those days, the lamb, especially the horned lamb, was the symbol of great victory. Judas Maccabeus is described like this, and also Samuel, David and Solomon. The lamb – strange as it may sound – is the symbol of God's victorious champion. Therefore it is not a symbol of helpless weakness, but of victorious majesty and strength. Jesus was God's Champion who fought sin till death, and triumphed. Small wonder that the victorious Lamb is mentioned twenty-nine times in Revelation!

Lord Jesus, I heard Your voice calling me and by the grace of God I could answer, "O Lamb of God, I am coming!" Amen.

Read John 15:9-17

Forever Friends

"You are My friends if you do what I command" (John 15:14).

Jesus Christ is the Lord and Master. So in actual fact He should call us subordinates or slaves, but He doesn't. He not only rules over our lives, but also calls us His friends. If Christ is our friend, He is our friend forever. If we should obey Him as our Lord and Master, how much more should we be true to Him as a loyal Friend. Especially because He gave His life for us.

> What a friend we have in Jesus, all our sins and griefs to bear!
> JOSEPH SCRIVEN

Loyalty means obeying His instructions, namely to love one another as He loves us. If we do this, we are assured of His friendship until the very end.

There was a custom among the Roman emperors and Eastern kings. There was a hand-picked group in their palaces known as "the friends of the king" or "the friends of the emperor". They had access to the king at all times and could even enter his bedroom in the mornings. He spoke to them before he spoke to generals, rulers and statesmen. They had a close and intimate relationship with the king or emperor. They could go to him with any problem at any time.

Jesus, our Friend up until the very end, did an amazing thing; He gave us this intimacy with God so that God is not a distant stranger, but an intimate Friend until the very end!

Jesus, You are my Friend up until the end! I praise and thank You for this, my God and my Father. Amen.

Read Matthew 22:35-40

Neighborly Love

A second [command] is equally important: "Love your neighbor as yourself" (Matt. 22:39).

Jesus tells us that if we truly love God and our neighbor, we will automatically keep all God's other commandments as well. This indicates a positive approach to God's law. We shouldn't be constantly worried about everything we are not allowed to do, but rather focus on those things we may and must do to show our love for God. Jesus says that the most important of these things is to love our fellow human beings like we love ourselves.

Take careful note of the particular sequence in the commandment: We must love God above all else and then ourselves and our neighbor. Human beings are created in God's image (see Gen. 1:26-27). That is why we can love one another. Take the love of God away and all that remains is hate. Our love for our neighbor is firmly grounded in our love for God. To be truly religious is to sincerely love God. This is not a vague, sentimental love, but a powerful love accompanied by total surrender, and springs from our relationship with God and our service to our fellow humans.

> He who loves best his fellowman, is loving God the holiest way he can.
> ALICE CARY

There are many beekeepers in Wales and Ireland. Every three years beekeepers are expected to share their honey with their neighbors, free of charge, because their bees gathered the honey from the flowers in the neighborhood. Likewise, we owe a lot to our neighbors, because they contribute towards our happiness and prosperity. Consequently we are expected, according to the law of neighborly love, to share and distribute among them some of the honey of our own prosperity and comforts.

Help me, O Holy Spirit of God, to reveal, next to my love for God, a practical, day-to-day love for my fellow human beings. Amen.

Read Ephesians 3:14-21

Love Conquers All

And may you have the power to understand, as all God's people should, how wide, how long, how high, and how deep His love is (Eph. 3:18).

In this verse Paul prays that the Ephesians will know Jesus Christ's triumphant love, because this is the kind of love that conquers everything. He prays that the Father will enable them, through His Spirit, to get to know the victorious love of Christ in all its dimensions: in width, distance, height and depth.

If Christ and His love are in us, who can be against us? Then we can do battle with confidence and trust to be victorious if we fight for His cause and in His love.

A missionary was asked if he enjoyed his work in Central Africa. His answer was, "Do I like my work? No, because my wife and I do not like squalor. We have rather refined feelings. We don't like crawling into filthy shacks built behind stinking goat pens. We don't enjoy having primitive, barbaric and unrefined people around us as our only company. But does one do for Christ only the things one enjoys? May God have mercy on those who think so! Whether you like it or not has got absolutely nothing to do with it. God instructed us to go and we went. Our love drives us, and through our love we overcome anything."

> Take away love and our earth is a tomb.
> ROBERT BROWNING

It is in this attitude that we find the power that drives the best and most competent people to help with the salvation of souls for the Kingdom. They do it in the firm knowledge that love conquers everything.

Beloved Lord Jesus, purify and refine my love so that I may gain victory, to Your glory. Amen.

Read Matthew 24:36-44

Ready at All Times

"You also must be ready all the time, for the Son of Man will come when least expected" (Matt. 24:44).

Because we do not know when Christ is coming, we are forced to be ready at all times. This means that our lives must be constantly tuned to this event so that we are ready to receive Christ every day.

Jesus' second coming is presented as something that will happen suddenly and quickly. Therefore people are warned not to postpone their decision to accept Him as their Savior.

Jesus didn't tell us about His second coming so that we can speculate about the date, but so that we can be ready for it. Would you be faithfully busy with His work the moment that He comes? The only solution is to obey Him every day and be ready for His arrival.

> Christ planned the day of His second coming in such a way that it will remain hidden from us until we are constantly on guard as it were, waiting in eager anticipation.
> —MARTIN LUTHER

There is a fable of three of the devil's apprentices who were preparing to come to earth in the service of Satan. They were discussing with Satan their plans to bring about the fall of humankind. The first one said, "I will tell them there is no God." The devil answered that it would not work as they knew there is a God. The second said, "I will tell them there is no hell." Again the devil said this would not fool them, because everybody knew about hell where sins are punished. The third one said, "I will convince them they still have plenty of time." "Go!" Satan replied, "You will deceive tens of thousands of people." Therefore we must always be prepared. The Lord is coming!

Glorified Lord, keep me alert every day so that I will look forward with excitement to Your glorious second coming. Amen.

Read Matthew 25:31-40

God Blessed Us

Then the King will say to those on His right, "Come, you who are blessed by My Father, inherit the Kingdom prepared for you from the creation of the world" (Matt. 25:34).

What we believe shows best in our deeds. It is not easy to treat everyone we come across like we would treat Jesus. The way we treat others clearly shows how we feel about Jesus' command to feed the hungry, provide shelter for the homeless and visit the sick.

> If Jesus be God and He died for me, then no sacrifice can be too great for me to make for Him.
> C. T. STUDD

This parable is about love and compassion that we should show others every day. It has nothing to do with wealth, intelligence or physical strength, but simple things we do for others without expecting anything in return. Jesus expects all His disciples to work together in meeting another's need. And He confronts us with the wonderful truth that all the help we offer others in need – or hold back – we give Him or withhold from Him. We will be blessed to the extent that we do this. The best way to bring joy to a parent's heart is to help their child. God is our Father, and by helping His children in need, we bring joy to His heart.

Francis of Assisi was rich and of noble descent. Yet he was unhappy because his life was unfulfilled. One day he met a leper along the road which brought home to him the full horror of the disease. Something made him get down from his horse and with love in his heart, he embraced the leper. This was the turning point in his life, because from then on, life made sense to him.

Holy Jesus, I cannot earn Your blessings, but give me a sensitive heart for the need of my fellow human beings and the will to do something to ease their pain. Amen.

Read John 7:32-39

Pure Water

On the last day, the climax of the festival, Jesus stood and shouted to the crowds, "Anyone who is thirsty may come to Me! Anyone who believes in Me may come and drink! For the Scriptures declare, 'Rivers of living water will flow from His heart'" (John 7:37-38).

Jesus invites everyone to come to Him and receive pure water. This invitation goes hand in hand with the portions of Scripture that deal with the Messiah's life-giving blessing (see Isa. 12:2-3; 44:3-4; 58:11). The promise that He would give believers the Holy Spirit is unmistakable proof that He is the Messiah because only the Messiah is able to do this. The "living water" indicates eternal life (see John 4:10).

Water is one of our most essential needs. No living creature can exist or survive without water. What is the word on the cracked lips of the desert traveler who has lost his way? "Water!" What is the word the feverish man utters on his deathbed? "Water!" What is the heart-rending cry of the wounded lying on the battlefield? "Water!" How indescribably encouraging for each of us is the Master's invitation to the Living Water. If you are thirsty, come to Me (see John 7:37).

> I have a great need for Christ; I have a great Christ for my need.
> CHARLES H. SPURGEON

As the body needs pure water to survive, the soul must also have the pure water of life. The Bible ends with an invitation to all to receive that water, "Let anyone who is thirsty come. Let anyone who desires drink freely from the water of life" (Rev. 22:17).

Wellspring of Living Water, I accepted Your invitation and You gave me the pure, life-giving water. I pray for grace so that I will make it available to others as well. Amen.

April 21

Read Matthew 25:1-13

Be Watchful

"So you, too, must keep watch! For you do not know the day or hour of My return" (Matt. 25:13).

Jesus uses this parable to impress on us once again that we must be prepared when the Bridegroom comes. Spiritual preparation cannot be bought or borrowed at the last minute. Our personal relationship with God must be right all the time and therefore we must be permanently watchful.

In Jewish culture an engagement lasted a long time and the engagement vows were just as binding as marriage vows. On the wedding day, the bridegroom went to the bride's house and the ceremony was performed there, but he could also take her along to his own house for the festivities. No fixed time was set for his arrival; as becomes clear from this parable. The festivities could carry on for a week or even longer.

The ten bridesmaids in the parable waited up for the arrival of the bridegroom. They wanted to attend the wedding. However, when the bridegroom didn't turn up at the expected time, the lamps of five bridesmaids went out and they didn't have any extra oil. While they went to buy oil, the bridegroom arrived and they were too late to be allowed at the marriage feast. So be on the alert! Make sure you are ready for the Bridegroom's arrival!

> Repentance is a change of willing, of feeling and of living, in respect to God.
> CHARLES G. FINNEY

When Mary of Orange was on her deathbed her chaplain tried to explain the way of salvation to her. Her sorrowful answer was, "I have waited too long to put the matter right. It is too late!" Being too late because you were not watchful is always a tragedy.

Living Savior, keep me from missing the marriage feast of the Lamb because I was not watchful. Amen.

Read Joshua 1:1-9

Success Favors the Brave

"Be strong and courageous, for you are the one who will lead these people to possess all the land I swore to their ancestors I would give them" (Josh. 1:6).

The Lord set Joshua the task of leading Israel into Canaan. Because of Joshua's courage he had already been Moses' assistant a long time. He was also commander of Israel's army. He and Caleb were the two spies from twelve who were positive and confident after scouting out Canaan.

> Take heart. God is stronger than the devil. We are on the winning side.
> JOHN CHAPMAN

Now the time had come to take possession of the land, and the Lord would prove through Joshua that success favors the brave. God promised that He Himself would give them the country. With this assurance Joshua could act with purpose and without hesitation. However, our courage must be born from our faith. We must live from God and for God.

A Chinese boy in Singapore was going to have himself baptized as a Christian shortly before his graduation ceremony. To his surprise the University of Hong Kong awarded him a scholarship of five hundred dollars a year. One of the conditions was that he would become a follower of Confucius. He was a poor boy and was sorely tempted to cancel his Christian baptism, but he resisted the temptation and in front of everyone, knelt down to be baptized. A fellow student, a follower of Confucius, was then given the scholarship, but he was so impressed with his classmate that he declined it with the words, "If Christianity is worth so much to my classmate, it can mean just as much to me." He also became a Christian and was baptized.

Courage is always rewarded.

Gracious Father, grant that I will always be bold enough to defend Your name and honor by faithfully obeying only You. Amen.

Read Matthew 12:22-32

You Are for Us or Against Us

"Anyone who isn't with Me opposes Me, and anyone who isn't working with Me is actually working against Me" (Matt. 12:30).

It is impossible to be neutral in our relationship with Jesus Christ. If my presence doesn't make the congregation stronger, my absence certainly contributes to making it weaker. There isn't a no-man's-land of indecision. If my country is at war and I remain neutral I am actually helping the enemy by withholding my contribution to the battle.

In all things in life we must take sides. Refusing to make a choice, delayed action, is not the easy way out of a problem, because the very fact that I refuse to act and support a side means that I strengthen the opposition.

> In this war against Satan's strongholds there are only two sides, for Christ or against Him, gathering with Him or scattering with Satan.
> W. C. ALLEN

We choose to stay neutral because of our human nature. We would rather remain uninvolved and neutral than to actively take a stand. It could of course also be because of natural fearfulness. Many people refuse to make a stand for Christ, because it requires bold action from them. They always wonder what others will say and think. Then the world's voice is stronger than God's voice.

Or it might be that they prefer security rather than adventure. A challenge always includes adventure. Christ comes to us with a challenge, but often we prefer a life of comfort, without challenges. This is why Christ seriously cautions us, "You are for Me or against Me."

Give me the courage, Holy Jesus, to be on Your side at all times and to do it in such a way that the world will know that I have chosen You. Amen.

Read Matthew 5:3-12

Blessed Are the Peacemakers

"God blesses those who work for peace, for they will be called the children of God" (Matt. 5:9).

Christ uses the word "peace", meaning good relationships between man and man. Unfortunately there are people who are storm centers of trouble, bitterness and strife. Wherever they are, we find quarreling and hostility. They are called troublemakers and are found in practically every community or congregation. They merrily go about doing the devil's work.

On the other hand, there are people in whose presence bitterness cannot survive. They build bridges, clear up misunderstandings and turn bitterness into sweetness. They do heavenly work, because their job is God's great task of bringing about peace between man and man and between God and man. The person who brings division among people and creates strife does the devil's work, but those who reconcile people do God's work. Because of their efforts to fulfill God's plan for peace, they will be blessed and be called God's children (see Rom. 12:9-21).

Some people are true peacemakers through their relationship with Jesus. They are merciful, loving and helpful. They enter our lives and hearts with the quiet footsteps of peace. They do it without fuss. It doesn't disturb our course of life any more than sunlight coming through the window, spreading its rays; or dawn quietly announcing a beautiful, new day. They are the peacemakers who come and go and leave behind a lingering fragrance of blessed peace. They live like their Master did; they are happy and are called children of God.

> To be of a peaceable spirit brings peace along with it.
> THOMAS WATSON

Prince of Peace, I am enchanted by Your heavenly peace. Make me a peace messenger through Your Holy Spirit, in the part of the world You have placed me. Amen.

Read Matthew 5:3-12

Absolute Dependence

"God blesses those who realize their need for Him, for the Kingdom of Heaven is theirs" (Matt. 5:3).

What this blessing says to us is that the exceptionally happy person is the person who realizes his absolute dependence on God and has placed his complete trust in Him. This is the only way in which he can offer God that total obedience which makes him a citizen of the kingdom of God.

The person who becomes aware of his own helplessness and inability and places his trust completely in God, will find that two things happen in his life. Firstly, earthly things cannot give him happiness or blessings and he will not commit himself to these. Consequently he commits himself totally to God because he knows that only God can help with strength and hope. The person who acknowledges his dependence on God also realizes that earthly goods mean nothing and that God means everything.

> The kingdom of God which is within us consists in our willing whatever God wills, always, in everything, and without reservation.
> FRANÇOIS FÉNELON

Secondly, we need to reveal more practical wisdom to be heirs of the kingdom of God. All of us realize that we must make an effort to be successful in any sphere of life. We specialize in a certain field to gain more knowledge of a specific subject. We know that our success depends on the extent to which we focus on the subject. We know that without this we will never be achievers. It is essential that we focus on our dependence and concentrate on reaching the kingdom of God.

Lord, I confess once more my dependence on You and Your love and grace. Enable me to concentrate on this up until the end. Amen.

Read Revelation 2:1-11

Live a Good Life

"Don't be afraid of what you are about to suffer. The Devil will throw some of you into prison to test you. You will suffer for ten days. But if you remain faithful even when facing death, I will give you the crown of life" (Rev. 2:10).

The church in Smyrna was called upon to hold on to Jesus and remain faithful in a time of persecution. God is still in control and His faithfulness and promises stand firm. The sincerity of our faith comes to light in our faithfulness in the midst of persecution and disappointment.

> A man may lose the good things of this life against his will; but if he loses the eternal blessings, he does so with his own consent.
> ST. AUGUSTINE

All earthly life must die, believers as well as unbelievers; just as every human being will be raised from the dead. Believers will rise to live with God forever, while unbelievers will rise to suffer everlasting punishment. Thus they will die a second time, being separated from God spiritually and forever (see Rev. 20:14; 21:8; 22:15). Those who lived good lives and died in Christ will rise and live a second time. They will not be struck down by the second death.

A general and his troops were busy looting a palace. A soldier found a beautiful leather bag which contained the crown jewels. They were worth millions, but the ignorant soldier emptied the bag on a garbage dump. He boasted to his friends about the beautiful bag he found to keep his meager lunch in. He wasn't aware of the immense value of the priceless treasure he had thrown away. Many of us also throw away the treasure of eternal life because we are not prepared to live for God in this life.

Eternal God and Father, give me the strength and the wish to live to Your glory here and now so that I may receive life as a crown, through faith and obedience. Amen.

Read Psalm 19:1-11

The Heavens Proclaim God's Glory

The heavens proclaim the glory of God. The skies display His craftsmanship (Ps. 19:1).

In this psalm about creation, God reveals Himself to us in nature. We see the wonders of our Creator God. The skies are proof of His omnipotence, His love and care. It is ridiculous to claim that the universe came into being by chance. The order, the way everything is interwoven and the trustworthiness of nature is already enough proof that it all comes from the hand of a Creator who is involved in His creation. We need to take note of these things and thank God for the beauty He created, but also for revealing the truth about Himself to us.

> Nature is a good name for an effect whose cause is God.
> WILLIAM COWPER

Paul refers to this psalm in Romans 1:19-20 where he explains that everyone knows about God because His existence and Sovereignty are revealed in nature. Everyone who really sees nature *must* come to faith in the loving Creator. The most desperate and tragic people on earth are the fools who say there is no God.

When one is inside the breathtaking Cathedral of Milan, or in Westminster Abbey, or the Cathedrals of Winchester and Salisbury, one's soul is inspired by the architectural splendor of these buildings. Attending a service in such a cathedral can lift your soul until you feel you are flying with angel wings. These are awesome mountaintop moments to experience. And we call them mountaintop moments because it was there where the transfiguration of our Master took place and where His disciples wanted to stay forever.

It is at sea, in the mountains, in fields covered with flowers that we come closest to God and reach His heart of love.

Lord, I praise Your name because I hear You speak to me in Your Word and in nature and my soul is refreshed. Amen.

Read James 3:2-12

Watch What You Say

The tongue is a flame of fire. It is a whole world of wickedness corrupting your entire body. It can set your whole life on fire, for it is set on fire by hell itself (James 3:6).

We are warned against the terror of the tongue. James says the tongue can light a destructive fire which is kindled in hell itself. For this reason, believers must control their tongues. The person who manages this and never says the wrong thing, is perfect and he will be able to keep his whole body in check. This is why the role of the tongue is so important in controlling our bodies. Apart from all the positive things the tongue can do, James also mentions a negative side that makes it essential to be extremely careful of what we say, when we say it and to whom.

We cannot control our tongues ourselves. But Christ can and He created a method to help us. Because the Lord lets His Holy Spirit live in us, He gives us a bridle for our tongue, as it were. He enables us to take the bit between the teeth and control the tongue so that it doesn't rage on like a destructive fire. The Holy Spirit sees to it that your tongue is not a slave to your natural disposition any longer, but that it is governed by the liberating rule of the Holy Spirit.

> Our words are a faithful index to the state of our souls.
> FRANCIS DE SALES

In the days when fountain pens were still in use, the following tip was given in the instructions for use: "If this pen flows too freely, it is a sign that it is almost empty and must be refilled." This advice can be put to good use if applied to our tongues. If the tongue works too freely, it is time for it to be refilled with God's Spirit.

Lord, my Keeper, set a watch before my mouth, so that I will always be careful of what I say, when I say it and to whom I say it. Amen.

Read Hebrews 11:1-5

Things We Cannot See

Faith is the confidence that what we hope for will actually happen; it gives us assurance about things we cannot see (Heb. 11:1).

In the third century BC Tertullian said in his writing *De Carne Christi*, "It is certain because it is impossible." In this document he warns readers not to believe the evidence of their ears and eyes in matters of faith. Because we are insignificant human beings, with limited understanding, the fact that the supernatural truth appears impossible to us is all the more reason for accepting this truth rather than rejecting it.

> Faith is the sight of the inward eye.
> ALEXANDER MACLAREN

Our faith regarding the promises of God in our lives works like a title deed in the case of property. It guarantees that we are in possession of God's promises. In this dispensation His promises are still invisible. This includes matters like forgiveness of sin, our eternal justification and our salvation. All of it is still invisible and we do not have it in our hands yet.

However, what we do have is the title deed of the actualization of those promises, namely our faith. Our faith must be our proof of the reality of God's promises. Because it seems so impossible to the sinful human being that Christ saves us, our faith tells us that it is certain.

We go through life daily with faith in things such as airplanes, banks and bridges. But suddenly, when it comes to faith in God, we have a huge problem with it. This is why Jesus said to Thomas, "Blessed are those who believe without seeing Me" (John 20:29).

Loving Jesus, with You the impossible is always possible and certain. Thank You that I may cling to You and Your promises through faith because You saved me. Amen.

May

*Then, when our dying bodies
have been transformed into bodies
that will never die,
this Scripture will be fulfilled:
"Death is swallowed up in victory."*
   1 CORINTHIANS 15:54

Our old history
ends with the Cross;
our new history begins
with the Resurrection.
WATCHMAN NEE

Risen and Living Savior and Redeemer,
We rejoice in the knowledge that Your tomb is empty
and that You are alive!
We jubilantly confess:
"I believe in Jesus Christ – who was raised
from the dead on the third day, ascended to heaven,
and sits at the right hand of God, the Almighty Father."
Together with the psalmist we rejoice:
"Open up, ancient gates and let the King of glory enter!"
Lord Jesus, we worship You as the Conqueror of sin,
death and hell.
We thank You that You reopened the gates of Paradise
through Your ascension, not only for Christ the Conqueror,
but also for us, lost sinners that we were!
The gates of Paradise that swung shut behind Adam and Eve,
have opened up once again for us.
Thank You that You plead with the Father on our behalf;
Thank You that You went to prepare
a place for us in the Father's house;
Thank You that You sent us the Holy Spirit
as Comforter to glorify You and to lead us in all truth,
to comfort us and stay with us forever.
We pray this in the name of Jesus who waits for us in heaven.
Amen.

Read Acts 17:21-34

I Think, Therefore I Am

For in Him we live and move and exist. As some of your own poets have said, "We are His offspring" (Acts 17:28).

I think, therefore I am. This is one of the most well known of all philosophical axioms or principles. Descartes used it in his *Discourse on Method* as the point of departure of his philosophical system. But this is obviously not in agreement with Christian convictions because we live and exist by virtue of God's love and grace.

In our Scripture reading today Paul tells us that God is not made, He *is* the Maker! Therefore, He who made everything cannot be worshiped by anything created by human thinking.

God directs history. He is behind the rise and fall of the nations of days gone by. His almighty hand is at the helm to this day.

> Human beings must be known to be loved; but Divine beings must be loved to be known.
> — BLAISE PASCAL

God created human beings in such a way that they instinctively long for God. There is something in us that makes us reach out to our Creator in our darkness. As long as people search in the shadows of their own thinking, they cannot get to know God.

But now, in Jesus Christ, the full ray of the light of knowledge of God shines on our whole lives. The truth about life came with Jesus Christ. We no longer serve an unknown God, but He becomes the very reason for our existence. Thus the reason for my existence is not in me, but in Jesus Christ through whom I exist, live and think. Without Him I don't live, I merely am.

I praise and thank You, living Savior, that I have found in You the true reason for my existence. Thank You that through the Holy Spirit You give meaning and purpose to my life. Amen.

Read John 14:1-12

Jesus Christ Is the Way

Jesus told him, "I am the way, the truth, and the life. No one can come to the Father except through Me" (John 14:6).

The most essential requirement for our salvation is that we go to the Father through Jesus Christ. The living Christ is the road to God and there is no substitute! In Him alone we see the Father, and through Him alone we have access to the Father. He can show people what God is like, and only He can lead people into the presence of God without fear and shame. This is the most essential requirement of salvation.

Christ is the only way to the Father. Some people might think that this path is too narrow, but that is not true. It is so effective that the whole world can walk on it if only they would accept this road in faith. We must be unwavering in our belief that there is only one way to the Father and that is through Jesus Christ. Jesus Christ, who connected heaven and earth through the cross for those who believe.

> Salvation comes through a cross and a crucified Christ.
> ANDREW MURRAY

On earth Jesus is the visible image of the invisible God. He makes God fully known to us. Philip wanted to see the Father in person, but Jesus explained to him that knowing Jesus also means knowing the Father. The search for God the Father, and for reality and truth begins and ends with Jesus Christ (see also Col. 1:15; Heb. 1:1-4). Jesus is essential in finding God.

Savior and Redeemer, I bow before You in thankfulness because I can go to the Father through You and become His child. You will always be the Way, the Truth and the Life. Amen.

Read 1 Corinthians 15:1-11

By the Grace of God

> But whatever I am now, it is all because God poured out His special favor on me – and not without results. For I have worked harder than any of the other apostles; yet it was not I but God who was working through me by His grace (1 Cor. 15:10).

This verse illustrates Paul's humility: by God's grace alone he received a ministry he didn't think he was worthy of. But he worked harder than the other apostles. This is in no way a boastful statement. He knew that his power and strength were from God (see v. 10). It didn't matter to him who worked hardest (see v. 11).

Paul's conversion caused a great stir because he was a former Pharisee and this resulted in him being persecuted more than the other disciples. So he had to work harder than them to achieve the same results. Paul's former enemies now had to become his friends and confidants.

Paul was aware of his own worth, but his humility was not insincere. He spoke about what he did as if it was not his own doing, but was made possible by the grace of God.

On occasion, Gypsy Smith hosted an evening of testimony, where a man stood up and said, "I was in prison for murder for twenty years, but by God's grace I was saved." Another testified, "I was a drunk for twenty-five years, but by God's grace I was saved." Then Gypsy Smith got up and said, "People, listen to me: God performed miracles for you, but don't forget that He did more for this gypsy by His grace than for all of you together. He saved me while I was still searching for Him."

> Grace is the free, undeserved goodness and favor of God to mankind.
> — MATTHEW HENRY

Loving God, we praise Your name because Your grace is enough for us in all circumstances and at all times. Amen.

Read Philippians 1:12-25

My Best for God

For I fully expect and hope that I will never be ashamed, but that I will continue to be bold for Christ, as I have been in the past. And I trust that my life will bring honor to Christ, whether I live or die (Phil. 1:20).

For unbelievers this life is all there is because they refuse to give God their best. Instead, they pursue things like money, power and popularity. However, for Paul life held much more, because he gave his best, his life, to God. The things he did had eternal value and consequently Christ enabled him to view life with an eternal perspective. This is why he could say he was ready and willing to die. Because he gave God his best, God gave Paul His best: eternal life!

If you are not prepared to die for Christ, you are not prepared to live. Only when you know you have given God your best can you give your best to life without fearing death (see Heb. 2:14-15).

The missionary, Stanley Jones, said that he often stood at the Ganges River in India and saw mothers feed their children to crocodiles who they regarded as gods. One morning a young mother came along to the river, holding a skipping child by the hand and carrying a disabled child in the other arm. She put the disabled child down and threw the beautiful healthy child to the crocodiles as prey. In dismay he asked her why she hadn't rather thrown the handicapped child to the crocodiles. She answered him with tears in her eyes, "We give only our best to our god. What do you give yours?"

> It is our best work that God wants, not the dregs of our exhaustion.
> — GEORGE MACDONALD

I want to give You only my best, O God, because You gave me Your best, with love: Your Son as Savior. Amen.

Read Psalm 67:1-7

May God Have Mercy on Us

May God be merciful and bless us. May His face smile with favor on us (Ps. 67:1).

The psalmist's prayer links up with the priestly blessing that had to be pronounced on the people, according to Numbers 6:24-26. He prays that God will bless the people by redeeming them and having mercy on them. This not only gives them new possibilities in life, but also a new command: His salvation work must be made known to all nations so that they will turn to Him and believe in Him. They must know that He is the Lord. The psalmist confirms the fact that God's grace towards us is equal to the extent to which we share His grace with a lost world.

William Carey, a pioneer missionary in India, was a shoemaker before he became a missionary. As a shoemaker he traveled from town to town, preaching, because his heart overflowed with the love of God. One day someone said to him, "You are neglecting your job, traveling and preaching like this. If you pay more attention to your business instead, you will prosper and live a good life. You are a good shoemaker. The way things are now, all you are doing is neglecting your business." Carey's answer was, "Neglecting my business! My business is to proclaim the grace of God to all people. I make shoes just to cover my expenses."

> The church exists by mission, as fire exists by burning.
> — EMIL BRUNNER

May God give us the grace to reveal this attitude in His service.

How can we ever thank You enough for Your mercy, O God! Help us to share it freely with others through Your love that burns in our hearts. Amen.

Read James 4:11-17

God Willing

How do you know what your life will be like tomorrow? Your life is like the morning fog – it's here a little while, then it's gone. What you ought to say is, "If the Lord wants us to, we will live and do this or that" (James 4:14-15).

The future is not in our hands and no one dare arrogantly claim that he has the ability to decide about the future. Some people plan their future self-confidently and proudly without taking God into account. This arrogance is often seen in those who have achieved success and forget that what they have achieved was by the grace of God and not their own abilities.

> Change and decay in all around I see. O Thou who changest not, abide with me!
> HENRY FRANCIS LYTE

James points out how foolish this haughty self-assurance can be. You who don't even know what tomorrow will bring think you can boast about the future. You don't even know if you will still be alive tomorrow. When you speak, your attitude must always be: God willing. Your plans for the future show how dependent you are on the Lord.

When Robert Louis Stevenson, a well-known English author, was searching for spiritual light and eventually found it, he wrote his father a letter and mentioned among other things that no one can say that they have achieved success in life before they can write in the journal of their lives, the words: "God rules our destiny!"

The holy finger of God writes His command for our lives across all our earthly plans, of which He determines the outcome. Understanding this makes one humble, but also gives one courage to meet the future.

Father of love and grace, it is good to know that You decide about our lives. Help me to follow wherever You might lead. Amen.

May 6

Read Philippians 2:1-11

United in Christ

Then make me truly happy by agreeing wholeheartedly with each other, loving one another, and working together with one mind and purpose (Phil. 2:2).

The greatest danger that threatened the church in Philippi was division. Satan's tactics to divide and rule are evident in all the churches of Jesus Christ. The greater people's enthusiasm for a cause, the easier they clash. The most vindictive critics of church people are church people! Selfish ambition, personal prestige and focus on the self are the main characteristics Satan uses to divide and conquer.

We need to remember that we are one in Jesus Christ. No one who lives in unity with Jesus Christ can live in disunity with his neighbor. Christ's love will keep us united. If we love one another, the world will know we belong to Him. Submitting ourselves to the Holy Spirit will also keep us united in Christ. Compassion and empathy with each other will prevent disagreement. The church cannot grow and carry out its task as long as there is disunity amongst its members.

A man worked hard for many years to save enough money to buy a house and furnish it. He did this in order to marry the woman of his dreams. During their honeymoon he received a telegram with the news that his house had burnt down and that he had lost everything: all the toil of so many years in vain! His young wife read the telegram over his shoulder, looked into his eyes and smiled: "Never mind, my dearest husband, we still have each other!" If the devil tries to divide us, love is the anchor that stabilizes us.

> Every moment of resistance to temptation is a victory.
> F. W. Faber

Lord Jesus, You resisted so many of the devil's efforts and temptations. Help me to do the same because of my love for You. Amen.

Read Psalm 23:1-6

The Lord Is My Shepherd

He renews my strength. He guides me along right paths, bringing honor to His name (Ps. 23:3).

In life we get to know true contentment only when we pray: "Lord, guide us!" If however, we prefer sin to His guidance, we choose to follow our own road and then we cannot blame the Lord for the company we find ourselves in. Our Shepherd knows where the pastures and waters are that renew our strength. We will find our way there if we follow Him obediently. If we start to rebel against His guidance, we do ourselves and our future great harm. We must remember these things next time we choose to go our own way and refuse to be guided by our Shepherd.

The dolphin occupied a prominent place in the sculptures and adornments on the walls of the catacombs, as well as in the symbolic works of early Christian art. Dolphins were called "the arrows of the sea". In Greek mythology they were the guides and protectors of people who were in danger at sea. Consequently they were often depicted on coins of early times.

> Faith and obedience are bound up in the same bundle; he that obeys God trusts God; and he that trusts God obeys God.
> CHARLES H. SPURGEON

There are many stories of dolphins guiding shipwrecked and drowning people to safety and life. In Christian symbolism, the dolphin represents Christ as Guide and Savior. Those who trust in Him can rest assured that they have a Guide who will save them from the raging seas of the world and bring them safely to the Father's house. Therefore our sincere prayer must always be, "Lord, guide us!"

Lord, guide me, through earthly darkness, please lead the way! Amen.

May 8

Read Luke 23:36-42

Where There Is Life, There Is Hope

Then he said, "Jesus, remember me when You come into Your Kingdom" (Luke 23:42).

The salvation of the dying criminal on the cross is proof that where there is life, there is hope. His faith was stronger than that of all the disciples put together. They still loved Jesus, but their hopes and expectations for His kingdom were shattered. Contrary to their flimsy faith, this criminal looked at the dying Man next to him and said, "Remember me when You come into Your kingdom."

> To follow the Savior is to participate in salvation, to follow the light is to perceive the light.
> — IRENAEUS

This criminal, who was aware of his own sin and Jesus' innocence, accepted that Jesus' destiny would differ from his, and that is why he appealed to Jesus' mercy. He took Jesus' kingship seriously even if it was at a very late stage in his life. We are amazed at the faith of this man who, with deep insight, looked past the shame of the moment and saw the coming glory. He was the first fruit of Jesus' salvation work and that day he was led into the kingdom of God, holding Jesus' hand.

However, this is not a free pass for those who delay. The longer you know about the Gospel but persevere in sin, the easier it is for you to hear the message of salvation without any emotion. In the town where I grew up, the blacksmith had a dog that slept where the blacksmith worked with hot iron on the anvil. The dog lay there fast asleep, while the sparks rained down on him. He became so accustomed to his environment that he didn't notice his surroundings anymore. We must seize life while there is still hope. The time of grace will pass.

Merciful Master, it is wonderful to know that there is hope where there is life. Help me not to postpone ensuring my salvation. Amen.

Read Ephesians 4:1-16

One from Many

Make every effort to keep yourselves united in the Spirit, binding yourselves together with peace (Eph. 4:3).

One from many: The original motto of the United States, because they formed a country from many states. In the same way the Holy Spirit binds the children of God together in close unity.

> As we draw nearer to Christ, we shall be drawn nearer to His people.
> G. T. MANLEY

Creating unity is one of the Holy Spirit's most important tasks. We are called upon to maintain the unity He forged (see John 3:6; Acts 1:5; Eph. 1:14). This unity must be maintained because we as believers are one in all the aspects mentioned in Ephesians 4:4-6. Evidence of this unity must be seen in our relationships with each other.

God has authority over all of us because He controls the universe. He works through everybody and He uses believers to do His work. He lives in us and He is not closer to some than others. If we allow division among believers, we defy these facts. It often happens that believers are divided because of trivial doctrinal differences or even political viewpoints. If believers agree on the essence of the Gospel, they dare not allow other differences to drive them apart. The secular world gloats gleefully when Christians are at odds with one another.

In order to safeguard our unity we must live together in peace by always being humble, friendly, patient, tolerant and loving toward one another.

Holy Master, I would like to glorify You by making a contribution to the unity of Your children here on earth. Let Your Holy Spirit teach me daily how to do it. Amen.

Read Psalm 27:1-7

The Lord Is My Light

The LORD is my light and my salvation – so why should I be afraid? (Ps. 27:1)

This psalm is about the psalmist's faith that God will protect him from his enemies while he takes shelter in the temple. He expresses his unconditional confidence in the Lord.

Jesus Himself said, "I am the light of the world. If you follow Me, you won't have to walk in darkness" (John 8:12). He came to bring light into the darkness of this sinful world. The Lord is the light on every unknown road and His light shines down like the rays of the sun and purifies our hearts.

We will have our share of dark roads and the powers of darkness will surround and threaten us. But it became dark for Christ at Golgotha so that we would never again have to face the darkness of life alone. Together with the psalmist we can rejoice, "Even when I walk through the darkest valley, I will not be afraid, for You are close beside me" (Ps. 23:4).

In recent excavations at the former Gezer, hundreds of lamps were found, some of them carrying the inscription: "The Lord is my Light!" Since the earliest times of human existence, food, water and weapons have been necessities. But gradually the thought developed that light was necessary in the dark places of life. This gave rise to the lamp becoming the symbol of Light in the world in the early Christian period. Jews and Christians lit candles and lamps at funerals.

> Words which do not give the light of Christ increase the darkness.
> MOTHER TERESA

It is comforting to know that if we follow Jesus we will never walk in the dark.

Thank You, Lord Jesus, for lighting the way, so that I don't need to walk my life's road in darkness. Amen.

Read John 20:26-31

Trust God

Then Jesus told him, "You believe because you have seen Me. Blessed are those who believe without seeing Me" (John 20:29).

God expects His children to trust Him. Thomas doubted, but this was his way of getting to the truth. He didn't take pleasure in his doubts, and believed and trusted God implicitly when he found answers to his questions.

It is all right for us to have doubts sometimes, as long as it doesn't become a way of life. Doubting is healthy if it makes one think again. It can give us an answer to a question that helps us make a decision to trust God. We mustn't get lost in doubt, but use it to strengthen our certainty and faith. We must accept God's challenge: "Trust Me!"

A theological student, experiencing great spiritual confusion, went to Dr. Archibald Alexander for help and advice. He had started doubting whether he was a born-again child of God. Dr. Alexander said to him, "My young friend, you know what confession of sin is and what faith in Christ is. You think you confessed your sins in remorse once. Don't fight your doubt now; do it all over again. Confess your doubts and sins remorsefully, believe in the Lord Jesus and trust Him. This is the way to remain certain that you are God's child." This is a good remedy for doubt: work at it and trust God!

Jesus didn't reject Thomas because of his doubts. However, when doubt becomes stubborn and uncompromising, and this obstinacy becomes a way of life, it becomes a stumbling block in your faith.

> Every step toward Christ kills a doubt.
> THEODORE CUYLER

My Lord and God, You know everything: You know that I trust and love You. Let the Holy Spirit strengthen me in my moments of doubt. Amen.

Read James 2:14-26

Actions Speak Louder Than Words

> What good is it, dear brothers and sisters, if you say you have faith but don't show it by your actions? Can that kind of faith save anyone? (James 2:14).

Faith without deeds is dead. In our Scripture reading James implies that faith without deeds is not true faith. He uses the example of a corpse to illustrate it. Just as a body is dead without breath, so also faith is dead without good works. James is talking to practicing Christians who claim to have a good relationship with God.

No one can be saved by good deeds; only Jesus Christ can save us. Likewise, no person can grow spiritually without doing good works out of gratitude for his salvation. We are not saved *by* good works; we are saved to *do* good works. There is nothing as dangerous as repeatedly experiencing a beautiful emotion, without making an attempt to put that emotion into action. You can take pleasure in an emotion, but through effort, discipline and sacrifice it must take concrete shape in your life in the form of good deeds. After all, actions speak louder than words!

> If any man should ask me what is the first, second, and third part of being a Christian, I must answer, "Action!"
> — Thomas Brooks

There is a fishing village on a dangerous part of the coast of Wales and many lives have been lost in the treacherous sea. The inhabitants decided that they needed a lifeboat. First they built a beautiful boathouse, but by the time it was finished, they had no more funds. There the boathouse stood, painted and completed – but without a lifeboat.

This is symbolic of so many Christians: they have good intentions, but no powerful action to put those intentions into practice. In the meantime, many are drowning in the sea of sin.

Faithful God, make me a doer. Let my actions honor Your name and build Your kingdom. Amen.

Read Matthew 6:5-15

Your Will Be Done

"May Your kingdom come soon. May Your will be done on earth, as it is in heaven" (Matt. 6:10).

When we pray that God's will be done, we are not simply submitting ourselves to fate. We are praying that His perfect purpose will be fulfilled in this world, just as it is in heaven, and that we will do what He expects from us to make this possible. When this Scripture verse is read together with the foregoing part of the prayer, the request is that God will grant that He is known and obeyed.

> A man's heart is right when he wills what God wills.
> THOMAS AQUINAS

The kingdom of God is a community on earth where God's will is implemented just as perfectly as in heaven. We could pray this prayer in an attitude of defeat. You don't say it because you want to but because God is stronger than you. You can also say it with bitter resentment and in smoldering rage towards God. However, God wants us to pray it in complete love and trust because we know that God only has our best interests at heart.

To produce a perfect chord in music, it is essential that the instruments used must harmonize. Unless there is this perfect conformation as the note is touched, a discordant, jarring sound will be heard instead of flawless chords. Before we can be in perfect harmony with God's will and live in communion with Him, we must be tuned to His perfect will in loving submission.

Gracious and loving God and Father, my deepest desire is to live within Your will like Your Son, Jesus Christ, did. Let Your Holy Spirit enable me to do so. Amen.

Read 2 Timothy 1:3-14

In Faith and Love

Hold on to the pattern of wholesome teaching you learned from me – a pattern shaped by the faith and love that you have in Christ Jesus (2 Tim. 1:13).

When you are in doubt, you must cling to Jesus in faith and love. You need confirmation that the road you are on is the right one. Paul confirms this to Timothy in two ways and by using himself as example. Firstly, it means a lot to you if you have a role model to follow. It is as if the footsteps you place your feet in give you extra courage and conviction.

Secondly, Paul reminds Timothy of the fact that through faith and love, he has something good to hold on to. He must not doubt it, but work to the utmost for Christ through the power of the Holy Spirit. Faith and love enable one to carry out one's task fearlessly.

A man was trying to scrape frost from his window. A neighbor watched this and asked him what he was doing. "I'm getting rid of the frost, because I can't see through the window." The friend realized how foolish his neighbor was and good-naturedly gave him some advice, "Light your fireplace and let it burn well. The heat it generates will let the frost disappear on its own." It was good advice; also for us if our hearts have become frozen by the ice-cold atmosphere of doubt and a lack of love.

> The whole being of any Christian is faith and love.
> MARTIN LUTHER

Pray that God will light the fire of love and faith in your heart through the Holy Spirit, and your view of life will change radically.

Loving Master, strengthen the faith and love in my heart so that all doubt is allayed, and I can spread Your love in the world. Amen.

May 15

Read John 15:9-17

Faithful Friend

"I no longer call you slaves, because a master doesn't confide in his slaves. Now you are My friends, since I have told you everything the Father told Me" (John 15:15).

Jesus calls us His friends and also friends of His Father! This is an amazing gesture of love. It means that we don't need to longingly yearn for God from a distance anymore; we are not like slaves who don't have the right to enter into the presence of their master. We are not part of the crowds that only see the king on state occasions. Christ makes intimacy with God possible for us and we become friends of the Father's Son.

The living Christ is our Lord and Master. He should treat us like subordinates, but He doesn't! We must obey Him because He is our Lord and Master, and we must be loyal to Him because He is our friend. Especially because this Friend gave His life for us. Loyalty to Him means obeying His command to love one another.

> It is mutual loyalty that makes lasting friendships.
> JOHN NEWMAN

Luigi Rossini (1790-1857), the French artist, received a precious clock from the king as a gift, and for many years he was very proud of it. When he showed it to a friend years later, the friend told him that although he had owned the clock for such a long time, he hadn't yet realized its full value. He then pressed a hidden spring on the clock and the container opened and displayed one of Rossini's paintings inside. The king's signature was at the bottom as well as the words: From a friend. Many of us have not experienced Christ's friendship yet, although we have been members of His church for many years.

I bow in thankfulness before the wonder of Your friendship, O Lord. I will strive to stay worthy of this friendship. Amen.

Read Luke 2:8-20

Glory to God in the Highest Heaven

"Glory to God in highest heaven, and peace on earth to those with whom God is pleased" (Luke 2:14).

The story of vast hosts of angels singing the praises of God, and heavenly music resounding across the fields of Ephrata has inspired composers for 2000 years. It is often called "Gloria", arising from the first word in the Latin translation of the song. It is also the point of departure in numerous contemporary choirs, traditional Christmas carols and liturgical chorales.

> Praising God is one of the highest and purest acts of religion.
> THOMAS WATSON

The Gloria is the song the angels sang at the arrival of the Messiah. Many Jews thought He would free them from Roman domination and in doing so make the kingdom of God visible. He surpassed all expectations. People often draw up their own agenda for Jesus and then expect nothing more from Him.

His work extends far beyond what any one of us could think or dream of. He paid the price for our sins and opened the door to God's presence. He offers much more than superficial politics or physical change. He offers us a new heart that will carry us into eternity, and renewal in all spheres of life. So together with the angels we rejoice: Gory to God in the highest!

The glory of God is revealed in two ways: In His creation and all its glorious wonders. But we also marvel at His honor and glory through Jesus Christ in His unfathomable love and unselfish sacrifice. Therefore we rejoice: *Gloria in excelsis Deo!* The Word became flesh and came to live among us!

Jesus, we glorify You! Jesus, we praise You! Together with the angels we want to sing a song of praise: accept our thanks! Amen.

Read Psalm 147:1-11

God Heals All Wounds

He heals the brokenhearted, and bandages their wounds (Ps. 147:3).

For the Christian it is not time that heals all wounds, but God. The psalmist calls on us to praise God for His healing miracles. The time of nursing our wounds must pass, otherwise we might get stuck in our grief. Sorrow must spill over into praise because it brings acceptance of God's actions. Then a new spring dawns in our garden of life.

> Jesus did not come to explain away our pain and suffering or remove it. He came to fill it with His presence.
> Paul Claudel

Worship is the action through which our entire being is concentrated on God so that we can ponder and sing about His greatness and holiness. Worship sets us free from the pain of sorrow and grief. By the grace of God our perspectives are broadened by pain and sorrow. In this way worship allows the healing balm of God's grace to flow over our wounds and heal them.

Take Job, for example. After the loss of all his children and possessions and his health, Job was in deep mourning. First he tore his clothes in a demonstration of shock and dismay. This is a natural human response. Next he shaved his head, in a tribute to those who died, but also humbling himself before God. Even when experiencing immense sorrow, Job clung to God. Finally Job fell to the ground before God, worshiping Him because he had learnt that God heals all wounds, "Praise the name of the Lord!" (Job 1:21). It is on this condition that God heals all wounds.

God, open my eyes so that I will see Your greatness; open my heart so that I may love; open my lips so that I may glorify and praise You. Amen.

Read John 19:17-27

Inhumanity towards Others

Carrying the cross by Himself, He went to the place called Place of the Skull (in Hebrew Golgotha). There they nailed Him to the cross. Two others were crucified with Him, one on either side, with Jesus between them (John 19:17-18).

Crucifixion was the Roman form of the death penalty and a typical example of the inhumanity of humanity. Jesus had to carry the crossbeam of the cross on His flogged back along the main road up to the place where He would be crucified. At Golgotha He was nailed to the cross which was then lifted up by soldiers and dropped into the hole where it was to be planted. The nails tore into His flesh. He had to endure long and intense agony. He was in pain, and He was thirsty. It was a humiliating and an excruciating death.

The irony is that God sent His Son to earth because He loved the world (John 3:16). The response to that love was the worst form of brutality any human being could inflict on another. Those who have not found Christ yet are ruled by the law of the jungle: survival of the fittest. To them it doesn't matter which gruesome methods the "fittest" apply to survive. Christianity places us under the rule of love where we care for, and serve one another with compassionate hearts.

> Christ's blood is heaven's key.
> THOMAS BROOKS

When our Master died on the cross because of the inhumanity of humankind, He could say, "It is finished. The work You gave Me to do, I did." In this way He brought about the salvation of the world, in spite of the brutality of humankind.

Risen Savior, You taught us to love our enemies and to pray for them. In this way we make the world a better place. Amen.

May 19

Read Luke 22:47-53

Betrayal

Jesus said, "Judas, would you betray the Son of Man with a kiss?" (Luke 22:48).

In certain parts of the world it is still customary for men to greet one another with a kiss. Judas's kiss was however the sign by which the soldiers would identify Jesus. One shudders at the thought: one member of the small group of disciples Jesus trusted betrayed Him with a kiss in exchange for a small amount of money! The Scribes didn't capture Jesus in the temple, because they were afraid that the people who supported Jesus would stir up a rebellion. They captured Jesus in the dark by means of Judas's betrayal.

This is a manifestation of the hour of darkness. Jesus' enemies rejected an open, reasonable and fair debate. This, together with Judas's bitter betrayal, is a story one shudders to tell. William Hazlitt writes in his well-known essay *Of Persons One Would Wish To Have Seen*, "As far as Judas Iscariot is concerned, my reasons are quite different. I would have liked to see the face of him who dared to put his hand in the dish with Jesus' during the meal, and could betray Him just afterwards. I find it difficult to picture, and have never seen a painting (not even Leonardo da Vinci's *Last Supper*) that could even closely personify it." If we could have seen his face, we would possibly form a vague image, and understand why he did something we shudder to talk about. Therefore we should take note of Jesus' words, "Keep watch and pray, so that you will not give in to temptation. For the spirit is willing, but the body is weak" (Mark 14:38).

> O Lord my God, give me understanding to know You, diligence to seek You, wisdom to find You, and a faithfulness that may finally embrace You.
> THOMAS AQUINAS

Savior and Redeemer, help me through the work of the Holy Spirit, to remain faithful to You and never to betray Your love. Amen.

Read 1 Peter 5:5-11

Enemy of the Human Race

Stay alert! Watch out for your great enemy, the devil. He prowls around like a roaring lion, looking for someone to devour (1 Pet. 5:8).

Satan is the deadliest enemy of the human race. This is why Peter calls on all believers to be careful and alert, keeping the promise of God's power and grace in mind. If you know that your enemy is like a roaring lion, looking to devour you, you will always be on your guard. Peter also warns against evil desires and that they will destroy you if you give in to them (1 Pet. 2:11). The devil and your human nature will consume you if you are not prepared to handle unjust treatment with dignity. You resist this enemy if you remain steadfast in your faith and do not allow unfair suffering to motivate you to take the law into your own hands. Keep your eyes on Christ and resist the enemy, then he will flee from you (see James 4:7).

> The devil's snare does not catch you, unless you are first caught by the devil's bait.
> St. Ambrose

Henry Stanley, who traveled with David Livingstone in Africa, wrote that when they journeyed through the dark jungles of Africa they didn't see many snakes, but when they lived in a certain place for a long while and wanted to clear a piece of ground for themselves to plant corn, they found snakes all over the place; under tree stumps, rocks, leaves, weeds and in the ground. The snakes were destroyed, the land cultivated and corn sowed. Soon they had their first harvest.

In this way, he says, evil is hidden in all of us and is revealed by our temptations. If we are serious about eradicating them, fruit from the Holy Spirit will grow in the same soil.

Once again I confess my sin, Lord Jesus, and pray for Your forgiveness, and the ability to resist the powers of evil. Amen.

Read Luke 24:25-35

Behind Closed Doors

"The Lord has really risen! He appeared to Peter" (Luke 24:34).

Jesus' love and grace is revealed when He appeared privately to Peter after His resurrection (1 Cor. 15:5). This appearance is not described in the Gospels, probably because it was such an intimate and private conversation. Jesus was concerned about Peter, who felt unworthy after denying Christ. Peter was remorseful about this and Jesus forgave him. The Lord would shortly help him to build the church.

> Love is the greatest thing that God can give us, for He Himself is love and it is the greatest thing we can give to God.
> JEREMY TAYLOR

This conversation was undoubtedly the most special moment in Peter's entire life. It is astounding that Jesus appeared (both after His resurrection and before His ascension) in private to the disciple who denied Him. The glory of Christ's mercy and love is demonstrated in His decision to appear to Peter in private. If Christ had not done this, Peter would have hated himself for denying Christ. The Savior's goal was to get this impulsive disciple back on his feet again. He did this by having a private conversation with Peter.

Peter had committed an offense against Jesus and shed bitter tears of remorse. The one great desire Jesus had was to comfort him in the pain of his disloyalty. Love cannot go much further than to think of the hurt of the person who wronged him, lovingly and with a forgiving heart. Don't you think it's time that we also have private conversations with our Master about all the times we disappointed Him, and to treat those who offended us with kindness?

Forgiving Master, Your mercy is beyond our comprehension. Help me to follow Your example toward those who wrong me. Amen.

Read Galatians 6:6-14

Victory through the Cross

As for me, may I never boast about anything except the cross of our Lord Jesus Christ. Because of that cross, my interest in this world has been crucified, and the world's interest in me has also died (Gal. 6:14).

We all want to be winners. There are many inviting practices and viewpoints that can make us winners. Daily and in subtle ways we are tempted to give in to our sinful nature. There is only one way to overcome these self-destructive influences. You must realize that the old you died with Christ on the cross and that you yourself no longer live, but that Christ lives in you (Gal. 2:20).

If you try to be a winner through any other way than the way of Jesus' cross, you will fail. Only when you have died with Jesus, the Holy Spirit will rule in your life and you become a new person. For this reason you must, like Paul, no longer allow anything or anyone to take the place of Christ's cross in your life. Are there things in your life that take the place of the cross?

In the darkest hour of the war with Germany, when the future of western civilization was being threatened, the Congress of United Women met in Paris and accepted a striking slogan: "Believe in victory! Think victory! Preach victory! Live victory!" Where western civilization is once again under severe pressure in our day, we can adapt this slogan: "Believe in victory through the Cross! Think victory through the Cross! Live and preach victory through the Cross!" Because in the Cross we will triumph.

> By the Cross we know the gravity of sin and the greatness of God's love towards us.
> JOHN CHRYSOSTOM

Lord, we not only exult in the cross, but also in Your victory on the cross. Together with You, we are certain of victory. Amen.

Read 1 Corinthians 1:1-9

Father, Son and Holy Spirit

May God our Father and the Lord Jesus Christ give you grace and peace (1 Cor. 1:3).

Paul uses a Greek and Hebrew greeting. The Greek word for grace emphasizes God's goodness as the basis for salvation and peace. The Hebrew greeting "peace" is the result of God's goodness; the abundance of His blessings.

Paul tells us about God's grace and peace which is the blessing that rests on His faithful children. He also exults the name of Jesus Christ for those near and far: their Lord and our Lord! No human being, no church, has the exclusive right of possession of Jesus Christ. He is *our* Lord, but also the Lord of all people and consequently everyone shares in His blessings. It is the amazing wonder of Christianity that all people have a right to Christ's love and that God loves every one of us as if we are the only ones He has to love.

The Holy Spirit is automatically included in this benediction because He is our Comforter, our Guide and our Leader to God and Christ. It is through the Holy Spirit that we share in the blessings of the Father and the Son. Therefore the devoted child of God always prays in the name of the Father and the Son and the Holy Spirit.

> Our salvation is free in the Father, sure in the Son, ours in the Spirit.
> THOMAS MANTON

God of grace and peace, thank You that I may daily receive Your abundant blessings, through Christ and the Holy Spirit. Amen.

Read Matthew 25:1-13

Always Ready

"But while they were gone to buy oil [the foolish bridesmaids], the bridegroom came. Then those who were ready went in with him to the marriage feast and the door was locked" (Matt. 25:10).

This parable contains two universal warnings. Firstly, it warns us to be ready for anything. There are certain things that cannot be postponed until the last moment. To start preparing for an examination on the day you start writing would be foolish. Similarly, you cannot perform a task that requires specialized training, before receiving training. It is too late to start building character the day you need it. It is easy to postpone your salvation to the point where you can't prepare for Christ's second coming any longer.

> We are not a post-war generation; but a pre-peace generation. Jesus is coming!
> CORRIE TEN BOOM

Secondly, it also teaches us that there are certain things that cannot be borrowed. The foolish bridesmaids realized too late that there was no oil to borrow when they needed it. You cannot borrow a relationship with God; you must possess it. You cannot borrow character; your own must be formed. You cannot live indefinitely on another's spiritual capital. There are things that you must possess yourself in order to be ready for all things.

Heaven will be filled with people who were ready for Christ's glorious second coming. Hell will be filled with people who postponed preparation for Christ's second coming. So let us make sure that we are always prepared for when He comes again!

Risen and Living Christ, You promised that You would come again. Help me to remain watchful, so that I will be ready for this glorious event. Amen.

Read John 21:15-19

Word for Word

After breakfast Jesus asked Simon Peter, "Simon son of John, do you love Me more than these?" "Yes, Lord," Peter replied, "You know I love You." "Then feed My lambs," Jesus told him (John 21:15).

Did Peter say this to Christ? Yes, word for word! And by repeating these words three times, he erased his threefold denial of his Master.

> Little keys can open big locks. Simple words can express great thoughts.
> WILLIAM ARTHUR WARD

Peter's whole life changed when he eventually realized who Jesus really was. He went from full-time fisherman to full-time disciple of the Master. His lifestyle also changed. His impulsive nature gave way to a more stable and reliable one. And all of this was the result of his words, "You know I love You!" His relationship with Jesus changed as well, because he had been forgiven and understood the meaning of Jesus' words about His death and resurrection.

As He did with Peter, Jesus also asks us, "Do you love Me?" If we could answer exactly as Peter did, our love for the Master will bring about a task for us: to look after His lambs and sheep. The only way we can show that we love Jesus is by loving others. Love is a privilege, but also a responsibility.

Peter's love for Christ came at a price. He died because of the exact words he spoke on this occasion. We don't truly love Christ unless we are willing to do His work and take up our cross. Otherwise our words mean nothing.

Lord, You know everything. You know that I love You. Amen.

Read Matthew 5:13-16

Work for God

"Let your good deeds shine out for all to see, so that everyone will praise your heavenly Father" (Matt. 5:16).

The greatest victory we can achieve with work is to glorify God with it. All other work is inferior to this. Work is only victorious if it is done to the glory of God alone!

If we wish to live for Christ, our work will be like a light that reflects Christ. Our work is in vain if we keep quiet when we should speak or witness; if we go with the flow; if we deny that we have received talents from God; if we allow sin to dim our light and zest for work; if we don't explain to others that our work and strength are from God. If you are a bright beacon of truth, your work will always prevail, and be to the glory of God.

We must make sure that our work does not focus the attention on us, but on God. The great preacher Dwight L. Moody once attended a conference where a diligent group of young people prayed through the night. As they were leaving the room, they met Moody and told him in excitement that they had prayed through the night. Then they added, "Just look how our faces are glowing!" Moody muttered to himself, Moses wasn't aware that his face glowed (Exod. 34:28-29). Good work accompanied by overestimating of the self can never be blessed, because it draws attention to us instead of glorifying our Father in heaven. If He gets the credit, the work we do for Him will overcome everything!

> We should always honor and reverence Him as if we were always in His bodily presence.
> — THOMAS À KEMPIS

Faithful Lord, let the work of my hands bring honor and glory to You, so that I can be victorious in Your name. Amen.

Read Luke 19:37-43

Christ's Tears

But as He came closer to Jerusalem and saw the city ahead, He began to weep. "How I wish today that you of all people would understand the way to peace. But now it is too late, and peace is hidden from your eyes" (Luke 19:41-42).

The Jews rejected their King. The spiritual leaders rejected God's offer of grace in Jesus Christ and for that reason God would hand them over to their enemies. And about forty years later Jerusalem was destroyed by Titus. This verdict was given at the time of Jesus' triumphant entry into Jerusalem when the crowds wanted to crown Him as king. When He saw the city, and foresaw its future, Jesus cried. He did not shed sentimental tears because Jerusalem was precious to Him. The tears He shed were on account of everybody who rejected Christ as their Redeemer and Savior.

This episode is just a short flashback on Jesus' road of suffering. He came to proclaim the grace of God to people and to get that message across He died on the cross. There His Via Dolorosa reached both its peak and its end when He breathed His last words, "It is finished!" He had completed everything God instructed Him to do. It was accompanied by blood and tears, but in obedience to His task, He persevered until the end.

> The purest suffering produces the purest understanding.
> JOHN OF THE CROSS

We often lack passion for lost souls, so that we do not have the ability to shed tears for a world on the road to hell. Jesus' tears are a shining example of empathy with a sinful world, that rejects its Savior.

Thank You, Lord Jesus, that I may share in Your suffering by having compassion with a lost world. Let my tears culminate in action. Amen.

Read Matthew 5:38-42

An Eye for an Eye

"You have heard that it was said, 'Eye for eye, and tooth for tooth'" (Matt. 5:38 NIV).

This is about retribution according to the law of the jungle. When we are wronged, our first reaction is revenge. But Jesus said we must do good to those who wrong us. We mustn't keep count of those who wronged us, but respond with love and forgiveness.

> "I can forgive but I cannot forget," is only another way of saying, "I cannot forgive."
> HENRY WARD BEECHER

This is not a response that comes naturally to human beings. Only God can enable us to love others like He loves us. Don't plan revenge, but rather pray for those who hurt you.

One morning when a little boy saw his friend next door, he greeted him happily, grabbed his cap and ran to the front door for their regular morning play session. His grandpa said jokingly, "What? Are you playing next door again? What about your fight last night when you said you would never have anything to do with each other again? You have a short memory." "Never mind, Grandpa," he answered, "Kevin and I are good at forgetting!"

If only we could all be as forgiving as children and not only forgive, but also forget, the world would be a better place.

You graciously forgave me, Lord Jesus. Help me to forgive others in the same way and refrain from nursing a grievance. Thank You for Your holy example on the cross. Amen.

Read Luke 18:9-14

Sincere Confession

"Two men went to the Temple to pray. One was a Pharisee, and the other was a despised tax collector" (Luke 18:10).

James warns us and says, "God opposes the proud but favors the humble" (James 4:6). Here Jesus points out two people who went to the temple to pray. Whatever they felt about each other and whatever the world thought of them, they were both people that had to stand before God and confess their sins. Their status, standing in the community, possessions and education, counted nothing before God. According to the world, the Pharisee was a God-fearing man and the tax collector a sinner. But God knew the attitude of their hearts when they stood before Him, confessing their sins.

> We must lay before Him what is in us, not what ought to be in us.
> C. S. Lewis

They revealed two types of attitudes. Everyone went to the place of confession with a certain attitude. The Pharisee claimed a prominent place before God, as if it was due to him. He stood before God, an egoist filled with pride. The tax collector almost didn't dare appear before God because he was deeply aware of his sin.

They also prayed two prayers. The Pharisee gave God a letter of recommendation, so to speak. He didn't thank God for His grace, but told Him how much better he was than others. We must however be careful of saying, "I thank God that I am not like the Pharisee!"

The tax collector went to confession with sincere motives. He stood at a distance and simply pleaded for mercy and confessed his sins.

When the renowned Lord Simpson was asked what his greatest discovery was, he answered humbly, "My sin!"

Gracious Redeemer and Savior, give me the heart and attitude of the tax collector so that I will appear before You in sincere confession. Have mercy on me, a sinner. Amen.

Read Matthew 25:14-30

Use Your Gifts Well

"The master was full of praise, 'Well done, my good and faithful servant. You have been faithful in handling this small amount, so now I will give you many more responsibilities. Let's celebrate together!'" (Matt. 25:21).

The money that we read about here doesn't refer to personal talents or gifts. It is more about the practical faithfulness and personal responsibility of believers in carrying out their task until Jesus returns. It is not about how much we receive, but what we do with what we have received.

Jesus' second coming doesn't mean we must resign our jobs to work for Him. It means that we must faithfully use our time and talents and all the means at our disposal to serve God, wherever we are and whatever we do. For most of us it means that we do our normal work faithfully every day and make sure we are ready for His second coming.

We can also use the gifts and talents of our personality, voice or heart in God's service. A good-looking woman may devote her beauty and grace to the service of God. A man with social tact and insight may emulate Christ and become a fisher of people by means of his warm-heartedness and compassion. Everything in everyday life that is clean and virtuous fills life around us with a delightful fragrance if it is an offering at the feet of the Master like the nard oil that Mary anointed Jesus' feet with. Then His reaction is always, "Well done!"

> A man can only do what he can do. But if he does that each day he can sleep at night and do it again the next day.
> ALBERT SCHWEITZER

I devote my spirit, my soul and my body to You, O Lord. I offer myself as sacrifice to You forever. Amen.

June

Since we are living by the Spirit, let us follow the Spirit's leading in every part of our lives.
GALATIANS 5:25

Lord, when we are wrong, make us willing to change. And when we are right, make us easy to live with.
PETER MARSHALL

God of love and grace,
we thank You for the outpouring of the Holy Spirit
that teaches and leads us in truth.
Let Your Spirit inspire us to demonstrate pure love,
and help us to forget what we did for others,
but to remember what others did for us.
Spirit of God, let us remember above all,
what Jesus Christ did for us.
Help us to forget what the world owes us
and remember what we, as Your children,
are indebted to the world.
Let us keep our rights and demands in the background,
and our duties as the King's children in the foreground.
Help us realize that other people
have the same needs that we do,
so that we will see their hearts,
masked by their outward appearance.
Let us shut the complaints book and look around us to see
where we can sow a seed of gratitude and hope.
Open our eyes, O Spirit of God,
to look around us with love and to see
those who are sad, lost, hurt and miserably alone.
Help us to reveal Your goodness and grace to them.
Let Your love urge us to be messengers of Your hope,
reconciliation and peace.
This we beg of You in the name of Jesus our Lord and Master.
Amen.

Read Luke 15:11-23

My Sin

"I will go home to my father and say, 'Father, I have sinned against both heaven and you, and I am no longer worthy of being called your son. Please take me on as a hired servant'" (Luke 15:18-19).

Sin dragged this young man down to the lowest level of humiliation. It was unheard of for a Jew to feed pigs and even more of a disgrace to be forced by hunger to eat pig feed. This young man truly landed up in the mire and all he could do about it was to call out, "I am guilty!"

Some people must sink to the lowest level before coming to their senses. This young man's problems were caused by a wrong perception of what true freedom was. His interpretation of freedom was in fact extravagance. We see the same thing happening around us today. People often have to end up in sorrow and misery before they turn to the only One who can help them.

> Sin is not hurtful because it is forbidden, but it is forbidden because it is hurtful.
> BENJAMIN FRANKLIN

Are you perhaps trying to arrange your life to suit yourself; to your own liking? Are you trying to find happiness in satisfying your own selfish desires? Don't allow the false portrayal of freedom presented by the world to mislead you. Glitter and glamour, and things that seem like good fun, do not necessarily bring happiness and peace.

God's love for us never changes and He is waiting for us to come and confess our guilt. He is constantly looking out for us and gives us the opportunity to respond to His love, but He never forces us to turn back to Him. He waits patiently for us to come to our senses so that He can embrace us with His forgiveness. All we have to do is to confess: "I have sinned!"

O Jesus, my Savior, I have a song of praise in my heart because I came to You and received forgiveness. Amen.

Read Genesis 3:14-24

To Dust You Will Return

By the sweat of your brow will you have food to eat until you return to the ground from which you were made. For you were made from dust, and to dust you will return (Gen. 3:19).

When God called Adam and Eve to account for their behavior, He started with the man whose job it was to take care of the garden. Without hesitation the man laid the blame on the woman God gave him. Indirectly he suggested that it was actually God's fault. On her turn, Eve blamed the snake.

> Men fear death like children fear to go in the dark; and as that natural fear in children is increased by tales, so is the other.
> FRANCIS BACON

As soon as sin is exposed, the human being's first reaction is to find excuses and look for a scapegoat to take the blame. We are quick to blame other people and circumstances for our sins and failures.

Adam and Eve learnt the hard way that the Lord punishes sin because He is holy. We read of many cases in the Bible where people's lives were destroyed because of disobedience to God. Sin breaks up our relationship with God and causes disharmony on all levels of life. At worst it brings about death.

However, God does not want to punish us (see Ezek. 18:23; 2 Pet. 3:9). He wants to save us because He loves us, no matter how badly we've sinned. He wants to forgive us so that our relationship with Him can be restored and we can have eternal life. Longfellow says in his song of lament, *A Psalm of Life*:

Life is real! Life is earnest! And the grave is not its goal; dust thou art, to dust returnest, was not spoken of the soul.

I bow in thankfulness before You, Jesus, because Your resurrection guarantees eternal life. Amen.

Read Amos 4:8-13

Remember That You Must Die

"Therefore, I will bring upon you all the disasters I have announced. Prepare to meet your God in judgment, you people of Israel!" (Amos 4:12).

God called Israel to repentance through various military and natural disasters. Some of their cities like Sodom and Gomorrah were destroyed completely and the signs of God's judgment were on them like wood scorched by fire. However, nothing could bring them to their senses. God walked the entire road with them to remind them that they would have to die one day and stand before Him, the great Judge, to be sentenced.

God makes His will known to people and He is even able to cause a complete disturbance in the laws of nature to impose His will on them. We must realize who our Lord is and what He is capable of.

The perceptions that people in biblical times had of death were clearly depicted in the catacombs in Rome, and in other cemeteries in this city. Heathen epitaphs never mentioned a belief in immortality, but described death as an endless sleep. To them death was final and their cemeteries were filled by an atmosphere of endless sorrow. Contrary to this, the epitaphs of Christians in the catacombs and elsewhere testified of abundant hope. You can read the words: "Rest in Peace!", "Forever with the Lord!", "He rests until Christ comes!", "Do not grieve; death is temporary!" and "Alexander is not dead, but lives beyond the stars!"

For those who are ready to appear before their God, death holds no fear. To them it is the wonderful passageway to everlasting life.

> When the time comes for you to die, you need not be afraid, because death cannot separate you from God's love.
> CHARLES H. SPURGEON

Lord of life, we praise You because we don't have to mourn the death of a loved one like people who have no hope. Amen.

Read Matthew 4:1-11

Code of Conduct

Then Jesus was led by the Spirit into the wilderness to be tempted there by the Devil (Matt. 4:1).

Even in our Savior's life, temptation was Satan's modus operandi. But Jesus did not give in to the temptations. We may feel sinful if we are faced with temptations, but temptation in itself is not sinful; only if we give in to it. If we keep this in mind at all times, it will be easier to resist temptation.

Jesus was tempted in the wilderness where He was tired, lonely and His resistance at its very lowest. This is the devil's code of conduct. But Satan also likes tempting us when we are strong and easy prey for pride. So we must be alert at all times, because Satan never rests and never gives up.

Satan's modus operandi is aimed at getting us to question God's words. It will be easier for him to achieve his goal if we start doubting God, because then we are vulnerable to his temptations.

> The devil does not tempt unbelievers and sinners who are already his own.
> THOMAS À KEMPIS

If you are searching for answers, you must protect yourself by constantly thinking about the unshakable truths of God's Word.

In the mechanical world there is probably no power greater than that of the wedge. Once the thin edge of the wedge has been forced into place, it is just a matter of time before it will cause a split. Neither the hardest rock nor the strongest wood is resistant to the thin end of a wedge. Watch out for the wedge of temptation; it is the thin edge of the wedge in Satan's method of attack. Constantly pray that God will help you resist temptation.

Almighty Father, I need Your strength and grace so much when I am faced by temptation. I take refuge in You and pray that Your Spirit will give me the strength to resist Satan. Amen.

Read John 10:1-13

A Living Sacrifice

"The thief's purpose is to steal and kill and destroy. My purpose is to give them a rich and satisfying life. I am the good shepherd. The good shepherd sacrifices his life for the sheep" (John 10:10-11).

Christ had to die so that we can live. This is the essence of the entire message of the Gospel (see John 3:16). As the shepherd cared for every sheep in his flock, the Good Shepherd not only cares for His flock, but even laid down His life for us (see Ezek. 34:23). His birth, suffering and death were all for our sakes, so that we can live!

> Without sacrifice there is no resurrection. Nothing blooms except through an offering. Whatever you aim to protect in you atrophies.
> — ANDRÉ GIDE

Christ taught us that self-sacrifice is at the center of worship. In obedience to God, He sacrificed His life for a world on its way to perdition, which gives us every reason to say: He died so that I may live!

The altar is the focal point in the church. It is placed in the most prominent position and has great symbolical meaning. The altar or the Holy Communion table is there to remind us that there can be no true worship without sacrifice and that sacrifice is not only the central point of our worship, but also of our entire lives. The altar also symbolizes that no life can be lived for the Spirit of Christ without sacrifice.

Christ died so that we may live. We must also be willing to make sacrifices for our brothers and sisters.

Loving Lord Jesus, Good Shepherd that sacrificed Your life for me, make me faithful in sacrificing my life for You and my fellow humans. Amen.

Read Proverbs 24:1-10

Knowledge Is Power

The wise are mightier than the strong, and those with knowledge grow stronger and stronger (Prov. 24:5).

One of the outstanding advantages of knowledge and wisdom is that they provide power. It was Sir Francis Bacon who created the sharp-witted saying "Knowledge is power!"

> Knowledge without integrity is dangerous and dreadful.
> — SAMUEL JOHNSON

The discovery of mechanical powers and the power of steam, multiplied power a hundredfold in proportion to physical strength. It keeps the king from waging unwise wars (see Prov. 20:18). If, however, he is forced to go to war and has the advice of good counselors to rely on, it will not be easy to defeat him.

Those with spiritual knowledge and insight are powerful giants. They combine the brute strength to draw a bow with the wisdom of a steady hand and a sharp eye to find their mark. Being aware of your ignorance is the first step on the road to true knowledge. The wise man says, "I am still young and inexperienced", and this humble wisdom establishes his kingdom (see 1 Kings 3:7).

The Christian is strengthened by all the wisdom and insight the Spirit provides and the glorious power of God that gives him all the patience and endurance he needs (see Col. 1:9, 11).

Through God's knowledge and omnipotence His disciples are also girded with power so that they will testify for Him (see Acts 1:8).

Good Father, grant that I will grow in the knowledge and love of the eternal God, so that I may be Your powerful witness. Amen.

Read Acts 9:10-19

A Leopard Never Changes Its Spots

Instantly something like scales fell from Saul's eyes, and he regained his sight. Then he got up and was baptized. Afterward he ate some food and regained his strength (Acts 9:18-19).

Horatio wrote in one of his letters that a leopard cannot change is spots. This proverb literally means that you can drive a person's nature out with a pitchfork, but it will return. This proverb has sparked a never-ending debate on which is stronger; heredity or environment.

Yet, figuratively speaking, it is possible that a leopard's skin can change. Paul was busy persecuting the church of Jesus like a leopard on the prowl until his experience on the road to Damascus, when God changed this leopard into a lamb. In one moment of illumination Saul was chained to the cross forever and even his name was changed to Paul. Instead of being a persecutor and murderer of Christians, he became an apostle of Christ and had a deep-rooted influence on the church through all the ages.

Paul's meeting with Jesus changed his whole life. He was still a high-spirited and zealous person, but as from that moment on he used his strength to spread the Gospel.

Bryan Green says that during the last service of one of his crusades in America, he asked people to stand up and say what the crusade had meant to them. A Negro girl got up and said, "I found Christ through this crusade and He has enabled me to forgive the man who murdered my father." Paul and Ananias, who were fierce enemies, united as brothers. So the leopard had in fact changed his spots!

> Every story of a conversion is the story of blessed defeat.
> C. S. Lewis

Almighty God, I honor and praise You that You can make everything new and that You do it in my life by Your grace. Amen.

Read Colossians 2:6-15

Slaves of the Flesh

You were dead because of your sins and because your sinful nature was not yet cut away. Then God made you alive with Christ, for He forgave all our sins (Col. 2:13).

Seneca claimed that no one who is a slave of the flesh is free. This was directed at those who reveled in the uninhibited pursuit of pleasure, lust and other perversities and decadence. As long as your base desires are dominant in your life, you are a slave and don't know true freedom.

Before we accepted Christ, our prospects in life were bleak and we were slaves of our sinful nature. However, the born-again Christian receives new freedom and opportunities when he accepts Christ. God nailed our old and rebellious natures to the cross and enabled us to shake off the shackles of the old nature and to live in freedom. God declared us not guilty and we no longer need to live under the tyranny of sin.

He doesn't remove us from the world and He doesn't change us into robots either. We will still sin and sometimes yield to temptation. The difference is that where we were slaves of our bodies and our sinful nature before, we now choose to live in Christ. We are free because Christ sets us free.

> There are two freedoms: the false where a man is free to do what he likes; and the true where a man is free to do as he ought.
> CHARLES KINGSLEY

Thank You, Holy Master, that You set us free from the fetters of lust and base instincts. Grant that we will appreciate our freedom and handle it responsibly. Amen.

Read 1 Timothy 5:3-15

Idleness Is the Parent of All Vice

They will learn to be lazy and will spend their time gossiping from house to house, meddling in other people's business and talking about things they shouldn't (1 Tim. 5:13).

The dangers of idleness are the same for any age or gender. There is the danger of restlessness for young widows who don't have enough to do and then visit from house to house for meaningless social chatter. Unfortunately they become gossips because they have nothing significant to do. The stories are then repeated from house to house; every time a little more detailed and with more malice.

The best way to avoid gossip is to fill your life with action and your mind with knowledge so that you always have something worthwhile to talk about. Idle people also start interfering in other people's affairs. Just as it was true back then, it is true to this day. Satan gives idle people something to do with their tongues. A full life is always a safe life and an idle life is always dangerous.

Once, bees were transported to Barbados to make honey, but after the first year they stopped producing honey. The island's climate was so pleasant that it over-stimulated the bees' honey production. They produced too much honey and after a while their nectar didn't have any effect anymore. So they kept themselves occupied by flying around in sugar factories and stinging the workers. Many people are like those bees. Because they are not forced to work, they not only become idle, but also nasty.

> God, I pray Thee, light these idle sticks of my life, that I may burn for Thee. Consume my life, my God, for it is Thine. I seek not a long life, but a full one, like You.
> SOCRATES

Creator God, thank You for a task that keeps me occupied every day so that the devil is not given the chance to keep me company. Amen.

Read Matthew 21:28-32

Willing or Reluctant?

"But what do you think about this? A man with two sons told the older boy, 'Son, go out and work in the vineyard today.' The son answered, 'No, I won't go,' but later he changed his mind and went anyway" (Matt. 21:28-29).

We can say of this son that he was the better of two bad brothers, and rightly so. At least he did what he didn't really want to do, whether willingly or reluctantly. This parable tells us that there are two kinds of people in the world. Firstly, there are those whose words speak louder than their actions. They will promise anything, they pride themselves on their devotion and trustworthiness, but in practice their words come to nothing.

> In the Kingdom of God service is not a stepping-stone to nobility: it is nobility, the only kind of nobility that is recognized.
> T. W. MANSON

Then there are those whose actions speak louder than their words. They appear to be harsh, stubborn materialists, but are quick to do friendly and compassionate deeds even though they seem to be a bit embarrassed about it.

Both groups act as if they are doing something they don't really want to. True Christian goodness is found in people whose actions and words, what they do and what they say, complement each other meaningfully. The Christian way of doing is by means of actions, not promises. The mark of a Christian is to do what God gives him to do, obediently and respectfully, and joyfully. It is dishonest to pretend you want to be obedient to God if you don't feel the same way in your heart. After all, God knows every person's heart and because of this, your words and actions should be aligned.

Faithful Lord and Master, grant that I will enthusiastically do what You expect me to, and that I will enjoy doing it. Amen.

Read Matthew 6:16-24

All That Glitters Is Not Gold

"Don't store up treasures here on earth, where moths eat them and rust destroys them, and where thieves break in and steal" (Matt. 6:19).

In our daily lives the sensible thing to do is to acquire things that will last. Jesus tells us to concentrate on things with eternal value, and to remember that all that glitters is not gold! He illustrates this by using three examples of great wealth in Israel:

- Smart clothes were very important to everyone. But we mustn't place too much value on this, because moths can eat the clothes and ruin them.
- Watch out for things that can be spoilt by rust. In those days this referred to corn and flax that were kept in large but perishable sheds. Rust caused holes in sheds and rats, mice and worms devoured the contents. This isn't a lasting option either.
- Don't set your heart on things that you can be robbed of or that thieves can steal.

> Let temporal things serve your use, but the eternal be the object of your desire.
> THOMAS Á KEMPIS

What is the glitter that is not gold? The best outfit can be destroyed by moths. All pleasures of the flesh are temporary. It is a foolish person that finds pleasure in things that don't last. There are also pleasures that lose their attraction as one grows older. Do not set your heart on pleasures that the years can take away from you, or things that can be stolen from you. No material possession is safe, and if you build your happiness on that, you are going to lose out, because all that glitters is not gold.

Only treasures that we store in heaven are real "gold"!

Keep me, Lord Jesus, from losing my heart to earthly glitter. Amen.

Read Romans 8:9-17

Know Yourself

For His Spirit joins with our spirit to affirm that we are God's children. (Rom. 8:16).

How wonderful God's grace is to allow us to be His children. And what a tragedy that so many people don't know who they are. It is the Spirit of God who guides you to know yourself. Because of the Spirit, your relationship with God is not that of a slave, but of a child who says, "Abba! Father!"

If you realize that you have a heavenly Father who is better than the best earthly father could ever be, and in addition to His love for you, is also almighty, you have truly managed to get to know yourself. God knows what is best for you and He can and will let it happen as long as you realize that you are His child.

Many people have an identity crisis; they don't know who they really are. Some people admire themselves, like the Greek mythological figure, Narcissus, who fell in love with himself and pined away and died. Self-admiration is the death knell of your true self.

> Our main task in life is to give birth to ourselves, to become what we potentially are. The most important product of our effort is an own personality for each of us.
> — Erich Fromm

Others look at themselves with great expectation, but live in uncertainty about who they really are. For them there is only one road: the road to God. He makes sinners His children. He makes Saul a Paul, and Simon, the rock Peter.

Then there are those who refuse to look at themselves because they are afraid of what they might see. This is the road of despair. But Jesus makes us what God meant us to be, His children. Only then do we really know ourselves!

Thank You, Holy Spirit, that You taught me to know myself and that through Your sacrifice I may be God's child. Amen.

Read Romans 11:11-24

Take Note

Notice how God is both kind and severe. He is severe to those who disobeyed, but kind to you if you continue to trust in His kindness. But if you stop trusting, you also will be cut off (Rom. 11:22).

"Please note" is a well-known written term used in documents to bring something very important to the reader's attention. The well-known abbreviation is NB and the literal meaning: "Please note!"

Earlier on in the book of Romans Paul emphasized God's absolute power, but here he emphasizes the responsibility of the human being. He says that the Israelites were "cut off" like branches because they didn't believe, and the unbelievers from heathen nations were "grafted into" a branch because they believed. Here we see that humans are not passive pawns that are moved around by blind fate. We must "take note" of both the goodness and severity of God. If we want to share in His grace, we must live from His grace.

> Ideals are like stars: you will not succeed in touching them with your hands, but like the seafaring man on the ocean desert of water, you choose them as your guides.
> CHARL SHURZ

A man and his wife were traveling on a very dangerous road in a horse-drawn cart. At a very narrow and dangerous part of the road, the woman became frightened and grabbed the rein closest to her out of her husband's hand. Quietly her husband gave her the other rein as well. Then she was more afraid than ever and called out, "Don't let it go!" He replied, "Two people can't control one horse cart. Either I must drive, or you must." Immediately she handed the reins back to him and he took them safely past the danger.

If we want God to rule in our lives, we must leave everything in His hands. NB: Either God rules in our lives, or Satan will do it!

Lord Jesus, today I place my life under Your control. Amen.

Read Matthew 25:1-13

Be Prepared

"Later, when the other five bridesmaids returned, they stood outside, calling, 'Lord! Lord! Open the door for us!'" (Matt. 25:11).

This parable is a warning to us all to be ready for the coming of our Savior. Its theme is marriage, but actually also the fate of the unsaved. Jesus was speaking to the Jews in the first place. They were the chosen people; their whole history was meant to be in preparation of the arrival of the Messiah. They were supposed to have been ready by the time He came, but instead they were not ready at all and that is why they were locked out. This is a dramatic illustration of the unprepared Jews.

> Whatever resistance we see today offered by almost all the world to the progress of the truth, we must not doubt that our Lord will come at last to break through all the undertakings of men and make a passage for His Word.
> JOHN CALVIN

There are also two universal warnings in this parable. Certain things you just cannot get hold of at the last minute. The foolish bridesmaids found it impossible to borrow oil when they discovered they needed it. You can't borrow a relationship with God from someone at the last moment; you must be in possession of one.

You can't borrow character; you must already have your own. You cannot live on someone else's spiritual capital. Certain things we must get for ourselves in time, because we cannot borrow them.

Merciful and gracious Master, grant that I will always be ready for Your Second Coming; whether it is on my knees or behind the plough. Amen.

Read Psalm 55:1-23

Every Word a Lie

His talk is smooth as butter, yet war is in his heart; his words are more soothing than oil, yet they are drawn swords (Ps. 55:21 NIV).

After reading the whole of Psalm 55, one realizes that this psalm is more than a short account of the psalmist's personal history. Here every believer comes up against the representatives of God's enemies. But we stand firm in the wonderful knowledge that God will take care of us (v. 22). The power of the believer, as well as that of the church, lies in the confession: "I trust in You" (v. 23).

The psalmist talks about those who reached the deepest depths of betrayal by breaking their promises. They stabbed their friends in the back and violated covenants, in this way desecrating something holy because God was called as witness in such covenants. With their buttered tongues they were deceitful and disloyal. Consequently they would live out only half of their lives.

David was convinced that in spite of the betrayal and deceit of people with a smooth tongue, God was still in control. He would trust in the Lord. He would trust in the Lord because God is faithful to the very end. He believed it was just a matter between him and God, therefore he could confidently say, "Give your burdens to the LORD, and He will take care of you. He will not permit the godly to slip and fall" (v. 22). We must not become panic-stricken by the talk of the smooth talkers, but just trust in the Lord.

> You must live with people to know their problems, and live with God in order to solve them.
> PETER T. FORSYTH

Keep me, Lord, from putting my trust in polished liars, but rather to trust in You under all circumstances and at all times. Amen.

Read Colossians 2:20-3:4

Beyond the Stars

Think about the things of heaven, not the things of earth. For you died to this life, and your real life is hidden with Christ in God (Col. 3:2-3).

What Paul is saying is that with our baptism we die with Christ and rise again with Him in a new birth. As a new person, our thoughts are focused on heavenly things.

This does not mean that we can neglect our duties here on earth. We must put effort into carrying out our task on earth, but we must also put effort into "reaching for the stars". We should now see everything in the light of eternity and not as if earthly things are all that matter. The things of Christ are now of primary importance to us.

The artist, Frank Dicksee's painting titled *Ideal* is strikingly apt in this context. It portrays a young mountain climber who leaves the green sunbathed valley to ascend the mountain. Even if he would reach the highest peaks, he would still not achieve the ideal he longed for. The beautiful "figure" that inspired him, had disappeared into the clouds and the mist. The young man, one knee on the peak of the rock, passionately reaches out with both hands to grasp and possess the "figure". The painting does not convey the message that the ideal is unreachable, but that the struggle of making the effort to reach for the stars, continues into the hereafter.

> The Christian ideal has not been tried and found wanting; it has been found difficult and left untried.
> G. K. CHESTERTON

There all our ideals will be realized and we will receive the prize of our high calling in Jesus Christ when we see Him face to face.

I want to focus my thoughts on Your things, Father, without neglecting my earthly duties and responsibilities. Help me, through the Holy Spirit, to make the effort and reach for the stars. Amen.

Read 1 Corinthians 15:50-58

Stand Firm

So, my dear brothers and sisters, be strong and immovable. Always work enthusiastically for the Lord, for you know that nothing you do for the Lord is ever useless (1 Cor. 15:58).

At first, it seems as if Satan gained a victory in Eden (see Gen. 3), and also with Jesus' death at Golgotha (see Mark 15:22-24). However, God changed this apparent victory into a dismal failure when Jesus was raised from the dead (see Col. 2:15; Heb. 2:14-15). We needn't fear death anymore because Christ defeated death and our hope goes beyond the cross.

> The final heartbeat for the Christian is not the mysterious conclusion to a meaningless existence. It is, rather, the grand beginning to a life that will never end.
> — JAMES DOBSON

The fear of death terrifies human beings. In what is this fear founded? It lies partly in our fear of the unknown. It is caused by our awareness of our sin. We are afraid to meet God and account for our sins. Our awareness of sin springs from the knowledge that we stand under God's law. But this is precisely what Jesus came for. He came to tell us that God is not law, but love; that we are saved by grace from sin and from death! The fear of death disappears when we think of God's love!

Paul ends this chapter with a challenge: the death caused by sin has finally been defeated. Suddenly his theology becomes a practical challenge. The Christian life might be difficult at times, but be determined and endure, because you know that your effort in the service of the Lord is not in vain. Eternal life is your destination.

God of love and life, in life and in death I will remain true to You and look forward to being united with You! Amen.

Read Matthew 27:3-10

Sorry, Too Late!

When Judas, who had betrayed Him, realized that Jesus had been condemned to die, he was filled with remorse. So he took the thirty pieces of silver back to the leading priests and the elders (Matt. 27:3).

Judas tried to undo his betrayal because he regretted what he had done. Sorry, it was too late! Perhaps Judas decided to betray Jesus in the first place to force Him to lead an uprising against Rome. Of course it didn't work. Whatever his motivation, Judas changed his mind, but too late.

> Most Christians are being crucified on a cross between two thieves: Yesterday's regret and tomorrow's worries.
> WARREN W. WIERSBE

It often happens that we start things which we want to stop afterwards, but cannot. This is why it is so much better to think of all possible consequences of an action before we act. In this way we will have no regrets afterwards.

An incident during the last hours of Joan of Arc's life illustrates this incident painfully well. After she was condemned to burn at the stake as a result of false testimony, the young girl, dressed in white, walked up to the stake, dignified and fearless. She was calm, her eyes turned up to heaven. The crowd and soldiers around her waited in silence. Suddenly a man forced his way through the crowds and threw himself at her feet, begging for her forgiveness. It was Loiseleur, her priest and confessor, but also the man who had betrayed her. He was torn apart with remorse, but it was too late!

Faithful Friend and Savior, keep me from betraying Your holy name in any way and under any circumstances. May remorse in my life never come too late. Amen.

Read Psalm 30:5-12

God's Silver Lining

For His anger lasts only a moment, but His favor lasts a lifetime! Weeping may last through the night, but joy comes with the morning (Ps. 30:5).

This psalm bears testimony to the fact that every dark cloud has a silver lining. The psalmist expresses great thankfulness because the Lord saved him. He was ill and dying (vv. 2-3). Death is portrayed here as a dark pit, but even there the silver lining of God's grace and love is not absent. "Even when I walk through the dark valley of death, I will not be afraid, for You are close beside me. Your rod and Your staff protect and comfort me" (Ps. 23:4).

This concept which is captured so beautifully in verse five, is followed up in the New Testament: the fact that sorrow brings forth joy under God's loving hand (see 2 Cor. 4:17; John 16:20-22). A contrast is created between the monumental and the eternal; between "light" troubles and glory that "outweighs" them all. This is God's silver lining to our dark clouds.

> Everything that is done in the world is done by hope.
> MARTIN LUTHER

Bonar Law went to France, a broken and sorrowful man, to visit the place where his son died in an airplane crash. There he was shown the wreck in which his son had died. It was riddled with bullet holes. Bonar climbed into the wreck and sat in the seat where his son had died. He sat there a long time while his friends waited on one side. Finally he climbed out with a new expression on his face; a new light in his eyes; a new spring in his step. He went back to London and resumed his work with zeal.

By God's love and grace he had found the silver lining to the dark cloud of his life of pain and affliction.

Holy Father, grant that I will always keep hope burning in my heart! Amen.

Read 1 Timothy 1:1-11

Promoter of the Faith

This letter is from Paul, an apostle of Christ Jesus, appointed by the command of God our Savior and by Christ Jesus, who gives us hope (1 Tim. 1:1).

Paul was par excellence a promoter of the faith. Even before his conversion, the fanatical way in which he persecuted Christians contributed indirectly to the rapid advancement of the early church. Paul's personal meeting with Jesus radically changed his life. With his characteristic enthusiasm and zeal, he devoted all his strength to the spreading of the Gospel.

Up until his conversion, not much was done to proclaim the Gospel to Gentiles. Paul promoted the Christian faith among Gentiles in an active way in various places. Afterwards he undertook three missionary journeys and proclaimed the Gospel across a substantial part of the Roman Empire. There was a marked difference of opinion in the early church about the question whether Gentiles had to maintain the Jewish laws and practices once they accepted Jesus as their Savior. Paul worked hard at convincing the Jews that Gentiles were acceptable to God, but he had to work just as hard to convince the Gentiles. The people that Paul came into contact with did not doubt for a moment the special place Christ had in Paul's life.

> Go not to those who want you, but to those who want you most.
> JOHN WESLEY

God did not allow a single shred of Paul's capabilities to go to waste. He used Paul's background, his citizenship, his mind and even his weaknesses. Paul was indeed a "promoter of the Christian faith". Are you willing to let God do the same for you?

My spirit, my soul, my body, I dedicate to You, O Lord. I lay myself before You forever as sacrifice. Amen.

Read Proverbs 23:9-18

Discipline Is Essential

Don't fail to discipline your children. They won't die if you spank them (Prov. 23:13).

Christian parents don't always understand the scriptural standards of discipline. Both parents and children come into the world as sinners. Therefore discipline and even punishment are essential. But we must always remember, "He who loves well, disciplines well."

The word "discipline" stems from the same word as "disciple". A disciple is someone who follows in your footsteps. Therefore, discipline must always be accompanied by self-examination, prayer, faith and the correct upbringing. It is hard to cause pain to those we love. But we cannot raise a child without discipline. Eli is a disturbing example of how even a man of God can fail in the upbringing of his children.

> We have neglected to discipline our children and called it building self-esteem.
> JOE WRIGHT

Doesn't this make us cruel? No, we are cruel if we fail to discipline (v. 13). Which parent that wants to rescue his child from eternal death will withhold loving discipline? It is better for the body to hurt than for the soul to die. How would a parent be able to deal with the guilt all through eternity if his children ended up in hell?

Some parents threaten all the time but never do anything. They use punishment as a method of frightening their children and it quickly becomes powerless. Because we love our children, we must punish them in the right way. Later in life they will thank us for doing this because "he who loves well, disciplines well".

Father, You are our perfect Example of the way to discipline our children whom we love. Help us to faithfully follow Your example. Amen.

Read 1 Timothy 6:1-18

The Root of All Evil

The love of money is at the root of all kinds of evil. And some people, craving money, have wandered from the true faith and pierced themselves with many sorrows (1 Tim. 6:10).

Money is not the problem here, greed is. In spite of people saying the direct opposite, they act as if the amount of money they have determines the measure of their happiness. People who long to be rich usually never reach a point where they feel they have enough, and it is precisely this tendency that leads them into temptation.

For many it ends in their downfall. Test your own attitude toward money by the following principles:

> Nothing I am sure has such a tendency to quench the fire of religion as the possession of money.
> J. C. Ryle

- Wealth will have no meaning in life hereafter (v. 7).
- Be content with what you have (v. 8).
- Think of what you are prepared to do for money (vv. 9-10).
- See to it that you love people more than money (v. 11).
- See to it that you love God more than money (v. 11).
- Give generously (v. 18).

Let your prayer always be: "Give me neither poverty nor riches! Give me just enough to satisfy my needs" (Prov. 30:8).

An Arab who survived after getting lost in the desert without food and water, described his feelings when he found a bag of pearls just when he wanted to give up all hope: "I will never ever forget the joy that came over me when I thought it was corn that I could eat; and my disappointment and despair when I discovered the bag contained only pearls."

Lord Jesus, to me You are the pearl of priceless value that I would never want to exchange for any earthly treasure. Amen.

Read 2 Kings 22:11-20

Rest in Peace

"I will not send the promised disaster until after you have died and been buried in peace. You will not see the disaster I am going to bring on this city." So they took her message back to the king (2 Kings 22:20).

Josiah, the king, sent a high-ranking delegation to the prophet Huldah. This is a sign of his regard for God's judgment of the people's disobedience. Although Zephaniah and Jeremiah acted as prophets during this time, the king sent a request to Huldah, the prophetess.

Huldah couldn't give them news that would soften the blow. It was not that God wanted retribution. The curse on disobeying the covenants (see Deut. 28:15) would automatically come into effect. If you place yourself above the demands of the covenants, you place yourself outside the protection of the covenants. This does not apply only to the old covenants with Israel, but also to the new covenants in Jesus Christ (see John 15:5-8).

For Josiah, the most devout king that Judah ever had, there was a word of comfort. Because he took the words of the code of law so seriously, he would not experience the disaster that would be brought onto Judah. He would die and rest in peace because of his obedience to the law of God.

> Where there is peace, God is.
> GEORGE HERBERT

Christ's wish for all His children is that they will rest in peace after the earthly struggle. By means of His death and sacrifice He made it possible for us. May you also rest in peace at your God-given time.

John Bunyan writes in *The Pilgrim's Progress*: "They laid the pilgrim down in a room of which the window was opened in the direction of the rising sun; the name of the room was 'peace' and there he slept until the eternal dawn would come."

Lord Jesus, Prince of Peace, thank You for Your peace that surpasses all understanding. Amen.

Read 1 Corinthians 15:12-27

I Will Rise Again!

Just as everyone dies because we all belong to Adam, everyone who belongs to Christ will be given new life (1 Cor. 15:22).

Christ's triumphant resurrection from death is the guarantee for God's children to say, "I will rise again!" We as believers stand or fall by the resurrection of the Lord Jesus Christ. He became the Firstfruits and we who belong to Him, will share in His resurrection.

Death came as a result of Adam and Eve's sin (see Rom. 5:12-21). However, Christ's resurrection brought life again to all who believe. The new heaven and the new earth will be heralded by a flourish of trumpets. The Jews would understand the meaning of trumpets because all their important festivals and other major events were announced in this manner (see Num. 10:10). Trumpets announced judgment or festivity.

Edward Burne-Jones, a renowned English author, attended the funeral of his colleague, Robert Browning in Westminster Abbey and returned from it very disappointed. The service was morbid and dismal. "I would have given anything for a colorful banner or two," he wrote, "and I would have wanted a soloist to make the dome reverberate with the sound of a trumpet!" He is of course quite right because this is the way a Christian should meet death: with banners and a flourish of trumpets.

> The cross of Christ is Jacob's ladder by which we ascend into the Highest Heaven.
> THOMAS TRAHERNE

It is fundamental to Christianity that death was devoured and defeated in Christ's victory. The world will pay attention again when the Christians leave the world with a flourish of trumpets and the cry of victory: "I will rise again!"

Risen Savior, I praise You for the privilege to live because of Your resurrection. Amen.

Read Matthew 4:1-11

Get Out, Satan!

"Get out of here, Satan," Jesus told him. "For the Scriptures say, 'You must worship the LORD your God and serve only Him'" (Matt. 4:10).

The concept of Satan as arch-tempter is part of the Judeo-Christian tradition. The noun "Satan" in Hebrew, which we translate through Greek and Latin to *satanas*, means "opponent". He is involved in our lives every day. Jesus said to him, *"Apage, Satanas!"* (Be gone, Satan!) Today anybody with a little knowledge of Latin can do the same.

> Like a good chess player, Satan is always trying to maneuver you into a position where you can save your castle only by using your bishop.
> — C. S. LEWIS

Many legends are linked to the name of Satan. One of them is as follows: "A priest in Avignon was busy with a confession. Among the members of his congregation he noticed an attractive young man, broad-shouldered with a graceful neck and golden locks; lean and tall with a fiery look in his eyes. When it was his turn to confess, he confessed so many horrific evils that the priest's hair stood on end and he said, "Young man, you must have lived a hundred years to commit so many evils!" "I lived thousands of years," the young man said. "I was cast out of heaven at the beginning of time and want to go back there."

The priest had a merciful heart and told him it was possible. He didn't even ask him to show remorse, but wisely said, "Repeat the following words after me: 'Only God is great and perfect!'" The young man turned his back on the priest and walked away. He refused to humble himself before God. This is why his work continues unceasingly today and we have to say all the time: "Be gone, Satan!"

Lord, I praise and thank You that You protect me from Satan's deceit. Help me to persist, through faith and prayer. Amen.

Read Psalm 103:14-22

Earthly Pleasures Are Short-lived

Our days on earth are like grass; like wildflowers, we bloom and die. The wind blows, and we are gone – as though we had never been here (Ps. 103:15-16).

In this part of Psalms the poet writes about fading earthly glory and short-lived human existence. The Lord knows what to expect from humankind. In contrast to the brevity of the human being, whose life is like grass that loses its glory too soon, stands the everlasting faithfulness of the Lord.

> People nowadays take time far more seriously than eternity.
> THOMAS KELLY

The Lord saved the poet of this psalm from certain death (v. 4). The Lord granted healing and forgiveness (v. 3). As testimony of this event in the life of an individual, is the story of Israel with whom the Lord had made a covenant since Moses' day (vv. 7-8). According to the New Testament, God's grace came to us in Jesus Christ. Therefore we can praise Him as the Eden whose glory will never disappear, while we are made deeply aware of it that our earthly glory will disappear.

The glory of grass and flowers is short-lived. This is a popular theme in the Bible. Earthly pleasures pass, but heavenly glory remains forever.

So we shouldn't set our hearts on earthly things, but rather on things Above; the things that benefit our eternal welfare.

Eternal God, You exist from everlasting to everlasting and I would rather be united with You than be attached to the temporary things of this world. Amen.

Read Hebrews 3:7-19

Without Delay

That is why the Holy Spirit says, "Today when you hear His voice, don't harden your hearts as Israel did when they rebelled, when they tested Me in the wilderness" (Heb. 3:7-8).

These words refer to Psalm 95:7-11 where the Israelites rebelled against God and Moses in the desert (see Exod. 17:1-7; Num. 20:1-13). Their punishment was that they would not enter the Promised Land. The writer of Hebrews applies it to people who disobey God's voice and revolt against Him; who miss out on eternal life as a result of their rebelliousness. It is said by implication that we must accept God's invitation "without delay".

The writer cautions us that while we are able to talk about "today", God must get the trust and obedience due to Him. "Today" means "while there is still life". God's warning is clear: He makes us an offer, just like He offered Canaan to the Israelites. To accept the offer, two things are necessary. Trust in God and the belief that everything He promises is true, and secondly, obedience to God and His Word. It is like the doctor who says, "I can heal you if you use the prescription I give you."

There is a time limit to God's announcement. This offer stands as long as we live and we never know how long we will live. We so readily speak about tomorrow. Tomorrow might never come for us! All we have is today. God's offer must be accepted today and without delay.

> God has promised forgiveness to repentance, but He has not promised tomorrow to your procrastination.
> ST. AUGUSTINE

Thank You, Lord, that I accepted Your offer without delay and made Your salvation my own while there was still time. Amen.

June 27

Read Matthew 7:15-23

Later Than You Think

"Not everyone who calls out to Me, 'Lord! Lord!' will enter the Kingdom of Heaven. Only those who actually do the will of my Father in heaven will enter" (Matt. 7:21).

People always think of Judgment Day as an occasion in the distant future and something they don't really have to worry about. Jesus Christ taught us time and again that it is later than we think and that we must be prepared for His Second Coming and Judgment Day. There are a few vital truths in this Scripture passage:

- There is only one way in which our sincerity is tested and that is by our deeds. When the time has run out and we have to appear before God, good words can never be a substitute for good deeds.
- Only one thing is proof of true love, and that is obedience. There is no sense in saying we love someone and then do things that break that person's heart. Especially not if it is the God of love.
- It is easier to recite a confession of faith than to really live a Christian life. Faith without actions is a contradiction in terms.

> Revival is a clean-cut breakthrough of the Spirit, a sweep of Holy Ghost power.
> NORMAN GRUBB

Behind this warning lies the reality of the second coming of Christ, and God's judgment. To what extent are your spiritual confessions and practical life in line with what Christ expects from you?

Risen Lord, grant in Your unfathomable grace that I will be ready when You come again. Amen.

Read Colossians 4:2-6

Watch and Pray!

Devote yourselves to prayer with an alert mind and a thankful heart (Col. 4:2).

Paul never wrote a letter without making an appeal for watchfulness and persevering prayer. He regarded these as cardinal components of our Christian faith lives.

He also tells the Colossians to persevere in prayer. Even the most devoted Christians have times when it seems as if their prayers are powerless and don't go further than the ceiling. Especially then, the solution is to persevere in prayer, because a prayer drought doesn't last long for those who persevere. God is faithful.

> In prayer it is better to have a heart without words than words without a heart.
> — JOHN BUNYAN

He also calls on them to be watchful. Paul encourages them, literally speaking, not to fall asleep when they are praying. He was possibly thinking of the occasion on the mountain of transfiguration when the disciples fell asleep (see Luke 9:32). Or of the garden of Gethsemane when Jesus prayed and His disciples slept. When the body is tired, it happens that we fall asleep during prayer. Then a long prayer is not necessary. God will understand and answer a sincere prayer.

Our prayers must express gratitude. It is good to be watchful and to pray, but if our prayers are only lists of requests in which we pray for favors, our approach is wrong. We have so much to be thankful for that we won't have much time for other topics once we start giving thanks. Let us listen to what Paul wants to say to us from many centuries past, and carry it out promptly: "Persevere in prayer! Together with that, be watchful and thankful!"

Faithful Father, make me faithful, persevering and thankful in my prayer life so that my conversation with You will be meaningful. Amen.

Read Philippians 1:12-26

Hope for the Future

> So I rejoice. And I will continue to rejoice. For I know that as you pray for me and as the Spirit of Jesus Christ helps me, this will lead to my deliverance (Phil. 1:18-19).

On what are your eyes focused when the worst happens to you? Some people look back and find comfort in memories of beautiful and peaceful days in the past. Others picture how wonderful it will be when the present mess has been resolved and they can move on to some or other dream they cherish about the future. The latter are more positive. They hope, and their hope keeps them on their feet and motivates them to prepare for the fulfillment of their dreams.

> He that lives in hope dances without music.
> GEORGE HERBERT

Paul had hope. He was imprisoned for spreading the Gospel but he knew that the people of Philippi were praying for him. He also freely tapped into his faith in Christ and refused to give in to despair. The Holy Spirit, the Comforter, helped him to look ahead to the dreams and plans that he savored for when he would be set free. He refused to get stuck at the victories and successes of the past, but instead looked ahead with hope in his heart.

Follow Paul's example. If you struggle with difficulties and problems, look forward to a better future with hope in your heart. Fix your eyes on a goal in the future that you believe God called you for. Whether it is small and personal, or big and community related, let it dominate your thoughts. Write down plans and steps for achieving your goals. Set time limits and firmly believe that your dreams will come true. Then let nothing stop you to move on with hope in your heart.

Lord Jesus, thank You that through Your grace I can look ahead with hope in my heart. Amen.

July

But if we confess our sins to Him, He is faithful and just to forgive us our sins and to cleanse us from all wickedness.

1 JOHN 1:9

Faith and obedience are bound up in the same bundle. He that obeys God trusts God; and he that trusts God obeys God.

CHARLES H. SPURGEON

Almighty, Holy and Eternal God,
You dwell in magnificent light,
Your omnipotence is too high
and too majestic for us to grasp.
We cannot determine the heights of Your wisdom,
or fully understand the depths of Your grace.
We cannot come within sight of Your glory with uncovered eyes.
But with humble hearts, O Lord, we come to You in silence;
we wait upon You in hushed excitement!
Heavenly Father, we want to look deep down into our hearts,
so that we may discover where we failed in living the life
You meant for us, through Your Son, Jesus Christ.
We confess in sorrow and remorse our sins toward You, O Lord.
While we search our souls, we plead in all sincerity and honesty,
Father, help us, through the Holy Spirit,
to see the truth about ourselves.
Point out our weaknesses and selfishness.
Keep us from hypocrisy and superficial words.
Grant that every confession of sin
will be like words spoken on a deathbed.
Grant us, undeserving sinners,
Your forgiveness because You are a merciful God.
Grant us unshakable courage to lay bare
our lives to Your bright light.
Gracious God, we pray that You will forgive our sins
in the redeeming name of Jesus our Savior.
Amen.

Read Proverbs 9:1-9

Constructive Criticism

Leave your simple ways behind, and begin to live; learn to use good judgment (Prov. 9:6).

There are two forms of criticism. Constructive criticism, when expressed in love, benefits those involved and enriches their lives. Negative criticism appears to be much more common. Being constructive calls for mental energy and a spirit of helpfulness. Being destructive requires a negative attitude only.

Why do people lean towards negative criticism? Normally it is because they are not sure of themselves. They see others overtaking them in the race of life and are overwhelmed by a feeling of incompetence. Instead of being happy for others about their success, they make snide remarks on how their success was achieved. No one can develop to full maturity while they have an attitude that prevents them from sharing in another's joy.

Another reason, and probably the most common, why people criticize in a negative and destructive way, is because they allow jealousy to dominate their lives. Jealousy is a monster that destroys the personality and violates the person's relationship with God and his fellow human being. It might start in small measures but will quickly influence and control the person's thoughts.

The answer to destructive criticism is to allow God's Spirit to take possession of your spirit so that you are able to share in another's joy and success and take note of the good things in their lives.

> You have not fulfilled every duty, unless you have fulfilled that of being pleasant.
> CHARLES BUXTON

Keep me, Spirit of God, from the curse of destructive criticism and always make my opinions constructive. Amen.

July 1

Read Isaiah 4:1-6

A Spirit That Purifies

The Lord will wash the filth from beautiful Zion and cleanse Jerusalem of its bloodstains with the hot fiery breath of judgment (Isa. 4:4).

One of the main tasks in maintaining public health is getting rid of the large amounts of refuse in the modern packaging system.

In ancient Jerusalem, the city's garbage was dumped in the valley of Hinnom where it was burnt. The fire got rid of the garbage and also purified the city of possible sickness and contamination. Fire and cleansing are inextricably linked.

But there is another kind of cleansing that only God can do: the inner purification of people's thoughts and hearts. It is essential that they be purified from sin. Isaiah believed that the Spirit of God would both judge and purify their hearts by burning away their sins, just like the fire of Hinnom purified the city.

> I pray Thee, O God, that I may be beautiful within.
> SOCRATES

When the Holy Spirit came at Pentecost, what looked like tongues of fire appeared. This symbolizes, among other things, God's powerful purification. Wherever His Spirit comes, He not only empowers, but also purifies. He also wants to burn the filth of sin out of your life and mine – if we would only allow Him.

O God, penetrate and know the black and hidden depths of my heart, and seek deep down inside me where You may detect a harmful way. Guide my uncertain steps to the way of everlasting peace. Amen.

Read Psalm 18:30-42

How Well Equipped Are You?

You have armed me with strength for the battle; You have subdued my enemies under my feet (Ps. 18:39).

Wars are usually won by armies with the most soldiers, the best equipment, the most powerful weapons and the sharpest generals. Sometimes smaller and weaker forces triumph over bigger armed forces, but this is the exception to the rule.

David, who wrote this psalm, was a strong man. He was a hardened warrior and became strong through years spent outdoors as a shepherd, and in caves as a fugitive. He became the greatest general of Israel's army. He attributed his strength to God, and his success in battle to the Lord.

> Christianity does not remove you from the world and its problems; it makes you fit to live in it, triumphantly and usefully.
> CHARLES TEMPLETON

We also have to fight many battles and some are battles of endurance – we must carry on struggling and wrestling with some or other problem or weakness. There are battles where everything seems to go against us. Even if they don't seem to be connected in any way, problems are crowding in on you from all directions and you start wondering if someone is conspiring against you. There are people who wage a long battle against illness and they feel that their faith is tested on purpose.

One must be well-equipped to fight these battles. One part of your armor is your faith in God. Make sure it is strong and sincere. Another is your knowledge of the Bible and your prayer life. Then there is also the Christian community you are part of. It is necessary to be supported by their love in some of the battles you fight.

And finally, you must nurture an attitude of faith that God will deal with the future for your good.

Leader to life, help me to wear God's full armor. Amen.

Read Psalm 22:23-31

Join in the Feasting

The poor will eat and be satisfied (Ps. 22:26).

There is a campaign that focuses on the enormous issue of poverty in the world today. Figures report that millions of people have to get by with practically no money. On the other hand, there are those who are well off and throw away their leftovers that could feed the poor.

> You can give without loving, but you cannot love without giving.
> AMY CARMICHAEL

The slogan of those who want to put an end to poverty is: "Make poverty history." The writer of Psalm 22 was not dreaming of a time that poverty would be eradicated. In his joy of being healed from his illness, he was preparing to go to the temple to give thanks to God. In some offerings the sacrificial animal was placed on the altar and killed, and after it had been sacrificed, it was cut open and returned to the worshiper and his family to eat. This is probably what the psalmist had in mind, and he intended to invite the poor to join in the feasting.

It is always praiseworthy when those who have plenty, decide to share their meal with the needy. It is much easier to be selfish and just ignore the less privileged. The psalmist here sets an example worth following. He says to us, "If you are thankful to God for His blessings, prove your gratitude by being generous." This is a pure Christian way of thinking.

Christ fed the crowds. It won't be possible for you to make poverty history, but you can turn someone's poverty into a feast.

Grant that I will share Your gifts with the less privileged, Lord Jesus. Amen.

Read 1 Timothy 2:1-15

The Only Savior

There is only one God and one Mediator who can reconcile God and humanity – the man Christ Jesus (1 Tim. 2:5).

In our modern, fast-paced, secular world it is very easy to lose sight of God completely. It is also possible to lose contact with Him. In many circles God's name is just mentioned as a swearword. He seems almost distant and isolated, without any contact with this world. He could easily be referred to as "the forgotten God"!

In the ancient world He was also distant and detached. But they believed that there were mediators, or at least beings that were half-God and half-human. They were regarded as God's representatives in the world. Some religions still believe to this day that there are such mediators. Paul, however, forced this idea out of Christian thinking. "There is only one Mediator," he said with conviction – and that is Jesus Christ. God says to humankind, "I will meet you in Jesus Christ and nowhere else!"

When God seems distant to you, don't go and look for Him in strange, wonderful and impossible theories; not even in solitary and beautiful places. Look for Him in Jesus. He is the human image of God. And remember, no matter how distant God may seem to you, this is of your own making, not God's. Jesus Christ embodies God for you. Jesus is *where* you find God and *how* you find God. When Jesus has found you, you have found God.

> You are saved – seek to be like your Savior.
> CHARLES H. SPURGEON

Thus, focus on Jesus. Think often of His words, His actions and His love. Talk to Jesus and tell Him how you feel – even when you don't feel close to Him.

Jesus, Mediator, help me to experience Your presence – here and now, so that I may find God. Amen.

July 5

Read 1 Timothy 3:1-16

In the Flesh

Christ was revealed in a human body and vindicated by the Spirit (1 Tim. 3:16).

Today pilgrims from all over the whole world visit Israel and they represent diverse approaches of Christian discipleship. They go to Bethlehem and see where Jesus was born – or somewhere very close to it. They visit Nazareth, Canaan, Capernaum and Jerusalem. They even sail in boats across the Sea of Galilee where Jesus Himself sailed once. Many of them go home and declare, "Everything looks so much more real. I actually walked where Jesus once walked." One person even said, "Now I can believe!"

The Christian faith is founded on the supposition that in Jesus of Nazareth's lifetime of thirty-three years He took on the stature of God; the God that created heaven and earth. He lived, breathed, worked, ate, slept, suffered and died just like any other human being. He who placed the stars in their orbit, created the planets and controlled the sun also sailed in a boat, quieted the storm and wept at the grave of his friend, Lazarus. We go as far as to say that His life followed the pattern of all human life, and that He should be the mold for our own lives.

> If ever the Divine appeared on earth, it was in the person of Christ.
> JOHANN WOLFGANG VON GOETHE

People came forward with all kinds of theories that explained why Jesus was not really what He pretended to be, but none of them held water for very long. The belief that He was God in human form, that He lived a real life and that His life can make your life more of a reality, changed the lives of millions of people in the past and still does, to this day. Your life will make very little sense if you don't believe it.

Jesus, I don't always know how You did it, but I believe with conviction that You did it. Amen.

July 6

Read John 1:1-18

Before Bethlehem

In the beginning the Word already existed (John 1:1).

If Christian believers would step out of life in the fast lane for a while and meditate on Jesus whose birth we commemorate annually, it would enrich spiritual lives beyond measure.

John tells us, "In the beginning the Word already existed." These are also the words used at the beginning of the book of Genesis to describe how God created the universe. Jesus, the Baby that was born in Bethlehem, was much more than just a human baby. He was the Son of God and therefore He is just as eternal as God the Father. John says that He was "the Word".

> Our Lord Jesus Christ,
> the Word of God,
> of His boundless love,
> became what we are
> that He might make us
> what He Himself is.
> — IRANAEUS

A word is something that people use to express an inner thought or to convey a message. It might be in the speaker's thoughts long before he expresses it. So John says that the Word (note the capital letter – it is Christ's name) existed before anything else, except God. Therefore, even before God started with His creation, the pronouncement of God, or Christ, already existed. Theologians call this insight "the pre-existence of Christ". Then, because of His indescribable love, He sent His Word to become a living being in human form. This is why we celebrate Christ: Christmas.

Therefore, greet His arrival joyfully every day of your life. If you can't understand how He could have existed, don't worry. Just believe! Forget about all the detail; simply thank the Father and the Son for this miracle of love.

I kneel in wonder and worship before You, the Word. Amen.

Read Ephesians 3:14-21

True Faith

May you experience the love of Christ, though it is too great to understand fully. Then you will be made complete with all the fullness of life and power that comes from God (Eph. 3:19).

Facts have proved that many Christians are not happy with their faith. It is not that they have become antagonistic towards what they first regarded as holy; but as a result of a changed attitude and negative circumstances they have become unconcerned about issues of spiritual life. Gradually they started feeling that Christianity had lost its appeal, with the result that they don't acknowledge the rule of the living Christ over their lives anymore.

> It is harder to conceal ignorance than to acquire knowledge.
> ARNOLD GLASOW

How is it possible for someone who was an enthusiastic Christian to cool down to such an extent that his former glorious faith has become a mockery? There can be many reasons. The neglect of fellowship with believers; inability to develop a prayer life; neglecting to read the Bible and group pressure – these are just a few things that can lead to spiritual apathy.

A famous philosopher claimed that it is possible to know all about Christianity without being a Christian. Many people study the different religions and they are outspoken when they reason about some or other dogmatic issue. Yet their lives reflect nothing of the beauty and love of Christ.

To experience the fullness of a positive and living faith requires personal surrender to Jesus Christ that rises above the theory of religion, and enfolds your entire being.

Lord Jesus, may my knowledge of You lead to an ever-deepening appreciation of Your holy character. Amen.

Read 1 Timothy 1:12-17

Why Did Jesus Come?

This is a trustworthy saying, and everyone should accept it: Christ Jesus came into the world to save sinners (1 Tim. 1:15).

We can give a good number of answers to the question, "Why did Jesus come to this world?" Some will say He came to demonstrate God's amazing love to us. Others will say He came to explain the truth about God the Father. Or that He came to open the road to heaven so that people can understand the meaning of death, and are able to receive eternal life. It could also be said that He brought the work of the Kingdom of God to this world.

The main reason why Jesus came to earth, however, was to save sinners; to make bad people good. One of the most popular hymns is *Amazing Grace*. It was written by John Newton who was involved in many sinful things in his youth. He later became a sailor on a slave ship that traveled between West Africa, the West Indies and America. Then Newton came to know Jesus, became wholeheartedly converted and was ordained as a priest of the Church of England. He wrote his own epitaph: "John Newton, Clerk, once an infidel and libertine, a servant of slaves in Africa, was, by the rich mercy of our Lord and Savior Jesus Christ, restored, pardoned, and appointed to preach the faith he had long labored to destroy." This is the glory of the Gospel of Jesus Christ that declares that those who are slaves of sin are given salvation.

Perhaps you need Jesus Christ's saving grace today. If you haven't done it already, open up your heart and life for Him and allow Him to save you – today!

> Only in Jesus Christ do we have assurance of salvation, forgiveness of sins, entrance into God's family, and the guarantee of heaven forever when we die.
> — LUIS PALAU

Thank You, Redeemer and Savior, that I may experience Your saving grace. Amen.

Read John 10:22-42

The Son of God

"Why do you call it blasphemy when I say, 'I am the Son of God?' After all, the Father set Me apart and sent Me into the world" (John 10:36).

Many people are of the opinion that Christianity is just about being a "good" person, living a decent life and being generous. Others again believe that it's all about being "religious": to say many prayers and regularly read the Bible. Then there are those who think it's all about knowledge: the ability to know several Bible verses off by heart, to know the names of the kings of Israel, to name the faith heroes, or to understand the theology of the Holy Trinity. However, there is something of each of these aspects in true Christianity.

Yet there is much more. It is about personal knowledge of Jesus Christ and a living relationship with Him. Knowledge of Jesus means you know who He is – and who He is not. He is *not only* a great Prophet, a brilliant Teacher and a wonderful Physician. He is not only an exceptional Leader or a Rebel with a good cause. He is the Son of God! It is clear that Someone who could feed the multitudes, tell people about God, cast out demons and contradict respected religious authorities, was from God. In our spoken language He was the real McCoy: perfectly genuine and trustworthy.

> Jesus Christ is not a good way to heaven – He is the only one.
> KARL BARTH

Whatever you think or believe about Jesus, you must first of all be convinced that He is the Son of God. Build your faith around Him. Make Him the central point and sum total of your life. Plan your lifestyle and your deeds according to His teaching. Allow Him to be your Example; make Him the foundation of your life and you will become a child of God.

Father God, thank You that You sent Your Son, Jesus Christ, to this world and to me. Amen.

Read John 1:1-18

A Life of Gratitude

We have seen His glory, the glory of the Father's one and only Son (John 1:14).

It is understandable that some people think Christianity is mainly about good actions, because this is what we are constantly told. The message we often hear is, "God is love, so show more love." It is true that God is love and that we must therefore be more loving. But it is merely one small sub-section of the Christian Gospel.

> God's gifts are meted out according to the taker, not according to the giver.
> MEISTER ECKHART

The message that gripped the world in Christ's time was the announcement of what God did. He spoke through the prophets. He came in the image of His Son. He raised Jesus from the dead. He sent His Holy Spirit. He will come again. Therefore, believe in Him, accept Jesus' rule and obey Him. Grace and truth are not things we have to do. These are gifts that God gave us in and through Jesus. When He came to the world, grace and truth were brought within reach of human perception. Like His glory, these gifts came from the Father. They were made public by the life of the God who became Man.

As Jesus' disciple, you must always live in the awareness that it was God who came to earth in Jesus and in everything Jesus said and did. Your share is to react to all those mighty deeds, as well as in all the mighty deeds you see Him do today. He is the same God today as He was then. He reveals His loving goodness and truth in the same way.

How do *you* respond to His loving goodness and truth?

Holy Spirit of God, help me to live in gratitude so that I can experience God's goodness and truth every day. Amen.

Read Luke 2:22-32

Wait on God

At that time there was a man in Jerusalem named Simeon. He was righteous and devout and was eagerly waiting for the Messiah to come and rescue Israel (Luke 2:25).

There is always great excitement building up before a special occasion. When it finally happens we can hardly believe it. But not everything we look forward to happens. Some people buy lottery tickets and wait for their "lucky day". For most of them that day never comes. In some countries people wait for a corrupt and evil government to be overthrown.

> We must wait for God, long, meekly, in the wind and the wet, in the midst of thunder and the lightning, in the cold and the dark. Wait and He will come. He never comes to those who do not wait.
> F. W. Faber

God's children wait on Him. Sometimes He answers prayer quickly and unexpectedly and then we are surprised. In other cases God takes His time and His disciples are kept waiting for a long time. Simeon, who was already an elderly man, was typical of many good and devout people in Israel who longed for God to free the people from their bondage. When God sent His Son, many failed to recognize and accept Him. But not Simeon. Patiently and humbly he obeyed the whisperings of the Holy Spirit and he welcomed Jesus. He knew that his long wait was over. When he welcomed the Child of Bethlehem, he praised God.

If you are waiting for God to fulfill His promises, don't become impatient. No amount of calculations and research will speed up His coming. He will come in His own time. Wait on Him patiently and trust Him.

Holy Father God, give me the grace to wait patiently and faithfully for You to return. Amen.

Read 1 Timothy 1:1-11

Jesus Christ Our Hope

This letter is from Paul, an apostle of Christ Jesus, appointed by the command of God our Savior and Christ Jesus, who gives us hope (1 Tim. 1:1).

Do you have any hope for our world today? If you look at the crime rate, the threats of terrorism, the impact of HIV/AIDS, the problem of global warming, poverty, the failure of political initiatives to solve the world's problems, you could easily land in the depths of despair.

However, there is more to consider than human problems and crises. Because of Jesus' ascension to the Father's right hand, He directs us beyond the dimensions of time and space. He says to us, "I defeated sin, pain and death and I am a part of the final reign of God the Father in this world."

Once during a flight from Cape Town in rain and cold weather the pilot announced, "After take-off we fly through the clouds. High above the sun is shining, and we expect a pleasant flight to Johannesburg." His confidence in the weather forecasters made him believe that the poor weather conditions below the clouds were just a local problem.

> Hope is nothing else than perseverance in faith.
> JOHN CALVIN

Look beyond the clouds of today's problems and see Jesus sitting on the throne of the universe. Jesus shines with love, hope, truth and power. He is the King of love and Conqueror of death. Put your trust in Him.

Lord Jesus, we praise and thank You because You always give us hope. Amen.

Read 1 Timothy 1:12-17

Faith and Love

> But God had mercy on me so that Christ Jesus could use me as a prime example of His great patience with even the worst sinners (1 Tim. 1:16).

It is a very sacred experience to visit an old cemetery, especially if it is centuries old. There you see the names of people who lived and died and are mostly forgotten. It is not likely that you would know any of them. Inevitably the question arises: "What kind of life do they have now? Are they simply names engraved on stone? Or was there and is there something more?"

The Bible's message is that it is the presence of God's omnipotence that makes human life more than just the passing of a time span of labor, love, suffering and joy. It declares that when God touches your life, He fills it with a portion of eternity. It is faith in Jesus Christ that makes your existence "alive" and lifts you up from the daily grind of human existence. Having everlasting life means that God has taken hold of you and given you seventy or eighty years on earth with the power, love, joy and hope that reflects life in heaven.

> Once a man is united to God, how could he not live forever?
> C. S. Lewis

Life, true *life*, is about faith, and faith is about receiving God's life. Your earthly life is merely a brief earthly journey. The phrase "eternal life" indicates something bigger and better, unlimited and ongoing: a journey that does not end when you leave this earth. But it starts here! Has it started for you yet?

Holy God, raise my earthly life to the level of Your eternal life. Amen.

July 14

Read 1 Timothy 2:1-15

How God Wants Us to Live

This is good and pleases God our Savior, who wants everyone to be saved and to understand the truth (1 Tim. 2:3-4).

Most people have their own conviction of how God wants them to live. This is, however, limited by our personal behavior and our family life. We think that God has no idea how we should act at work, in our relationships, toward local or national matters, or in our leisure time and money matters.

> You can't lead anyone else further than you have gone yourself.
> GENE MAUCH

By appealing to Timothy to pray for all rulers, Paul shows us that God is interested in our lives and expects us to pray for our community and for the world. As Christians we can't cut ourselves off from the big, pulsating world with its tension and stress, its terrorism and crime, its poverty and unemployment and its fast-growing technology. Paul's message is that God is present in everything that happens, even if we aren't. Paul also points out to us that he wants us to be caught up in prayer for the sake of this world. God loved the world and Christ died for it. We must live for it and not use our faith as an excuse to detach ourselves from it.

Therefore, let your devotion to Jesus Christ and your faith make you an inseparable part of God's world. Be knowledgeable about climate change, social affairs, nuclear weapons and terrorism. Bring everything to God in prayer and ask Him for solutions. Pray that world leaders will realize their responsibility toward God and accept that they must live the way He expects them to.

Creator God, please bring order to this chaotic world. Amen.

Read Genesis 17:1-8

A Bright Future

"I will make you extremely fruitful. Your descendants will become many nations, and kings will be among them" (Gen. 17:6).

One never knows what the future holds! Even while the darkest, most threatening clouds of disaster appear on our horizon, they bring showers that yield the richest crops.

William Barclay tells the story of an old German teacher who was in the habit of lifting his cap as he entered the classroom in the mornings and then ceremoniously bowed to the learners. One day a learner asked him why he did this. His answer was, "You never know what one of these boys might become one day." He was quite right because one of those boys was Martin Luther.

> Those who keep speaking about the sun while walking under a cloudy sky are messengers of hope, the true saints of our day.
> HENRI J. NOUWEN

God made Abraham a promise: not only would he have many descendants, but some would be important – even kings. The angel made Mary a similar promise. Her Son would become the Savior of the world. God had His salvation purpose to fulfill and He would keep to His promises to Abraham and his descendants. One of those descendants became the King of all kings.

Don't be too sentimental about the past. Don't be overcome by pessimism because of current problems. God is the God of the future. Therefore, look forward with excitement and expectation to what God is still going to do. He might do it through people, events or movements. But most of what He does will be through ordinary and dedicated people. Some of it He will even do through *you*.

Lord Jesus, please fill my heart with hope every day. Amen.

Read Isaiah 5:1-7

God's Vineyard

> My beloved had a vineyard on a rich and fertile hill. He plowed the land, cleared its stones, and planted it with the best vines. In the middle he built a watchtower and carved a winepress in the nearby rocks (Isa. 5:1-2).

While coping with the tension of this fast-paced world of today, its instant communication and complex problems, it happens quite easily that you forget that faith provides some of the simplest and most straightforward ways of looking at things.

Isaiah tells a parable about the song of the vineyard. It is very simple. God is the "Beloved" who owns the vineyard and the vineyard is Israel. The people are the grapes cultivated there. The owner of the vineyard goes to great trouble to prepare the soil, to plant the best vines and to cultivate them. He also has the equipment ready and waiting for the harvest.

Today we can look beyond the parallel of Israel as the vineyard. The entire earth is in fact God's vineyard. He provided everything humankind could possibly need. He showered planet earth and its inhabitants with love and care. In our discovery of the earth's resources, the development of its abundant minerals and materials, we easily forget that it is God's vineyard and not ours.

> When we ponder creation, the how and what does not matter as much as the why and wherefore.
> RAMON DE CAMPOAMOR

Believers try to look at the world from God's eyes and treasure it. This is the way Jesus looked at the world. He loved the world that God created and saw Himself as a laborer in God's vineyard. We are also His laborers and we have the privilege and duty of looking after God's vineyard with dedication and care.

Father, make us diligent laborers on the planet that You have given us. Amen.

July 17

Read Isaiah 12:1-6

Who Is Your Savior?

See, God has come to save me. I will trust in Him and not be afraid. The LORD GOD is my strength and my song; He has given me victory (Isa. 12:2).

From time to time we read in the newspapers about someone who had a terrifying experience while driving a car. It was once reported that the driver of a car was stranded and that a friendly stranger stopped and helped him. In his shocked condition the driver forgot to take the helper's name. He wanted to let the good Samaritan know that he appreciates his/her timely help sincerely. In those circumstances the unknown helper was a "savior".

In the Bible the words "save" and "redeem" convey the idea of deliverance. Their time of slavery in Egypt showed the Israelites that God was their "Savior". When they had lost all hope after four hundred years of slavery, their God stepped in and saved them from their misery. He made a road through the Red Sea and stopped the pursuing Egyptians. From that moment on they knew that they could trust God because He delivered them from their misery.

These characteristics of God became the essential ingredients in Jesus Christ's mission. The angel who appeared to Joseph at the time of Jesus' birth declared that the Child that was to be born would "save His people from their sins" (Matt. 1:21). He did it then and He still does it to this day. He saves you when you give your life to Him by confessing your sins of the past and accepting His forgiveness. This removes the feelings of guilt from your soul. But He carries on saving you by helping you to overcome obstacles and to show you the way to serve Him and your fellow man, and to testify about Him.

> Salvation is God's work for us, not our work for God.
> LEWIS SPERRY CHAFER

Thank You, heavenly Father, for saving me through Jesus Christ. Amen.

Read Psalm 19:1-15

A Word of Warning

How can I know all the sins lurking in my heart? Cleanse me from these hidden faults. Keep Your servant from deliberate sins! (Ps. 19:12-13).

How well do you know yourself? Most of us have an exaggerated opinion of our own abilities, but we diminish our weaknesses and pretend that we either don't have faults, or that they don't matter so much. It also happens that many of us exaggerate the weaknesses of others, and degrade their good points.

Someone said on occasion that there are parts of us that everyone can see, including ourselves. Then there are parts that others see but we don't. Thirdly there are the secret parts of us that only we see – and probably do our best to keep hidden from others. Then there are parts of us that are unknown to ourselves and others – the deep, hidden secrecies of our personality.

> Lord Jesus, let me know myself and know You, and desire nothing save only You.
> AUGUSTINE OF HIPPO

The person who wrote today's psalm was honest and humble enough to admit that he didn't know about the hidden sin inside him – he probably had no way of knowing about it. When you are tempted to judge someone else who revealed a weakness, remember these words. It is better to be careful than judgmental because you never know when your own hidden sins may come to light.

Rather be glad that God accepts you and loves you with all your faults, weaknesses and failures. Remind yourself that Jesus Christ accepted sinners and that He accepts you. Just think how wonderful it is that He is helping you triumph over your weaknesses and that He can turn your weaknesses into something good. Ask Him for insight into your own character so that you are aware of areas where you can improve.

Holy Spirit of God, help me to know myself better. Amen.

Read Jeremiah 3:19-25

The Lord Our God

"Yes, we're coming," the people reply, "for You are the LORD our God" (Jer. 3:22).

It seems as if religion is pushed to the outside borders of human activity and that God is not taken into account anymore. If you are a believing Christian you may feel at some stage that everybody around you thinks of you as a freak.

> Before me, even as behind, God is, and all is well.
> JOHN GREENLEAF WHITTIER

The ancient community of Israel was not at all secular. But they worshiped gods that were not God. The result was deterioration in morality, government and national life. Jeremiah yearned for the people to repent and worship the Jehovah God again. He dreamt of the day that they would answer God's invitation: "Yes, we're coming, for You are the Lord our God!"

It makes a big difference who your God is. To Christians, Jesus Christ is the Son of the living God. The God of the Israelites made a covenant with them. They were His people and He was their God and they were not allowed to serve any other god. They would find their calling and fullness of life in His service.

Don't get sucked in by the surrounding community's values, misplaced faith systems and half-truths that are accepted as "wisdom". As innocent as this life might seem, it will rob you of your spiritual strength, of truth and of the virtues born of knowledge of Him who is "the Lord our God".

Heavenly Father, lead me in the knowledge of You as the true Lord and God. Amen.

Read Jeremiah 10:1-11

The True God

The LORD is the only true God. He is the living God (Jer. 10:10).

About thirty years ago a group of theologians came up with a new doctrine: "God is dead!" It caused an uproar at the time and people who spread this did well with their book sales. However, it didn't last very long. Their books had barely appeared in book shops when the charismatic renewal began. God revealed Himself as very much alive and the Holy Spirit showed them exactly how alive God was.

Many of the gods that people worshiped in Jeremiah's time were made of stone, wood or metal – that's why Jeremiah could brand them as dead objects. They had no life and couldn't produce any life. They were indeed lifeless.

Israel's God was the living God. He did great works and said great things. He breathed life into humankind, provided them with food and He led His people through the wilderness to the Promised Land. If they did something wrong, He punished them. The other gods were fakes, but this God was real and true.

It is essential that we distinguish between the true and living God, Jesus Christ, and the fake and lifeless gods that are worshiped today. Even money, although it is an essential commodity, is the source of many problems when it is sought for its own sake. It easily becomes a god.

Many people see no further than their bodily needs. Others again raise their nation to the status of a god and lose sight of all other things. Only Jesus gives real life because He is the true and living God.

> Wherever the Father is (and He is everywhere) there the Son is also, and wherever the Son is, there the Father is.
> CYRIL OF ALEXANDRIA

God, we thank You that we may worship You as the true and living God. Amen.

July 21

Read Romans 7:14-25

You Are Worthy

Oh, what a miserable person I am! Who will free me from this life that is dominated by sin? (Rom. 7:24).

There are people who have such a high opinion of themselves that they are blinded to the truth of who they really are. What people think they are, and what they really are, often differs considerably. Then, contrary to people who have a high opinion of themselves, there are those who can think of nothing good about themselves. While humility is a virtue, this truth can be taken to extremes and become a stumbling block and a burden that destroys initiative.

If you constantly slate yourself and your talents, don't be surprised if your fellow humans accept that you are as unworthy as you think. If you are always belittling yourself and saying that you are just a very ordinary person, don't be surprised if you are treated that way.

Each individual has bright prospects, and you are the one who must develop your life to its full capacity. This is done best by realizing that you are not an isolated entity that has to do everything in your own strength. You are a child of God and your reason for living is to glorify God and carry out His will for your life. To enable you to do this, God gave you His Holy Spirit so that He may live in you and express Himself through you.

> There is only one small corner of the universe you can be certain of improving, and that is your own self.
> — ALDOUS HUXLEY

Having such a wonderful God means that you dare not think of yourself as unimportant and unworthy. God's indwelling Spirit makes you worthy and purposeful.

I thank You, O Holy Spirit of God, that You live in me and make me worthy. Amen.

Read Isaiah 66:1-9

When God Speaks

"When I called, they did not answer. When I spoke, they did not listen" (Isa. 66:4).

Not many people have heard God's voice. The average person has to receive and understand His guidance in other ways. It takes time and discipline, but a time may come that you will experience the wonderful assurance that you are busy doing God's will; that you can say with conviction, "This is what the Lord says!"

In order to receive God's guidance it is necessary to wait on Him in silence. This takes discipline, because as soon as you start seeking His presence, evil powers start causing confusion in your thoughts and spirit. You constantly need to re-focus your thoughts on the living Christ until you become aware of your unity with Him.

> The will of God will never lead you where the grace of God cannot keep you.
> THOMAS AQUINAS

As you surrender yourself to Christ more and more, you will discover that you become more sensitive to His guidance. Things start happening in many ways. Even if there are problems that don't go away, you are able to handle them constructively; you understand the problems so much better, and you become aware of the godly power and wisdom at work in your life and your actions.

God has not changed. As He led those who trusted in Him in days gone by, He still does today for those who love and obey Him. He gives them the assurance that they are within His holy will.

Holy Father, even if I can't hear Your voice, I rejoice in the awareness of Your guidance in so many different ways. Amen.

Read Job 36:22-33

Is Your God Great Enough?

Look, God is greater than we can understand. His years cannot be counted (Job 36:26).

One of the hurdles in spiritual growth and development is a limited concept of God. You believe that He loves you and cares for you. You accept that He is almighty, omnipotent and omniscient. But when disaster looms and you are confronted with problems and daunting challenges, God is given a less important position and you fail to make use of His wisdom, peace, power and courage.

> Don't pray when you feel like it. Have an appointment with the Lord and keep it. A man is powerful on his knees.
> CORRIE TEN BOOM

Unless you constantly remind yourself of the sources God makes available to you and regularly make use of them in trying times, you will find that your trials are greater than your God.

When life runs smoothly, you must broaden your vision of God. This can be done by intensifying the time you spend with God; by expanding your interest in the world around you. Be determined to develop a greater awareness of God's presence and His greatness. Make use of the grace that He places at your disposal to get to know Him better. And then, when the storms come – and they will certainly come – you will have a spiritual reserve that enables you to stand firm, no matter how tough the times.

When you have become one with God, you will find that He gives you strength in moments of temptation; that your faith is no longer just a feeling. He assures you of His presence at all times. Know that God is great and your faith will be great as well.

Eternal Father, grant me a deep appreciation of Your greatness so that I may also have great vision and a great spirit. Amen.

Read Romans 16:17-27

Satan Crushed

The God of peace will soon crush Satan under your feet (Rom. 16:20).

It might sometimes seem to you that crime and violence reign supreme in the world today. Widespread despair, greed, abuse, violence and murder cast a grim shadow over the entire community. Every day we hear about child molestation, rape, serial murders, drug abuse, robbery and corruption on a staggering scale. We ask ourselves: "Will it ever end?"

God's promise is that it will come to an end. On a high wall, just as you enter the Coventry Cathedral in the English midlands, a sculptor created an image from the Bible. It is based on Revelation 12. It is a huge bronze figure of Michael, the archangel, crushing Satan under his feet. The message is that evil might reign a while but that God will triumph.

In Paul's time evil was rampant in many guises in Rome. Christians would soon be thrown to the lions in arenas and devoured. But God's promise remained: "The God of peace will soon crush Satan under your feet."

That message is just as relevant today as it was then. Ultimately, evil in all its forms will be defeated by God's omnipotence. He can and wants to triumph over evil. Jesus' resurrection is the guarantee that this is so.

As a Christian you must react to the evil of our day with the calm assurance and faith that Satan will be crushed. Unceasingly fight all evil in your area: the final victory belongs to God's children.

> If you cannot hate evil, you cannot love God.
> STRUTHERS BURT

Lord Jesus, keep me from despairing of evil around me. Amen.

Read 2 Samuel 24:18-25

True Discipleship

I will not present burnt offerings to the LORD my God that have cost me nothing (2 Sam. 24:24).

It is a widely known fact that the things we worked hardest for are the things we appreciate most in life. In most cases the achievements that we put the least effort into, are soonest forgotten and we lose interest in them. We find that we don't appreciate their influence on our lives that much.

True discipleship is not achieved easily and without sacrifice. No one who bears Jesus Christ's name can do it without total surrender of his or her life to Him. If you choose to serve God in your own way, in your own time, and on your own conditions, you will quickly be disillusioned.

To grow in the grace of Christ and experience a fulfilled life on your Christian pilgrimage, it is absolutely vital that you give yourself to Jesus completely, without reserve. There is no room in a Christian's life for half-hearted surrender. You enter into a relationship with Jesus Christ on His terms and not your own.

When you surrender yourself to Christ unconditionally, you will experience the wonder of a special feeling of amazement and fulfillment that more than compensates for anything you sacrificed. As reward you receive the gift of His Holy Spirit.

> When we have, through Christ, obtained mercy for our persons, we need not fear but that we shall have suitable and seasonable help for our duties.
> JOHN OWEN

Lord my God, I give myself to You again, unreservedly, to do with me as You please. Amen.

Read 2 Peter 3:1-16

God Is Patient

> He is being patient for your sake. He does not want anyone to be destroyed, but wants everyone to repent (2 Pet. 3:9).

It seems that some people have amazing patience and they never become upset or rushed. They can struggle ahead and go to great lengths to make sure that every detail of a project is in place. They see things through until the end. Others again are impatient and if things go wrong they lose their temper.

Peter says that God is patient. Sometimes He acts with amazing speed. But He is not limited to the span of a human life. He has eternity in which to complete His holy plans. One of those plans is to bring people to their senses, to repentance, to confession of sin, forgiveness and to accept a new life in Jesus Christ. As the father waited for his prodigal son to return, his heart broken by love and compassion to have his son safely home, God also waits. He doesn't want only one or two of His stray children to be saved. He does not want to lose even one.

> We can only achieve perfect liberty and enjoy fellowship with Jesus when His command, His call to absolute discipleship, is appreciated in its entirety.
> DIETRICH BONHOEFFER

Every day is an opportunity for you to repent. Every day that God lets you breathe and live, is an opportunity to put the past behind you and take hold of His undeserved grace with both hands; to start a new, better life in Jesus Christ – eternal life. And if you have slid back to your earlier life, it is not too late. God is patient with such people in particular. Take your chance today!

I thank and praise You, Father, for the many chances You give me. Amen.

Read 1 Peter 5:1-11

Like a Lion on the Prowl

Stay alert! Watch out for your great enemy, the devil. He prowls around like a roaring lion, looking for someone to devour (1 Pet. 5:8).

You are sought-after prey! You may lead a quiet, peaceful life and probably see yourself as someone without any enemies. But you are mistaken. You have at least one deadly enemy, and that is the devil.

> The best protection against Satan's lies is to know God's truths.
> THOMAS BROOKS

The Bible is very serious about sin. Throughout the entire Bible there are many references to the presence and power of the Evil One. He lurks around every corner and waits at every turn, ready to attack his innocent prey.

We are at our most vulnerable when we think we are strong and powerful, or when we make light of spiritual dangers as if they don't exist. They come in the form of moral temptations, like David who became the prey of another man's wife, Bathsheba. They come in the form of doubt, like Thomas who refused to believe that Jesus had risen from the dead. They come in the form of false doctrine like people who try to spread false viewpoints about Jesus. Peter knew the power and strength of temptation. That is why he portrays Satan as a roaring lion, looking for someone to devour.

Never underestimate the devil – he is alive and well, very active and very powerful. He is totally destructive. He is in the world to make trouble. One wrong move from your side and he will pounce on you and overpower you. But you have Jesus on your side, working for you and protecting you.

Jesus is the "Lion of Judah!" Put your faith in Him and trust His omnipotence.

Holy Spirit of God, thank You that You showed me who my real enemy is. Amen.

Read Isaiah 6:1-10

The Voice of God Is Calling

Then I heard the Lord asking, "Whom should I send as a messenger to this people? Who will go for us?" (Isa. 6:8).

What makes a railway worker with hardly any schooling take up the books again and study until he passes high school? What urges him to battle through the preacher's theology examination and start the Christian ministry? What causes him to study at a theological seminary for five years until he is ordained? What is the reason for him continuing his studies at a university after he has been ordained? The answer? The voice of God calling him.

It came to Isaiah as the climax of a vision that God revealed to him in the temple. It came as a call to the ministry of prophecy. It carried him through many years as adviser in the king's court. Isaiah didn't ask himself, "What shall I do now? Will I be a builder, or a baker, or a soldier?" He didn't choose his calling in life; God chose it.

This is the fourth largest qualification for spiritual leadership — that God calls the leader. He doesn't think he can do something big for God; he or she knows that God wants to do something big through them.

To this day God calls people. Perhaps He also wants you to serve Him. Do you hear the voice of God calling?

> It is a privilege, a responsibility, a stewardship to be lived according to a much higher calling, God's calling. This alone gives true meaning to life.
> ELIZABETH DOLE

Lord, speak clearly to those You want in Your service. Amen.

Read Isaiah 6:1-10

I Will Go – Send Me!

I said, "Here I am. Send me" (Isa. 6:8).

Christian believers today have faith because one person – or many persons – through the ages, responded to God's voice by saying, "Here I am. Send me."

Gordon MacDonald tells the tale of how his wife once went to a certain dry cleaning business in New York. The first time she visited the place she noticed that it was somewhat different to other dry cleaners. Because the work was done so well, she went again. By her third visit they knew her name and recognized her. Somehow she started feeling that she was looking for excuses to visit the place again.

One day she ventured to say, "There is something about this place. You make it a pleasure coming here. What is it?" Larry, the person in charge, said to her, "I am a Christian and I think this is how Christians should treat their customers." Larry, who was aware that his business was the place where he preached the Gospel, was one of the people who said, "Here I am. Send me."

God called Isaiah to bring His message and truth to the rebellious people of Israel and Judah. He called Paul to bring His truth to the heathens of the first century. God is continuously sending people, and He is always looking for someone to send. He sends some to work in stores, to build up families, to teach, to drive a bus, to make political decisions, to present TV programs, to work with computers and to sell groceries.

> If a man is called to be a street-sweeper, he should sweep streets even as Michelangelo painted, or Beethoven played music, or Shakespeare wrote poetry.
> MARTIN LUTHER KING, JR.

When He calls you, will you be ready, like Isaiah, to say, "Here I am. Send me."

Lord, my God, I am ready and willing. Send me! Amen.

Read Philippians 1:1-11

Knowledge and Understanding

I pray that your love will overflow more and more, and that you will keep on growing in your knowledge and understanding (Phil. 1:9).

There are people who grow spiritually for a long time — and then stop. It seems like they hit the ceiling of their professional development, their intellectual growth, their spiritual progress, whatever. Sometimes they even deteriorate spiritually.

Paul wanted the people of Philippi to grow spiritually. He didn't want them just to make a lame effort and then stop. He urged them to grow and to keep growing. He knew that human capacity for love and growth in spiritual knowledge and insight were closely connected.

God gives you knowledge and insight and that obliges you to love even more. But Paul had enough experience of God's love to know that the love that Christians should reveal is not only sentimental love, but wise love. This wise, mature, Christian love is sensitive to the needs of people, and at the same time respects their need to grow. This love is fully thought through and promotes the growth of self-worth in others and also seeks to promote their spiritual growth.

> If I find in myself a desire which no experience in this world can satisfy, the most probable explanation is that I was made for another world.
> C. S. LEWIS

If you grow in this kind of love you will gain knowledge and insight on a number of fronts in life. You will be more devoted in prayer; you will read the Bible with greater understanding and your faith will be strengthened. You will care more for others and worry less about yourself — and Christ will grow and take shape in you more and more.

Lord Jesus, help me to think more about You and others and to lose myself in Your love. Amen.

August

*The grass withers
and the flowers fade,
but the word of
our God stands forever.*
   Isaiah 40:8

I know the Bible
is inspired because it
finds me at a greater
depth of my being than
any other book.
Samuel Taylor Coleridge

All-knowing God who speaks to us through Your Word,
we thank You for Your Word that is like You:
eternal, unfathomable and indispensable.
Thank You that You sent Your Son
as Word Incarnate so that we can live through Him.
We thank You for the Holy Spirit that opens up Your Word for us
and teaches and leads us in its truth.
We thank You for entrusting Your Word to writers of old
and that Your Spirit inspired them to pass it on to us.
Thank You that Your Word is available in so many languages
and that even little children can understand it.
We thank You for translators, printers and publishers
that eternalize and distribute Your Word.
Thank You that even the neediest among us
can possess the Bread of Life.
We praise You for Your Word and for its saving power.
We thank You for preachers that help us to understand it;
for Your Spirit that sees to it that the Word
is a light for our path and a lamp for our feet every day.
We pray this in the Name of the Word Incarnate.
Amen.

Amen

Read Philippians 1:1-11

The Things that Really Matter

For I want you to understand what really matters (Phil. 1:10).

In all fields of life, decision-making plays a crucial role. An outstanding figure in the economic field was appointed head of an organization. He served at conferences and on commissions and this took up much of his time. Someone who knew him well remarked to a friend that he wondered if he ever put in a full day's work for his employers. The friend answered, "It doesn't really matter. He was appointed for his productivity, he was appointed to make decisions. If he makes one good decision a month on his level, he has earned his salary."

> Good and evil both increase at compound interest. That is why the little decisions you and I make every day are of such infinite importance.
> C. S. Lewis

Paul knew that it was necessary for Christian believers to make good decisions. They had to make choices between right and wrong every day. All kinds of false doctrines were doing the rounds and they had to know how to discern between the true and the false, the good and the bad. Often there were relationship problems in the local community and it took wisdom and compassion to solve them. Christians would only be able to deal with these problems if they lived close to God, had knowledge of Christ and could consequently make wise decisions about these issues.

You and I must often make choices about all kinds of issues. We need to prioritize the use of our time, our money and our energy. Especially if we have to choose between pleasure, acquiring possessions and wealth, the role we will play in social life, and our family relationships. We will not only make many decisions, but also many important decisions.

Lead me, O Holy Spirit of God, in all the decisions I have to make. Amen.

August 1

Read Philippians 1:18-30

Together in the Midst of the Struggle

We are in this struggle together. You have seen my struggle in the past, and you know that I am still in the midst of it (Phil. 1:30).

The task of spreading the truth about Jesus Christ, worldwide, was a daunting one. In Paul's time not a single one of the modern means of communication, like printing presses, the radio, movies or television existed. Physically, the task was enormous, but the biggest problem by far was the fierce opposition of the Roman authorities, of other religions and false preachers from inside the Christian faith itself.

Paul knew that Satan was behind the opposition he had to face. So he saw the whole setup as a vicious war. But he wanted his fellow combatants in Philippi to know that although he was far away from them, he was with them in this bitter struggle.

You and I are not lonely warriors. Wherever you might be, you are part of a task force of "soldiers of the Cross", busy fighting to overcome the problems and setbacks in the struggle of getting the Gospel to the people in today's world, and resisting the devil. Be encouraged by their boldness. Behind them are crowds of people praying for you. They are with you in the midst of the struggle – just like Jesus at the Throne of God!

> Christianity is a battle, not a dream.
> WENDELL PHILLIPS

Holy Leader, thank You for the multitude of believers all over the world. Amen.

August 2

Read Philippians 2:1-11

Encouraged and Comforted

If you have any encouragement from being united with Christ, if any comfort from His love, if any common sharing in the Spirit, if any tenderness and compassion, then make my joy complete by being like-minded (Phil. 2:1-2 NIV).

Some people have amazing strength. In 1970 John Wesley started his journal for the year with the words, "I am now an old man, decayed from head to foot. My eyes are dim; my right hand shakes much; my mouth is hot and dry every morning; I have a lingering fever almost every day; my motion is weak and slow. However, blessed be God, I do not slack my labor: I can preach and write still." He was eighty-seven years old at the time and left for England on a preaching campaign a few weeks later.

> It will do us good to be very empty, to be very weak, to be very distrustful of self, and so o go about our Master's work.
> CHARLES H. SPURGEON

Paul knew that he received his strength from Christ. The missionary journeys he undertook would have been too much for people considerably younger than him. His young assistant, John Mark, did in fact leave him at some stage. Paul did his work in the name and the strength of the Lord. Christ empowered him physically, spiritually and mentally. Paul wanted the believers in Philippi to draw their strength from Jesus so that they would not be defeated by the forces of evil.

Christ not only makes you whole, He also makes you holy and strong. He makes you strong to handle life's problems. He makes you strong in the face of fierce opposition, ridicule, sickness, setbacks and frustration. He enables you to go ahead when your human resources have dried up. Remember how weak you are in your own strength and hold on to the strength Christ gives you – and never look back.

I thank You, Lord Jesus, for the strength You give me. Amen.

August 3

Read 1 Timothy 2:1-7

Jesus Sets You Free

He gave His life to purchase freedom for everyone. This is the message that God gave to the world at just the right time (1 Tim. 2:6).

William Barclay tells the story of a man who lost his son in a war. He was a man who had lived a reckless and ungodly life, but his son's death brought him to his senses, and face to face with God, like never before in his life. One day he stood at the local wall of remembrance and looked for his son's name on it. When he found it, he said to himself, "I think he had to die so that I could live."

> Let the fact of what our Lord suffered for you grip you, and you will never again be the same.
> OLIVER B. GREENE

In biblical times slavery was practiced worldwide. Most people became slaves when their country of birth was defeated in a war. The winning nation took some of the local inhabitants back to their country where they were bought and sold as slaves. A slave could, however, be freed from slavery if someone was prepared to pay the ransom.

With Jesus' death, He paid the ransom to free us from sin – He had to die so that we could live. He gave Himself in exchange for us, so that we could be set free from sin.

If you are aware that Jesus Christ forgave your sins, rejoice in the fact that He set you free. Never allow your sense of gratitude for this wonderful gift to fade or die. If you don't yet know if your sins have been forgiven, ask Jesus to forgive you now and accept the glorious truth that you are a freed sinner.

Hallelujah, Lord Jesus, You set me free – please keep me free forever. Amen.

Read Isaiah 11:1-11

The Omnipotence of God

In that day the LORD will reach out His hand a second time to bring back the remnant of His people (Isa. 11:11).

There is something very special about homecoming. Soldiers returning home after the war are welcomed with open arms and great joy. Exiles kiss the ground when they return to their homeland. Families that were spread far and wide, celebrate their reunion.

The people of Israel were scattered across the entire ancient world and some of them were exiled as slaves after Israel was defeated in war. Throughout the Old Testament the people's faith, especially that of the prophets, fostered the hope that God would take them all home again. It wouldn't only be a national family homecoming. It would mean that those who had become "lost" to God would be restored again to their original faith. There was little hope that their homecoming would be made possible by human effort. God would have to step in to release them and bring them back again. This He would do in His omnipotence.

In the face of our human inability to do the big things, we tend to forget that God has always been almighty. He used His omnipotence to free the Israelites from slavery in Egypt. He raised Jesus from the dead. He protected His followers during horrific Roman persecution, and made the Christian faith the official faith of the Roman Empire. He has proved His omnipotence time and again.

Trust Him. Believe in His ability to achieve His goal of salvation. Do everything you can to advance His salvation task.

Almighty Father God, thank You that You still show Your omnipotence today. Amen.

> He can only give according to His might; therefore He always gives more than we ask for.
> MARTIN LUTHER

August 5

Read Genesis 17:1-8

It Never Stops

"I will confirm My covenant with you and your descendants after you, from generation to generation. This is the everlasting covenant: I will always be your God and the God of your descendants after you" (Gen. 17:7).

Not all covenants last. Sometimes one of the parties in a covenant fails to keep his promise. Many marriages don't last forever. Friendships fade and die as time goes by.

In making His covenant with Abraham, God pledged Himself to His servant. It was a decision God made of His own free will. And the covenant was not one that God would withdraw from, deny or forget about. It was not even a "till death us do part" agreement. It would outlive Abraham himself and continue with his children and grandchildren, for endless generations.

At the Last Supper, Jesus made a new covenant founded on His own death and resurrection. That covenant still holds true and will last forever if believers surrender to Him. Whatever sins may be rampant, whatever evils may thrive, no matter how disloyal the church may become, how badly believers may be misled, into whatever tragic condition the world may degenerate, God's covenant of love, grace and peace will remain.

> You are mine and I am Yours. So be it! Amen.
> JOHN WESLEY

Human kingdoms may come and go, but no matter to what extent things change, whatever headway is made in the name of progress, whatever violence people are guilty of, God's covenant to protect, provide and redeem will remain because it is everlasting. It is the only covenant that will last forever. For your sake and mine, God is also forever!

Lord my God, help me to be true to You until the end. Amen.

Read John 10:22-42

The One Who Was Sent

"Why do you call it blasphemy when I say, 'I am the Son of God?'" (John 10:36).

Communities take great pride in people who grew up with them and then become famous. Chris Barnard, the heart transplant pioneer was born in the town of Beaufort West, in the middle of the South African Karoo. Today there is a Chris Barnard Museum in this town to pay homage to his achievements. He is the most famous resident of this town.

This is how some people think of Jesus Christ. They see Him as the greatest Son of humankind. They believe He was the most famous Man that ever lived.

> He is the greatest influence in the world today. There is a fifth Gospel being written – the work of Jesus Christ in the hearts and lives of men and nations.
> W. H. GRIFFITH THOMAS

The Bible has a different view. The Bible doesn't see Him as the greatest example of what a human being can achieve. It says that He was sent into the world of human existence, strife and dispute from the outside. He was sent here from somewhere else in a way that science fiction portrays the arrival of people from Mars. Jesus is not *our* most famous product. He is God's greatest gift. Salvation comes from outside – from God!

Jesus is still the One who was sent. Not only was He sent, He is still being sent. He is sent to the traumas and problems of human communities, as well as the depths of your own heart. He is God's gift in your sorrow and your joy, in good times and bad. He is sent to hold you and to help you, to comfort and inspire you. Today and always!

Lord Jesus, send me like You were sent, and always make me willing to go. Amen.

Read Philippians 3:12-21

Enemies of the Cross

For I have told you often before, and I say it again with tears in my eyes, that there are many whose conduct shows they are really enemies of the cross of Christ (Phil. 3:18).

> The cross is proof of both the immense love of God and the profound wickedness of sin.
> JOHN MACARTHUR

There are people who openly challenge God. They say, "There is no God. Let us enjoy life while we still can, because tomorrow we die." Others go even further and say, "Let us use every possible moment to get the most out of our community. After all, we are in control." Then they exploit their fellow human beings and make many lives miserable. Others do their very best to silence the Christian faith and even prevent its members from carrying out their task.

This is nothing new. They did the same in biblical times. There were two kinds of "enemies of the cross" in Philippi. One kind believed that Jesus had set them free from the necessity of obeying the Jewish laws so that they could go ahead and do anything they wanted to celebrate that freedom. The other group thought that because God loves us and forgives sin, we can sin without worrying about it because God will forgive us anyway.

Following any of these views is denying Christ who came to make it possible for us to live holy lives.

Make sure you live like a servant of Christ and not like an enemy of the cross. Do not forget or deny your surrender and devotion to Christ. A Christian disciple is a person with discipline and self-control. Guard against becoming an enemy of the cross. Live a holy, Christian and responsible life.

Keep me, Holy Spirit of God, from ever becoming an enemy of the cross. Amen.

Don't Blame God

People ruin their lives by their own foolishness and then are angry at the LORD (Prov. 19:3).

God is often blamed for things He is not responsible for. It is His wish that everyone will live with Him in harmony and lead peaceful, productive lives. Yet there are several people who cannot adapt in a community and then blame God because they are miserable. And it won't enter these unhappy people's minds that if they lived close to the Master and obeyed His will, their lives would have been quite different.

The truth that a person is responsible for his own attitude and happiness should have a great influence on us. The saying that you reap what you sow is an unchangeable law. The fact that this truth is often forgotten or ignored doesn't influence its effectiveness.

If you are unhappy or miserable and you have developed an aggressive attitude towards life and towards God, be sensible enough to come to your senses for a moment. Then, in your disappointment and bitterness, ask yourself where exactly you lost your way.

Instead of fighting life, start cooperating with it. This can only happen if you acknowledge Jesus Christ's sovereignty over your life and are willing to work together with Him and allow Him to lead you.

He has invited all of us to share His life with Him, and those who do so discover a totally new dimension of life. Problems are approached in a constructive way, essential values take their rightful place and life becomes meaningful when it is seen from Christ's vantage point.

> The value of life lies not in the length of days, but in the use we make of them.
> MICHEL DE MONTAIGNE

Lord Jesus, be my Guide and my Friend and lead me until the end of my pilgrimage. Amen.

Read Jeremiah 15:10-18

Cheerful Obedience

When I discovered Your words, I devoured them. They are my joy and my heart's delight, for I bear Your name, O LORD God of Heaven's Armies (Jer. 15:16).

Robert Louis Stevenson immigrated to Samoa for health reasons. One evening he felt very tired and went and sat down in a chair. He thought how good a cup of coffee would taste. The next moment the door opened and his servant entered with a cup of coffee on a tray. "This is wonderful," Stevenson said, "your thoughtfulness is exceptional." "No Sir," replied the servant, "my love is exceptional." Some people serve and obey out of a sense of duty. Others do it out of love.

In spite of the burdens that Jeremiah's submission to God entailed, he served the Lord willingly and joyfully. No matter how strict the demands made on him, he accepted them cheerfully. He knew that it was a privilege to belong to God, and to serve Him was a joy.

Some of the demands God makes on you will be pleasant and you will carry them out with excitement. But others will be taxing. Your obedience to Christ will sometimes satisfy Him, and also you. At other times you will only be able to serve God by renouncing yourself. The parents of a sick child may spend hours taking care of the child, losing a lot of sleep in the process. But the parents would never count the cost of it or complain.

Do you serve the Lord cheerfully – or do you constantly grumble and yearn for more enjoyable things you could have been doing?

Father God, grant that it will always be pure joy for me to serve You. Amen.

> To give real service you must add something which cannot be bought or measured with money, and that is sincerity and integrity.
> DONALD A. ADAMS

Read Isaiah 1:1-10

Listen!

> Listen, O heavens! Pay attention, earth! This is what the LORD says: "The children I raised and cared for have rebelled against Me" (Isa. 1:2).

In spite of the fact that we have only one mouth and two ears, we find it much easier to speak than to listen. Usually it doesn't really matter whether we have something worthwhile to say. And when someone speaks to us, we concentrate more on what our answer will be than on what they want to say to us.

God speaks. If we are at all interested in building a relationship with Him, we have to listen, so that we can hear what He wants to say to us. God spoke the universe into existence. He spoke when He gave the Ten Commandments. He spoke through His servants and prophets. He spoke in and through Jesus. In the Scripture passage He was speaking to His people. He called on heaven and earth to be silent so that they could hear what He had to say about the condition of the nation. He often spoke in grace, but sometimes in judgment.

> However devoted you are to God, you may be sure that He is immeasurably more devoted to you.
> MEISTER ECKHART

It is still essential for the world to listen when He speaks. Unfortunately it happens very seldom. You and I must also listen. Sometimes God may try to say something to you in the most ordinary circumstances. Sometimes He has to condemn and warn. At other times He may speak words of comfort. There are times He wants to warn you. And there are times when He makes a promise that will give you hope. He often speaks in grace and mercy. It is therefore of the utmost importance that we will listen. Are you listening?

Lord, my God and Father, silence my chatter so that I can hear what You want to say to me. Amen.

Read Isaiah 1:1-10

Are You Also Living in Ignorance?

"Even an ox knows its owner, and a donkey recognizes its master's care – but Israel doesn't know its master. My people don't recognize My care for them" (Isa. 1:3).

Often people carry on their merry way, unaware of the dangers and problems lurking around the corner. Political leaders suddenly discover that a revolution is going on to get rid of them. Marriage partners find out that their spouse is having an affair – and they are the last to know.

> The recipe for perpetual ignorance is a very simple and effective one: be satisfied with your opinions and content with your knowledge.
> ELBERT HUBBARD

Isaiah spoke to the people of Israel and told them that even animals have a good relationship with their owners. They know who feeds them and they respect and obey their masters.

But the people lived in ignorance of God, who was their Father. They conveniently forgot that He provided food for them and met their every need. They didn't respect or trust Him and went their own way in blatant disobedience.

Don't ever forget what God did for you. Stay close to Him and count your blessings. Remind yourself all the time of what Jesus means to you. Be happy that you have grown in grace and give God the credit. Listen to His voice and respond by following wherever He may lead you. Look up to Jesus for your daily joy and take note of His warnings when He wants to protect you against dangerous temptations and snares. Always be wide awake to hear Jesus' voice and learn from Him every day so that you will not be ignorant when God speaks.

Lord Jesus, may I never become ignorant about Your place in my life. Amen.

Read 1 Timothy 1:12-17

The Glory of God

> Glory and honor to God forever and ever! He is the eternal King, the unseen one who never dies; He alone is God. Amen (1 Tim. 1:17).

There are two sides involved in all Christian experiences. They are sometimes referred to as the objective and subjective aspects of religion. We can see the objective part of religion as things "outside". God, Jesus Christ, the Holy Spirit, the Bible and the church. The subjective aspects are the workings of God "inside" our hearts, our thoughts and our feelings. One aspect is not more important than the other because we need both.

Paul often spoke about the way he experienced the subjective aspects of his own faith. He talked about his own sin and referred to himself as the "greatest of all sinners". But this led him to speak about eternal life and that guided him back to God. Here he is jubilant and praises the glory of God, and in doing so, returns to the objective aspect which is the foundation of his faith.

We must be careful of being so busy with the subjective aspect of our religious experience that we forget about God's glory. Be sure to carry on placing the emphasis on God, and constantly honor Him. Ponder the glory of God regularly and remind yourself of your insignificance compared to Someone who is immortal and eternal. Focus on the Lord in His glory, His majesty and His uniqueness. He will help you to keep your own subjective experience in perspective. Never stop singing about the greatness of God. Make sure you maintain a good balance between the objective and subjective in your religious perceptions.

> The radiance of the divine beauty is wholly inexpressible: words cannot describe it, nor the ear grasp it.
> PHILIMON

Holy and Almighty God and Father, help me to glorify You alone. Amen.

Read 1 Timothy 1:12-20

Fight the Good Fight

Timothy, my son, here are my instructions for you, based on the prophetic words spoken about you earlier. May they help you fight well in the Lord's battles (1 Tim. 1:18).

Many images are used to describe the spreading of the Gospel and the Christian faith. Sometimes it is referred to as the "sowing of the seed", an image taken from farming. In other places it is described as a "spreading of the light" or the "teaching of the truth".

Here Paul reminds Timothy of the task of not only spreading the faith, but of maintaining it in the face of fierce opposition. Paul knew that there were enemies set on undermining the true Christian doctrine and destroying the church. Paul thought of this as fighting a battle against Christ. By using war terminology and talking about a fight, Paul was declaring that he took the enemies of the church seriously, because they were serious in their onslaughts on the church. Thus, defending the faith wasn't just a trifling matter. In his time Paul had a lot to do with false teachings and he knew it would also happen to Timothy. It was always a case of spiritual warfare and it still is.

> The devil does not sleep, nor is the flesh yet dead; therefore, you must never cease your preparation for battle.
> — THOMAS À KEMPIS

Don't make light of the task of the Christian community all over the world today. The enemies of Christianity are strong, mighty and determined. They would very much like to see the Christian faith totally wiped off the face of the earth. Only an approach of dedicated, courageous and persevering warfare from all Christians will take the task to victory. Wear the full armor of God and make sure your armor is ready and clean.

Holy God, help me to persevere and fight the good fight in Your strength. Amen.

Read 1 Timothy 3:14-16

All over the World

He was believed in throughout the world and taken to heaven in glory (1 Tim. 3:16).

Christianity is regarded as one of the world's religions along with Judaism, Hinduism, Islam and Buddhism. Christianity is regarded all over the world as the religion of the "west" because it was the dominant religion of this part of the world for many centuries. Some thirty or forty years ago however, a shift took place. The missionary work of Christians was so effective that the number of Christians in the developing world has increased tremendously.

> Remember, a small light will do a great deal when it is in a very dark place.
> DWIGHT L. MOODY

When Paul said that Christ was "believed in throughout the world" he was obviously talking about a very small world – mainly in the vicinity of the Mediterranean Sea. Barclay calls this pronouncement of Paul, "A glorious truth put in the greatest simplicity". After Jesus died and was raised from the dead and ascended to heaven, His followers numbered 120 (Acts 1:15). All His followers had to offer was the story of a Galilean carpenter who was crucified as a criminal on a hill in Palestine. And yet, before seventy years had passed, that story was taken to the ends of the earth and people of every nation accepted the crucified Jesus as Redeemer and Savior.

The task of spreading the Gospel is an ongoing task. It is every believer's responsibility. No matter how personal your faith may be, or how small the Christian group you belong to, you are part of a global religion with a worldwide community. This includes automobile manufacturers in Korea and mineworkers in South Africa, bus drivers in Birmingham and students in California. You and I are inseparably linked to them as Christians.

I thank You, Lord Jesus, that I may be part of Your family because You saved me. Amen.

All of Creation Made Holy

For we know it is made acceptable by the word of God and prayer (1 Tim. 4:5).

There is a tendency among people to see the earth and everything around us as a commodity that we can use as we please. This means that it is often abused. People are, however, becoming increasingly aware of the importance of caring for nature.

> The glory of God, and, as our only means to glorifying Him, the salvation of human souls, is the real business of life.
> — C. S. Lewis

The Bible says that the physical universe belongs to God. After creating it, God appointed the human race to conserve and manage it. This is why there is something holy about creation and we must respect it and regard it as God's gift to us. God's right of possession and His ownership of the world, as well as the hold He has on it, make it something much more than a handy resource. Paul goes a step further. He says it is made holy by the word of God and our prayers. Creation started with God's commands (Gen. 1:3). Creation came into existence through His word. And our response is prayer. We don't worship creation itself, we worship the God that created it. We pray in thankfulness for it, and for all God's gifts to us, including the gift of life itself.

We express this gratitude in two ways. Firstly, we say grace before every meal and thank God for the food He provided for us. Secondly, we make His creation holy when we partake of the bread and wine (produce of His creation and our labor) and make these signs holy because they mean that Christ has given Himself to us anew. In this manner we are brought back repeatedly, and in many ways, to the holiness of His creation.

Let me never deny the holiness of Your Creation, my Creator God. Amen.

Read John 1:1-18

The Creative Word

God created everything through Him [the Word], and nothing was created except through Him (John 1:3).

Scientists have different theories about how creation came into being. Their point of departure is, "What evidence is there to prove how things originated?" The Bible has a different approach and asks the question, "Who started it all?" And the Bible's answer is, "God!"

But seeing that the Son, or the Word, or Christ was already there before the beginning, and was therefore present at creation, He was there at the beginning as the Father's partner in the act of creation. Creation in itself is a miracle of God, and when the Word became part of the created world in Bethlehem, it was another miracle of God's love. By taking on a human form, God took it upon Himself to become part of the physical matter that He created Himself. In this way He made the created world holy. He did it out of love for us, the people He created – we who are part of the same creation.

Therefore, we should always honor the glory of God's creation made holy by the birth of Jesus Christ. We must celebrate the joy and miracle of God's creation. We must celebrate God's physical "gift" of Himself and His love in the birth of the Child of Bethlehem and all other children.

> No philosophical theory which I have yet come across is a radical improvement on the words of Genesis, that "in the beginning God made heaven and earth."
> — C. S. LEWIS

Decide to delve deeper and develop understanding that is much more precious than the ignorant theories of the world.

Creator God, I kneel in wonder before Your love which is visible in everything You made. Amen.

August 17

Read Philippians 1:1-11

Complete Your Work in Me, O God

And I am certain that God, who began the good work within you, will continue His work until it is finally finished on the day when Christ Jesus returns (Phil. 1:6).

Many people approach the future with the intention of doing something good. Some start a business, others work with the youth, others fight for social improvement or political justice. Many find it easy to start good things, but hard to persevere until the task is completed.

When Paul wrote to the people of Philippi, he rejoiced in the way they shared in his work of spreading the Gospel. But he admitted that what they did was actually God working in them. They were just instruments in God's hands, like Paul himself.

Paul had a long-term vision for what was happening. He knew that God had hardly even started His work in them and that there was still much to do. They could certainly not afford to sit back now and relax. There was work to do and God had promised that He would carry on with it until completion.

> Love not what you are, but what you may become.
> MIGUEL DE CERVANTES

God is also at work in you. If you have given Christ your life then He has begun to form and reform your life according to the dream He has for your life. At this very moment He is working continuously to make you see new truths, to stimulate you to learn more about Him, to inspire you to live and act in line with His will and His love. He is busy shaping Christ's image in you. God does not pay a life a single visit. His work continues until it is completed.

Lord Jesus, help me to complete the tasks God has given me. Amen.

August 18

Read Isaiah 1:10-20

What God Really Wants

Give up your evil ways. Learn to do good. Seek justice. Help the oppressed. Defend the cause of the orphans. Fight for the rights of widows (Isa. 1:16-17).

There is much more to the Christian faith than just attending church services and associating with people who think the way you do. There is even more than just prayer and meditation. God wants you to go much further than that. He sends you out of the church and into the market places of the world, there where the action is.

> The center of God's will is our only safety.
> BETSIE TEN BOOM

The problem that Isaiah saw in the Israel of his day was that people were faithfully busy going through all the rituals and ceremonies of their religion, but didn't manage to put their religion into action. The people were blind to the needs of those around them. The rich exploited the poor. Widows and orphans were abandoned. The poor, the weak and the outcasts of life were suffering. The rich brought offerings and thought that they would find favor with God in this way.

God has always expected us to love Him and to extend that love for Him to our fellow human beings. Justice is more than catching criminals and putting them behind bars. It is managing the community in such a way that justice is done to the poor and the weak. In today's world it means to knuckle down and accept the responsibility to help orphans, street children, the desperately poor and downtrodden. It is much more than one-on-one help. It is about laws, budgets, health schemes, education and security. Jesus said in Matthew 25:40, "When you did it to one of the least of these My brothers and sisters, you were doing it to Me." Do you honestly realize what God expects from you?

Merciful Father, show me what I must do and help me to obey You. Amen.

Read John 1:1-11

Life and Light

The Word gave life to everything that was created, and His life brought light to everyone. The light shines in the darkness, and the darkness can never extinguish it (John 1:4-5).

At Christmastime there are lights everywhere. They glitter all around us: in trees, in shops and in the streets. Many people look around to see if they can spot the star of Bethlehem.

> Love is the sum of all virtue, and love disposes us to do good.
> JONATHAN EDWARDS

God is the source of life. But the first action performed in creation, according to the book of Genesis, was the call for light. Then there was light and it shone in the dark, brooding chaos that was there before "the beginning". Creating light was God's first act to remove this chaos or drive it away. Thus God the Creator and God the Word brought light into being – and life also has its origin in God. He is the Source of both life and light, because without light there can be no life. And without light we can't see the glory and acts of God in this world.

Christmas is also a celebration of God's light that came into this world. When places that had no electricity before are given power, it is celebrated as a giant step forward for those people, because it changes a part of their night into day. Likewise, we rejoice in the fact that Jesus came; in the fact that we received His light. We must also be grateful for receiving the gift of life itself. We can look beyond the terrifying dark blotches of disruption and chaos that sometimes threaten our world. If it hadn't been for God's almightiness and love, the darkness would have overpowered us long ago.

Father God, I thank You for the new life that You gave me in Christ and for Your light that lightens up my path in life. Amen.

Read Isaiah 1:14-20

Cleansing

"Wash yourselves and be clean! Get your sins out of My sight. Give up your evil ways" (Isa. 1:16).

After eating, humankind's most common activity is probably washing. We wash our bodies, our clothes, our dishes. It makes us feel good to wash and it gives us confidence. It is a perfectly normal act of human decency and it is also a healthy practice. We feel uncomfortable when we know we are dirty.

Hence, it is not surprising that the whole idea of cleansing has become part of our religion. The sacrament of baptism is symbolic of cleansing. A well-balanced worship service will enable us to get rid of feelings of guilt and we will be left with a sense of being cleansed. In ancient Israel, cleansing became a preparatory stage in the act of offering a sacrifice to God. When God, through Isaiah's words, appealed to the people to cleanse themselves, He simply asked for a normal activity. He didn't, however, expect them to cleanse their bodies; He appealed to them to cleanse their souls and lives.

Not only your body and clothes get dirty, but also your soul. It is necessary that you turn to God time and time again for cleansing. You do it by confessing your sins before God and laying them at the foot of the cross. Sometimes they will be horrific and major sins and on other occasions they will seem insignificant. But all of them damage and contaminate your conscience. There's no getting away from them. They cannot be wished away, they are washed away. God, and only God, can do it and make you pure and holy.

> Our sanctification did not depend upon changing our works, but in doing that for God's sake which we commonly do for our own.
> BROTHER LAWRENCE

Wash me in Your blood, Lord Jesus, then I will be pure. Amen.

August 21

Persevere in Doing God's Will

Epaphras, a member of your own fellowship and a servant of Christ Jesus, sends you his greetings. He always prays earnestly for you, asking God to make you strong and perfect, fully confident that you are following the whole will of God (Col. 4:12).

It is not easy to stand firm in all circumstances. Many people change their opinions, viewpoints and convictions and sometimes it is necessary for them to do so. The opinions they had were wrong in the first place. But many people change their opinions because they are weak and are easily swayed from one side to another.

It was much more difficult for the Christian believers of the early Church to stand firm than for disciples today. They didn't have a New Testament to guide them. This is why Paul wrote letters to the different churches: to help them believe in the true faith and keep them from backsliding. There were many bad people who proclaimed half-truths, false dogmas and doubtful teachings. They wanted to lead believers in Christ away from their Lord. Epaphras prayed earnestly that the disciples in Colosse would stand their ground and not be lured away from Christ.

> Great men are they who see that spiritual is stronger than any material force.
> RALPH WALDO EMERSON

We must also be aware that there are many popular schools of thought and teachings doing the rounds in the world of our time. They are not really Christian in their being, even if they have a "religious flavor". Teachers of false doctrines, unsavory faith and wicked thoughts also abound. They want to lure us away, often to fill their own pockets. Avoid them. Stand firm in your faith and do God's will. Study the Bible. Make sure you know the difference between what is good and what is bad – and then stand firm in what is good.

Holy Spirit of God, help me to stand firm in what is good and do what God wants. Amen.

Read Colossians 4:7-18

How Mature Are You?

Epaphras, a member of your own fellowship and a servant of Christ Jesus, sends you his greetings. He always prays earnestly for you, asking God to make you strong and perfect, fully confident that you are following the whole will of God (Col. 4:12).

Paul wanted young Christians to grow in their faith. He said to the Christians in Ephesus, "Then we will no longer be immature like children. We won't be tossed and blown about by every wind of new teaching" (Eph. 4:14). Here he was talking about his friend Epaphras, who prayed earnestly that God would lead the Christians in Colosse to maturity. To be able to do this they would have to stand firm in their convictions of who Christ was and what He did. They would have to remain loyal to Him in all circumstances. They would have to love Christ sincerely and deeply and be aware of the needs of their fellow human beings. Furthermore they would have to look ahead, beyond present problems, and see a future abounding with possibilities for the Gospel of Jesus Christ. Christ was and always will be the grindstone for Christian maturity.

> For you know that when your faith is tested, your endurance has a chance to grow. So let it grow, for when your endurance is fully developed, you will be perfect and complete, needing nothing.
>
> JAMES 1:3-4

How does God manage to lead you to Christian maturity? How strong is your faith in Jesus Christ? How sincere is your mercy for your fellow human beings? How will you overcome the traumas that threaten to undermine your faith in God? How often do you use your spiritual gifts to the glory of God? Do you persevere in prayer for others? Is there perhaps a long road ahead of you? Pray that God will lead you to spiritual maturity.

Holy God and Father, lead me closer to spiritual maturity every day. Amen.

Read Psalm 19:1-14

The Lord's Law Revives

The instructions of the L<small>ORD</small> are perfect, reviving the soul (Ps. 19:7).

In an attempt to solve the problem of people who don't pay their TV licenses, the South African Broadcasting Commission came up with an advertisement that ends as follows, "Pay your TV license. It's the right thing to do." It's not only right, it is also sensible. Wise people stay on the right side of the law. Many people think it clever to break laws, as long as they aren't caught in the act. They feel exactly the same about God's laws.

> Every virtue is a form of obedience to God. Every evil word or act is a form of rebellion against Him.
> S<small>TEPHEN</small> N<small>EILL</small>

God's precepts however, are more profound, far-reaching and sensible than the laws of any country. They concern your relationship with God, obedience to the laws of your country, your family life and the role you play in the community. They revive because they shine in a world of evil and trouble. They light your path in a world dominated by the darkness of sin, disobedience and unhappiness. Following God's well-planned lifestyle is the sensible thing to do because it leads to true, revitalizing life when you obey Him.

Jesus is the Light of the World. He helps you to find your way in a confusing, difficult and deceptive world. Dark dangers lurk at every turn. He will protect you from all disaster. Obey God's precepts – it's the right thing to do and it will revive you.

Heavenly Father, thank You for the life-giving power I draw from obeying Your laws. Amen.

Read Psalm 19:1-14

The Road to Happiness

The commands of the LORD are clear, giving insight for living (Ps. 19:8).

Recently a lady joked, "Everything I like is either against the law, or immoral, or fattening." Many people think if you keep to everything lawful and moral, you will be bored to tears. But this is not true. On the contrary, exactly the opposite is true. Those things that are unlawful, immoral and not beneficial, cause unhappiness, dissatisfaction, and are bad for your health.

The psalmist knew this. The guidance God provided when He gave the Ten Commandments to the children of Israel focused on leading the people to what philosophers call "the good life". Furthermore, this virtuous lifestyle was the "right" way to live. Failure to follow God's guidance would lead to a wrong and unhealthy way of life and wrong relationships in the community. Disobedience to God was a recipe for disaster and unhappiness.

Nothing has changed. There are unhappy people around you and many of them contributed to their own distress by deliberately disobeying God's laws. This unhappiness is made worse by their feelings of guilt. God knew what He was doing when He gave the people the Ten Commandments. He charted the route He wanted humanity to follow to real, deep and ongoing joy and happiness. Jesus didn't change these laws, but simply emphasized the law of love that converted the Commandments to positive instructions to love God and your neighbor. Whether you obey God's laws or not, will determine how happy or unhappy you wish to be in life.

> Complete happiness is knowing God.
> JOHN CALVIN

Spirit of God, teach me to trust and obey God so that I may find happiness in life. Amen.

Read 2 Peter 1:16-21

Trust the Message

Because of that experience, we have even greater confidence in the message proclaimed by the prophets. You must pay close attention to what they wrote, for their words are like a lamp shining in a dark place (2 Pet. 1:19).

People sometimes complain that the Bible is old and deals with things that happened such a long time ago that we can't really relate to it. At the time Peter wrote his letter to the early Christians, the first written messages of the Old Testament prophets were already 800 years old. They were hand-written for hundreds of years and the art of copying was a highly developed art. They protected the true and real message, and the original messages to the prophets came from God Himself through the Holy Spirit that worked in them.

You and I can trust in the Bible's message. Its physical preservation was led and protected by what can only be seen as an act of God and His goodness. But even more important: What it says touches the hearts and lives of people all over the world and it becomes possible for God to speak to them by means of His message. People have always found guidance, comfort, strength, hope and peace through the truth of the message of the Word. It speaks to them of God's transformational love, His omnipotence and His willingness to make broken people whole again. People feel they can trust the Word because it speaks to them in their personal situation; it touches them in their fear and leads them in their confusion. The Message stood the test of time and calls on us to do the same, to the honor and glory of the Supreme God.

> The Scriptures alone are the foundation of our beliefs as Christians. I stand on the Word of God as recorded in the Bible.
> MARTIN LUTHER

Eternal God and Father, thank You for Your message that leads me daily and helps me to choose the right way. Amen.

Read 2 Peter 1:16-21

A Light in the Dark

Their words are like a lamp shining in a dark place – until the Day dawns, and Christ the Morning star shines in your hearts (2 Pet. 1:19).

We live in a world of pitch-dark gloom. There is darkness in the political sense of the word where world leaders are looking for solutions to a myriad of problems. Wars, poverty and sickness are threatening to destroy humankind. There is moral darkness where humankind is in danger of being flooded by the enormous occurrence of violence, escalating at an alarming rate. There is spiritual darkness where uncountable numbers of people haven't heard about Christ yet and are confused by the cults around them.

> An age is called Dark, not because the light fails to shine, but because people refuse to see it.
> JAMES A. MICHENER

God's message always shines like a light in this darkness. It brought light when God gave Moses the Ten Commandments. The message of the prophets showed people the way out of the darkness surrounding them, to the light of God's future for them. The message of Jesus and the apostles brought light into a world of political darkness, oppression, and religious confusion.

In the darkness of our day, God's message is still, as always, a light. It is a light for the poor who wonder if there is still any hope for them to rise above their desperate circumstances. It radiates a message to the rich when it recommends that they rather put their trust in God than in their earthly possessions. It is a light for the lonely because it tells them about an ever-present Friend. It offers hope to those without hope, guidance to the mighty, strength to the weak, comfort to the despondent and joy to those in mourning. Do not curse the dark, follow the Light!

Holy Father God, I can find my way through the darkness of this world with Your light. Amen.

Read Genesis 17:1-8

I Will Give ... I Will Be

"I will give the entire land of Canaan, where you now live as a foreigner, to you and your descendants. It will be their possession forever, and I will be their God" (Genesis 17:8).

It's not surprising that we sometimes become confused about who exactly God is. He is at the same time the "Good Shepherd" and the "Great Savior". He is the "Friend of sinners" but at the same time the "Judge of the entire world". In some of His titles He gives us something and in others He demands that we give Him something.

> God is more anxious to bestow His blessings on us than we are to receive them.
> AUGUSTINE OF HIPPO

When He appointed Abraham as His special servant, God made a covenant with Him and He made certain promises. He would give His servant many descendants and also a country that we know today as Israel. At the same time that He gave Abraham the blessing of a large offspring and a country, God also demanded from Abraham that He and all his descendants serve Him as their God. Abraham didn't make this up. He didn't go through a long list of possible gods and then decide which one would be the best. God appointed Himself as their God in His omnipotence, sovereignty and glory.

God always comes to us with an offer and a demand. Some believers accept the gifts, but try to sidestep His demands. Accepting the gifts requires an enormous commitment and obedience from us. Those who first meet Him in His demands, find out that the commitment this requires, turns out to be more of a gift and a blessing. Enjoy what God gives you with love, and also give Him whatever He might ask of you.

Help me, Heavenly Father, to discover Your blessings by meeting Your demands. Amen.

Read Genesis 17:9-14

Obey the Terms of the Covenant

Then God said to Abraham, "Your responsibility is to obey the terms of the covenant. You and all your descendants have this continual responsibility" (Gen. 17:9).

There are two parties in every covenant. Sometimes there are more, but there must be at least two. Things are disrupted if one of the two doesn't honor the promises made. Sometimes both parties fail to uphold their end.

God bound Himself to Abraham and his descendants, and He expected them to honor their side of the covenant. They had to obey God and submit to His authority as Lord. Later He would give them the moral and religious responsibilities of what we call the Ten Commandments. This was the foundation of their entire way of life – and still is. The Old Testament is largely the long and sad saga of their failure to keep to the stipulations of their side of the covenant and of God's continuing appeal for them to be "His people" and to obey His laws.

Likewise, we fail to keep our side of the covenant we entered into when we gave our lives to the Lord the first time. We most probably fail in honesty, in purity, in integrity and in love. We might not even have reached the standard we set for ourselves, let alone what Christ expected from us. We may, however, renew our covenant. This is done by first admitting that we broke the covenant. Then we must allow the forgiving and renewing grace of Christ to restore us. Then we must earnestly promise to be more faithful in future. And most likely we will have to do it again and again and again.

> I know the power obedience has of making things easy which seem impossible.
> TERESA OF AVILA

I thank You, Lord my God, that I may renew the covenant with You. Lead me to faithfulness. Amen.

Read Hosea 5:1-15

Your Sins Are Forgiven

Your deeds won't let you return to your God (Hosea 5:4).

Of all the destructive experiences that have a negative influence on your spiritual and emotional well-being, feelings of guilt and regret are probably two of the most important and most dangerous. Anybody who has suffered the pangs of a guilty conscience will know it affects you mentally and physically, and how difficult it is to control these circumstances.

The worst effect of feelings of guilt and remorse is your estrangement from God. This is not because the Lord distances Himself from you because He certainly does not do this. On the contrary, it is the person who feels so unworthy and undeserving that he feels he cannot face Christ, and consequently he tries to hide from God's light that exposes everything. Because of his shame and regret he would rather hide than look Christ in the eye. Consequently he moves farther and farther away from the One who has the ability, and who is waiting to take him back.

> It is always the case that when a Christian looks back, he is looking at the forgiveness of sins.
> — KARL BARTH

Don't ever forget that God is love and that His love for you was so big that He sacrificed His Son for your sake. If it was worthwhile dying for you, it is logical that Jesus wants you to follow Him irrespective of what you did or how wicked you may be. Turn to Him now – for the first time or once again, and be reassured of His forgiving love that He proved on Golgotha.

Just as I am, filthy, wicked and troubled, I come to You, Lord. You will never disown me. Amen.

Read Psalm 22:23-31

Return to God

The whole earth will acknowledge the LORD and return to Him. All the families of the nations will bow down before Him (Ps. 22:27).

Most of us think mainly in local terms. Even when we look ahead, we do it from the more narrow-minded vantage point of our own nation's interests and from within our own cultural context. We are much more concerned about the interests of our local soccer or rugby team than about global warming or the problem of clashing civilizations.

In ancient times this was also the way people thought about religion. Their god was for their nation and only for their nation. The Hebrews, however, developed a way of thinking and saw their Almighty God as Lord of all other nations. While they felt very strongly about the prosperity of their own nation, they knew deep in their hearts, that they worshiped a global God. They yearned for the time when people all over would reject their idols, would turn to the true God and worship only Him.

> Oh! for a spirit that bows always before the sovereignty of God.
> CHARLES H. SPURGEON

Christians know that Jesus Christ came to save the whole human race. They long for the day that every tribe, race and nation will acknowledge Him as Savior and worship Him as Lord. There is an international dimension to the Christian faith. Jesus came for all people. He died and rose for all. The Holy Spirit united people of diverse languages and cultures in Christ – and He still does. Don't stop praying that a people will come into being who are united in Christ, and never stop working toward it.

Redeemer and Savior, grant that people all over the world will get to know God and worship Him. Amen.

August 31

September

The flowers are springing up, the season of singing birds has come, and the cooing of turtledoves fills the air.
SONG OF SONGS 2:12

If we're not growing, we must feel guilty because we are not fulfilling Christ's command.
EVAN BURROWS

Holy and Almighty Creator God,
We worship You as the Origin and Sustainer of all life.
Everything You have created is so breathtakingly beautiful
and great joy surges through me.
Source of life and Creator,
touch my heart and bring new life
and growth to my everyday existence.
I feel a song of praise bursting forth from my inner being:
Praise the Lord, O my soul.
Help me strive with my entire being,
to nurture a life
of growth and spiritual maturity.
Grant me Your grace so I can set a practical example
of awakening faith, hope and love.
Call the faithful from the ranks
of Your believing Christian warriors
to continue Your glorious work on earth.
Open up all of our hearts to this abundance
of Your goodness and beauty.
This we pray in the name of our Great Guide to life,
Jesus Christ our Lord.
Amen.

Read Psalm 22:23-29

The Power and the Kingdom Forever

Praise the LORD! He rules all the nations (Ps. 22:23, 28).

From time to time individuals who want to try and control the world appear on the scene. In ancient times the Roman and Greek Empires were extensive and their emperors were strong and mighty. More recently, Napoleon, and then also Hitler, made every effort to achieve military victories so that they could control the world. Undoubtedly other candidates will emerge in the future, because there will always be a power struggle, or an impending one.

It was the same in biblical times. Egypt, Babylon and Assyria took turns to dominate. The question was always how good or how bad the winners would be, and who would be next. The issue of where the next wave of victory would come from was important to the Israelites. They were a small nation among mighty neighbors. In their weakness they looked up to God and noticed that He ruled over the power games of the strong. They knew that He was almighty and had authority that no human dictator could ever overthrow.

> If you do not wish for His kingdom, don't pray for it. But if you do, you must do more than pray for it; you must work for it.
> JOHN RUSKIN

Today's leaders yearn for the limelight. They have their say and they do their thing – and then disappear from the scene. But people of faith know there is more to life than politics. God Himself reigns supreme! Jesus is at His right hand, and one day He will come again to rule with authority and peace, love and righteousness. Don't be upset by temporary rulers; no matter how mighty they might be, their influence is limited and their reign short-lived.

Almighty God, I rejoice because the whole world belongs to You. Amen.

Read Psalm 18:1-16

Are You Strong?

I love You, LORD; You are my strength (Ps. 18:1).

Because there is such a strong emphasis on moral behavior in the Bible, we often think Christianity is just about being "good". Much of what the youth is taught emphasizes this element as well.

> The acknowledgment of our weakness is the first step in repairing our loss.
> THOMAS Á KEMPIS

The Bible also has a lot to say about the God who makes us strong. Part of the message is that God Himself is strong, and images of His strength abound in the Bible. God is a fortress or stronghold, a high tower, a rock, a warrior, a mighty king in battle.

In addition to this He empowers His people and makes them strong. One of the last promises Jesus made to His disciples was that the Holy Spirit would be sent and that through Him the disciples would "receive power" (Acts 1:8).

God makes you strong to resist evil. No matter how you look at it, once you believe in Christ and surrender your life to Him, you are involved in a struggle with evil – both an inner struggle, and in the world around you. It is essential that you are empowered to be ready for the battle. You must also be strong in love. The love that Jesus equips you with is not a feeble and timid kind of love. It is strong, wise and cares for others. It is the only thing that defeats the world and will ultimately make God's kingdom a reality.

Lord, strengthen me in Christ so that I will stand firm in faith's struggle. Amen

Read Psalm 18:1-15

My Mighty Savior

The LORD is my rock, my fortress, and my savior; my God is my rock, in whom I find protection. He is my shield, the power that saves me, and my place of safety (Ps. 18:2).

Even the strongest among us sometimes need to take a breather. Heavyweight boxers are thankful for the break between rounds. Champion sportsmen sometimes need time to regroup, and the same goes for the defense force. Lions take a rest in the shade of trees in the heat of the day.

It is most probable that King David wrote today's Scripture reading. He was the greatest king in Israel's history. He won more battles than any other king. There was, however, a time that he fled the wrath of King Saul and lived in exile. His faith in God was deep and sincere and he was humble. He feared for his life and knew the rocky mountains of Israel because he slept in caves and hid behind rocks. He found the physical nature of his hiding place symbolic of his God's great protection. The strongest man in the history of Israel needed protection – not only in wartime, but in everyday life. He knew where to find protection and shelter – in his God!

> There is no more urgent and critical question in life than that of your personal relationship with God and your eternal salvation.
> BILLY GRAHAM

Do what David did. See God as your fortress, your shelter, your refuge and your rock where you find protection. Make use of human help as far as you can, but in the end make sure that you have found the mightiest Rock – your Redeemer and mighty Savior, Jesus Christ.

Jesus, You are my Rock. I trust You and know that You will never forsake me. Amen.

September 3

Read Psalm 18:31-42

The Only God

> For who is God except the LORD? Who but our God is a solid rock? (Ps. 18:31).

There are many gods, but there is only one God. Therefore it is inaccurate to claim that "all religions are the same". It is, however, true that besides all mainstream religions in the world, many pseudo-religions are competing to get people to accept their religion.

"The Lord!" This was the name of the God of the people of Israel. They knew that they were His chosen people and that He called them to be His people. He was also their Mediator who defended them. He saved them from slavery and called them to testify to the world around them. He produced kings, priests, prophets and leaders for them. There were also other gods around and they were mainly worshiped by other nations. The Egyptians had their gods, the Canaanites theirs, as did the Babylonians, the Greeks and the Romans. Some had more than one god. To this day there is still a circular building in Rome called the Pantheon, where the ancient Romans worshiped all their gods.

Jesus' early disciples gave Him the name "Lord!" In this way they acknowledged Christ's uniqueness as they acknowledged God's uniqueness of God the Father, before Jesus came.

> There is but one God, the Maker, Preserver and Ruler of all things.
> JAMES BOYCE

Don't allow other gods to come between you and the Lord Jesus. Money and wealth will try to do this; patriotism; your sports team; your favorite pastime; your possessions – car, house or shares. All these things will compete to take Christ's place in your life. And your health and beauty can do the same. Be alert and take care: Christ alone is God! David knew who God was. Ask yourself in all honesty if you share his conviction.

Lord, You alone are God. Grant that I will never forget this. Amen.

Read Luke 4:14-30

Things You Take for Granted

When He came to the village of Nazareth, His boyhood home, He went as usual to the synagogue on the Sabbath and stood up to read the Scriptures (Luke 4:16).

Life is full of precious things we take for granted and often claim as our right. Few people think about the origin and meaning of the Sabbath. For the majority it has no spiritual meaning at all. We have forgotten the sacred meaning behind the day.

On a more personal note, it is dangerous to take our loved ones for granted. It is a tragedy when married couples can no longer remember when they last told their spouses that they loved them and confirmed it with a little gift. Love is very easily taken for granted and when this happens, love dies.

> Gratitude is the most fruitful way of deepening your consciousness that you are not an "accident," but a divine choice.
> HENRI J. NOUWEN

If you sit down and recall the precious things in your life that you take for granted, the result might surprise you. Make time to count your endless blessings and thank God for them one by one and you will discover a fountain of wonderful inspiration. The more we appreciate God's goodness, the more it will grow in scope and power.

Go through your life in search of God's everyday gifts and you will find it a fascinating pastime, as well as a spiritual asset. It will create an awareness of God's presence in your life and it will become more and more of a reality.

Thank You, Holy Spirit, that You make me aware of Your wonderful, often hidden gifts. Amen.

September 5

Read James 1:19-27

Your Tongue

If you claim to be religious but don't control your tongue, you are fooling yourself, and your religion is worthless (James 1:26).

In an argument you might say, "I think …" while in truth you haven't given the matter under discussion much thought. You are simply expressing your emotions at that given moment. If people would only think before they speak, our world would be a much better place.

How you feel and what you say are very closely related to each other. When your feelings take over your tongue, you are living dangerously. The possibility exists that you will say something you will regret later. You are an exceptional person if you have never said anything that you later regretted.

> Helping others, that's the main thing. The only way for us to help ourselves is to help others and to listen to each other's stories.
> — Eli Wiesel

Keeping a tight rein on your emotions is of the utmost importance in life. It is not always easy, because when you are insulted it is only natural to feel that you want to react. In personal matters of this kind it is wise to remember that you are hurt only to the extent that you allow it to happen.

There are times that the tongue must be used firmly and constructively. When an innocent person is being slandered, or when an animal is ill-treated, keeping quiet about it is a sin. It is true that there are times that your words soothe and heal, but there are also times when it is necessary to be firm. During Jesus' earthly ministry He spoke harsh words when necessary. He was angered by religious hypocrisy. He was extremely sharp with those who mistreated children. The way you use your tongue is your responsibility. So make sure your emotions are under Jesus Christ's control.

I praise and thank You, Holy Father, for the gift of speech. I pray that I will always use it carefully. Amen.

Read Philippians 1:1-11

Peace

> May God our Father and the Lord Jesus Christ give you grace and peace (Phil. 1:2).

In spite of all the prayers for world peace and all the movements and organizations that strive for peace, the world appears to be hovering on the brink of war. From time to time war does break out. Still, all people long for peace, on condition that they are in control of it.

In days gone by it was exactly the same. At the time the New Testament was written there was a form of peace. It was called the *Pax Romana*. It was the peace that resulted from one great kingdom enforcing its will and its rulers on others, and sending its armed forces to confirm its dominance.

The peace Paul wished his readers was, however, the peace that existed in war and peace. This peace is the result of reconciliation with God. The Bible is convinced that we live as God's enemies until we become reconciled with Him. This reconciliation is made possible by Jesus Christ's mediation. It has far-reaching consequences. We get to know peace with God that makes us feel that we have the right relationship with Him. Consequently we lose our feelings of fear and guilt in His presence. This enables us to be at peace with ourselves and to experience inner harmony. Instead of living in enmity with others, God gives us an attitude of peace and the desire to become reconciled with other people.

> Peace reigns where our Lord reigns.
> JULIAN OF NORWICH

This peace is only possible if you know Jesus as your Redeemer and Savior. When you reconcile with God, it makes a big difference because you are a new person and you live in a new world.

Prince of Peace, grant that I will know Your peace in my heart and life. Amen.

Read Philippians 1:1-11

Thank God

Every time I think of you, I give thanks to my God (Phil. 1:3).

When little children pray, they usually thank Jesus for their parents and their pets. Older people probably thank Him for a home, a daily job, for love, family members and for good health.

Paul thanks God for the people of Philippi. Just the thought of them gives him joy. They were the first people who responded to the message of Jesus and His love when Paul started his mission in Macedonia. All of them were triumphs of grace, converts to Jesus, and people who started to grow in their knowledge of God the Father and Jesus Christ the Savior. Each of them had a story to tell about how God worked in their lives. Paul loved them like brothers and sisters in Christ and they expressed their love and support for him, especially when he was in prison. This is why Paul thanks God for the people He gave him to work with.

> The person who has stopped being thankful has fallen asleep in life.
> ROBERT LOUIS STEVENSON

Try to extend the list of blessings God gives you beyond your domestic and personal interests, no matter how important these may be to you, so that you can also be grateful for others.

Thank Him for the Gospel of Jesus Christ, for fellow believers that you have fellowship with; for the preachers who open up the Gospel of Jesus for you and strengthen your faith. Thank Him for the host of faith heroes through the ages that passed their faith on to you. And don't forget to thank God for His personal love and salvation that He made available to you.

Heavenly Father, help me to always remain thankful to You. Amen.

Read Colossians 3:12-17

Sing!

Sings psalms and hymns and spiritual songs to God with thankful hearts (Col. 3:16).

People sing in various, and sometimes strange places. They sing during rugby games, at funerals, at political gatherings and birthdays. They sing in the shower, in concert halls and in churches, at music festivals and at Christmas. Music touches the deepest chords of the human heart and thoughts; places where conversation can't reach.

> The shepherds sing, and shall I be silent?
> GEORGE HERBERT

People receive, and teach others about Christianity through song. Christianity inherited the roots of song from the Jewish faith. When the Holy Spirit sent Jesus Christ's disciples out into the heathen world, they went with music in their hearts and others joined them in singing songs of praise with joy and thanksgiving. The early martyrs died at the stake while singing songs of praise to the glory of Christ.

It's likely that you learnt more about your faith from psalms, hymns and spiritual songs than from any sermon. Your faith becomes stronger because of the singing that accompanies it.

Song feeds your thoughts, awakens emotions and speeds up the will to act. It is not surprising that appeals to surrender to Christ are always accompanied by song. If you don't already do it, it would be a good idea to start glorifying God with song now. One day, when the struggle of life has passed and you arrive in heaven, you will be surrounded by angel choruses. Seeing that you will have to take your place among them, you will be far better equipped if you learn to sing to God's honor now.

Holy Spirit of God, teach me to continually sing to the glory of God. Amen.

Read Colossians 4:7-18

Our Dear Doctor

Luke, the beloved doctor, sends his greetings (Col. 4:14).

People from all walks of life approve of the Christian faith. Fishermen were the first to follow Jesus, but farmers, academics, clerks, teachers, train drivers, attorneys, laborers and many others responded to His call to follow Him.

> Use your gifts faithfully, and they shall be enlarged; practice what you know, and you shall attain to higher knowledge.
> MATTHEW ARNOLD

One of the earliest disciples was a doctor named Luke. It appears that he became a follower during one of Paul's missionary journeys, and then became a colleague and co-worker of the great apostle. Because of his medical training he probably cared for the physical health of the group of workers traveling with the apostle Paul. Paul was not always in good health and it is possible that, if it hadn't been for Luke, he would not have been able to carry out the taxing task God called him for in the way he would have liked to. By listening so often to Paul's teachings and preaching he learnt a lot about Jesus. He was also in possession of the Gospel of Mark, where he probably gathered more knowledge of Jesus. Luke also wrote one of the four Gospels that we have today. Then he went ahead and wrote about the early history of the church in what we know as the book of the Acts of the Apostles. What a gift his ministry of medicine and writing was to all believers.

Christ can make very good use of any gifts you might have, to spread His Gospel among people. The first services of the Methodist Church in South Africa were not led by missionaries or pastors, but by soldiers. No matter how talented you may be or how very ordinary and mundane your gifts might be, use your gifts to glorify God.

Lord Jesus, I lay all my gifts at Your feet and ask that You use them to Your glory. Amen.

Read Colossians 4:7-18

The Unknown Followers

Please give my greetings to our brothers and sisters at Laodicea (Col. 4:15).

In many places in the world there are sites known as the "Tomb of the Unknown Soldier". They remind us of all the soldiers who died in action and were buried in some unknown place in the world.

In his letter to the Colossians, Paul asked them to give his greetings to the neighboring town, Laodicea. We don't know anything about the church in Laodicea and there are no indications that Paul ever visited the place. It is mentioned in the book of Revelation. Paul's letter to the Colossians should be read there as well. So Laodicea could be seen as the prototype of all the other churches. Like a "Tomb of the Unknown Soldier" in the sense that Paul's message to them applies to us, and all Christians throughout the ages.

Thousands of Christians met Jesus and accepted Him as their Redeemer and Savior. They schooled and uplifted each other in the faith. They would sometimes get together in small groups in prisons, villages, secluded settlements, on farms and under trees. Others gathered in large churches, cathedrals or temples. All wanted to win people for Christ and all professed His sovereignty. Simply gathering in His name served as a visible testimony of Jesus' authority, and testified about the power of the Gospel to neighboring communities.

> The form of the church in any age is prescribed by the Holy Spirit.
> A. SKEVINGTON WOOD

Perhaps you are part of such a community. If so, you are part of the countless fellowship groups that span the world and cross all boundaries between heaven and earth. You have one thing in common with the rest of the world – Jesus Christ.

Grant, Lord Jesus, that all Your followers will join together as one huge community. Amen.

Read John 20:19-23

Filled with Joy

> They [the disciples] were filled with joy when they saw the Lord! (John 20:20).

Many of the things we perceive fill us with joy and excitement. A child's smile excites a parent. When someone we love smiles at us we are excited and happy. When friends suffer hardships and finally overcome them, we are happy for them and filled with admiration.

Here the disciples were looking at the Jesus whose crucifixion they had witnessed. He came through the locked door of the room they were gathering in. They saw His pierced hands and the wound in His side and they knew that He was not only alive, but that it was the beginning of a new world. The things He had taught them about the kingdom of God were true. The miracles He had performed, before their eyes, were true acts of God, who could raise Jesus from the tomb. The life that God gave triumphed over death, the final end to the world's evil.

The abundant life that He came to give was there again, in abundance – and it would overcome all onslaughts of human weakness, doubt and despair. Everything they had sacrificed their daily life for was true and now it was even worth dying for. There was not only truth; there was also power in God's love. And outside a world was waiting that longed to hear about Jesus and His life.

> There is real magic in enthusiasm. It spells the difference between mediocrity and accomplishment.
> — NORMAN VINCENT PEALE

See Jesus in your mind's eye as the disciples saw Him. Let your heart become excited and joyful about the change He brought about in your life, about the love that filled you with hope and inspired you to serve Him. And thank God.

Holy God, I thank You for the joy You brought to my life. Amen.

September 12

Read John 20:19-23

Have You Been Sent?

He [Jesus] said, "Peace be with you. As the Father has sent Me, so I am sending you" (John 20:21).

The advent of satellite television opened up a whole new world for sport. Because of worldwide audiences, TV advertisements became more expensive. Sports bodies were also paid well for televising matches. Often a new invention changes the entire character of human activities.

Jesus Christ's resurrection was a much more important and significant change for which He devoted His whole life to. Up until that moment He drew disciples to follow Him and He gathered them together. After His resurrection He changed their whole direction. Instead of drawing people to Him, He now sent them out into the world to spread His message, to confirm His truth and offer His salvation and life to everyone who wanted to hear. But it was merely a continuation of a movement that had already started. God the Father started it, by sending Jesus to earth. The resurrected Jesus changed it to a movement characterized by risks, dangers, and expansion.

> We cannot hesitate to believe that the great mission of Christianity was in reality accomplished by means of informal missionaries.
> ADOLF HARNACK

Jesus still sends His disciples to spread the truth that Jesus proclaimed, to tell the story of His life, death and resurrection and emphasize God's mighty deeds. There was also another task: to gather groups of people around the Word and, with love and compassion, teach them to love the Word. In this way new Christians would be formed and equipped to spread the Word. Do you merely listen to the Gospel, or do you know that God has sent you?

Lord Jesus, send Your disciples into the world with renewed vigor and faith in their mission. Amen.

Read John 20:19-23

God Still Breathes Over Us

Then He breathed on them and said, "Receive the Holy Spirit" (John 20:22).

When someone is critically injured or seriously ill, it is sometimes asked, "Is he still breathing?" For people without a medical background, breathing is an indication of life or death. But when we speak of God who breathes, we don't mean that "God is alive"! But that He is the Source of all life. His breath gives people life, like it did in the Garden of Eden during creation (see Gen. 2:7).

> The Holy Spirit is not a blessing from God, He is God.
> COLIN URQUHART

God did something completely new when He raised Jesus from the dead. He did not restore Jesus to His former human form in which He would grow old and die (like Lazarus). Jesus received a completely new form of life that had never been known before. There in the room with locked doors, He who was dead breathed new life into those who were alive. The word "breath" is the same word used in the original act of creation.

God breathes new life into everybody who believes in Jesus and trusts in Him. If your hope has died, He will inspire you with new hope that transcends. If your faith has died, or if your love for God is waning, or if bitterness has destroyed your emotional and spiritual health, or if addiction has stripped you of all human dignity, He will put you in full control of your life again. Let God's breath and the resurrected Christ reinvent you.

Breathe new life into me, O God. Amen.

Read John 20:24-30

The Absent Disciple

One of the twelve disciples, Thomas (nicknamed the Twin), was not with the others when Jesus came (John 20:24).

We sometimes miss important events because we just couldn't be there at that moment. We feel bad about it and wish we had tried a little harder to attend. It might have been a family member's birthday, a funeral, a sports event or an exhibition of some kind. Afterwards people might say, "You don't know what you've missed," or "Why weren't you there? You let us down."

This is what happened to Thomas. Was he upset? Was he angry? Was he disillusioned? We can only guess, but he wasn't there! He missed the opportunity of meeting Jesus and receiving the Holy Spirit. He did not hear the Master's instruction when He said, "As the Father has sent Me, so I am sending you" (John 20:21). He missed out on the joy of seeing Jesus appear through the locked door. He missed out on the fellowship and support of his fellow disciples and also the opportunity of having his faith restored. Just because he wasn't there when Jesus came.

> Three things come not back – the spoken word, the spent arrow, and the lost opportunity.
> PROVERB

How do you and I miss out on our spiritual pilgrimage? If you allow trivialities to keep you from worshiping with other believers; if you choose to miss opportunities of communion with God; if you stop reading your Bible and don't pray anymore; if the pleasures of the world mean more to you than spiritual activity: any way in which you fail to be there when Jesus comes. Then you are the one who loses out.

Lord Jesus, today we pray for everyone who avoids fellowship with Your disciples. Amen.

Read John 1:1-18

The Choice Is Yours

He came to His own people, and even they rejected Him (John 1:11).

It is so easy to get carried away by the beautiful stories in the Gospel that we often fail to see them as reality. If we move on from the wonder of Christ's birth, John helps us to see the Gospel for what it really is. He doesn't ignore its dark side or get carried away by the charm of the stories.

He reminds us that one aspect of Jesus' mission was a failure. The people God called to be His special people and His representatives in the world, refused to accept the Son of God. God spoke His Word to them in Christ. They couldn't and wouldn't listen. The people who were specially prepared to receive the Light in His fullness, did not receive it at all. We should never forget that this aspect of His work and testimony was a great disappointment and we may never forget that Jesus was a Jew.

This was an indication of what was still to come. The people who had to receive Him, had to believe in Him, who had to experience salvation through Him, decided not to do so. They preferred a life without Him.

> Darkness cannot drive out darkness; only light can do that.
> MARTIN LUTHER KING, JR.

You are not forced to know Him or believe in Him. God gives you the opportunity, but He leaves the choice to you. You have to choose if you want to accept Him, but you can just as easily reject Him. The choice is yours! You can say Yes to Jesus and walk in the Light for the rest of your life, or you can say No to Him and live in spiritual darkness for the rest of your life.

Redeemer and Savior, I accept You and want to walk in Your light forever. Amen.

Read John 1:1-18

A Special Group

> But to all who believed Him and accepted Him, He gave the right to become children of God (John 1:12).

How does one come to accept the Christian faith? The vast majority do it because they are raised to believe in God and consequently find it easy when they meet God themselves. Others don't really give it much thought, but then, with one major intervention they meet God. He claims them and they are converted. Others argue and wrestle with confusion and problems concerning their spiritual lives.

> For a soul to come to Jesus, is the grandest event in its history.
> JOSEPH ALLEINE

It was not easy for the people in Jesus' time to believe in Him. He came from a humble background. He was not acknowledged by the religious leaders of the time. On top of that He refused to be the popular political figure or revolutionary that lived up to people's expectations. Yet some saw in Him the true image and presence of God: either by listening to Him, watching what He did, or experiencing His crucifixion and resurrection. This group said, "This is the man; the Messiah of God. We will surrender ourselves unconditionally to Him." The total mission of Christ on earth rested on these few believers. He dedicated His work to them, taught them and instructed them and when the ongoing mission was handed over to them, He left them. Without them there would have been no Christian movement; it would have ended then and there in Palestine.

Humbly thank God if you are privileged to be a member of the group that accepts Him and believes in Him. Be thankful that it happened to you and that in one way or another He touched your life; that you are one of that small group that takes responsibility to pass the faith on to future generations.

Lord, use me as an instrument to encourage others to believe in You. Amen.

September 17

Read John 11:45-57

One for Many

It is better for you that one man should die for the people than for the whole nation to be destroyed (John 11:50).

Sometimes it seems as if the history of all of humanity comes to a standstill while one man or woman takes the stage and advances history. When Neil Armstrong landed on the moon he said, "One small step for man, one giant leap for mankind." At that moment he held history in his hands. The eyes of all of humankind were focused on him.

> In His love He clothes us, enfolds us and embraces us; that tender love completely surrounds us, never to leave us.
> JULIAN OF NORWICH

The High Priest, Caiaphas, was ready to sacrifice Jesus in a fruitless effort to keep the peace with the Roman authorities. Little did he know that the death of that one Man, a death that he instigated, would be one of the turning points in the history of humankind. It would be the event that would ensure salvation for everybody that would meet Christ as a result of this crucifixion. It was not one Man for the whole nation. It was one Man for mankind – for all times. Caiaphas wanted to get rid of Jesus. The rest of the world needed Jesus as their Savior – and soon they would find Him.

Soon afterwards a man with a razor-sharp intellect would testify about Jesus, "I live in this earthly body by trusting in the Son of God, who loved me and gave Himself for me" (Gal. 2:20). Later, people in Italy, Greece, France and England would say the same. They knew that they owed the new life they found in Him to the Man who died for all. Today they say it in Russia, Africa, Australia, in the Americas and Asia, as well as on the most remote islands of the world. Can you say what they say?

Thank You, Lord Jesus, that You gave Your life for me too. Amen.

September 18

Read John 11:45-57

The Universal Mission

He did not say this on his own; as high priest at that time he was led to prophesy that Jesus would die for the entire nation. And not only for that nation, but to bring together and unite all the children of God scattered around the world (John 11:51-52).

Some people think small while others think big. Some preachers become so obsessed with their own small flock that they lose sight of the universal church. John Wesley founder of the Methodist church, whose only congregation was a small town north of Lincolnshire said that he saw the whole world as his congregation.

The general idea of the people of Israel during Jesus' stay on earth was that God had a special purpose with Israel, and that He would one day send His Messiah to help rid them of the Roman yoke. But Jesus had a different idea of God's purpose with His mission.

God's purpose for sending Jesus as His Messiah did not include the people of Israel only. By the time John wrote his Gospel, many years had passed since Christ's death, His resurrection and the outpouring of the Holy Spirit. The Gospel had been preached to heathens who responded positively and believed in Jesus, and they became united with their Christian friends that were converted to Christianity from the Jewish religion.

> The Church is her true self only when she exists for humanity.
> DIETRICH BONHOEFFER

The "gathering" of people from many nations, backgrounds and cultures into a united community of believers has always been Christ's mission and aim. He died for everybody. He prays for everybody and He unites them in His body. Look beyond your own limited horizon, broaden your tunnel vision and rejoice in the knowledge that you are part of a universal community.

Continue, O Holy Spirit of God, to gather Christ's flock from all over the world. Amen.

Read John 11:17-32

Not a Theory, But a Person

"I am the resurrection and the life. Anyone who believes in Me will live, even after dying" (John 11:25).

Death is one of the greatest mysteries of our existence; some people see it as the greatest mystery. In an effort to come to terms with it, people have different theories. One is that you don't die at all, but live on in the memory of your family members and friends. Another is that only your body dies while your spirit, which is indestructible, is set free to live on in a different form, probably another person or an animal. Another theory has it that there is nothing after death.

The Christian's understanding of death is by no means a theory. It is a strong belief in Jesus Christ who said, "I am the resurrection and the life." Christians don't theorize about life and death. They don't speculate about the form it might take. They don't philosophize, wonder or worry. They see only Jesus.

> Through a tree we were made debtors to God; so through a tree we have our debt cancelled.
> IRENAEUS

Christians know that Jesus is the life and that His life that He shares with them, is a lasting, enriching and empowering life that regards death as an enemy that Christ defeated. They believe in Jesus, the risen Savior and Redeemer. They trust Him and look up to Him. Their life and hope are in Him.

Christians are not interested in stories about people who died and came to life again because they need no further proof than Jesus Himself. The mere fact that He said He is the resurrection and the life is enough for them. How about you? Is He enough for you?

Risen Lord Jesus, all I need now and in the future, is You! Amen.

Read John 10:22-42

Do You Believe?

"I have already told you, and you don't believe Me. The proof is the work I do in My Father's name. But you don't believe Me because you are not My sheep" (John 10:25-26).

Many people think that life is good while you enjoy it, but when it is over, it's over. There is nothing on the other side. You can decide if you want to accept this point of view.

The Bible teaches us that there is more to life than meets the eye. It says when you decide to believe in God, you see a totally new picture of yourself and the world, and acquire a new understanding of life itself.

> A little faith will bring your soul to heaven, but a lot of faith will bring heaven to your soul.
> Dwight L. Moody

It says that you are more than an intelligent animal, and that the world is more than a coincidental accumulation of random elements. The faith factor ensures you that you are born in the image of God and that His creative hand has a determining influence on your life; that your origin in the world is God.

The Bible says that God is also your final destination. It says that God's Son, Jesus Christ, is the image of what a human being can be, and that you will experience something of His quality of life if you believe in Him. Like Him, you will also see death as a minor pause on the way to God, your eternal destination. Faith takes you past superficial appearances and artificial interpretations. Faith really does make all the difference. Do you believe?

Lord, through Your Spirit, help all who are confused in their faith. Amen.

Read John 12:41-50

What Is Your Reaction?

"I will not judge those who hear Me but don't obey Me, for I have come to save the world and not to judge it" (John 12:47).

Without realizing it, we condemn ourselves in different ways. This usually happens when we take a stand on a subject we know very little or nothing about. A tourist gazed fixedly at the Chapel of Christ in Gethsemane, and then at the newly built Coventry Cathedral. She stared through the big wrought iron crown of thorns at a colorful mosaic of Christ, kneeling as He drank the cup of sorrow. This was part of an architecture competition. The tourist grimaced, "Really! I can't stand modern art." Her opinion didn't say anything about the work of art, but a lot about herself.

> The decision we all face is this: whether to consciously lock God out of our lives or open the door of our heart and invite Jesus Christ to come in.
> LUIS PALAU

In a way our reaction to Christ is the same. He is not judged before the bench, but we are. We also judge ourselves in the manner we hear the message of the Gospel. Furthermore, we stand condemned for hearing Him or not, and putting our trust in Him or not. His message and His Person force us to take a stand. People in Christ's time thought they were busy deciding whether Christ was the One from God, but this was not a decision they had to make. They were deciding about their own eternal destination by either accepting Jesus, or rejecting Him.

To hear about Jesus and to meet Him, to answer His call, is a crucial and life-altering event. It is not Christ who judges you – you judge yourself according to the way you react to His message.

Lord Jesus, once more I see the importance of meeting with You. Grant me the grace to make the right choice. Amen.

Read John 12:41-50

The Great Mission

"I have come to save the world and not to judge it" (John 12:47).

One of the most important tasks of a management team is to determine the exact nature of their business. They do this by asking the question: "What is our business about?" Superficially it sounds simple, but it is not always as obvious as it seems. If an electrical contractor describes his business as "bringing light to people", does this mean he runs around with candles and lamps during a power outage?

Jesus could have said His mission was "to get people to obey the Ten Commandments". This is what religion was about in His day. He might have seen His task as solving the world's poverty and health problems; or to free the Jewish nation from Roman dominion. But He didn't. He probably had to consider whether He should condemn the mistakes and offenses of the religion of His time. He decided to avoid this as well. He knew it wasn't His task to judge, but to love people and to save them. He came to earth to focus on people, not problems. His mission was salvation, not solutions. He knew it and refused to allow anyone to distract Him from His great mission.

> Remember, sinner, it is not thy hold of Christ that saves thee – it is Christ.
> CHARLES H. SPURGEON

It is just as important for us, as His disciples, to know the essence of Jesus' work. Tempting as it might be to condemn the evils of the world, it is not what Jesus saw as the focal point of His task. His task was to bring wholeness (or salvation) to the world.

Lord Jesus, help me to stay focused on my calling to be Your witness. Amen.

Read John 13:1-17

Walking towards Your Destination

Before the Passover celebration, Jesus knew that His hour had come to leave this world and return to His Father (John 13:1).

People often have a sense of foreboding about the future. When someone dies, the family will recall something the deceased said a few days before. It would then appear that this person had a foreboding of future events. Most of us, however, have no such feelings about the future because we are too busy with the present.

Jesus lived very close to God the Father. He thought the Father's thoughts, knew about the Father's plans and breathed the Father's life breath. They worked together very closely. By the time Jesus attended the Passover celebration, He knew that He would soon die. Jesus looked at this in a completely different way than anyone else. If His disciples had known, they would have seen it as the failure of a dream. The people simply saw it as the end of yet another prophet. The authorities saw it as fair punishment for a dangerous rebel. Theologians of a later time saw it as the completion of His sacrifice for our sins. Some claimed it was victory over evil. Jesus, however, saw it as the time to leave the world and return to the Father. Whatever others might have thought, Jesus knew He was fulfilling His destiny.

> The only possible answer to the destiny of man is to seek without respite to fulfill God's purpose.
> PAUL TOURNIER

When you walk with Jesus, you can be sure that you are fulfilling your destiny. He might send you on a new mission at any time. Or He might bless you in a way you could never have imagined. But He will always point you to the Kingdom of God which is in His future and in yours.

I am grateful, Father, because I know that my destiny is in Your loving hands. Amen.

Read John 13:1-17

Lasting Love

> Having loved His own who were in the world, He loved them to the end (John 13:1 NIV).

In the book *The Hiding Place,* the touching story is told of two devout German sisters who were witnesses of God's grace in atrocious wartime situations. There is a description of their mother who endured great pain as a result of cerebral hemorrhage. "It is truly amazing," writes Corrie ten Boom, "how she could live the quality of life she did in that crippled body. To see her in the three years she was paralyzed brought me to a new discovery of love."

> He loved us not because we're lovable, but because He is Love.
> C. S. LEWIS

"Mama's love had always been of the kind that proved itself at the soup pot and the sewing machine. But even now that these things were taken from her, her love still seemed as healthy as ever. She sat in her chair at the window and loved us. She loved the people she saw in the street and even farther away. I learnt that love is bigger than the walls that enclose it."

Jesus loved His disciples deeply and sincerely. Later generations saw Him as the embodiment of God's love. And He went on loving them. If people persevere in loving like Jesus loved, the positive effect of their love continues even after their death. Even the memory of them fills us with thankfulness to God.

You and I are His disciples and He loves us. Whether you are up or down, good or bad, successful or a failure, mediocre or brilliant, sickly or healthy, He loves you! He always loves you! He will always love you! Make this truth the foundation of your faith and hope, forever.

Lord Jesus, make me more and more loving each day and help me to follow Your example. Amen.

Read 1 Peter 4:12-19

An Unexpected Blessing

Be happy when you are insulted for being a Christian (1 Pet. 4:14)

God often blesses us with beautiful and pleasant gifts. A child is born and brings love, beauty and joy into a family. A new job is found and someone's livelihood is ensured. Someone recovers from a serious illness and experiences new strength and hope.

> You will never be the person you can be if pressure, tension, and discipline are taken out of your life.
> JAMES G. BILKEY

When unpleasant and unwelcome things happen to us, we may find that God concealed a blessing in our misfortune that we never noticed at first.

No one really wants to suffer. The early Christians that Peter wrote to didn't want to suffer either. They wanted to carry on with their lives and be God's people in His world. They also wanted to share their faith with the heathens around them. But it was not as easy as they thought at first; sometimes it was very inconvenient. Simply being a Christian incited the wrath of the Roman authorities. In some cases Christians were killed for their beliefs. But if they suffered in this way, they were given new status – they became martyrs and witnesses for Christ. Then the glory of God surrounded them. By dying for Christ they became powerful witnesses for Him.

If it happens that you must suffer for Christ, know that you will also receive unexpected blessings from Him. No matter how badly you are criticized, how severely you may be oppressed or punished, they will also see something strong and powerful in your willingness to suffer for Christ. You will also experience the presence and power of Christ that support and keep you in ways you never would have thought possible. You will get to know God and draw closer to Him more than at any other time in your life.

Lord Jesus, strengthen me so that I will pay the price of my discipleship joyfully. Amen.

Read 1 Peter 4:12-19

The Working of the Spirit

"Be happy when you are insulted for being a Christian, for then the glorious Spirit of God rests upon you" (1 Pet. 4:14).

Some people think that when the Holy Spirit comes upon you, He changes you into a strange character. You then do strange things, like speaking in tongues, performing miracles and predicting the future. True, some people in whom the Spirit lives do have these gifts, but others don't, even if the Holy Spirit lives in them.

Peter says here that the Spirit comes to you when you are subjected to rejection or persecution in Jesus' name. Then the Spirit does two things. First He works at your character and personality and changes you by bringing Jesus into your heart and thoughts. You become more and more like Christ. The second thing He does is to make you stronger so that you can withstand opposition and persecution.

It is not necessary to bear the mockery, rejection or persecution with your own futile strength. The Holy Spirit is God's encourager. He gives you courage that exceeds your own. When you are afraid, He encourages you and in this way He empowers you to resist opposition far better. This is precisely how Christ accepted His cross, and you become like Christ when you take up your cross and bravely carry it for His sake. Christ suffers persecution when you are suffering persecution; He feels your pain; He suffers when you are ridiculed. In this way the Holy Spirit is busy forming and perfecting Christ in you.

> God, who foresaw your tribulation, has specially armed you to go through it, not without pain, but without stain.
> C. S. LEWIS

Holy Spirit, empower me for suffering and for action. Amen.

Simple Faith and Pure Truth

And I have been chosen as a preacher and apostle to teach the Gentiles this message about faith and truth (1 Tim. 2:7).

There are people who think that the Christian faith is riddled with complicated dogmas and far-fetched teachings that only the highly educated can understand. In addition, the worship disciplines are so demanding that only professional preachers and a few fanatics are able to uphold them.

Basically Christianity is a matter of simple faith and pure truth. It need not be difficult or impossible for simple people to follow. Paul says this here, in so many words. His total lifework was taking the story of Jesus to heathen nations who knew nothing about Old Testament traditions, and to teach them how to know Jesus and believe in Him. He devoted his life to teaching them about Jesus and instructing them on the way to live a Christian life. Everything he taught and did, he did with that purpose in mind.

> It's easy to be clever. But the really clever thing is to be simple.
> JULE STYNE

Never allow yourself to be confused by people who try to make Christianity a daunting and complicated, or highly intellectual exercise. A farm laborer who knows nothing about Anselm's theory of confession can be just as good a Christian as the theology professor who knows all about it. Keep your faith simple. Believe in the pure truths of the Christian faith – God, Jesus Christ, the Holy Spirit, Creation, the Cross and the Resurrection. Don't allow yourself to become bewildered by all kinds of theories on Jesus' relationships with the opposite sex or the moral weaknesses of Christian leaders. Stick to the solid facts. Read your Bible and pray as often as you can. Walk with God – to the very end!

I thank You, Savior and Friend, that even the most simple among us can be Your followers. Amen.

Read Isaiah 4:1-6

Undying Hope

In that day, the branch of the LORD will be beautiful and glorious; the fruit of the land will be the pride and glory of all who survive in Israel (Isa. 4:2).

On the high plateaus that form a large part of central Africa (better known as the Highveld), a strange weather phenomenon can be observed. The clouds often gather in summer after a perfect, sunny morning. By midday they will be dark and threatening. Lightning and thunder will be seen

> We must always change, renew, rejuvenate ourselves; otherwise we harden.
> JOHANN WOLFGANG VON GOETHE

and heard and then rain will come pouring down. Sometimes it even hails. Then it suddenly stops, the clouds disappear, the sun shines brightly and it will be a perfect evening.

God's judgments that Isaiah prophesied were something like this. They were harsh and unsympathetic. Then the silence of renewal followed and out of the havoc and devastation, God would let a branch grow again. From the branch new growth would sprout, new shoots, and finally the tree would bear fruit again. There would be new life, fertility and hope. Beyond God's judgments a new era would dawn for His people and they would enthusiastically look forward to making progress and growing.

Judgments come in the form of wars, revolutions, floods, droughts and revolts. But there is a future for humankind because God loves them and God reigns. Never lose heart in judgment, no matter how dark it might be or how long it lasts. He who brings forth the storm also brings forth the branch that comes afterwards. After the crucifixion, the resurrection wholeness and glory will follow!

Heavenly Father, give me insight to understand the strange way in which You work with the human race. Amen.

September 29

Read Isaiah 4:1-6

Wholeness and Holiness

All who remain in Zion will be a holy people – those who survive the destruction of Jerusalem and are recorded among the living (Isa. 4:3).

We are inclined to make a distinction between economic development, political events, the cycle of nature, religion, family life, morality and scientific progress. The ancient Hebrews linked them all together because they believed that God reigned supreme over all these things and therefore they were all connected.

> Holiness is a process, something we never completely attain in this life.
> — Jerry Bridges

Isaiah saw hope for a new life on the other side of God's judgment. But it would be a different kind of life. Together with a new beginning, God would bring new fertility to the earth because nature would be made whole. It would bring about a new form of wholeness in the lives of the people. And to this, God would add the dimension of holiness. When God heals, He heals completely and leads people into a new quality of life – a quality on which the word "God" is written. Isaiah's dream didn't only predict that there would be a new future of abundance. He dreamt of holiness – the quality of godliness in everyday life. If the community should choose to serve the Lord, He would give abundantly and they would be totally devoted to Him. Hope, holiness and wholeness were all one.

Finally Jesus came to make people holy. He Himself was holiness in a human life. His dream is that you will also be holy one day. By conforming to Him, you will become holy. The more you seek Him, the more He will take possession of you. By walking through the labyrinth of evil with Him, you hold tight to Your Guide until the people around you don't see you anymore, but only Him.

Lord Jesus, make me whole and make me holy. Amen.

October

*Show me the right path,
O LORD; point out the road
for me to follow.*
　　　　　PSALM 25:4

Where there is much prayer, there will be much of the Spirit; where there is much of the Spirit, there will be ever-increasing prayer.
　　　ANDREW MURRAY

Faithful Leader and Master,
the year is speeding to an end
and we are in urgent need of You, O Lord.
There are many things we thought were high priority,
and can now readily do without –
but we can't take on the rest of the year without You.
We need You if it was a successful year,
in case we forget You in our smugness and pride.
We need You if the shadows of failure and sorrow
fell on our path, so that we will not lose heart
but keep on trusting in Your love and omnipotence.
In our insecurities, disappointment, despondence and despair
we need You to keep us on our feet, through Your Spirit.
We need You when the sun shines warmly on our path,
so that we will never forget in whose grace we live and work.
Thank You for the strength and courage
that You have granted us.
In Your grace, please forgive our negligence that is written
in burning letters across so many of our good intentions.
Talk to us often through Your Word and Spirit,
so that we will remain courageous to the very end,
and have enough strength for the road ahead.
Help us to live with all people in Your love,
because we live from Your love.
In the name of Jesus, whose love overcame the world.
Amen.

Read Psalm 17:1-9

How Sincere Are Your Prayers?

O LORD, hear my plea for justice. Listen to my cry for help. Pay attention to my prayer, for it comes from honest lips (Ps. 17:1).

Not all prayers are real prayers. Some are just empty words. Others are a repetition of words; over and over again, until they lose all meaning. St. Augustine was one of the great Christian leaders. He once prayed, "Lord, make me pure, but not right now." Some prayers are boastful, and some negotiate with God. There are people who try to fool God with their prayers, and in the end, only succeed in deceiving themselves.

David, who wrote the prayer in today's Scripture passage was undoubtedly being very honest with God. He was close enough to God to know that the Lord could see right through the masks and pretense that he tried in earlier years. He knew that he had to live in all sincerity so that his prayers could be supplemented by his actions.

> Prayer is not a matter of getting what we want the most. Prayer is a matter of giving ourselves to God and learning His laws, so that He can do through us what He wants the most.
> AGNES SANFORD

How sincere are your prayers? When you pray, "Forgive us our sins, just as we forgive those who have sinned against us," are you really ready to forgive those you bear a grudge against, or do you prefer nursing your grievances?

It is pointless to pray for world peace, if after you have prayed, you criticize all the political leaders you disagree with and blame them for all the problems in the world. Likewise, it serves no purpose to ask God to provide you with a job if you have done nothing to qualify yourself for one.

Holy Spirit of God, help me to be honest and sincere in my prayer life. Amen.

October 1

Read Psalm 17:1-9

Spotting the Truth

Declare me innocent, for You see those who do right (Ps. 17:2).

> Truth is the greatest gift of life and love is the exercise of that truth.
> — ANONYMOUS

We live in a world where it is not always easy to see the truth. International leaders make statements about issues, while behind the scenes, conspiracies are being planned which contradict the public statements. Few things are really what they seem.

Religious leaders also tend to create the impression of innocence, while in secret, they play power games. Advertisers promise products with amazing benefits while the only ones that benefit from it are the manufacturer and the retailer. Some people have perfected the art of using the media to their personal advantage and know how to please a crowd.

The fact is that our human perception of most aspects of reality are distorted by the habit we have of choosing only those things that are compatible with our objectives, and ignoring those that aren't. We see the world – and God – through spectacles we made ourselves. This means that we very seldom fully understand the truth. Often, when we discover that we were wrong, we still cling to our theories and ideas because we don't want to admit our mistakes. This is by no means something new. The psalmist had learnt that the truth, according to human beings, is merely more or less what it really is. But God is different. He can, and does see the truth. Jesus later said, "I am the truth."

Be careful of accepting anything at face value and watch out for those who always try to please the crowd. Learn as much as possible about the world and the people around you. Trust God and be humble about knowledge you might later have to revise or adapt.

Jesus, You are the Truth. Teach me to see things the way You do. Amen.

Read Colossians 4:7-18

The Truth in Part

These are the only Jewish believers among my co-workers; they are working with me here for the Kingdom of God. And what a comfort they have been! (Col. 4:11).

When a champion racing driver crosses the finish line as winner he is applauded by millions. Few people keep in mind that behind the scenes, a whole team of people worked very hard to ensure the winner's success. It takes more than one person to win a Grand Prix.

Paul also had his team of co-workers. He even managed the church of Christ in Rome from prison. He could do this because of the people who worked with him. Jesus didn't do everything Himself. The disciples were there and a group of women followed them faithfully and were probably responsible for their meals. One member of Paul's support group was Jesus Justus. We have only his name, but what exactly it was that he did is not mentioned. Like the others he was a team player, and that was enough for him. All of them probably supported Paul in prayer and helped with the training of converts. In this way they took a great burden from Paul's shoulders so that he could be free to give them guidance. Paul appreciated their efforts – he knew how much they encouraged and comforted him, especially during the time he was imprisoned.

> It is not your business to succeed, but to do right: when you have done so, the rest lies with God.
> C. S. Lewis

Some Christians, especially those in leadership positions, enjoy their status. They try to avoid working behind the scenes. Can you keep your ego in the background, offer others wholehearted support, recognition and appreciation, and work for the Good Cause, knowing that teamwork ultimately leads to victory?

Grant by Your grace, Lord Jesus, that I will be a good teammate in Your service. Amen.

Read Psalm 20:1-9

Answer to Prayer

May the LORD answer all your prayers (Ps. 20:5).

It is always exciting and heart-warming to hear that Christians prayed about a certain matter and that their prayer was answered. It is also disappointing and upsetting to hear about some people's unanswered prayers.

The people of Israel appealed to God to richly bless their king, and this prayer included the wish that God would answer all his prayers. Don't we all wish that our prayers will be answered in the way we want? On the other hand, not all prayers are requests for God to do something. Sometimes we offer prayers of thanksgiving and praise, and both kinds are on an equal footing. Not all the prayers in the Bible were answered in the way people asked.

In the Garden of Gethsemane Jesus asked that the bitter cup would pass Him by – but it didn't and He was crucified. But Jesus prayed that particular prayer in an attitude of submission, and in the end He asked that God's will be done. And God's will was done, because He used Jesus' self-sacrifice to bring about the salvation of the entire human race.

> Prayer is absolutely necessary to a man's salvation.
> J. C. RYLE

The question whether God always answers all our prayers is a great mystery. We will only know for sure how God works when we meet Him face to face in heaven. Up until then we can only trust Him because He knows what's best for us.

Holy Spirit of God, teach me how to pray and how to accept God's will. Amen.

Read Psalm 20:1-10

You Are God's Anointed One

Now I know that the LORD rescues His anointed king (Ps. 20:6).

From time to time things happen that amaze people. When a new monarch is crowned in London, the ceremony is performed by the Archbishop of Canterbury who, among other things, anoints the monarch with oil. This part of the ceremony recalls biblical times when the prophet Samuel anointed Saul as the first king of Israel. Samuel was God's human representative in the choice and appointment of the king.

> True dignity is never gained by place and never lost when honors are withdrawn.
> PHILLIP MASSINGER

Anointment with oil in this manner implies that the one who performs the anointment ceremony is passing some of their authority and power on to the anointed one. The Israelites understood very clearly that the king's position was from God and he was often referred to as "God's anointed one". Gradually it was applied to "the king that would come," the Messiah. When the disciples realized that Jesus was the Messiah, they acknowledged the fact that God could anoint people who were not political kings. And when the Holy Spirit came at Pentecost, He anointed them with power from on High.

So it happens that every Christian is anointed by God and called to be a priest, a prophet and a king. While you live your humble life, are devoted to Christ and testify about Him, you declare that the sovereign King, God Himself, lives in you and works through you. He anointed you by making you His special person and He calls you to spiritually live like a king or queen – with dignity and authority.

Lord and Master, help me to live every day with dignity and authority, as Your anointed one. Amen.

Read John 11:33-44

Empowerment through Prayer

So they rolled the stone aside. Then Jesus looked up to heaven and said, "Father, thank You for hearing Me" (John 11:41).

People have many ideas about what they should do to be successful. Some focus on food and what they eat, others on physical exercise. Most emphasize hard work. Others have ingenious methods to make the most of the time available to them. The views on what it takes to be successful are wide and varying.

> Prayer is not a substitute for work, thinking, watching, suffering, or giving; prayer is a support for all other efforts.
> GEORGE BUTTRICK

Jesus lived for a life of prayer. The Gospel often refers to occasions where He made time for prayer, or withdrew to a quiet place to pray. To Him this was the secret of His power. Success in the sense that we think about it was not important to Him. Power and authority were, and prayer was His channel to the empowerment that He knew God the Father wanted Him to exert by means of His life, teachings, death and resurrection. In Bethany, before the most dramatic miracle of His entire ministry, He became quiet to pray to God. In Himself He could do nothing. He knew it, but He wanted the spectators to be aware that the power He was about to reveal was from God and not in Himself. Jesus was not a magician, a miracle-maker, a stuntman or an entertainer. He was a human channel for God's almighty power. Prayer was His constant contact with that power from Above. This was the secret of His success.

Don't pray just to ask for gifts. Ask God to reveal His omnipotence and His power through you. Simply acknowledge your complete dependence on God and obediently focus on Him. Then, the minute you achieve success, give Him the credit.

Holy Spirit, make me a praying person. Amen.

Read John 11:33-44

The Son's Prayer

"You always hear Me, but I said it out loud for the sake of all these people standing here, so that they will believe You sent Me" (John 11:42).

Many people find it difficult to pray because they don't know how to put their prayers into words and they think that poor wording makes a prayer worthless. Then there are those who feel that it is wrong to make use of written prayers because they don't really originate in the heart. Others feel guilty because they don't spend enough time in prayer. Then there are those who think they don't know the proper "religious language" to pray. Some people don't pray because they don't believe that God hears their prayers.

In Christ's prayer He simply thanked God for listening to Him. He prayed in obedience, and to God's glory. He also prayed thankfully. Most likely He had already prayed about Lazarus beforehand, and He confirmed that He prayed often. These words make His concern clear to the bystanders. The purpose of the miracle God was about to perform was to convince people that Christ was indeed who He said He was – the Son of God. It was necessary for them to see that He and God the Father were one. He wanted to strengthen their faith.

You and I must also keep our prayers simple. Don't worry if you don't use "church" language. Always thank God; it will help you to focus on what He has done for you with love. Pray obediently and always try to find out what God wants to do in you and through you. Always glorify and honor God and ask Him to give you strength and power for everything you must do in His name.

> Every great movement of God can be traced to a kneeling figure.
> Dwight L. Moody

Holy Spirit, support me in my efforts to pray the right way. Amen.

October 7

Read Psalm 18:17-30

You Can Charge an Army

In Your strength I can crush an army; with my God I can scale any wall (Ps. 18:29).

Sometimes you need more strength than you believe you have. You have to bear an extra burden and take on new responsibilities. Sometimes it takes a lot of effort to muster more reserves of courage, endurance and perseverance.

David, who wrote today's psalm, was a former soldier. He knew what it was to give his all. He knew that wars were not won by keeping strictly to the rules and neither by giving up when it got tough. He was successful because he knew where to find that extra source of strength. He found it in his God. God gave him a lot of practical help. He needed extra physical strength when he was outnumbered by overpowering enemy forces. On occasion he had to scale a wall and charge the enemy – with God's help and support.

You can find strength beyond your abilities. Connect to God's strength; He rules everything. Paul said, "I can do everything through Christ, who gives me strength" (Phil. 4:13). Perhaps you need physical strength. But it could also be courage, perseverance or merely the will to do something you find difficult. You might need mental orientation to tackle something you have never done before. No matter how high the wall you have to climb or how overwhelming the army you must charge, do it in the strength that Jesus gives you and He will make sure that you are victorious.

> Without courage, wisdom bears no fruit.
> BALTASAR GRACIAN

Savior and Lord, never let me shy away from a challenge because of fear or weakness. Amen.

Read Hebrews 11:1-12

What Do You Look Forward To?

Abraham was confidently looking forward to a city with eternal foundations, a city designed and built by God (Heb. 11:10).

As children, we looked forward to birthdays and Christmases. We were excited to see what gifts we would get. As school children, we looked forward to leaving school one day and venturing into the world. We always had something to look forward to, but as we grow older we tend to yearn for the past.

> Trust Jesus, and you are saved. Trust self, and you are lost.
> CHARLES H. SPURGEON

Abraham was a pioneer who left his comfort zones and the security of his home to explore new areas, not only in Israel, but also in his faith. This is enough proof of the fundamental dynamics of hope. God made Abraham certain promises and he looked forward to the fulfillment of those promises with hope and faith in his heart. Abraham was sure they would be kept and he knew there would be much to experience in the future: a bigger, better life, founded on God's promises. The Hebrews writer calls it the city that God has prepared for them. Jesus called it eternal life. It always has a dimension of the future, even if it already exists.

This is what life is about when it is dedicated to God. It came as a gift, but there is much, much more to come. Whether you look forward to retirement, comfort or family joy, make sure you include the bigger and more glorious life in Christ as part of your hope.

It won't be limited to earthly horizons and neither will it have to live through the insecurities of this earthly life. It will be built on a strong and firm foundation, because God is its Builder and Designer. Look forward to the future with hope in your heart.

Lord God, help me to look at the horizon with hope in my heart. Amen.

Read Jeremiah 31:15-22

A Merciful God

"Is not Israel still My son, My darling child?" says the LORD. "I often have to punish him, but I still love him. That's why I long for him and surely will have mercy on him" (Jer. 31:20).

There are many different and distorted opinions of who God really is. Some see Him as a strict officer of the law, ready and waiting to punish anyone who disobeys Him. Others see Him as a nice bearded old man, high up in the clouds. There are also those who think He is an exceptional conjuror who can sometimes be persuaded to come up with a miracle or two.

> Man may dismiss compassion from his heart, but God never will.
> WILLIAM COWPER

One of the truly great themes, central to the Bible, is that God is a compassionate Father to the people of Israel, and to everybody who believes in Him and His Son, Jesus Christ. Even if the children of Israel disappointed God time and time again, by disobeying His laws and worshiping other gods, He still loved them. He felt endless patience and compassion for them. His desire for them to be loyal to Him went deeper than they could ever have imagined.

God feels just as much compassion for you. No matter how sinful you might have been, how many times you did the wrong thing, how little love you showed others, how unfriendly you were – His heart still longs for you. His compassion for you has not reached breaking point yet. Jesus Christ was that same Compassion, in human form.

No matter how "tired" you might be of religion, how little you trust Christian leaders, how sinful your desires and ambitions, He still loves you and offers you His mercy, love and undeserved grace. Isn't it time for you to start accepting it gratefully?

Holy Spirit, grant that the fruit of compassion will also be visible in my life. Amen.

Read Jeremiah 31:23-35

Something New and Different

This is what the LORD of Heaven's armies, the God of Israel, says: "When I bring them back from captivity, the people of Judah and its towns will again say, 'The LORD bless you, O righteous home, O holy mountain!'" (Jer. 31:23).

When automobiles were invented, they were referred to as "horseless carriages". The automobile was not necessarily celebrated as something novel – simply a horse cart without the horse; a refined method of transport. The fact is that it was a revolutionary new invention. The incentive to create something new continually spurs humankind on to cross previously unexplored borders of development and expertise.

It is a strong biblical thought that God is a mighty and progressive Creator. He not only created the universe, but is still busy creating new things. His ability to bring forth the new is unlimited. The role of the human race is to work together with Him in creating these things. This means He is going to create a cure for cancer, a way to put an end to HIV/Aids, and a solution to the problem of poverty.

In Jeremiah's time the new and different things He would create included a new Israel that was determined to obey God, in this way discovering a new life. This "new thing" was merely the hope in Jeremiah's heart and thoughts because it never happened. But God can do new things. He proved it when He sent Jesus and when He brought the Church into existence.

> It is in the nature of man to long for novelty.
> PLINY THE ELDER

God can also create new things in you. When He called you to be His disciple, He made you a new person. He gave you new thoughts, new hope and new gifts to serve Him with. He showed you new ways of being a witness for Him. Never underestimate God's ability to create new and different things. What a prospect!

Creator God, use me to create new things for You. Amen.

Read 1 Samuel 7:3-17

The Stone

Then Samuel took a stone and set it up (1 Sam. 7:12 NIV).

Today, people set up stones of all shapes and sizes all over the world. There are mighty triumphal arches and tall pillars, impressive monuments, obelisks, sphinxes and pyramids and then also a good many tombstones. All these stones speak; they have something to say to us. They are solidified words and the words are interlinked with the moment. The words are set in the stone. The stone preserves the words and carries it through time for later generations.

Samuel not only picks up a stone, he puts it upright and writes on it. This widens and fortifies the scope of the stone's function. It prevents the stone from being trampled on and turned into dust on the road of life. Thus it forces passers-by to notice the word that is written on it. It brings them to a stop, encourages them and drives them ahead on their path.

This stone that Samuel set up is something special. Our stones sing the praises of dead or living people and because of this they are regularly torn down. What today's people see as glory, tomorrow's people find shameful. Samuel's stone, however, sang God's praises. Here stood a man (and behind him a whole nation) who praised God. Although Israel's men fought bravely and the actions of their commanders were heroic, this stone says nothing about it. To God alone all the glory! Ebenezer! Thus far God has helped us! We could also set up a stone to the glory of God because we have reason to rejoice so each day.

> One single grateful thought raised to heaven is the most perfect prayer.
> G. E. LESSING

Rock of Ages, thank You that I may find shelter in You and may glorify You for it. Amen.

Read 1 Samuel 7:3-17

Thus Far!

Up to this point the LORD has helped us! (1 Sam. 7:12).

Samuel came to a standstill for a moment: "Up to this point!" He was certainly not there yet. He knew it was still a steep climb up the mountain. But this was not central in his thoughts at the moment. He would attend to that presently. Soon he would say, "From now on." But now he said, "Up to this point!" With these words he looked back on the climb he had already completed.

> The next moment is as much beyond our grasp, and as much in God's care, as that a hundred years away.
> C. S. LEWIS

Everything he had gone through came to mind now. It was not an easy climb. It was a hard and difficult journey and many things happened. Obviously there were also parts that were sunny and easier to climb, and joy and gratitude flooded his soul when he thought of these times. Yet ... he also remembered the hard parts and dangerous moments. But he didn't give up.

All this went through Samuel's mind and he didn't say, "Up to this point we made it in our own strength!" or "We made it up to this point because of our own energy." When Samuel looked back on the past with the words, "Up to this point!" he knew ... "the Lord helped us." When we didn't know what to do anymore, the Lord was our help and strength. Before we fell, He took our hands.

The Lord has helped us faithfully through a difficult past. His help was always wonderful. It was more than emergency aid because it embraced everything in our lives – for time and eternity. And God's help has a concrete form: the greatest and most wonderful help we could ever hope for, the Lord Jesus Himself.

Thank You, Father, that the past, the present and the future are in Your hands. Amen.

The Stone between Mizpah and Shen

Then Samuel took a stone and set it up between Mizpah and Shen. He named it Ebenezer, saying, "Thus far the LORD has helped us" (1 Sam. 7:12-13 NIV).

The stone Samuel set up has long since been destroyed by wind and weather conditions, but the name he gave the stone remains to this day. It is spread all over the world and repeated on thousands of gables and walling. It is also engraved in millions of hearts: Ebenezer – "Thus far the LORD has helped us!"

> The love of God is broader than the measures of man's mind.
> F. W. FABER

Samuel placed the stone upright between Mizpah and Shen and he had good reason for doing so. One doesn't set up memorial stones in random places, because they focus one's thoughts on a certain place for a specific reason. Samuel did it between Mizpah and Shen.

We know a lot about Mizpah. It is the place where God helped Israel in a miraculous way. It is the place the entire Israel talked about. We don't know anything about Shen because it is never mentioned in Israel's history.

Thus, when Samuel set up his stone an equal distance from both Mizpah and Shen, it was his way of thanking the Lord for His known and unknown help, for big and insignificant things, for things that everyone talks about for a while and is soon forgotten. Samuel placed equal value on both places.

From this we learn that we must not forget about Shen when we remember Mizpah. Count all your blessings – the important but also the insignificant ones. Who decides what is big and what is small? We so easily say, "Nothing of importance happened today." As if the ability to work, live, and come home safely at night is of no importance!

I thank and praise You, Father, for the big and small things. Amen.

Read 1 Thessalonians 5:12-28

No Matter What Happens

Be thankful in all circumstances, for this is God's will for you who belong to Christ Jesus (1 Thess. 5:18).

When we have thanked God for His good gifts, we haven't finished our thanksgiving yet. This is the first step, but this ladder has many more steps. We must not only thank God for abundance, we must also thank Him for everything else. There is no doubt about this and the apostle makes it quite clear when he says, "in all circumstances." In his letter to the Ephesians he places even more emphasis on it, "And give thanks for everything to God" (Eph. 5:20). It means that we should not only thank God in good and joyful times, but also when storms rage in our lives and we have to carry our child's coffin to the grave. Not only when the acre is fertile and the barns full, but also when the harvest is poor and the cattle die. It is true that some have more of one than the other, but we all get our share. Every home has its trying times and every heart its sorrow. Some people are shattered by their misfortune, but still, we must thank God – even then. We must thank God no matter what happens.

The apostle stresses it in Ephesians, "For everything!" Take note: Not "After everything!" Not when looking back on troubled times. Then we are behind with our thanksgiving. We didn't find it at all difficult to thank God *after* He had rescued us, but it was quite hard while we were still in the thick of things. Here Job is an example to us. When he had lost everything he said, "The LORD gave me what I had, and the LORD has taken it away. Praise the name of the LORD!" (Job 1:21).

> If I was a nightingale I would sing like a nightingale; if a swan, like a swan. But since I am a rational creature my role is to praise God.
> — EPICTETUS

Holy Father, may I sing Your praises in adversity and prosperity – in all circumstances. Amen.

Read Hebrews 13:7-17

Those Who Confess His Name

Through Jesus, therefore, let us continually offer to God a sacrifice of praise – the fruit of lips that openly profess His name (Heb. 13:15 NIV).

A "confession" is required of us here. This means proclaiming the glory of His name. The name of Him who loved us first, gave His life for us, delivered us from perdition. He who made us new and spiritually rich and happy. We must promote His name and get people interested. Whenever we get an opportunity, we must let His name shine through the light of the windows of our lives to everyone passing by.

The apostle goes on to say that we must do it with our "lips". This most certainly doesn't mean that our testimony must be idle words. The fruit of our lips is a fruit that, although it grows on the lips, comes from the heart. Therefore our confession may only be proclaimed by the lips if it comes from the heart, and it must bear spiritual fruit in our lives. Our entire life must be a confession: our marriage, the way we raise our children, our relationships with our fellow humans, our business life, our sorrow and our joy.

It is very important that our confession bear fruit. A fruit is not made, it grows spontaneously and naturally from a plant. In the same way, the confession of Christ's name also comes up spontaneously in living Christians who get their life juice from Christ. They are confessors, whether they want to be or not, and they cannot keep quiet; they must witness for Christ. If this fruit is good and healthy, it draws people to Christ.

> Faith is not belief without proof, but trust without reservations.
> ELTON TRUEBLOOD

Lord and Savior, make me Your faithful witness in all circumstances. Amen.

Read Acts 20:13-24

Job Satisfaction

But my life is worth nothing to me unless I use it for the work assigned me by the Lord Jesus – the work of telling others the Good News about the wonderful grace of God (Acts 20:24).

Paul was undoubtedly a cheerful person. He often mentioned cheerfulness in his letters and found it very important. He also encouraged the churches to be joyful, "Always be full of joy in the Lord. I say it again – rejoice!" (Phil. 4:4).

It is important to understand that our Scripture passage today is solely about joy. Paul did his job joyfully and therefore he experienced job satisfaction. Is it possible that this is the same man speaking about this same work in 2 Corinthians 11? We are at a loss for words because that is an appalling account of hardship and suffering. And yet he was able do his daily task joyfully amidst all the trials and tribulations. Even though he was in prison in Philippi with his feet in chains, he sang a song of praise to God at midnight.

> To be simply ensconced in God is true joy.
> C. C. COLTON

Without a doubt, Paul experienced this joy also in his job as a tentmaker. He not only joyfully proclaimed the Gospel, but sang songs of praise while he was making tents. He was cheerful and joyful when dealing with others. In spite of the thorn in his flesh and Satan's angel harassing him, the sound of his songs of praise could be heard all day long. The Source of his joy was Jesus Christ and that is why he could walk his path in life joyfully.

We should be like this. It is not enough that we are Christians – we must be joyful Christians, because joy is welcomed everywhere!

Savior and Redeemer, let me be a cheerful person no matter what the circumstances. Amen.

October 17

Read John 9:24-34

The Meaning of Our Existence

God should get the glory (John 9:24).

The Jews asked the man who Jesus so miraculously healed from blindness, to give glory to God for his healing. Their purpose was to get Jesus out of the picture. They didn't realize that God and Jesus were the same person. It is very important because this is what makes our lives meaningful. It is after all why God created us.

> Before I begin to think and consider the love of God and the mercy and compassion of God, I must start with the holiness of God.
> — MARTYN LLOYD-JONES

It is good when parents teach their children to be respectful. But it is even more gratifying when parents discover that their children have learnt to glorify God and that they give all the glory to God in life and in death.

After Jesus healed the blind man, he gave glory to Him. Without detracting from this miracle, it is necessary that we give God all the glory, even without the miracle. We shouldn't wait for miracles before we do this. Not all blind eyes can see again and not all crosses are taken from us. Such burdens can often add new dimension of meaning to our lives. Those who stay blind must also glorify God because God always deserves to be glorified, whether we are sick or healthy. Otherwise life becomes pointless. Unceasingly the command is repeated, "Give glory to God!"

It is necessary for every person, in whatever circumstances they might find themselves, to give glory to God if they are at all interested in making their existence meaningful.

Holy God, may my words and deeds always bring You honor and glory. Amen.

Read Matthew 28:11-20

To the End of the Age

"And be sure of this: I am with you always, even to the end of the age" (Matt. 28:20).

Henri Nouwen was a well-known Christian author and a trustworthy guide in spiritual matters. On a dark winter morning in 1989 he was involved in an accident and narrowly escaped death. It brought him to that place of shadows between life and death, and also led him to experience God in a new way. In his remarkable book *Beyond the Mirror*, he describes this experience in death's entrance hall:

"What I experienced then is something I had never encountered before: pure and unconditional love. Even better: what I experienced was an intensely personal presence; a presence that pushed all my fears aside and said, 'Come, don't be afraid. I love you.' A tender, non-judgmental presence; a presence that simply asked me to trust, and to trust completely. Before the accident I spent many hours studying the Bible, listening to lectures and sermons, and I read spiritual books. Jesus was always very close to me, but yet also very far away; a friend, yet at the same time a stranger; a source of hope but also of fear, feelings of guilt and shame. But now, after skirting the gates of death, all the double meanings and uncertainties were gone. He was there, the Lord of my life, and He said to me, 'Come to Me, come.'"

> God is always near you and with you; leave Him not alone.
> —Brother Lawrence

He continues, "This experience was the fulfillment of my oldest and deepest desires. Since the first moment of consciousness, I had the desire to be with Jesus. Now I've experienced His presence in an almost tangible way, as if my whole life had come together and I was enfolded by love."

God will also be with you and with me at the gates of death.

Thank You, Lord Jesus, that You are always with me. Amen.

Read Jeremiah 1:11-19

A Branch from an Almond Tree

Then the LORD said to me, "Look, Jeremiah! What do you see?" And I replied, "I see a branch from an almond tree" (Jer. 1:11).

Different objects have different meanings, depending on the interests of the people looking at them. To the artist, the oak tree is an object of beauty that he can use to make a beautiful painting. The carpenter will see it as a valuable source of wood for making furniture. A bird will see it as a place to build a nest, and consequently it will become a home. The prophets saw things everybody saw, but they looked at these things in a different way. They saw them as message-bearers from God, as signs of His almightiness, control and creativity.

After the winter months, the almond was the first tree to break into white blossoms, which announced spring. When the almond bloomed, it demonstrated new life. It announced the end of winter and the return of summer, warmth and growth. The arrival of spring promised future growth and fertility. It meant something was going to happen.

> A revival is nothing else than a new beginning of obedience to God.
> CHARLES G. FINNEY

Something is always happening under the surface. Behind the scenes God is busy designing a new spring. He might allow winter to cloak the preparations, but He does bring forth new life, new hope and new activity. If you battled to survive spiritual winter months, why not take note of the almond tree. Somewhere and in some way or another, God is waiting to send you into a new spring.

As cold as things might seem to you right now, they will break into joy, hope and love. Just be patient.

Lord Jesus, bring new life to those who have become spiritually cold. Amen.

Read Psalm 17:1-9

A God Who Listens

I am praying to You because I know You will answer, O God. Bend down and listen as I pray (Ps. 17:6).

One of the most common problems people have with prayer is the feeling that God just isn't there and that He doesn't listen. They feel like they are speaking to a stone wall. And even if He does hear, He doesn't answer anyway.

> Prayer is love in need, appealing to love in power.
> ROBERT MOFFAT

Our psalmist for today, however, knows God well. He knows that even if God is a glorious and sovereign Lord, He is a God who speaks to His people. He spoke the universe into being. He gave His Commandments to humankind by speaking certain "words". He has always yearned for His children to enter into conversation with Him and that is why they spoke to Him when they worshiped.

They spoke to Him through their actions. They also spoke to God in their prayers – and some of them really did speak! They not only presented long lists of requests to Him, they charged the gates of heaven. Abraham prayed for the wicked Sodom and Gomorrah. Moses prayed for rebellious people. David prayed for the purification of his own sinful heart. Job complained to God in his suffering and loss, and God heard it all. God was a reality to these people; He was part of their struggle to exist. He was with them in their hour of triumph. He held them in the darkest hours of their history. And during His suffering at Gethsemane Jesus knew that His Father was listening.

We still worship a God who listens. Answers to prayer are not points noted down on a scoring-board. They are the life stories of profits and losses, of pain and tension. Therefore, feel free to bare your soul to God in prayer: God listens!

Thank You, Father, that I know You hear when I call out to You. Amen.

Read Psalm 17:1-7

The Foundation of it All

Show me the wonders of Your great love, You who save by Your right hand those who take refuge in You from their foes (Ps. 17:7 NIV).

Religion is many things. It is a set of religious convictions: We believe in God, in Jesus Christ, in His resurrection and in the outpouring of the Holy Spirit. This also comprises a variety of activities: we worship, we pray, we give and we reach out to others. Thirdly it is a collection of experiences: conviction of sin, conversion, forgiveness and empowerment. Fourthly it has a certain outcome: our attitudes change, we build relationships with people, we give up certain habits, and so on.

> It is not after we were reconciled by the blood of His Son that God began to love us, but before the foundation of the world.
> JOHN CALVIN

At the root of it all, however, there is one inescapable fact – the love of God! All other things originate from it. Being aware of it, experiencing it, its outcome, the fellowship in communities, the change in behavior, obtaining faith and hope – all this is the result of God's love. The psalmist calls it "the wonder of Your great love". It is wonderful because it comes to us entirely from outside. It is wonderful because, when we receive it, it changes us. It is wonderful because it motivates us to worship and it compels us to show gratitude and mutual love. It is wonderful because it was the reason why God gave His only Son, and it was the reason why Jesus gave His life in sacrifice and suffering. It is wonderful because it makes our entire human existence meaningful; it fills our lives with purpose, direction and meaning. It is wonderful because it is available to every single person on earth. It is wonderful because it continues even after death. It is offered to you free of charge. Have you accepted it yet?

Holy God, thank You for Your wonderful love. Amen.

Read Isaiah 4:1-6

Hope through Cleansing

The Lord will wash the filth from beautiful Zion and cleanse Jerusalem of its bloodstains with the hot breath of fiery judgment (Isa. 4:4).

Not only individuals go through trauma, disaster, uprisings and decay – the same happens to communities and nations. A revolution and war, particularly civil war can cause these problems. Natural disasters and corrupt governments can also contribute.

The prophet Isaiah knew that his country and its people, its priests and its rulers, were under God's authority. But they didn't obey God's laws, and ignored His commands. He would punish them by bringing disaster over them. Afterwards He promised renewal. But before renewal, in fact as part of it, cleansing had to take place. Not only a few people were wicked; the whole nation was guilty and the whole country had to be cleansed. Part of the hope for the future lay in God's cleansing and purification of His people.

Do you or your community need cleansing? Does your country need to be healed again? Today there are many in all the countries of the world that need to be cleansed. As a Christian believer you have been called by God to be part of His priesthood. Your task is to lead others to God and to plead for them in front of God. Don't confess only your own sins before God; also confess those of your community and country.

> We are all patients in constant need of help.
> HENRI NOUWEN

Don't just complain about problems and shortcomings – go to God and seek His cleansing. Start with yourself, but don't stop there. Your country needs you.

Almighty God, cleanse our nation in the name of Jesus Christ. Amen.

Read Psalm 18:31-42

Where Is God?

They called for help, but no one came to their rescue. They even cried to the LORD, but He refused to answer (Ps. 18:41).

Most people cry out to God when they are in trouble or when they experience a crisis. That includes people who normally have no time for God, religion or the church. Many people even think that this is the very reason why God is there – to help them when all else fails. Many people, some with a lot of faith and others with little faith, are disappointed when God doesn't respond to their emergency calls.

King David wrote this psalm and he is referring to his enemies that he defeated with God's help. He says that God is there for him, but not for his enemies.

There are people who say the exact opposite, "He is there for other people but not for me. Why?" Nobody knows the right answer to this question. We will only know it when we meet Him face to face. The truth of faith is, however, that it doesn't give a person obvious solutions to all problems. If this was the case people would stream to this easy and speedy solution, without ever giving their lives to God.

> In the church we seem to have lost the vision of the majesty of God.
> JOHN STOTT

Jesus asked the Father to take the Cup of Suffering away from Him and God didn't do it. Sometimes He does what we ask and sometimes not. He wants us to trust Him in times of prosperity and adversity, because that is the real test of faith – to cling to God through thick and thin and in all circumstances.

Lord God, help me to trust You, even when I don't get the things I ask for. Amen.

Read Psalm 22:21-31

Hope and Gratitude

All who seek the Lord will praise Him. Their hearts will rejoice with everlasting joy (Ps. 22:26).

Hope is a strange phenomenon to some people. They think, "Things are just going from bad to worse." Then there are those people who are never thankful for anything. They moan and groan about everything. They are never satisfied and consequently make everyone around them unhappy too.

David, the writer of Psalm 22, had a very positive outlook on life, in spite of all his suffering during a period of misfortune. Because he worshiped God and experienced God's omnipotence, love and presence, he knew that God cared for him and loved him. After getting well again, he never forgot that God saved him. He was very thankful and knew that God would surround him with goodness and undeserved grace. This gave him hope for the future. He knew that whatever happened to him, God would protect him.

> The word which God has written on the brow of every man is hope.
> Victor Hugo

Christians should have the same positive outlook on the future. They should be sensible enough to realize that they will not escape the problems and troubles of life. But they also know that they have a Savior who helps them, who enables them to endure everything and who rescues them from every disaster and setback. They are thankful that they have this Savior who walks with them and who talks with them. They live in hope because they know that Jesus Christ promised them the crown of eternal life when this life ends. For this reason the Christian must live in gratitude and hope.

I praise and thank You, Lord Jesus, that You give me hope. Amen.

Read Philippians 1:12-26

The Importance of Courage

For I fully expect and hope that I will never be ashamed, but that I will continue to be bold for Christ, as I have been in the past. And I trust that my life will bring honor to Christ, whether I live or die (Phil. 1:20).

Christianity is sometimes portrayed as a weak, lukewarm way of life. Its followers are often labeled as spineless and miserable spoilsports. And because they are without joy, they want to see everyone around them despondent too. This is a false portrayal of Christians.

> Courage faces fear and thereby masters it; cowardice represses fear and is thereby mastered by it.
> MARTIN LUTHER KING

Jesus was strong and courageous and not afraid to be different. He took on authorities and met His death fearlessly. Paul, His most competent apostle, did not hesitate to declare war on secular authorities, those who taught false doctrines and his fellow Christians when they were wrong. He was taken prisoner and didn't waver in the face of opposition but used his circumstances to his own, and God's advantage. Whether he was on the road winning new places for Christ, or suffering persecution and punishment for his bold testimonies, he never lost faith.

You also need plenty of courage. Your faith in Christ requires that you be strong, positive and brave when defending the truth about Jesus. Continuously seek to be filled anew with the Holy Spirit, the encourager of Christians. He gives you spiritual strength no matter what your circumstances. Sometimes you need courage to start something God has called you for. On other occasions you need courage to carry on prolonged obedience to Christ.

Grant in Your grace, O Spirit of God, that I will never lack spiritual courage. Amen.

Read Psalm 141:1-10

My Refuge

I look to You for help, O Sovereign LORD. You are my refuge; don't let them kill me (Ps. 14:8).

"O Sovereign LORD, You are my refuge." Many people would really like to repeat what David said. Anyone can do with a secure refuge if he is under threat of being trampled in the dust on the path of life. A refuge in life's critical situations when he has nowhere else to go anymore. In our world of strife, where people do not pay any attention to God anymore, don't go to church, don't touch a Bible and don't pray, we yearn to die with the faithful.

The Lord wants to be a refuge for these people as well, if they would only come to Him – not only with their needs, but also with their hearts. He comforts the weeping heart that calls out to Him. David fled to the Lord in this way, and not in vain. David found a true refuge in the Lord, and in our text today, he expresses that glorious truth.

> When spiritual comfort is sent to you by God, take it humbly and give thanks meekly for it.
> THOMAS À KEMPIS

David said this in the Old Testament. We, who stand in the full light of the New Testament, may also say it. When Jesus Christ came to earth as refuge, God's master plan was revealed. In the most dangerous grottos of sin and guilt, shame and death, Christ was our refuge. On Golgotha we can say with confidence, "The Lord is my refuge." In suffering and death, Christ is our final and most important refuge.

Lord, thank You that I found refuge in You and that I am safe forever. Amen.

Read James 1:1-11

Use Adversity to Grow

Dear brothers and sisters, when troubles come your way, consider it an opportunity for great joy. For you know that when your faith is tested, your endurance has a chance to grow. So let it grow, for when your endurance is fully developed, you will be perfect and complete, needing nothing (James 1:2-4).

If the Christian faith could guarantee that the minute it is accepted, all stress and suffering would disappear from your life, everyone would want to make it their own. Christ and His teachings make no such promise. In fact, while Christ promised His disciples a new relationship with God, He made it very clear that they would still be tempted and would have to endure problems and suffering.

One of the most wonderful themes of New Testament Christianity is that disciples can grow in grace and understanding of their Master. The Christian is even encouraged to rejoice in difficult times, because every negative situation offers the possibility to prove God's omniscience.

To be able to face every difficult situation without running away requires positive faith in the purpose and goodness of God. It requires trust in Christ so that you can experience the inner joy that rises above the fear of the unknown. It is born from a life in harmony with God.

> Although the world is full of suffering, it is full also of the overcoming of it.
> HELEN KELLER

It is true that you as a Christian can grow spiritually when confronted with problems and temptations. If you face your troubles in a positive and constructive way, you will develop a deeper understanding of and love for the Master.

In Your power and strength, Holy Master, I will turn my disappointments into victories. Amen.

Read 2 Timothy 1:1-10

Discover God's Gift to You

This is why I remind you to fan into flames the spiritual gift God gave you when I laid my hands on you (2 Tim. 1:6).

Many people allow their lives to become dull and boring because they don't appreciate the gifts God gave them. They are overpowered by other people's achievements and convince themselves that they will never be able to do anything worthwhile. They never bother trying anything new and lack motivation, resulting in a life of inactive speculation instead of active participation.

> Your talent is God's gift to you. What you do with it is your gift back to God.
> LEO BUSCAGLIA

God gave each person at least one gift. Some gifts are developed and others are revealed. Unfortunately, there are many people who never discover the hidden talents inside them. This might be because of ignorance, laziness or because they don't know how to discover that talent.

Unfortunately, precious little can be done for those who are convinced that they received no talents from God. Their treasure will remain buried forever because of their unbelief. Those who are lazy will forever complain about lost opportunities. Only the Holy Spirit of God can reveal their weaknesses and create new life and growth.

To discover God's gift in you requires sensitivity to the Father's guidance and a willingness to be active in His name. It takes courage, but God never disappoints those who put their trust in Him. When you follow where He leads, He will enrich your life because you obeyed Him.

Lord God, give me the courage and obedience to discover the gift that You gave me. Amen.

Read 1 Peter 4:1-11

Use Your Godly Gifts

God has given each of you a gift from His great variety of spiritual gifts. Use them well to serve one another (1 Pet. 4:10).

One of the greatest setbacks on a person's Christian pilgrimage is the feeling of incompetence. The inevitable result is that in many cases we fail to follow God's guidance and then we are left with feelings of frustration and disappointment. The faith of countless numbers of Christians has lost its spark as a result of a lack of fulfillment because they didn't listen when the Master called them for service.

> God's gifts put man's best dreams to shame.
> — Elizabeth Barrett Browning

None of us is without a gift or talent of some kind. It might not be clearly visible, but you can be sure that God gave you a talent with which you can glorify Him.

Your gift may be a form of Christian ministry. It might be intercession or simply listening to others with a sympathetic ear.

Seek the Lord's guidance while you become still before Him. Ask Him to reveal His gift to you and help you glorify His name with it.

Then go out into the world in faith and use the gift you received by His grace.

Use me, Lord Jesus, according to Your will. Amen.

The Holy Spirit Reassures

> We know how dearly God loves us, because He has given us the Holy Spirit to fill our hearts with His love (Rom. 5:5).

We are certain of the facts of Pentecost. We believe in the outpouring of the Holy Spirit on Pentecost day and that it was accompanied by power and mighty signs. We believe what is written in God's Word and accept what is written in Acts 2:4, "And everyone present was filled with the Holy Spirit." We are certain of this and more. We are certain that the church as such received the Holy Spirit. The Scriptures teach us that we are God's Temple and that the Holy Spirit lives in us. This is what Paul said to the church in Corinth.

But something we are not completely sure of and that we often doubt is: "Was the Holy Spirit also given to me personally?" Yes, the catechisms proclaim that He was given also to me, among others. Our question mark is at "among others" personally receiving the Holy Spirit. Is it not merely upbringing, repeating what we have heard others say, and agreeing? We are certain that the Holy Spirit was given to the church on Pentecost day, but has it also been delivered at my address? Did I also receive Him personally?

> The Holy Spirit of grace desires to disturb your sleep. Blessed are you if you awaken.
> Lars Linderot

To celebrate Pentecost is to be sure of the Holy Spirit with a certainty that rises above all doubt. What a Source of immense power it is to be sure that we personally possess the Holy Spirit! Then we can carry any cross to the very end and we can take on any task with confidence. The Holy Spirit reassures us that we received the Holy Spirit.

Thank You, Holy Spirit, for the certainty that You are at work in my life. Amen.

November

Search me, O God, and know my heart. Point out anything in me that offends You, and lead me along the path of everlasting life.
PSALM 139:23-24

Lord, teach me to know Thee, and to know myself.
AUGUSTINE OF HIPPO

Eternal and unchanging God,
we worship You as the Alpha and the Omega;
the Beginning and the End.
As the First – but also the Last!
Bless those for whom this was a good year
and let them thank You and praise and honor You.
Bless those for whom it was a sad year
and keep them from despair and frustration.
Grant all of us the grace to face an unknown future
holding the hand of a known God.
Merciful Father and Comforting God,
have mercy on those whose year was filled
with tragedy and grief;
those who lost loved ones through illness and unexpected death.
Help us to remember at all times that every day
there is someone somewhere that is sad;
that morning never descends into evening
without a heart being broken somewhere.
Accompany us the rest of this year;
console our hearts, ease our longing,
renew our spirit and thoughts.
Forgive us when we confess lost opportunities,
love we could have given but never did.
Reinforce our intentions to seek Your will, and do it.
In the name of our Redeemer and Savior,
Jesus Christ.
Amen.

Read Proverbs 23:15-26

Who Has Your Heart?

O my son, give me your heart. May your eyes take delight in following my ways (Prov. 23:26).

The love that God poured out develops in our hearts. The Holy Spirit establishes it in our hearts and Pentecost is the time that a great appeal is made for our hearts – it actually costs us our hearts.

God demands a Pentecost heart from us. The Holy Spirit is not satisfied with the borders of our hearts. "My son, give Me your heart." Pentecost has no glory for us if we don't obey this call. We should receive and keep Pentecost blessings in our hearts. Who has your heart?

> The mark of a saint is not perfection, but consecration. A saint is not a man without faults, but a man who has given himself without reserve to God.
> W. T. RICHARDSON

The Holy Spirit wants us to give our hearts to God. Our hearts are the center of our entire lives. This is where the last and most important decisions in life are made. If you give God your heart, He also has your home, your state and your world. What do you have if you don't have your heart? What does confession, a church, a sermon mean without a heart? To the Holy Spirit it's all about surrendering the last stronghold: It's all about the heart. Who has your heart?

"Give?" To the Holy Spirit, it is ultimately not a matter of giving, but of taking. In the end, our hearts are not given, but taken; whether we want to or not. In this way the Holy Spirit becomes the great gift of inner grace.

The love of God is in our hearts too! What an overwhelming thought!

Thank You, heavenly Father, for accepting my heart. Amen.

November 1

Read Psalm 143:1-12

The Hands of God

I meditate on all Your works and consider what Your hands have done (Ps. 143:5 NIV).

Hands play an important role in the imagery of language. We "lend a hand" when we help or support someone. We say "the left hand doesn't know what the right hand is doing." We speak of "clean hands" as being innocent. "A hand in the till" indicates theft. When we worry about the future we sometimes say, "It is in God's hands."

The "hands of God" indicates God's work of creation. This means that they are expert and artistic hands with the ability of a master craftsman. When David writes in this psalm, "I consider what Your hands have done", he is probably admiring God's miracles in nature. As a shepherd, he probably spent a lot of time alone in the hills with his sheep. Unlike us, living in our fast-paced modern life, he had time to appreciate and meditate on nature.

> The higher the mountains, the more understandable is the glory of Him who made them and who holds them in His hand.
> FRANCIS SCHAEFFER

He might also have been thinking of how God miraculously freed the people of Israel from slavery in Egypt. They always saw it as an act of deliverance by God, in which God intervened to rescue them. He acted again when He gave them the Ten Commandments in the wilderness. They called it "the Law" and accepted it as the foundation of their new way of life. God's hands were busy while He brought about His mighty acts for His people.

God did not stop working. Perhaps we should come to a standstill for a moment and ponder the mighty works of God's hands in our own lives.

God, help me to see the work of Your hands in the world around me, every day. Amen.

Read Psalm 143:1-12

Empty Hands

I spread out my hands to You; I thirst for You like a parched land (Ps. 143:6 NIV).

Our hands should be the most useful, handy and serviceable parts of our body. We work and earn our daily bread with them. We use them to write, draw, play music, cook and drive our cars. We use our hands to indicate something or to wave friends good-bye or to welcome them. The traffic officer holds up his hand, indicating "Stop!" We clench our fists and fight with our hands but we can also embrace a loved one and show our love with our hands.

> The reason why we obtain no more in prayer is because we expect no more. God usually answers us according to our own hearts.
> RICHARD ALLEINE

David opened his hands in prayer. Our most natural way of praying is to fold our hands together. When David opened his hands and spread them out before God, he was indicating his emptiness. He was yearning for God like a dry land yearns for rain.

If you refuse to pray, your life will be spiritually poor and empty. It is beautifully symbolic to stretch your hands out to God, asking Him to fill you. Chances are that you will receive more from God if you go to Him with an attitude of emptiness, instead of making demands.

In the Gospels Jesus eagerly responded to people who were desperate for His grace. The deeper the need and the more intense the desperation of their cry for help, the more readily and abundantly He reacted. Do you honestly thirst for God?

O Hearer of prayer, fill me with Your undeserved grace and also do it for everyone calling out to You today. Amen.

Read Psalm 119:33-48

Emotions or Principles

I reach out for Your commands, which I love, and I meditate on Your decrees (Ps. 119:48 NIV).

Hasty decisions are not always very wise, and it is foolish to boast that once you have made a decision, nothing will change your mind. While firm convictions are to be admired, blind stubbornness must be avoided.

> Those who insist upon seeing with perfect clearness before they decide, never decide.
> — HENRI-FREDERIC AMIEL

When you are confronted with a problem that needs an urgent solution, you mustn't sidestep your responsibility by postponing your decision. Some problems don't require an immediate answer. If this is the case, time can be spent in prayer and meditation as you seek God's guidance. Then, when the time comes to make a decision, you can act confidently because you know your decision is in line with God's will.

When an immediate solution is required, you act according to one of two principles. You can evaluate the situation in terms of profit and loss and how it will affect you. This is how most people come to a decision. The alternative evaluation is not made according to your personal feelings, but by the principles that rule your life. These principles are not based on your emotions, but on what is right.

Emotional thinking doesn't always have positive results. When you make a decision founded on Christ's teachings, and you place God's will first, other people second and yourself third, you have reached a point where you discern between what you want and how you must act. There must be no hesitation in a Christian disciple's thoughts: God's will must always come first!

Holy Father, give me the power to obey Your will at all times. Amen.

Read Proverbs 9:1-12

Be a Blessing to Others

Fear of the LORD is the foundation of wisdom. Knowledge of the Holy One results in good judgment (Prov. 9:10).

The ability to share a problem with someone trustworthy, whose wise advice you can always trust, creates a feeling of relief. Even if the complete solution to the problem is not immediately forthcoming, the support you get from this person normally creates a feeling of stability and peace. This enables you to make the best of the situation. How then is it possible that such a person can bring calmness in your life?

When it comes to your relationship with God, it is important to build an intimate, personal relationship with Him. The more you obey Him, and the more intimate your relationship with Him becomes, the more He is able to guide your entire being. In this way you become an instrument that pronounces His words, communicates His power and reveals His wisdom in your dealings with other people.

> If grace does not make us differ from other men, it is not the grace God gives His elect.
> CHARLES H. SPURGEON

This privilege doesn't come easily or of its own accord, and requires that you discipline yourself to place God at the center of your life and dedicate yourself to Him unconditionally. It is necessary that you spend time in meditation before Him and empty your mind of all other distracting thoughts so that God can take control of your entire being.

The closer you grow to Christ, the greater your awareness of His influence on your life becomes. It enables you to be a blessing to others, in His name.

Lord Jesus, empower me with the power of Your Spirit, and work through me so that I will be a blessing to others. Amen.

Read Genesis 3:1-7

Deliver Us from Temptation

The serpent was the shrewdest of all the wild animals the LORD God had made. One day he asked the woman, "Did God really say you must not eat any of the fruit from any of the trees in the garden?" (Gen. 3:1).

How often a major catastrophe occurs in people's lives because they yielded to minor temptation. People with integrity and commendable principles behave in an exemplary way until, for some unknown reason, they stray from the path of honesty. Suddenly this apparently insignificant offense leads to worse transgressions so that they eventually fall prey to the temptation of becoming dishonest, untrustworthy and untruthful.

It is of the utmost importance to keep to the standards Jesus set, to follow Jesus' example, socially and in the business world, and to obey His commands. Just as the Fall was caused by what many people regard as a trivial act of disobedience, so many modern people are brought down as a result of this one seemingly trivial act. But this act was the beginning of a compromise of standards that led to more serious transgressions.

> Do not be harsh with others who are tempted, but console them as you yourself would wish to be consoled.
> THOMAS À KEMPIS

Your duty as a Christian is to keep to the highest code of moral conduct at all times. While you walk with God, His hand will guide you and His voice will always be there to encourage you to fight the good fight. You can do this because you know that Christ is your power and strength in every temptation.

Savior Jesus, with You at my side I can overcome every temptation. Amen.

Read Jeremiah 13:15-19

Give Glory to the Lord

Give glory to the LORD your God before it is too late. Acknowledge Him before He brings darkness upon you (Jer. 13:16).

Very few people don't stray from God at least at some time in their lives. Some drift through life and spend their time doing activities that are useful but not essential. Others turn their backs on Him deliberately and claim that they are able to take control of their own lives without God's help. Then there are those who fall prey to sin and find that their feelings of guilt prevent them from getting to know God.

> Fight to escape from your own cleverness. If you do, then you will find salvation and uprightness through Jesus Christ our Lord.
> JOHN CLIMACUS

The Bible is very clear about this, "For everyone has sinned; we all fall short of God's glorious standard" (Rom. 3:23). It is made just as clear that there is a path back to God. The Bible tells many stories of people who left God and returned again. The parable of the prodigal son (see Luke 15:11-24) is a classic example of one person who strayed, but returned to the right path. In today's Scripture Jeremiah appeals to the whole nation to turn back to God and to give Him the glory. He knew that they would find no peace until they did this and he warned them about the horrific consequences if they didn't.

If you have strayed from God, or if you've abandoned Him intentionally, take today's Bible verse as a friendly invitation. Turn back to God *now*. You will find that Jesus is not standing at the door, waiting to punish you. He is on the roof watching out for you, His heart beating warmly with excitement because you are on your way home.

Your voice is soft and tender, Lord Jesus. I am on my way home. Amen.

Read Jeremiah 1:1-12

What Do You See?

Then the LORD said to me, "Look, Jeremiah! What do you see?" And I replied, "I see a branch from an almond tree" (Jer. 1:11).

Our eyes see many things, especially on television. We see the exquisite beauty of a rose and the forked tongue of a snake, the architecture of a cathedral and the ruins of a wrecked house. We see others' body language and we try to determine what it means.

> God has given us two ears, but one tongue, to show that we should be swift to hear, but slow to speak.
> THOMAS WATSON

God not only communicates with us verbally, but also by means of what He shows us and by what we see. He knows that our eyes see more than what our ears hear because He created us this way. We take in more by seeing than by hearing. Perhaps it is of great importance that God first created light – the first step in creating order in chaos. When pondering the coming of Christ, John said of the Word that became flesh, "The one who existed from the beginning whom we have heard and seen. We saw Him with our own eyes" (1 John 1:1).

On occasion, William Booth walked down the streets of London's East-End, and when he saw the human decline he felt called by God to declare war on sin. He called his movement The Salvation Army. To this day they are still busy waging spiritual warfare.

What do you see? Perhaps God wants to give you insight into something you haven't thought of before, or send you in a direction that you have never considered taking.

Holy Spirit, open my eyes to what Christ wants me to see. Amen.

Read Psalm 119:65-80

God Knows Best

My suffering was good for me, for it taught me to pay attention to Your decrees (Ps. 119:71).

Often when we are going through a bad patch in our lives we can't understand why, and ask, "Why must it happen to me?" Countless people experienced this in the past, it is experienced in the present, and it will also be the case in the future.

It is necessary that you accept that God knows, better than you, what's best for you. Your view of life is limited to the present. God is eternal and consequently His view is eternal. His plan with your life will ultimately be the very best for you.

> Grace keeps us from worrying because worry deals with the past, while grace deals with the present and future.
> JOYCE MEYER

In order to accept this truth you have to demonstrate absolute and unreserved faith in the Lord. It means that you must lay down your life for Him and be willing to accept His will for your life – and stick to it.

Once you accept these facts and allow Him to dictate the pattern of your life, you'll experience a feeling of peace as you submit to His will. You will cherish the positive knowledge that Christ is leading you to perfect fulfillment.

Thank You, Lord Jesus, that You give me the courage to see the dark clouds in my life as signs of Your grace. Amen.

Read 2 Corinthians 6:1-13

The Deeper Values of Life

"At just the right time, I heard you. On the day of salvation, I helped you" (2 Cor. 6:2).

Some people see Christian life simply as an option; something they may accept or reject, depending on their emotional needs. They are of the opinion that in the end, it will make very little difference in their lives.

There are people who define life in terms of time while Christians see life in terms of eternity. A person can struggle through life without acknowledging God's supreme authority and guidance. He might even feel proud of what he has achieved and classify himself as "a self-made person". What happens when they pass on from time into eternity and realize that all their possessions and achievements are meaningless? A person's true worth cannot be determined by the things they owned or collected during their earthly pilgrimage. It all depends on what they are before God. Did they develop spiritually under the influence of godly love? Did they try, at all times, to be helpful toward those who needed help? Or did their spirit become so hard that they did not see beyond the boundaries created by their self-centeredness?

> Eternity is not something that begins after you are dead. It is going on all the time. We are in it now.
> CHARLOTTE PERKINS GILMAN

The wise person realizes that he has a spiritual final destination and he doesn't allow greed and the cares of life to separate him from God. He makes time to develop an awareness of eternity in his spirit. So when the time comes that he has to cast off the old body, he enters into a glorious life because he knows God.

Spirit of God, teach me the value of the present moment so that I may learn to seek the eternal values and appreciate them. Amen.

Read Jeremiah 33:1-11

Witnessing All Over the World

"Then this city will bring Me joy, glory, and honor before all the nations of the earth!" (Jer. 33:9).

We get the type of person that tells others how God works in them so that it makes them sound like they're very special people. They almost acquire an aura of pride.

When God promised, through the prophet Jeremiah, that He would restore the people of Israel and make Jerusalem safe and prosperous again, He did not mean that only the Israelites would be favored. God does His rescue work as He pleases, whether it's through people or an individual.

> Expect great things from God, attempt great great things for God.
> WILLIAM CAREY

They must, however, never see themselves as the sole recipients of God's love and saving grace. God has a bigger and wider audience in mind. He is not only the God of Israel. He is Lord of all of humanity and He used Israel as His agent to spread the truth all over the earth. He does His good works among His own people so that others will see what kind of God He is and will seek Him. His people are not selfish receivers of His grace: they must share the Good News of His grace with all people. They are missionaries witnessing about Him.

Jesus wants others to see His glory through you, so that they will surrender themselves to His saving grace. Always be aware of the message you pass on among those you live, work and relax with.

The more complete His work is in you, the stronger the message will be that you pass on. You are a witness of God's grace in this world.

Lord Jesus, make me a trustworthy witness of Your love and grace. Amen.

Read John 21:15-25

"Lord, You Know Everything"

"Lord, You know everything. You know that I love You" (John 21:17).

Here Peter appeals to the Master's omniscience. This turns his self-conscious and humble confession into an enormous and well-founded one. It becomes a confession before Him who examines and knows the deepest thoughts of the hearts and minds of people. It sets him free from the devil and also from himself. If our hearts should condemn us: God is greater than our hearts and He knows all things.

> I am nothing,
> I have nothing.
> I desire nothing but
> the love of Jesus
> in Jerusalem.
> WALTER HILTON

Now Peter's confession doesn't rest on his soul-searching anymore because it has been dealt with. He is still weak and deceitful. Our confession doesn't rest on what people say about us either. Sometimes they idolize us and sometimes they break us. It is all up to Christ. When Peter calls on Jesus because of his love for Him, he calls on the highest authority one could think of: on Jesus Himself. He bares his heart and life to Jesus' scrutiny, "Lord, I really don't understand myself. What I want to do, I don't; what I hate, I do. I hear myself saying, to my own utter amazement, 'I don't know Him!' And yet … and yet … No, I don't know – but Lord, You know everything."

He doesn't need to defend himself anymore; too much happened for that. He has learnt to be careful about his own judgment and his own words. Thus Peter's confession becomes a refuge-seeking confession. In his own weakness and unbelief he finds himself in the presence of Him who knows everything, "Lord, where to now? To You alone. You see through me and You know me. You know everything and You know that I love You!"

I love You dearly, O Lord! Thank You that You know it. Amen.

Read Jeremiah 29:10-23

Seeking God

"In those days when you pray, I will listen. If you look for Me wholeheartedly, you will find Me. I will be found by you" (Jer. 29:12-13).

It is an indescribable privilege to find God. There are, however, many people who never find God. Does God play hide-and-seek with us? Those who are still searching, claim that this is so. The words of Jeremiah, however, make it quite clear that it is precisely the other way around.

Seeking God is an extremely important and wonderful task. Today's verse makes it quite clear, "If you look for Me wholeheartedly, you will find Me." If you focus your entire being on seeking God, you can rest assured that your "seeking" will end in "finding". But the opposite is also true: If you don't find what you seek, then you alone are to blame.

All so-called "religious seeking" in which God is never found, and the seeker finds his satisfaction in the search, is typified as "self-willed religion". It means looking for God all on your own, in your own way. It is the work of an unbroken and unwilling heart that refuses to submit to God.

God is available to everyone who seeks Him in earnest. Surely God is not to blame if we can't find Him. He is not in hiding, or a secret God. He comes looking for you in His Son's crib and at the Cross of Golgotha. If you haven't found the God who is looking for you, then you are to blame because then you are not seeking Him in earnest. Then *you* are playing hide-and-seek with God.

> God often visits us, but most of the time we are not at home.
> JOSEPH ROUX

Loving Father, thank You that You found me and that You wrapped me in Your grace. Amen.

Read Jeremiah 29:10-23

"You Will Find Me"

"If you look for Me wholeheartedly, you will find Me" (Jer. 29:13).

The human heart is a wonderful thing, because it is so deep and big. Jesus says even if we gain the whole world, it will not benefit us. In fact, it won't benefit the heart at all. The heart is not satisfied by it and doesn't find rest in it.

The human heart was created for God and therefore it finds rest in God alone. "You cried to Me in trouble, and I saved you" (Ps. 81:7). Only the person who finds God finds real life, because God is life: true, full, lasting life. This is the highest aspiration. When a lost human being finds the great, glorious, gracious and merciful God, it is as if time comes to a standstill for a moment. To find God's veiled communion is the highlight of spiritual experience.

Those who do not rejoice in this, have not yet found God. They have found the means to grace, but have never tasted the grace of the means.

> Seeking with faith, hope and love pleases our Lord and finding Him pleases the soul.
> — JULIAN OF NORWICH

We must take note of the strong personal "Me". It is not enough if you have found the sacraments in the Bible, in the church, in preaching and in theology. In their own nature, all of these are outstanding. But Christ says, "All must drink from it!" It's not about the Cup or the wine; it's about Christ and God. Your heart can never be filled with less. You must find God. Have you found Him yet?

Holy God, in Your indescribable love, meet every seeking heart. Amen.

Read Colossians 4:2-6

Prisoner for Christ

Pray for us, too, that God will give us many opportunities to speak about His mysterious plan concerning Christ (Col. 4:3).

There are people who, in serving Christ, become involved in activities they would never have dreamt of taking part in. Mother Teresa became an icon worldwide because of her ministry to the poverty-stricken and suffering people in the streets of Calcutta. Billy Graham became a household name through his ministry. Dietrich Bonhoeffer, a German theologian, became a martyr when his religion got him involved in a conspiracy to kill Hitler.

> The strength and happiness of a man consists in finding out the way in which God is going, and going that way too.
> HENRY WARD BEECHER

The apostle Paul, a diligent Pharisee, became a missionary for Christ and this resulted in his imprisonment. In prison he wrote letters of guidance and encouragement to the churches he founded. The Gospel he preached brought deliverance for thousands, but at the same time restricted his own freedom. In spite of this, profound teachings emerged from that very prison, and guided and taught the Church of Christ and individual Christians through all the ages.

You never know where your discipleship of Christ might lead you. It takes some people to the most extreme ends of the earth. Nixon's right-hand man in the Watergate scandal was Charles Colson and his conversion led to a fruitful spiritual ministry among prisoners in jails.

For others, it leads to achievements in the fields of music, teaching, writing and prayer. You can, however, not prescribe to God where He must lead you. All you need to do is open yourself up to God. The key is always obedience to Him – even if your obedience lands you in prison.

Master, help me to obey You, whatever the consequences. Amen.

Read Colossians 3:12-17

Be Thankful

And always be thankful (Col. 3:15).

Some people find it difficult to express their thankfulness. They also find it hard to feel thankful. They don't like feeling obliged to admit that they owe the people they must thank.

> A thankful heart is not only the greatest virtue, but is the parent of all other virtues.
> CICERO

Much of a Christian's experience springs from the gratitude we feel toward God for everything He did for us. The Christians in Colosse were called on to be thankful. By hearing the Gospel and believing in Jesus, they were led out of heathendom into a healthy, enlightened, loving way of life. Furthermore, they were placed in a Christian community of love, truth and forgiveness. They knew about salvation through Jesus Christ and were filled with God's Holy Spirit. They had plenty to be thankful for.

All of us have a lot to thank God for. Thank Him for the provision of your daily needs, no matter how little they might sometimes be. Thank Him for your health and safety, for your family and friends and for all the other good things He gives you. Be especially thankful for the fact that you may know Jesus.

Thank Him for the Bible, for the church and for your pastor. Thank Him for all the help you receive in trying times. Thank Him for forgiving your sins and for restoring your relationship with Him, in peace. Be thankful that you may look to the future with hope and a life in the Father's eternal home.

Together with all Your other gifts, Father, give me a thankful heart. Amen.

Read Colossians 4:1-5

Make It Easy to Understand

Pray that I will proclaim this message as clearly as I should (Col. 4:4).

Chances are that you have also watched a television advertisement and wondered what on earth the link between the advertisement and the product is. Some are quite witty and entertaining, but the message is not always clear and understandable.

It is of the utmost importance for those who proclaim Christ's message to make it as clear and easy to understand as possible. It must never sound like a history lesson, or the speaker's personal opinion. The illustrations must highlight the truth. The message must bring the Gospel of Jesus Christ and not that of a theology student to the people. It must be simple and direct, keeping the audience's experience in mind. It must suit the specific occasion. Above all, God must be revealed in all His glory, Christ in His saving grace and the Holy Spirit in His empowering strength. Paul was an educated theologian and it was an immense challenge to him to contemplate Jesus' message and preach it in a way that his mainly illiterate audience would understand, accept and respond to.

As a Christian, you also have a message to proclaim: the same message Paul was given. You may carry it across by what you say, how you act or by the way you present it. Some people give mixed signals: their words say one thing and their acts exactly the opposite. Make sure that the message you carry across is clear, to the point and simple. Make sure it is the true message: Of Jesus, His love, His kingdom and His truth.

> Every sermon should be an agony of soul, a passion to beget Christ in the hearts of men.
> JOHN CHRYSOSTOM

Word incarnate, help all Your messengers to spread the message of salvation clearly. Amen.

November 17

Read Colossians 3:12-17

The Riches of Christ

> Let the message about Christ, in all its richness, fill your lives (Col. 3:16).

There are people who are obsessed with money and who think about it day and night. Everything they do is determined by how much it will cost them, or how much they can make out of it. They have not mastered money, money has mastered them.

There are different forms of wealth. In Charles Dickens' *A Christmas Carol,* the miser, Scrooge, who had a lot of money, was miserable and horrible in his relationships with other people. His servant, Bob Cratchit, who barely made a living, had a loving family and he cherished the abundance and richness these relationships gave him.

Paul saw his new life in Christ as his most important asset. He often wrote about the "riches of Christ". When you hear about Christ and He speaks to you, it is a source of richness you can count on and should cherish. If you regularly take in Christ's words in the Bible, you will become part of unprecedented riches. If that same Word stays in you, it will make you much richer than any goldmine. Spiritual riches will not be affected by inflation.

> If you want to feel rich, just count all the things you have that money can't buy.
> ANONYMOUS

As a believer in Christ it is necessary to know the worth of the different kinds of the wealth available to you. Knowledge, wisdom and health are all highly valued, and so are family, faith and friends. Let Christ's words guide you in determining the types of riches that should be most valuable to you.

Good Master, help me to determine the value of the spiritual riches You give me. Keep me from yearning for things that are of no value. Amen.

Read John 9:24-31

Does God Listen to You?

We know that God doesn't listen to sinners, but He is ready to hear those who worship Him and do His will (John 9:31).

Every day an elderly Jewish man went to the "Wailing Wall" to pray. Someone noticed him and watched him every day for twenty years. One day the person asked him how it felt to go and pray there every day. The old man's answer was, "What does it feel like? I'm talking to a wall." Perhaps you also sometimes feel like you are talking to a wall when you pray to God.

> You cannot alter the will of God, but the man of prayer can discover God's will.
> SUNDAR SINGH

The ancient Jews believed that the way to reach God was to live a good life. "God doesn't listen to sinners" was the customary wisdom of the day.

Jesus showed us that this is not so. God does listen to sinners. He listens in particular to those who know they are sinners and kneel before Him humbly and remorsefully. God by no means gives preference to the righteous and good people. In fact, God longs to hear your prayers, whether you are a devoted believer or a sinner, rich or poor, young or old, learned or not. It gives Him joy to listen to your prayers, whether you pray with confidence or struggle to put together one sentence. God doesn't give preference to people who speak well. He rejoices in answering prayers, even if they are simple, stumbling utterances.

Whatever your condition, your abilities or your problems may be, pray without ceasing!

Hearer of prayer, teach me how to pray. Amen.

Read Luke 1:26-38

Jesus!

"You will conceive and give birth to a son, and you will name Him Jesus" (Luke 1:31).

Today parents name their children after movie stars, sports heroes or other popular people. Sometimes they choose a name for baby girls because it "sounds pretty", or if it's a boy, because it "sounds strong". In biblical times names were normally used to indicate the parents' hopes and expectations of what the child would one day become. The family name was often also maintained in some adapted, altered way or another.

> The name of Jesus is in my mind as a joyful song, in my ear a heavenly music, and in my mouth sweet honey.
> RICHARD ROLLE

The name Jesus means Savior, Redeemer, Deliverer. It focuses on the role Jesus would play. He who came to save and set free. Of course He came to set us completely free. His salvation included forgiveness of sin, but also healing, making holy, renewal, joy, love and hope.

"Jesus" is the most loved name in the world. It means different things to different people. If you are lonely, it means friendship and love. If you are depressed, it means joy. If you are afraid it means courage; if you are sick, healing; if you are guilty, forgiveness; if you stumbled, recovery. If you are in trouble, it means light in the darkness. If you are dying, it means life after death.

When you are happy, successful and popular, it means the celebration of thankfulness. It is the name most of us use for God, and that is right, because without Jesus we would never have had the opportunity to get to know God better.

Jesus, most precious name in the universe, my Shield and Refuge, I worship You as my Savior and Redeemer. Amen.

Read Isaiah 9:1-7

Prince of Peace

> The government will rest on His shoulders. And He will be called: Wonderful Counselor, Mighty God, Everlasting Father, Prince of Peace (Isa. 9:6).

We refer to Christmas as a time of peace and goodwill. The message of the angels was indeed a message of peace. Our world, sick of wars, needs this message desperately. It is strange that in spite of all the progress in technology, international organizations and access to instant communication, we are still ravaged by war just like any other generation.

The Messiah that the Old Testament prophet dreamt about would be called the Prince of Peace. The Hebrew idea of peace was something much more comprehensive than ours. We usually think of peace in terms of conflict: The absence of armed conflict. The people of the Bible, on the other hand, thought of peace in a warm and positive way. It was the absence of strife, but it was much more. It was prosperity. Peace was going ahead to cultivate the land, the establishment of families, the development of community life and worshiping and glorifying God. Peace was well-being, moving ahead, the advancement of human prosperity, health and happiness. It started with the transformation of swords into plowshares, and continued up until the harvesting of a rich crop.

> Christ alone can bring lasting peace – peace with God – peace among men and nations – and peace within our hearts.
> — BILLY GRAHAM

Christ is a Greek word with the same meaning as the Hebrew word *Messiah*, which means God's anointed one. He is coming again: as Restorer of peace to all. Ponder today the way in which you can make a small contribution to the peace that our Prince of Peace brings about.

Jesus, let Your peace bloom across the entire earth. Amen.

Read Isaiah 9:1-7

The Kingdom That Will Come

His government and its peace will never end. He will rule with fairness and justice from the throne of His ancestor David for all eternity (Isa. 9:7).

If you are of the opinion that the world has declined into a sorry mess, you are probably right. It has always been the case. It is not a sign of the end of our world, it is normal. The important question is, "Will it ever get better?"

In spite of the Old Testament prophecies about a Messiah, which were fulfilled in Jesus, the world is still cursed with poverty, injustice, oppression, disease, famine, greed, crime, terrorism and threatening war. Do you courageously try, as a Christian, to counteract these things with a list of good things? Or do you despair and ask God to put an end to the world because it is so evil?

No, rather do what the Hebrew prophets did. They dared to hope, dream and pray for a new world where God would be the sole ruler. They painted their picture of God's coming in glowing terms. In a certain sense they were unrealistic – their dreams would never be fulfilled. In another sense they were very realistic because their hope was grounded, not in the skillfulness of people, but in God's saving and liberating omnipotence. It was the only way of looking at the future that gave true and lasting hope.

> There can be no Kingdom of God in the world without the Kingdom of God in our hearts.
> ALBERT SCHWEITZER

It has always been the case. No matter how wretched and chaotic humankind has become, always look forward to the coming of the Kingdom of God. Hope and pray for a time when God's omnipotence will be revealed, when peace will reign and justice and righteousness will triumph.

May Your Kingdom come, may Your will be done on earth as it is in heaven. Amen.

Read 1 John 3:1-10

Just Like Jesus

But we do know that we will be like Him, for we will see Him as He really is (1 John 3:2).

Human nature has the tendency to imitate someone else. A toddler will try to copy the expression on his mother or father's face. He laughs because an adult laughs, without knowing what the joke is about. Later we make heroes of entertainers and sports giants. Even adults are inclined to make a role model of a leading figure.

Jesus Christ is the Christian's role model. The Spirit works His fruit in our lives: love, joy, peace, patience, kindness, goodness, faithfulness, gentleness and self-control (see Gal. 5:22-23). These qualities are all present in Christ and those of us who best display these qualities of character, are more like Christ. They don't all develop together in equal measure. It normally takes many years for the Spirit to bring them all on an equal level. But even the youngest believer, in whose life Christ is starting to take shape, is on his way there.

> Jesus does not give recipes that show the way to God as other teachers of religion do. He Himself is the way.
> KARL BARTH

To form an idea of what you will be like when the grace of God's loving work is completed in you, and you are mature, it is necessary to take a look at Jesus. You will be nothing less than the person you are. Your personality will not be blotted out. On the contrary, you will be more *you*, and your own personality will be clearer and more unique than ever before.

Holy Father God, I would like to be like Jesus. Help me to achieve this through the work of Your Spirit. Amen.

Read 1 John 3:1-10

Keep Yourself Pure

But we do know that we will be like Him, for we will see Him as He really is (1 John 3:2).

When sportsmen go on extended overseas tours, there are always reserve players who stay home. Those reserves must keep themselves fit in case members of the touring team get injured. While the group on tour enjoys all the attention, the reserves back home must persevere and work hard in case they are called to take the place of an injured player.

> The responsible person seeks to make his or her whole life a response to the question and call of God.
> DIETRICH BONHOEFFER

In the same way Christian believers must keep themselves pure because the call to be with Christ can come at any time. There is no time off in a Christian's faith and there is no such thing as relaxing. You must practice at all times, not because it is sensible to do so or you are told to do so. It is because of the hope in you. You know that the future will come and you must be ready for it. You know that Christ is God's Holy One and that He lives in you. It is His holiness alone that protects you from backsliding. Therefore you must trust Him, even as you wait for Him to call.

To keep yourself without blemish requires constant attention to the disciplines that are demanded from His followers. Watch your habits, keep up prayer and meditation, and persevere in your faith and expectations. Always be sure of God's presence. Care for your fellow human beings and don't neglect Christian fellowship.

Lord Jesus, help me to prepare for Your call. Amen.

Read 1 Corinthians 1:1-9

Rich in Every Way

God has enriched your church in every way – with all of your eloquent words and all of your knowledge (1 Cor. 1:5).

There are many ways to get rich. Most people strive for material wealth. Some even see it as the most important thing in life. Then there are others who endeavor to gain academic knowledge and line up one degree after the other. Some become authorities in their chosen study fields. Some people are rich in friendships and build up a large group of people with whom they have hearty relationships. Some people are made rich by their collection of historical treasures of artistic beauty and value.

The people of Corinth who converted to Jesus were rich in a different way. They experienced spiritual prosperity. They were richly blessed with the gifts of the Spirit, for example with prophecy, healing, speaking in tongues, wisdom and miracles. The Holy Spirit worked in them in this dramatic way, not so that they could boast about their gifts, but so that the church as a whole could be enriched by it. Paul had much to say to this specific group of Christians about their division and bickering. And yet they were spiritually rich!

> It is not the fact that a person has riches that keeps them from heaven, but the fact that riches have them.
> — Dr. Caird

You can also be blessed by God in spite of your shortcomings. He makes you rich in love, faith and hope. Possibly He fills you with prayer and praise, or a deep sense of thankfulness for the grace He shows you. Perhaps He blessed you with good family relationships or with an enriching church community. Don't envy the riches of this world. Cherish the riches God gives you.

Loving Master, with Your love in my heart I am truly rich. Amen.

Read Psalm 77:1-20

When God Leads the Way

> You led Your people along that road like a flock of sheep, with Moses and Aaron as their shepherds (Ps. 77:20).

Does God also lead people who are in mortal danger as a result of disasters? Does He lead those who experience a terrifying tsunami or are the victims of terrorist bombs? Yes, God is always in control. His outstretched, pierced hands grab hold of their lives, and disaster passes. Yes, at first there is fear of God's unfamiliar footsteps, until they realize that these are the footsteps of God coming to their rescue.

To this day, God leads us just as He led the people of Israel: through deep waters to the pristine shores of eternity. Then the water grave and the bomb blast become a passage to heaven. And it is a sunny day once more. You can die in the Lord anywhere. If you die in the Lord it doesn't matter where you die – it is always a blessed death. Through a dark and fearful night, the Lord leads us to eternal light.

God leads the nation, even the abandoned and the deceased. They cannot go any further until God as the great Shepherd of His flock appears and lays His hand on them. He says that He will grab you with His rescuing right hand. He strengthens you. He also helps you. When God leads, we always reach our destination.

> If God sends us on stony paths, He will provide us with strong shoes.
> ALEXANDER MACLAREN

In Christ we are reunited with God the Father. There is only One to whom we can cling – even while sinking in floods and terrorism. Jesus said, "Anyone who has seen Me has seen the Father!" (John 14:9).

We cannot hold on to God, but in Jesus Christ, God can hold on to us in any circumstances.

Thank You, Good Shepherd, that I am in Your caring hand at all times. Amen.

Read Psalm 77:1-20

Like a Flock of Sheep

You led Your people along that road like a flock of sheep (Ps. 77:20).

Without exception, God's unfamiliar footsteps are the richest in blessings. They don't take God away from us, but bring God's grace and love closer to us. At the Dead Sea the Israelites realized that God was close by in their time of need. He didn't make it known by words, because God wouldn't reason with a terror-stricken human flock with fear in their eyes and anxious souls. God didn't explain His footsteps to them and neither did He try to make them acceptable. He did what we do with hesitant children: He took them by the hand.

> Christ, having sacrificed Himself once, is to eternity a certain and valid sacrifice for the sins of all faithful.
> HULDRYCH ZWINGLI

There they were, huddled together like an anxious flock, trapped by the sea, not knowing what to do. Then suddenly in the dark of the night, the rescuing, protective and guiding hand of the Lord was stretched out to them. Never before had God been as close to them as that terrifying night when they didn't recognize His footsteps. He took them by the hand and went through the depths with them, leading them past the threatening walls of water. God was leading them with His unfamiliar footsteps.

It was unbelief and distrust that caused them not to understand or know His footsteps. After all, they had every reason to trust God, even if He approached with unfamiliar footsteps. They were "His people". God never lets His people down. God's covenant with His people will never come to an end and God stands by the promises He made to His people. Even if God walks ahead of us with unfamiliar footsteps, He is always there. Those who are part of His flock always find refuge in Him.

Good Shepherd, thank You that I may belong to Your flock. Amen.

Read Psalm 119:169-176

God's Saving Hands

Give me a helping hand, for I have chosen to follow Your commandments (Ps. 119:173).

There are still many good, kind hands in this world of ours: The hands of a mother, of marriage partners and of sincere friends.

> Everything comes from love, all is ordained for the salvation of man, God does nothing without this goal in mind.
> CATHERINE OF SIENA

But after all is said and done, they are still human hands and human hands are weak. They cannot reach very far. There are times that these hands cannot help us, such as times of sorrow, death, loss and guilt. Then human hands are helpless.

But God is ready to help when human hands fail. God's hands are wonderful hands. When Elijah was in the desert they helped in the form of an angel that provided him with bread and water. It is comforting to know. But if you want to see God's hand completely stretched out to lost humanity, then you must look at the Child in the manger at Bethlehem. There Jesus' tiny hand waved us back to God. It is God's hand that wants to deliver humanity of its sin.

God's hands reach out to the fallen, to all who believe despondently and despairingly that life is not worthwhile. God holds out His hands to you in Jesus Christ. Like Elijah you might be fleeing from God and want to take your hand from God's. But God lovingly takes hold of you with His pierced hands and He will never let you go. God does not want you to die in desperation, but to really live abundantly.

Lord my God, hold me in Your loving hands when storms rage around me. Amen.

Read Isaiah 40:25-31

The Young Ones

Even youths grow tired and weary, and young men stumble and fall; but those who hope in the LORD will renew their strength (Isa. 40:30-31 NIV).

This scripture is about the renewal of strength. It is indeed a very important issue in our life-draining daily routines. At the moment there are many very despondent and helpless people, and normal periods of rest don't help them because the problem goes deeper than physical and psychological tiredness. We are existentially tired because our hearts are weary and we cannot cope with life anymore. The philosophy of existentialism (the theory that humans are free and responsible for their actions in a world without meaning) is the symptom of our culture of constant fatigue.

Young ones often think that they are able to live their lives without anyone else's help. Youth is the peak of youthful strength, humankind at its very best – and therefore they are humankind at its worst.

It can also be an elderly person who doesn't wish to be seen as old and tired. But keeping up is falling behind. These people who want to take on life in their own strength, tend to "stumble and fall". How impressive it is to see the way a young person walks, yet here is talk of stumbling and falling.

> For I can do everything through Christ who gives me strength.
> PHILIPPIANS 4:13

In our own strength we can do nothing, but God is almighty and can empower us if we put our hope in Him. Then we will "soar on wings like eagles", and run without getting tired.

Father God, I put my hope and trust in Your omnipotence. I want to do Your will. Amen.

Read Isaiah 40:25-31

Hope in the Lord

But those who hope in the LORD will renew their strength. They will soar on wings like eagles. They will run and not grow weary (Isa. 40:31).

"But!" A jubilant and joyful emphasis is placed on this "but". There are also people other than young people who hope in the Lord. In fact young and old should put their hope in the Lord. It is by no means the monopoly of the elderly. The distinguishing trait of people who place their hope in the Lord is that they don't rely on their own strength but on the Lord. They have used the last of their own strength and now they wait on the Lord for strength.

> We must not confide in the armor of God, but in the God of this armor.
> WILLIAM GURNALL

They place their hope in the Lord, the merciful God who demonstrated to this world the source of His strength at Golgotha. The strength with which God finally equipped the struggling human being is the reconciliatory blood of Jesus Christ. The fountain of God's strengthening power finally welled up in Christ's broken heart.

Do you want to renew your spiritual strength? It can happen because it is part of truly being a Christian. God's strength renews us and changes us into powerful human beings. The stream of God's power flows through our lives and into the essence of our being, and makes the dead wood of our spiritual life sprout new and fertile branches.

This strength is from God and has nothing to do with exercise or character. God alone gives strength to the weary.

In my weak and wretched state, I come to You, Lord. Amen.

December

*Glory to God
in highest heaven,
and peace on earth to those
with whom God is pleased.*
       LUKE 2:14

Bethlehem and Golgotha,
the Manger and the
Cross, the Birth and
the Death, must always
be seen together.
       J. SIDLOW BAXTER

Little Child of Bethlehem,
may You be born again in people's hearts every day.
Grant that Your Holy Spirit will infuse us
with pure love and that we will share it with others
so that it will be Christmas in our lives every day of the year.
We thank You for the privilege of celebrating this day
and for what it means to us:
That You came to this evil world as the Son of God
and became part of a humble household;
that You were raised and grew up just like any other child;
that You grew to adulthood and worked in a carpenter's shop;
that You became hungry and thirsty like we do.
Thank You that You knew temptation and sorrow;
that you were like us in everything but sin;
and struggled to make a living like we do.
We praise You for Your life and work, for Your love
until death and for the power of Your resurrection.
We share in Your transfiguration
and rejoice in Your divine intervention in our lives.
We make space for You in our hearts this festive season.
Let us rejoice all year round because we have found life in You.
We worship You, Lord Jesus, as our greatest gift from God.
Amen.

Read Jeremiah 2:1-13

Living Water

"For My people have done two evil things: They have abandoned Me – the fountain of living water. And they have dug for themselves cracked cisterns that can hold no water at all!" (Jer. 2:13).

Water is an extremely important commodity, especially in developing countries. Where water is not provided by means of water pipes, it must be fetched from rivers or pumped from deep underground wells. When water is scarce, living conditions are very difficult, and when there is a flood, lives are in danger.

A fountain with fresh water is nature's gift of life. A fountain sustains life just like God does. He not only gives life, He also enriches and renews it with His gift of spiritual energy. This gift of God empowers people, puts them on the right track and gives them direction.

> "If you only knew the gift God has for you and who you are speaking to, you would ask me, and I would give you living water."
> JOHN 4:10

It raises the level of society and brings joy, security and fruitfulness. A natural fountain is a mystery. There in the middle of nowhere, water bubbles up from the slope of a hill, its origin unknown. Even when the land is dry, it still provides its life-giving contents. God is also a mystery like the fountain on the mountain slope; His origin unfathomable to the human mind. He continually refreshes those who drink from His fountain.

Water is also a purifier. It is very satisfying to have a warm bath and get out nice and clean. The Lord purifies us spiritually, no matter how contaminated we may be. Like clothing that is worn too long, we are in constant need of cleansing. The only Source of this cleansing is the Fountain of Living Water that is the Lord Himself. Are you sustained and purified by this Source?

Lord Jesus, You are the Fountain that never runs dry. Amen.

Read 1 John 1:1-10

We Are Fooling Ourselves

If we claim we have no sin, we are only fooling ourselves and not living in the truth (1 John 1:8).

The Greek philosopher, Socrates, warned, "Know thyself!" This is extremely difficult. Most of us probably think more of ourselves than we should. We tend to make light of our faults. On the other hand, it is false modesty to belittle ourselves and run ourselves down.

> Nothing is easier than self-deceit. For what each man wishes, that he also believes to be true.
> — DEMOSTHENES

In some of the ancient religions the promise was made that the worshiper who went through certain rituals or religious ceremonies would gain access to God. All these procedures guaranteed a higher lifestyle, set them free from the everyday struggle that others went through, and raised them up to a level where they couldn't sin anymore.

The words of today's Scripture reading were meant to deny this kind of nonsense. No one is spared the temptation to sin. People who pretend they are never tempted are guilty of pride. They are fooling themselves and this is a dangerous practice.

If you are of the opinion that spiritually, you have "arrived", be very careful. There are those who will believe you, but it is unlikely that everyone will. If you think so highly of yourself, you can be sure that you will become entangled in a sin you never thought possible. Rather examine yourself in humbleness and honesty. Ask God to show you your weaknesses and blind spots. Ask for His light to shine brighter than yours and put your trust in His truth more than in your own.

Father God, help me to keep my eyes fixed on Jesus so that I will stop fooling myself. Amen.

Read 1 John 1:1-10

The Value of Confession

But if we confess our sins to Him, He is faithful and just to forgive us our sins and to cleanse us from all wickedness (1 John 1:9).

A friend of ours, who gave his life to Christ, found that it was impossible for him to forgive himself for a certain weakness in his life. He went to a trusted confidant and emptied his heart and confessed his sin in prayer. Very soon he was delivered from his feelings of guilt that tormented him so. He said later that he discovered if you confess your worst sins to God in the presence of someone else, you can never again claim to be good. You can stop wasting energy trying to convince people that you are so wonderful. You know there is at least one person who knows who you really are.

"Confession is good for the soul!" This is an old Scottish proverb. Confession enables you to part with the past and gives you a great feeling of relief and freedom. When God accepts the confession, your ministry to others improves, and you grow in understanding and grace. This is because you placed yourself under the healing grace of God.

If God's grace and forgiveness work in you and continue to work in you, you become a more complete person. You have learnt to live with your human nature and you have accepted yourself for what you really are – a sinner saved by grace. Perhaps the time has come that you start acting according to this spiritual truth.

> The final contribution of religious faith to freedom is the freedom to confess our sins.
> URSULA W. NIEBUHR

Savior and Redeemer, be with everybody who will hear another person's confession today. Help them to handle the ministry of forgiveness in Your name with love and compassion. Amen.

Read Romans 13:8-14

Respect Yourself and Others

Owe nothing to anyone – except for your obligation to love one another. If you love your neighbor, you will fulfill the requirements of God's law (Rom. 13:8).

Belittling yourself is not a Christian virtue. If you don't have a good opinion of yourself, you will not have a good opinion of your neighbor either. It is when you respect yourself that you respect others, who were also created by God.

Self-respect is in no way self-glorification. Self-glorification allows pride to exalt you, and that is bad for your spiritual life and robs you of the virtues of the Christian disciple.

Sincere self-respect is created by the knowledge that God loves you and that you are His child. This truth bans a groveling spirit and enables you to get your words in line with your actions in the life you live before God, and among your fellow human beings.

Self-respect means maintaining a high standard of dignity, and behavior that is worthy of Christ, because your life must reflect Him.

> Let me know myself, Lord, and I shall know Thee.
> AUGUSTINE OF HIPPO

When you see others as His creation, you will develop a positive attitude toward them. You won't look down on those the world sees as inferior and you will not envy those who think themselves better than you. You will see each person as someone whom God loves infinitely.

God of love and grace, grant me a deeper awareness of Your love, so that I will approach all people with love and respect. Amen.

Read Proverbs 19:1-10

Why Be Angry with God?

People ruin their lives by their own foolishness and then are angry at the LORD (Prov. 19:3).

How often one hears people rant and rave at God when disaster strikes! Someone dies in a car crash and God gets the blame, but what about the reckless, drunken driver? A person loses all his possessions and he and his family are destitute – and people question God's love. Nobody keeps in mind that this person was a gambling addict.

One of God's greatest gifts to humankind is our own free will. God set the example of the right way to live, but He leaves it to us to make the right decisions about the road we choose to travel.

> Trust the past to God's mercy, the present to God's love and the future to God's providence.
> AUGUSTINE OF HIPPO

In spite of the lifestyle you choose to live, God's saving love is so great that He is always at your side to help and support you when you turn to Him in your need.

Don't ever forget that you are responsible for your own actions. But in spite of this, whatever the consequences, the God of love is always there and ready to lead the lost back to His flock.

Thank You, Lord, that I may find rest in You. Allow Your grace to flow through me when I feel weak. Amen.

Read John 14:1-14

The Search for God's Peace

"I am the way, the truth, and the life. No one can come to the Father except through Me" (John 14:6).

Through the ages people have been searching for fulfillment and meaning. The situation is no different today. In fact, the search is even more intense while people wrestle with all the demands and distractions of our modern lifestyle.

> Who except God can give you peace? Has the world ever been able to satisfy the heart?
> GERARD MAJELLA

There is only one way in which this yearning will be satisfied and that is by entering into God's peace. This godly peace is not of this world, but is an experience that rises above all human understanding. It is that condition of the mind and the soul that you experience only when you are completely one with God.

The most important question in the minds of most of us is how to achieve this condition we so desperately search for. The answer lies in the Master's words in today's Scripture verse. He will lead us into the presence of God's peace, but only if we turn to Him and open up our lives and hearts to Him.

Invite the Living Christ once again to take possession of your heart and you will soon be filled with "God's peace, which exceeds anything we can understand" (Phil. 4:7).

Thank You, Lord Jesus, for leading me to God's peace. Amen.

Read Isaiah 63:1-12

Alone!

"I have been treading the winepress alone" (Isa. 63:3).

Christ trod God's winepress alone – even without his mother. When Christ was on the verge of bringing His sacrifice of atonement, He could not or was not permitted to turn to His mother. At that moment He could not ask for His mother's support. He trod the winepress completely alone.

When Jesus entered the valley, carrying the curse of our sin, even this last bond was broken. He no longer had a mother. Here Christ also bore the judgment of sin that separates children and mothers. This is the most terrible separation ever.

A person can break with everything in life, but who can tear themselves from their mother? *This* is Golgotha. *This* is the Cross! And *this* is what Jesus did when He saw His mother and said, "Woman …" With these last words Mary was not dishonored but saved.

And this was all that Mary needed. Mary did not have a son of flesh at Golgotha, because she was there, not as a mother but as a woman who needed salvation. All women need a Savior for their sins. At Golgotha we are all lost sinners and nothing more. There is room for no one else at Golgotha. At Golgotha no special prerogatives count anymore; not even those of motherhood. At Golgotha all importance comes to an end. Jesus died "alone" for our sins.

> There is no death of sin without the death of Christ.
> JOHN OWEN

Man of Sorrows, thank You that You even broke the ties with Your mother to save me. Amen.

Read Acts 7:46-60

The Secret of Heavenward

> But Stephen, full of the Holy Spirit, gazed steadily into heaven and saw the glory of God, and he saw Jesus standing in the place of honor at God's right hand (Acts 7:55).

Even in the face of death, some people never raise their eyes to heaven and acknowledge God. Only when we are filled with the Holy Spirit can we look to heaven and be filled with the hope of heaven. The Holy Spirit is the secret of "heavenward".

It was also Stephen's secret. "Stephen, full of the Holy Spirit, gazed steadily into heaven." Without the Holy Spirit, Stephen would not have been able to do it, because then he wouldn't have seen anything of heaven. Stephen would have gazed at his murderers in mortal fear, at his wife and children, at his world, and his young life that he was soon to lose.

Then Stephen would have looked down into the dark abyss of death, like so many people do. But because of the Holy Spirit, he could raise his eyes heavenward.

The Holy Spirit is the secret of looking heavenward. Each year at Pentecost, the Holy Spirit enables Christians to raise their eyes heavenward. The Holy Spirit must direct our eyes away from worldly desires, from possessions and temptation, cares and troubles, from anxiety and sorrow that cast shadows in our eyes. The Holy Spirit draws and forces our eyes heavenward so that we see through the stones raining down. Yes, through everything, we see Jesus "at God's right hand".

> There is not a better evangelist in the world than the Holy Spirit.
> Dwight L. Moody

Holy Spirit, I praise and thank You that You forced my eyes to look heavenward. Amen.

Come In

"I have opened a door for you that no one can close" (Rev. 3:8).

The words of this message were intended for the people of Philadelphia. They were originally outsiders, living without God in a cold, dark world. The first condition for coming in is to stand outside … and to know that you are standing outside.

"I have opened a door for you." When our door is locked, God opens His door. Jesus Christ is God's door in the dark passage of this life. "I am the Door!" This is how Jesus offers Himself to everybody who is still standing outside. It started in Bethlehem and the door continuously opened wider …until the broken heart of the dying Savior, the door of God's love, opened completely. So completely, so widely, that the needs and the sins of the whole world can pass through.

> Before an individual can be saved, he must first learn that he cannot save himself.
> M. R. DE HAAN

You needn't search for this door, the door searches for you. It is right in front of you, wide-open. You only have to walk through it. In your most desperate circumstances, Christ taps you on the shoulder and says, "It's cold outside, come in! I am the Door!"

Savior and Friend, thank You that I may pass through Your door. Amen.

Read Acts 2:14-21

Everyone!

Everyone who calls on the name of the LORD will be saved (Acts 2:21).

Everyone!" This is a welcoming and meaningful word and it includes the whole world. Jesus told His disciples to, "go and make disciples of all the nations" (Matt. 28:19). This means that everyone on the whole earth is to receive the Gospel message. "Everyone" makes it globally all-inclusive and yet strictly personal. Therefore it's as if you are personally spoken to. Everyone, you!

> Three things are necessary for the salvation of man: To know what he ought to believe, to know what he ought to desire, and to know what he ought to do.
> THOMAS AQUINAS

"Everyone" is also an extremely encouraging word. It means that the One who knows our souls assures us that we can be saved. No matter how sinful we are, or how far we have strayed from God, Christ can make the Father's reconciliatory grace available to all of us because He changes us inside and out. "Everyone" also means there is no discrimination against anyone. This word brings the Cross of Christ to every individual; not only to the devout and sincere, but also to sinners and tax collectors. This truth is for "everyone".

The Holy Spirit wants to bring every person to the Cross of Golgotha, but He can be refused. Everyone has a choice to say no to Him, "No, I don't want to be saved." It makes one shudder to hear that a person wants to ruin himself by choice. How great it would be if everyone gave their lives to the One who died to give us life.

I call to You in my trouble and misery, Lord, and I know You can save me. Amen.

Read Romans 5:1-11

The Outpouring of God's Love!

He has given us the Holy Spirit to fill our hearts with His love (Rom. 5:5).

The glory of the events at Pentecost is that they place life in the sunshine of God's love. Sunshine that doesn't come and go, but that is eternal. Our entire lives are interwoven in this love; in times of prosperity and joy, but also in the darkest depths of our lives where we experience disappointment and grief. Even the most serious sickbed is exposed to the sunshine of God's love.

Pentecost is the outpouring of God's love and this happens through the Holy Spirit alone. People or things do not come into play here. Not fantasy, philosophy, technique or art can bring forth even a shred of God's love, or pour out a drop of it in the human heart. Therefore the human being and the human spirit are not important where there is talk of the Holy Spirit. We are simply empty vessels that are filled by the Holy Spirit. We can do nothing but be filled by God's love.

Pentecost is the outpouring of the Holy Spirit, and in His outpouring, God gives the world the love of God. This love does not come drop by drop. It is not a feeble, thin trickle. It is a mighty, surging, roaring stream. It is "poured out". This indicates a tremendous quantity and power. When God unlocks the gates of heaven an impassioned torrent of God's love is released. It fills the valleys and the hollows of the world. It is a cascade of the love of God.

> God's love never imposes itself. It has to be discovered and welcomed.
> **Brother Roger**

God of love, who could ever adequately describe Your love in words? Amen.

Read Acts 1:1-11

Trustworthy Witnesses

"But you will receive power when the Holy Spirit comes upon you. And you will be My witnesses, telling people about Me everywhere" (Acts 1:8).

Our witnessing must be carried and driven by "power". Then our testimony comes from our very soul, from our deepest inner being; like a plant's surging vital force from the earth brings forth the most beautiful flower.

We cannot generate this power through deep meditation, an ascetic life or by creating our own culture in our souls. What a person brings forth in his own strength is seen by Christ as nothing more than abuse and self-contempt. This is why Jesus here refers to the power of the Holy Spirit.

The source of our power to witness does not come from ourselves. Our spiritual power comes from God and is in His hands and in the Holy Spirit. We cannot generate it – it is a gift from God!

Once we receive this power from the Holy Spirit, we become witnesses. If a flower has the power of growth in it, the plant must bud and flower. We are like that too. We just have to witness. It must surge from us like water from a fountain: I believe, so I have to witness. We cannot keep it inside or hide it.

Our love for Christ cannot be stifled. It has to be expressed and told to others so that they too can believe.

> Our power in drawing others after the Lord mainly rests in our joy and communion with Him ourselves.
> J.G. BELLETT

I will praise You, Lord, for as long as I live. Amen.

Read Jonah 1:1-17

Escaping from God

But Jonah got up and went in the opposite direction to get away from the LORD (Jonah 1:3).

Jonah was on the run from God. One would think he had just read Psalm 139:7, "I can never escape from Your spirit! I can never get away from Your presence!" This is what Jonah tried to do in his desperation and fear. Jonah was God's prophet and the messenger of God's specific words. God called His prophet – but there was no sign of him.

Many people find God too stern, but Jonah found Him too tolerant. Jonah was fed up that God wanted to show mercy to the people of Nineveh. Therefore, when God sent him to Nineveh, Jonah deserted his calling and his mission. He refused to do his job and became a deserter. Then Jonah ran away from God's hand and from God's land.

> If you seek the Lord Jesus in all things you will truly find Him, but if you seek yourself you will find yourself, and that will be to your own great loss.
> THOMAS Á KEMPIS

Jonah boarded a ship on its way to Tarshish and was soon fast asleep. He had separated himself from everything: his family, his people ... and his God. Jonah was alone now, without a mission, without Nineveh and without God.

But was Jonah really separated from God? Is man ever without God? Jonah would soon find out that no one can run away from God. God was sending a storm Jonah's way, God was already on his heels. The captain spoke to Jonah, saying, "Get up and pray to your God!" Jonah was being cast back to his God by a heathen. And when Jonah insisted the men to throw him overboard, God had a plan to get Jonah where He wanted him – in the stomach of a great fish. No human being can run away from God.

I bow down in thankful worship before God, who found me when I was looking for Him. Amen.

December 13

It Can!

Read Zechariah 4:1-14

"It is not by force nor by strength, but by My Spirit" says the LORD of Heaven's Armies (Zech. 4:6).

What the angel says to Zechariah here is of great comfort to us. It tells us, "It can!" No, it doesn't come by force or strength of any kind. By the spirit of a human being it can't, but by the Spirit of God it can.

> The solution of the riddle of life in space and time lies outside space and time.
> LUDWIG WITTGENSTEIN

It can! It *can* happen that things change for the better in this world of ours: in the church, in marriages and in the family — and also in our wounded hearts. Don't despair, no matter how hard the fall might have been, how deep the depression, how many dry bones are lying in the valley. We sigh and say, "Can those dry bones come to life again?" Humanly speaking it is impossible, but the Spirit can do it. He can make dry bones living people again.

Just do what the Lord commands. Follow His instructions carefully. The Holy Spirit has been poured out and the reservoir is full. God's river is in flood. The heavy burden of the Cross has been borne and completed by Jesus Christ. Prophesy to the dry bones, but especially, speak to the Spirit. Then Ezekiel's prophecy will also be fulfilled in our day, "Then the Spirit came!" The Spirit is always on His way somewhere and especially where He is called in earnest.

"It can!" What change this can bring about. Your heart, work sadness and happiness will all be given new life. Your husband, wife, children, grandchildren, neighbors and friends! Even the most despondent can be rejuvenated. They will be given new life by God. It can happen … but only through the Spirit of God.

Almighty God, anything is possible for Your Spirit, even that which looks impossible to us. Amen.

Read Ephesians 4:17-32

Do Not Sadden the Spirit

And do not bring sorrow to God's Holy Spirit by the way you live. Remember, He has identified you as His own, guaranteeing that you will be saved on the day of redemption (Eph. 4:30).

Perhaps you received a rich blessing from God through a human friendship. Still, no matter how faithful our friends might be, not one of them can be as faithful, patient or tender as the Holy Spirit. He defends us if we've done something wrong or land up on the wrong road. He wakes us up when we fall asleep on the edge of a precipice. When we can't find peace, and desolately look for people to comfort us, He wants to be our Comforter.

The Holy Spirit won't leave us alone before He has brought us into the haven of rest. Every time separation threatens, or has already come because of our guilt and sin, He secures the communication line between our Savior and us. How can we bring sorrow to this patient Guardian of our souls?

And we do it so often. Every time we resist His soft whisperings or give in to our own selfish and proud hearts. What incredible patience He has with us. He never gives up on the work that He started doing in our hearts.

> The Holy Spirit's great task is to carry on the work for which Jesus sacrificed His throne and His life – the redemption of fallen humanity.
> ALAN REDPATH

From the moment we accept Jesus' salvation and He marks us as His own, from the moment we belong to the Lord, He works in our souls. Do not grieve the Holy Spirit.

Lord my God, I once again place myself under the authority of Your Holy Spirit. Amen.

December 15

Read Mark 9:14-29

Belief and Doubt

I do believe, but help me overcome my unbelief! (Mark 9:24).

In our times, human hearts struggle with belief and doubt. There has seldom been a time in which doubt has made its influence felt in such an intense way. But on the other hand, belief is confirmed and insists more strongly than before to protect its existence. This wrestling match is taking place all around us. Like in the time when Jesus was on earth, we find this within the borders of the human heart.

Perhaps you have also experienced it. You probably also know gnawing doubt in times of a weakening of faith, despondency and despair. See this as a challenge to grow in religious courage and renewed love.

There were once days and hours in our lives when we could rejoice because we were so certain of our faith, "I know my Redeemer lives!" "I am born again and secure in Him." And then the dark days came again when the eyes of our faith were clouded. If only we could cry out like the boy's father, "Help me overcome my unbelief!"

> The way to grow strong in Christ is to become weak in yourself.
> —CHARLES H. SPURGEON

Our Savior understands this faltering prayer better than any other, and He promises us the comfort of His Holy Spirit in times like this.

I believe, Lord Jesus, help me not to doubt anymore. Amen.

Read Philippians 1:1-11

Be Courageous

And I am certain that God, who began the good work within you, will continue His work until it is finally finished on the day when Christ Jesus returns (Phil. 1:6).

This is a word of encouragement for the faint-hearted and despondent, but it is also a message for each one of us. In any case, which of us don't fall in this group? All of us, who confessed Jesus as our High Priest and our Savior, would like to see Him in all His glory.

> The greatest test of courage on earth is to bear defeat without losing heart.
> ROBERT G. INGERSOLL

When however, we take note of our sin and our wavering strength, of our small faith and our ingratitude, our grumbling and complaining, we fear the great day of glory. Then we sigh, "It is not for me, I'll never make it. Although I'm getting older, I'm not really making progress on the road of life. Although I receive much grace from God, I am bound with heavy chains by the world around me."

These sighs of faint-heartedness and despondency prove that we still rely completely on ourselves and not on Him who brings about the work of purification in us and wants to uphold it. The Word is clear in this case, "Let us hold tightly without wavering to the hope we affirm, for God can be trusted to keep His promise" (Heb. 10:23).

It is God who continues with the work, not us. Therefore we can be courageous.

Holy Jesus, strengthen all weak hands and paralyzed knees and do Your glorious work in us. Amen.

Read Proverbs 3:1-10

With Christ in the Business World

Seek His will in all you do, and He will show you which path to take (Prov. 3:6).

Businessmen and women are in the marketplace to make a profit. They take on responsibilities and maintain a healthy balance as security. Making a profit is not wrong, if it is the result of lawful planning and honest labor.

> Honesty is the first chapter of the book of wisdom.
> THOMAS JEFFERSON

The most important issue is how that profit is made. Many see profit as the ultimate goal of their business efforts and disregard a good name and the respect of other people. There are people in the business world who walk all over their opponents. They make a profit by saying offensive things about others.

A wise businessman fully appreciates the value and necessity of making a profit, at the same time realizing that business consists of more than grabbing everything within reach as quickly as possible. Honest business principles shape your character.

The view that it is impossible to be a Christian in the business sector is disproved by the large number of Christians that handle their business according to Christ's precepts: Treat others the way you expect them to treat you.

If Christ is your Senior Partner in any undertaking, your principles will never be compromised for the sake of convenience or profit. You would not want to deny your connection with Christ. While you unashamedly take your place in a competitive world, the Lord will richly bless your sincere efforts.

Father God, grant that all business transactions will be done according to Your will. Amen.

Read James 4:11-17

Don't Postpone

How do you know what your life will be like tomorrow? (James 4:14).

Our world is full of people with good intentions. People who intend visiting a sick or elderly person – tomorrow! People who are going to write a letter to a lonely person far from home – very soon! People who want to make contact with someone they became estranged from – as soon as my to-do list is empty! If this sounds familiar to you, it is because all of us experience this at some time or another.

Nobody, except the Almighty God, can see into the future and you never know what tomorrow has in store for you or for the person you plan to contact. You cannot even say if there will be a tomorrow for you or for them. That is why it is of the utmost importance to get your priorities straight.

Follow the guidance of the Master who found time for all people in His busy life on earth. He will help you put things in perspective again. Don't postpone the things you know have to be done. If you do them to His honor and glory, He will provide you with the necessary time.

> You cannot repent too soon, because you do not know how soon it may be too late.
> — Thomas Fuller

With Your help, Beloved Master, I will do everything that needs to be done, so that I can find peace of mind. Amen.

December 19

Read Romans 14:14-23

Control That Temper

So then, let us aim for harmony in the church and try to build each other up (Rom. 14:19).

Unless we are very careful, differences of opinion can get out of hand. This goes for individuals, churches and nations. Whatever the circumstances around these differences, they can lead to serious consequences if not controlled. Enmity and war among nations and feuds between people have often been the result of discord that was allowed to run riot and grow out of proportion.

If you differ from someone, it is necessary that you don't allow your emotions to get out of control. Jesus differed from many people, but His attitude and approach were always grounded in God's love. Empowered by that love He could handle any issue with patience and understanding. He was never insensitive or hot-tempered.

You will also be able to control your emotions in your negotiations with others if you respect the other person's right to an opinion – even if you don't agree with it.

> If you are to be self-controlled in your speech you must be self-controlled in your thinking.
> FRANÇOIS FÉNELON

Empowered by the Holy Spirit, you should handle every situation with an attitude of love, compassion, patience and self-control. Then you will find that you can talk matters through in a civilized way and with a feeling of peace in the presence of Christ.

Savior and Redeemer, stand by me in controlling my emotions and thoughts, so that I may live in harmony with others. Amen.

Read Exodus 4:1-17

No Excuses

O Lord, I'm not very good with words. I have never been, and I'm not now ... I get tongue-tied, and my words get tangled (Exod. 4:10).

When God calls you to carry out a certain task, don't make excuses. If God knew you were not up to the task, He would not have asked you to do it. The problem is that most people have the wrong idea of what they are capable of, and are quick to say, "I can't," instead of saying, "I'll try, in God's strength."

Then there are people who try to pass the task God gives them on to others. They run the risk that God will not give them anything to do anymore, because they constantly refuse to obey Him.

> God doesn't call people who are qualified. He calls people who are willing, and then He qualifies them.
> RICHARD PARKER

Persistent refusal to serve God in a way that is acceptable to Him can loosen your grip on Him because it implies that you are more eager to please yourself than Him.

It is very likely that when God gives you something to do for Him, it will seem very difficult, in fact almost impossible. Don't allow this to frighten you so that you make excuses, because God has already proven, time and time again, that when He calls someone to be of service to Him, He equips them to do it. In your weak moments He will continue leading you, even if you can't see the road. Never make excuses when God calls you, but do the task He gives you confidently and joyfully.

Lord, keep me from making excuses and give me the boldness and wisdom to obey You. Amen.

Read Jeremiah 6:16-21

The Crossroads

"Stop at the crossroads and look around. Ask for the old, godly way, and walk in it" (Jer. 6:16).

Crossroads can be misleading. You must make very sure that you know exactly which way to take. A couple, who were cycling in a national park, came to a crossroads. There were three roads but only two road signs. They chose the one that seemed to go in the right direction. After a while they were back where they started.

> Nature gives man corn but he must grind it; God gives man a will but he must make the right choices.
> FULTON J. SHEEN

God was busy talking to the people of Judah. They were on the wrong spiritual road: a dead end. It was leading them into a moral swamp. Now they had to choose once again. They could return to the swamp or they could walk the "good road", which was of course the road God wanted them to take. If they had obeyed Him they would have found spiritual peace, harmony with God and hope for the future. But they didn't.

You also have a choice at the crossroads. Jesus never forces you to follow Him. You can turn off and take any road, but it might be a dead end. You can choose the "old road" or the "best road". And then you will find rest for your soul.

If you stray onto one of the dead-end roads you will never know peace with God, but you will be lost and know only confusion and emptiness. The choice is yours.

Lead me, Friendly Light, through earthly darkness. Amen.

Read Jeremiah 6:16-21

The Watchmen

"I posted watchmen over you who said, 'Listen for the sound of the alarm!' But you replied, 'No! We won't pay attention!'" (Jer. 6:17).

In biblical times informal timetables were drawn up and people would take turns to be watchmen. The watchman was expected to do three things: He had to watch; his mere presence was often enough to frighten away criminals. Secondly, he had to sound the alarm when there was danger. Thirdly, he had to account for his actions, especially if he did not sound the alarm in time.

The true watchmen, appointed by God, were the prophets. They served a much more serious purpose than the community watchmen. The true prophets, like Jeremiah, had to warn the people against disobedience to God. Their call to the people sounded like a trumpet blast. The prophets had to warn the community about life-and-death choices they had to make. But the people didn't listen to their warnings and were destroyed.

To this day God has watchmen. One is the Bible itself, that always leads the way back to God again and shows us the road Jesus walked. Then there are priests, teachers and preachers who share God's message with us. Then there are the less formal watchmen – friends, Bible study group leaders, Christian songwriters – all of them constantly busy indicating the road of the Gospel. Do you listen for the sound of the alarm? Or are you perhaps meant to sound the alarm yourself?

> Destiny is not a matter of chance, it is a matter of choice. It is not a thing to be waited for, it is a thing to be achieved.
> WILLIAM J. BRYAN

Lord, let Your Spirit make it clear to me whether You are also calling me to be a watchman. Amen.

Read Romans 1:1-7

God's Good News

Paul, a slave of Jesus Christ, [was] chosen by God to be an apostle and sent out to preach His Good News (Rom. 1:1).

The word "Gospel" means "Good News". Good news comes to us in different forms. It is good news when a child is born to a family and everyone is overjoyed. It is good news when two people fall in love and decide to get married. It is good news when old disputes are settled and wars are ended. You might have your own idea of what good news means to you.

The Gospel that the Bible talks about is good news of a special nature because it comes from God. While most people would want to thank God for the kind of blessings they receive that bring them joy, this good news is even better. The message itself comes from God. It is not only something God said, but something God did. It is the message of His arrival in Jesus Christ and in doing so He brought salvation for all who believe in Him and accept Him as their Redeemer.

> Christ's riches are unsearchable, and this doctrine of the Gospel is the field this treasure is hidden in.
> THOMAS GOODWIN

This salvation includes the forgiveness of sin and the strength to live a life without sin. It invites the individual to be reconciled with God and to become an ambassador for Christ. It offers comfort in our sadness; joy in our suffering and hope for the future. It does not say to us, "You have failed! Try harder!" It says, "You have failed! Now you can start over again!" Have you heard the Good News and do you believe the Gospel?

Lord Jesus, give me the grace to spread the Good News of Your love and salvation. Amen.

Promised Long Ago

God promised this Good News long ago through His prophets in the holy Scriptures (Rom. 1:2).

You might have wondered why God sent Jesus to our world, and why at that specific period in history. Possibly you also wondered what it all has to do with you in your present circumstances.

God always meant to send His Son to us. This decision dates back to Adam and Eve's sin. His love began before the creation of the universe. Even at the creation of humankind, He knew that they would fall from grace and that He would save them. It was no afterthought or desperate last-minute attempt to sort out a mess He never could have dreamt would happen.

> What God promises, we ourselves do not through choice or nature, but He Himself does by grace.
> AUGUSTINE OF HIPPO

The long story of the Old Testament was already a preparation for the Gospel. Rescuing the children of Israel from slavery in Egypt was merely a promise and a preview of the greater deliverance of all people that would be fulfilled in Jesus. The prophets started the dream of what Jesus would do in the future and of the great age of the Messiah, when He would come at last.

Every life that has ever been lived has a bearing on that event – and this includes your life. Even if there was no other living person on earth, it would still have been necessary for Christ to come – for you. You can even build your life around Him today. God also had you in mind when He started it all. Even if your life might have fallen apart, He will help you to mend it piece by piece. This is the Eternal Good News – the Gospel.

Savior and Redeemer, help those who have failed in life to find mercy in Your healing grace. Amen.

Read 1 John 3:11-24

For Others

We know what real love is because Jesus gave up His life for us. So we also ought to give up our lives for our brothers and sisters (1 John 3:16).

The normal human instinct entails the quest for personal survival, and getting hold of everything we can for personal gain. We accumulate money, power, skills, land, resources and equipment to enrich ourselves and we expect others to do the same. If someone else gets in the way while we are gathering "things", there is conflict, and a battle ensues which is won by the strongest. Sometimes we will form a pact with others to our mutual gain.

> There is no joy in all the world like the joy of bringing one soul to Christ.
> WILLIAM BARCLAY

Jesus' way of life was to turn all of this around. He gave Himself to others. "Though He was God, He did not think of equality with God as something to cling to" (Phil. 2:6). In this He set an example for His disciples to follow. They went out into the world to tell everyone about His sacrificial love. Some of them died doing this. Other disciples crisscrossed the roads of the Roman Empire to bring the news of His love to others. Some served prison sentences because they proclaimed that love. Some wrote about it so that the story of Christ and His love would never die. Later, others travelled to distant countries to bring the Good News to heathens. There were those who braved raging crowds and endured physical violence to bring the message to those who needed it. Some also gave up wealth, their families and their personal freedom in obedience to the Man of Galilee. They gave themselves to others unconditionally without thinking of the consequences. What do you sacrifice for the sake of others?

Lord Jesus, strengthen those who make sacrifices to bring Your Good News to others. Amen.

Read 1 John 3:11-24

Compassion for Others

> If someone has enough money to live well and sees a brother or sister in need but shows no compassion — how can God's love be in that person? (1 John 3:17).

As a small boy, Thomas Carlyle was left home alone one day while his parents were out. A beggar came to their door and asked for money. With the impulsivity of a child, Carlyle went to his own money box which had a few coins in it, forced it open, and gave the beggar all the money he had saved. He afterwards said that he had never before or since, experienced as much joy as at that moment.

Giving money to the poor is not without its own problems. We are concerned that they will buy alcohol or drugs with the money. We know that if we help a person in need, they can easily develop an attitude of dependency and in some cases we actually do more harm than good.

We live in a world swamped with poverty and we believe one small act of kindness won't solve the problem. Yes, we can think of a thousand excuses not to help others and some of them are most probably valid.

A Christian believer might ask, "What would Jesus have done?" or "What does love, the love of God expect from me?" Even if you can't solve a major problem, you can at least bring a little relief. Someone could be helped by simply knowing you care.

> The world doesn't care what you know until they know that you care.
> DAVID HAVARD

Lord Jesus, give me a heart filled with compassion, that shares with others what You have given me. Amen.

December 27

Read 1 Corinthians 13:1-13

Love Is the Key

Now we see things imperfectly as in a cloudy mirror, but then we will see everything with perfect clarity (1 Cor. 13:12).

Because Jesus could penetrate the hearts and thoughts of people, He was able to discern between the sincere searcher and the hypocritical questioner. At some time or another, all Christians are confronted with questions they cannot answer. This can be confusing and perplexing, but we must keep in mind that not one of Jesus' sincere followers can complete their pilgrimage without wrestling with difficult problems concerning their faith.

The reason for this is that we are human and it is impossible for the human mind to fathom the mysteries of eternity. Can anyone understand the mystery of God or limit Christ's love?

You might get to a point in your spiritual life when, after probing your mind to its extreme limits, you confess, "Lord Jesus, I don't understand, but my love for You rises above my ignorance, and I trust You for what I do not understand." This does not mean that you should never ask questions, because there will always be questions. This means that you will place your love for Christ before those questions that separate you from Him.

> Nothing binds me to my Lord like a strong belief in His changeless love.
> CHARLES H. SPURGEON

Love is the key that unlocks God's heart to all who seek Him. Without love you cannot know Him and neither will you develop a better understanding of His ways. It is love that makes your faith real and secure.

Thank You, Lord my Redeemer, that even though I don't understand everything, I know without doubt that You love me. Amen.

Read Isaiah 33:1-9

Ensuring a Safe Future

But LORD, be merciful to us, for we have waited for You. Be our strong arm each day and our salvation in times of trouble (Isa. 33:2).

No one can deny that we live in turbulent times. All over the world events are taking place that make even the bravest optimists fear the future. In fact, there are those who wonder if there is a future ahead.

It seems that there is a daily increase in crime and violence. Nations are hostile toward one another and basic human rights are mercilessly trampled underfoot. The heartbreaking occurrence of human injustice towards fellow humans carries on unchecked.

> Keep us little and unknown, prized and loved by God alone.
> CHARLES WESLEY

World bodies debate these issues at tremendous costs but they seem unable to find a lasting solution to the problems we are faced with and which are posing a threat to the community.

Once again it is clear that, in so many cases, God is ignored in plans humans make for the future. The time has come for all people and organizations to place their trust in God, to submit to His will and obey His law of love. This is the only way that we will find peace.

God who is Love, grant that we will obey Your command to love one another. Amen.

December 29

Read Acts 17:24-34

How to Enrich Others

For in Him we live and move and exist (Acts 17:28).

When you lose sight of your spiritual purpose, you have lost an incredibly valuable treasure. Then life becomes monotonous and your faith loses its power and spark. Every one of Christ's disciples ought to know in which direction they are headed otherwise God will never become a reality to them.

> The first great gift we can bestow on others is a good example.
> THOMAS MORELL

There are many commendable spiritual goals: To live nearer to God, obey His will and to live a life of Christian love and sacrifice. It may be a challenge to you to live a more virtuous life and be of nobler service. It is undoubtedly true that God calls certain people for specific tasks and that they find great joy and fulfillment in performing those tasks.

All Christian disciples wish to be like their Lord and Master. You might be called for a certain task, and the privilege of carrying it out enables you to become more like Christ. Whichever task you are called to do for Him must then be done to reflect His glory. While you serve Him devotedly, other people will become aware of Him in your life, and your character and personality will be enriched and strengthened. To live so that you reflect Christ will let you grow in spiritual stature and even if you aren't aware of it, will be a source of enrichment to other people.

Help me, Holy Master, to live so close to You that I will enrich the lives of others. Amen.

Read 1 Corinthians 13:1-13

The Secret of Eternal Youth

Three things will last forever — faith, hope, and love — and the greatest of these is love (1 Cor. 13:13).

You must have noticed that there are forty-year-olds who look sixty, and that there are people aged seventy that look much younger. It is wrong to say that circumstances and conditions caused the difference, because it occurs in people from all walks of life. A youthful appearance is not always created by cosmetics, because if the spirit is hard and unforgiving, and bitterness erodes the soul, the most skillful application of expensive cosmetics makes no one look more youthful. It won't make the eyes sparkle or improve a despondent look.

People with a cheerful spirit have discovered the secret of sparkling youthfulness, which is produced by the thoughts and the heart that have experienced the reality of God's presence. To live with the awareness of the Holy Presence brings depth and light to everyday life, as well as an ever-deepening understanding of joyous faith.

In the same way you share all things with God, He will also share His treasures with you. This means that His greatest treasure, His Love, also becomes yours. It lives in your spirit and shines through your whole life, and because the Spirit of Love knows no age, you become ageless.

> Only love enables humanity to grow, because love engenders life and it is the only form of energy that lasts forever.
> MICHEL QUOIST

Even if your body changes with the passing years, your spirit will still reveal timelessness in the beauty and youthfulness sprouting from your heart.

Lord Jesus, may Your love be reflected in me always. Amen.

Text Register

Genesis
3:1-7 .... Nov. 6
3:14-24 .... June 2
17:1-8 .... July 16, Aug. 6, Aug. 28
17:9-14 .... Aug. 29

Exodus
4:1-17 .... Dec. 21

Joshua
1:1-9 .... Jan. 27, Apr. 23

Judges
16:15-18 .... Jan. 9

1 Samuel
7:3-17 .... Oct. 12, Oct. 13, Oct. 14

2 Samuel
24:18-25 .... July 26

1 Kings
19:3-8 .... Jan. 19

2 Kings
22:11-20 .... June 23

Nehemiah
4:1-8 .... Feb. 26

Job
1:1-12 .... Mar. 16
36:22-33 .... July 24

Psalms
17:1-7 .... Oct. 22
17:1-9 .... Oct. 1, Oct. 2, Oct. 21
18:1-15 .... Sept. 3
18:1-16 .... Sept. 2
18:17-30 .... Oct. 8
18:30-42 .... July 3
18:31-42 .... Sept. 4, Oct. 24
19:1-11 .... Apr. 28
19:8-12 .... Feb. 13
19:1-14 .... Aug. 24, Aug. 25
19:1-15 .... July 19
20:1-9 .... Oct. 4
20:1-10 .... Oct. 5
22:21-31 .... Oct. 25
22:23-31 .... July 4, Aug. 31
22:23-29 .... Sept. 1
27:1-3 .... Mar. 28
23:1-6 .... Apr. 13, May 8
27:1-7 .... May 11
27:7-14 .... Mar. 28
30:5-12 .... June 19
40:1-6 .... Jan. 20
42:1-11 .... Feb. 18
51:3-14 .... Feb. 12
55:1-23 .... June 15
65:1-13 .... Feb. 21
67:1-7 .... May 5
71:1-8 .... Feb. 8
77:1-20 .... Nov. 26, Nov. 27
84:1-13 .... Apr. 7
103:8-13 .... Jan. 7
103:14-22 .... June 26

118:24	Feb. 7
118:19-29	Mar. 14
119:33-48	Nov. 4
119:65-80	Nov. 9
119:99-105	Jan. 5
119:169-176	Nov. 28
124:1-8	Feb. 29
130:1-8	Jan. 13
131:1-3	Mar. 25
139:1-12	Mar. 22
141:1-10	Oct. 27
143:1-12	Nov. 2, Nov. 3
147:1-11	Apr. 12, May 18

Proverbs

3:1-10	Dec. 18
6:6-11	Feb. 7
9:1-9	July 1
9:1-12	Nov. 5
10:5	Feb. 4
14:12-16	Feb. 10
19:1-10	Dec. 5
19:1-11	Aug. 9
23:9-18	June 21
23:15-26	Nov. 1
24:1-10	June 6

Ecclesiastes

10:1-3	Feb. 4

Isaiah

1:1-10	Aug. 11, Aug. 12
1:10-20	Aug. 19
1:14-20	Aug. 21
3:19-25	July 20
4:1-6	July 2, Sept. 29, Sept. 30, Oct. 23
5:1-7	July 17
6:1-10	July 29, July 30
9:1-7	Nov. 21, Nov. 22
11:1-11	Aug. 5
12:1-6	July 18
30:12-18	Jan. 8
33:1-9	Dec. 29
40:25-31	Nov. 29, Nov. 30
49:1	Feb. 8
63:1-12	Dec. 7
66:1-9	July 23

Jeremiah

1:1-12	Nov. 8
1:11-19	Oct. 20
2:1-13	Dec. 1
3:19-25	July 20
6:16-21	Dec. 22, Dec. 23
10:1-11	July 21
13:15-19	Nov. 7
15:10-18	Aug. 10
29:10-23	Nov. 13, Nov. 14
31:15-22	Oct. 10
31:23-35	Oct. 11
33:1-11	Nov. 11

Lamentations

3:21-27	Feb. 3

Hosea

5:1-15	Aug. 30

Amos

4:8-13	June 3

Jonah

1:1-17	Dec. 13

Zechariah
4:1-14 .... Dec. 14

Matthew
2:1-9 .... Apr. 5
4:1-11 .... June 4, June 25
5:3-12 .... Apr. 25, Apr. 26
5:13-16 .... May 27
5:38-42 .... May 29
6:5-15 .... May 14
6:8-15 .... Apr. 1
6:16-24 .... June 11
7:15-23 .... June 28
12:22-32 .... Apr. 24
20:20-28 .... Apr. 9
21:28-32 .... June 10
22:35-40 .... Apr. 17
24:36-51 .... Apr. 4
24:36-44 .... Apr. 19
25:1-13 .... Apr. 22, May 25, June 14
25:14-30 .... Jan. 2, May 31
25:31-40 .... Apr. 20
26:47-54 .... Mar. 12
26:47-56 .... Mar. 19
27:3-10 .... Mar. 27, June 18
27:11-14 .... Apr. 14
27:20-26 .... Mar. 3
28:11-20 .... Oct. 19

Mark
1:23-28 .... Feb. 16
5:1-13 .... Apr. 3
8:1-13 .... Mar. 26
8:34-38 .... Mar. 9
8:34-9:1 .... Apr. 2
9:14-29 .... Dec. 16

Luke
1:26-38 .... Nov. 20
1:76-80 .... Feb. 28
2:8-14 .... Mar. 6
2:8-20 .... Feb. 1, May 17
2:22-32 .... July 12
4:14-30 .... Sept. 5
15:11-20 .... Jan. 4
15:11-23 .... June 1
15:17-24 .... Mar. 4
18:9-14 .... May 30
19:37-43 .... May 28
22:47-53 .... May 20
23:13-25 .... Mar. 31
23:36-42 .... May 9
24:1-7 .... Feb. 5
24:25-35 .... May 22

John
1:1-11 .... Aug. 20
1:1-18 .... July 7, July 11, Aug. 17,
.... Sept. 16, Sept. 17
1:29-34 .... Apr. 15
4:31-38 .... Feb. 25
7:32-37 .... Mar. 21
7:32-39 .... Apr. 21
8:12-20 .... Jan. 31
8:36 .... Feb. 11
9:24-31 .... Nov. 19
9:24-34 .... Oct. 18
10:1-13 .... June 5
10:22-42 .... July 10, Aug. 7, Sept. 21
11:1-11 .... Mar. 23
11:17-32 .... Sept. 20
11:33-44 .... Oct. 6, Oct. 7
11:45-57 .... Sept. 18, Sept. 19
12:41-50 .... Sept. 22, Sept. 23
13:1-17 .... Sept. 24, Sept. 25

14:1-12	May 2
14:1-14	Mar. 15, Dec. 6
14:25-31	Feb. 19
15:9-17	Apr. 16, May 16
16:25-33	Jan. 23
19:1-7	Mar. 7
19:17-27	May 19
19:28-33	Apr. 6
19:28-37	Jan. 30, Feb. 17
20:19-23	Sept. 12, Sept. 13, Sept. 14
20:24-30	Sept. 15
20:26-31	May 12
21:15-19	Feb. 6, May 26
21:15-25	Nov. 12

Acts

1:1-8	Jan. 12
1:1-11	Mar. 2, Dec. 12
2:14-21	Dec. 10
7:46-60	Dec. 8
9:10-19	June 7
15:1-15	Feb. 27
17:21-28	Feb. 24
17:21-29	Jan. 28
17:21-34	May 1
17:24-34	Dec. 30
20:13-24	Oct. 17
28:1-10	Mar. 13

Romans

1:1-7	Dec. 24, Dec. 25
1:16-17	Feb. 13
5:1-5	Jan. 16
5:1-11	Oct. 31, Dec. 11
6:15-23	Feb. 11
7:15-24	Jan. 11
7:21-8:1	Jan. 21
7:14-25	July 22

8:9-17	June 12
11:11-24	June 13
13:8-14	Dec. 4
14:14-23	Dec. 20
16:17-27	July 25
24-25	Jan. 21

1 Corinthians

1:1-9	May 24, Nov. 25
6:15-20	Feb. 15
13:1-6	Apr. 10
13:1-13	Mar. 17, Mar. 20, Dec. 28, Dec. 31
15:1-11	May 3
15:12-27	June 24
15:54-58	Feb. 20
15:50-58	June 17

2 Corinthians

5:16-21	Mar. 11
6:1-13	Nov. 10
8:1-7	Jan. 17
8:2-7	Feb. 23
11:23-30	Jan. 22

Galatians

6:6-14	May 23
6:11-18	Feb. 2, Apr. 11

Ephesians

3:14-21	Apr. 18, July 8
4:1-16	May 10
4:17-32	Dec. 15
5:15-17	Feb. 14
5:15-20	Feb. 9

Philippians

1:1-11	July 31, Aug. 1,

	Aug. 18, Sept. 7,
	Sept. 8, Dec. 17
1:12-25	May 4
1:12-26	June 30, Oct. 26
1:18-30	Aug. 2
2:1-11	May 7, Aug. 3
3:10-16	Jan. 3
3:12-21	Mar. 18, Aug. 8
4:4-9	Jan. 25

Colossians
2:6-15	June 8
2:20-23	Jan. 26
3:1-4	Jan. 10, Apr. 8
2:20-3:4	June 16
3:12-17	Sept. 9, Nov. 16, Nov. 18
3:23-25	Feb. 14
4:1-5	17 Nov.
4:2-6	June 29, Nov. 15
4:7-18	Aug. 22, Aug. 23, Sept. 10, Sept. 11, Oct. 3

1 Thessalonians
5:12-28	Oct. 15

1 Timothy
1:1-11	June 20, July 13
1:12-17	July 9, July 14, Aug. 13
1:12-20	Aug. 14
2:1-7	Aug. 4
2:1-15	July 5, July 15, Sept. 28
3:1-16	July 6
3:14-16	Aug. 15
4:1-5	Aug. 16
5:3-15	June 9
6:1-18	June 22

2 Timothy
1:1-10	Oct. 29
1:1-11	Mar. 24
1:3-14	May 15
1:6-12	Feb. 22
3:12-17	Jan. 29
4:1-8	Mar. 10

Hebrews
1:1-9	Mar. 29
3:7-19	June 27
9:11-14	Jan. 15
11:1-5	Apr. 30
11:1-6	Jan. 1, Jan. 14
11:1-12	Oct. 9
13:7-17	Oct. 16

James
1:1-11	Oct. 28
1:19-27	Sept. 6
2:14-26	May 13
3:2-12	Apr. 29
3:5-12	Jan. 18
4:2-7	Mar. 30
4:11-17	May 6, Dec. 19
4:13-17	Jan. 6

1 Peter
4:12-19	Sept. 26, Sept. 27
5:1-11	July 28
5:5-11	May 21
5:8-11	Mar. 5
4:1-11	Oct. 30

2 Peter
1:16-21	Aug. 26, Aug. 27
3:1-16	July 27

1 John
1:1-10 .... Dec. 2, Dec. 3
2:14-17 .... Mar. 1
3:1-10 .... Nov. 23, Nov. 24
3:11-24 .... Dec. 26, Dec. 27
3:18-24 .... Mar. 8

Revelation
2:1-11 .... Apr. 27
2:8-11 .... Jan. 24
3:7-13 .... Dec. 9